Bailey's Saving Grace

by

ERIN OSBORNE

Dedication

The first part of the dedication goes to my mom. Without her I wouldn't have accomplished half of the things that I have. She supports me no matter what I want to do and stands behind me when I need her to have my back. I love you and can't thank you enough for everything you have done for us and continue to do.

The second part of this goes to anyone that has ever lost a baby. Don't let anyone ever tell you that you have to get over the loss in a certain time frame, there is none. I don't care if that child was lost to a miscarriage, still born, or lost to an illness shortly after birth. You mourn for as long as you need to.

CONTENTS

Back Blurb

Bailey

I grew up in the Wild Kings MC. My dad and brother are both members. Since I was a girl, I wanted to do everything my brother and his friends did and prove to them that I could do it better than they did.

Everything changed for me when I started having feelings for Grim. He became the love of my life. Even though I am hurt on a daily basis by his need for club girls, I can't just shut my feelings off for him.

Brock 'Gage' Wilson is the President of a different chapter of the Wild Kings MC. I've known him my whole life and we started having a friends with benefits relationship. Am I using him to try to get over my love for Grim? In a way, yes. But, he has his own demons he's fighting. That is until tragedy strikes and we suffer a tremendous loss.

Grim

I am the President of the Wild Kings MC. My dad was in the club and I decided early on to follow in his footsteps. There's nothing like knowing you have a group of men, family, that have your back and will do anything to support you.

Growing up with Joker, Cage, Irish, and Glock they quickly became my best friends and I would lay down my life for them. Bailey, Joker's little sister, was always trying to copy everything we did. So, I took it upon myself to make sure she didn't get in trouble and didn't get hurt. In doing that, I started to have feelings for her that I have no business feeling. I don't want an old lady. Never have, never will! Club girls know what I want and don't pressure me for more. A different one every time ensures that they won't get attached.

That all changes when Bailey suffers a tragic loss. She pushes me away and my heart shatters. I don't know if I can live with Bailey gone and I don't know what to do to make all the pain I've caused better.

Can Bailey get past her pain and move on?
Is Grim too late to fix his mistakes?
Will more danger tear them apart for good?
Or can Grim and Bailey find a way to come together?

Chapter One

Grim

TODAY'S THE DAY the club's been working towards for a while now. We're opening a garage up today to the public. We still have ours at the clubhouse for personal use, but we wanted to give back to the community. After months of looking for the perfect location that was easily accessible to the public, getting all of the permits that are required, and then construction, today is the grand opening of Spinners. Bailey's gone all out and has a whole day of activities planned to draw the people of the town in. We're going to have a cookout in the parking lot, the guys have set up bikes that they've built in the garage to showcase some of the custom work we've done, there's going to be games and rides for the kids, and we're going to have a raffle to win a custom bike. It's a good thing that we built on a lot with an attached field so we have room to set everything up.

I've been up for a few hours now trying to make sure that everything is set for today. Spinners isn't going to only be a garage where we work on bikes, we're going to work on most everything. It's something that I've wanted to do for a while now and I'm thankful that the guys were on board with doing this. So, after kicking the club girl out of my bed, I go to my office in the clubhouse so that I can go over everything.

Every night it's the same thing. I drink and party with my brothers and then I find some easy pussy to try to get my mind off of the one person that I want to be with. Bailey is never far from my mind these days. Well, it's been that way for a while now. I've loved her for as long as I can remember, but I can't tell her that. I know she loves me and that I've let her down so many times by not going after her. But, I can't help but feel like I'd be disrespecting Pops and Joker if I did. Among other reasons that I can't take that step with Bailey.

I still remember Bailey wanting to do everything that Joker, Cage, Irish, Glock, and I did growing up. She didn't want to play with other girls, when one happened to be around. If we were doing something, she wanted to be right there with us. It didn't matter if we were playing cops and robbers, climbing trees, or riding our dirt bikes when we got older. There was a period of time that Bailey begged and begged Pops to have one. He said no and that she needed to do things that little girls did. Ma, however, didn't care what she did. She always encouraged Bailey to do whatever she wanted. I still remember the day that Ma told Bailey if she wanted to be in a motorcycle club like the boys, then she should start her own. Her reasoning was that all of us guys were pig-headed and refused to let a female in. Pops blew up and I think he spent a few days at the clubhouse because he was so pissed that Ma would tell Bailey something like that. Anyone that knows Bailey knows that if you tell her something like that, she's going to do it.

In those days, Bailey would get so upset if we wouldn't let her tag along with us. So, eventually, I started letting her go with me. The more time we spent together, the more I fell for her. That lasted until I started noticing other girls. Then all of a sudden, I wanted to hang out with her less and less. I could see the glimmer and life going out of her slowly when she couldn't hang out with the boys anymore. When I didn't want to spend all of my spare time with her. But, I knew that she wasn't ready for the kind of relationship that I wanted. In my eyes, I'll always see her as the little tomboy with pig tails and an attitude that thought she could do everything better than the boys.

I'm abruptly jarred from my head by a knock on my office door.

"Come in." I yell, looking up to see Pops entering my office.

"You got a second?" He asks.

"For you, any time."

2

"Ma was supposed to meet Bailey at the store to help her get the food for the cookout. But, she woke up with a migraine, so I was gonna see if you could meet her instead. That way I can go back and make sure Ma's okay before the grand opening."

"Yeah, I can do that. I was just about to head over to the garage. But, I'll get a hold of Bailey and meet her at the grocery store. Tell Ma I hope she feels better but if she's not up for comin' today, we'll all understand."

"It will kill her if she can't come. You know that as well as I do. She loves all you boys as if you were her own. Hell, sometimes it feels like you all are. Where one of you is, the rest are. Especially when it comes to gettin' in trouble. But, you were always different when it came to Bailey. You were her protector and hero." Pops says chuckling at his own memories.

"I don't think she'd agree with you now." I say looking down at my desk, not wanting him to see the pain in my eyes at how I've treated her for a while now.

"Son, I don't think you could ever push her away from you. I know things are strained and weird right now, but she'll come around. Hopefully before she decides to leave us all and move to Dander Falls with Gage."

"Pops, if it weren't for me, she wouldn't have started anythin' with Gage. We both know that. She's lookin' for somethin' from me that I can't give her."

"You and I both know that's bullshit!" He says standing up. "Since when have you ever been afraid to go after somethin' you wanted? Well, I'll let you get back to what you were doin'. Don't forget to get a hold of her to meet her for food."

"I'll see ya later Pops."

As soon as he shuts my door, I'm digging out my phone to call Bailey. It goes to voicemail, so I hang up and send her a text instead. I tell her that I'll be at the store waiting for her to get there.

Making my way outside, I straddle my bike and think about what Pops just said. Does he know more than

3

I've given him credit for? I've always tried to keep anything I was feeling for her hidden away. There are so many reasons that I shouldn't ever start anything with her. More reasons than even I've thought of.

Bailey is a rare gem that needs to be loved and cherished. I have no problem doing that, I've loved her for almost ten years now. My problem is that I don't think I'm the type of man to settle down. I'm the president of the Wild Kings, and while we've gotten out of a lot of the shit we used to deal in, there's still enemies out there. People want our territory or just don't like the fact that we don't run guns or drugs anymore. It would kill me if anything happened to her because of that. I mean it killed me knowing that she was taken when we were dealing with Sky's fucked up sister and ex. I will forever be in Sky's debt because she risked herself in order to make sure that Bailey didn't get hurt worse, that she got free while Sky was tortured and hurt more than she should have been.

Then there's the fact that Bailey's nine years younger than me. She should be with someone her own age. Someone that doesn't have all of the responsibilities that I do. I'd love for her to settle down with some citizen, get married, have babies, and be happy. Unfortunately, Bailey was raised in the club and that's where her life is. She doesn't want anyone that isn't a brother. And, if I know Bailey, she wouldn't be happy with a citizen that has a boring nine-to-five job, is home every night on time, and can't give her that adrenaline rush that she's always chasing.

With all of the fucked up shit I've done, hell the shit I still do when it comes to the club girls, I know that I'm no good for her. She deserves someone that hasn't had almost every club girl that's with the Kings. It doesn't matter that the main reason I fuck them is to get her off my mind for a little while. That doesn't even work anymore. Instead, I picture her while I'm with whatever girl is in my room.

4

Anyway, I'm almost in town when I see Bailey's truck parked outside of the pharmacy. Maybe Ma sent her to get something for her migraine. I park my bike behind her truck and make my way inside. Where I find Bailey has my heart breaking and racing at the same time. She's standing in front of the pregnancy tests looking green as hell, and like she doesn't know what she's looking at.

Bailey

Waking up this morning, I was so excited for the grand opening. Well, I was a little worried too. The last time that Gage and Grim were together, there was a fight. It might not have gotten to fists flying, but I know that Grim is just waiting to get his hands on Gage. It was stupid really. I mean I've made my feelings for Grim clear and he's made it clear that he doesn't feel the same way. You can't really get much clearer than sleeping with anything with a fucking pussy. Today I hope that they can be civil and let things settle until members of the community aren't around to witness their bullshit. Grim really has no say though. I mean, it's like he doesn't want me, but he doesn't want me with anyone else either. What the fuck is that about?

I woke up and started heading upstairs for breakfast. About half way up the stairs, I could smell the eggs, bacon, and toast cooking. Usually it's a smell that makes my mouth water. Today, all I want to do is throw up though. I quickly make my way back down to my bathroom and lose whatever I had in my stomach, which wasn't much. This can't be good.

I know that Gage and I haven't always used protection, but I can't be pregnant right now. Gage and I have decided to cool things down between us. Not that we were much to begin with. Mainly we were fuck buddies that spent a little bit of time together outside of fucking. He lives a few hours away and I don't want to move away and leave my family. Brock 'Gage' Wilson is the President of the Dander Falls chapter of the Wild

Kings. I know he's not looking for an old lady. We started as friends and a place that I could go once in a while when I needed to get away. When things with Grim get too hard for me to handle, Gage always makes sure that I have a room at his clubhouse and that the guys leave me alone. Not that any one of them really want to fuck with Pops and Joker by touching me.

If I were pregnant now, it would be the worst possible time. Gage isn't going to want to be tied down with a kid and woman that he's not even serious with. Plus, I'm only twenty-three. Gage is only a few years older than I am. I'm not sure this is a good thing at all to be happening. Well, I guess I better go get a test and figure out what I have to do next. I quickly shoot a text to Skylar and let her know that I won't be up for breakfast. Instead of telling her what I'm really doing, I tell her that I'm going to get an early start on shopping for today.

I do plan on getting a start on shopping, but first I'm going to go to the pharmacy and buy a test or two so that I can be sure. Then I can decide on what to do as far as Gage is concerned and what I want as far as keeping the baby. Making my way into the pharmacy, I go to the section with the tests. I'm standing there looking at all of my choices, trying to decide on one, when I feel someone come up behind me. Looking over my shoulder, I see Grim standing there. Oh shit!

"Hey!" I say, sounding overly enthusiastic to see him.

"What's up crazy girl? I'm supposed to meet you at the store. So, I saw your truck here and stopped by to see when you are goin' to head over there." He says.

"Oh. I was looking for something and when I got in here, I couldn't remember what it was." I say laughing. "We can go to the store now. I'm sure you have other things to do and I need to make sure things are getting set up at the garage."

"Bailey, babe, get what you need and we'll go to the store." He says, knowing what I'm really here for.

6

"Oh, um… okay." I say, quickly grabbing the first box I can reach and make my way up to pay.

"Crazy girl, I'll meet you outside." He says walking out the door.

After paying for my purchase, I walk out and get in the truck without looking at Grim. He's already on his bike so he's obviously ready to get going. I pull out and make my way to the grocery store. He follows me and parks next to me.

"I was going to say I'll go one way and you go another, but I think we'll just get this shit together." Grim says walking next to me grabbing a cart of his own.

"Whatever you want Grim. I'm heading over there as soon as we're done here so that I can make sure things are getting set up right and that people are showing up that need to get their stuff set up. I know that there are a few rides that arrived last night and the guys said they'll be back around ten to set them up."

"Everythin' you've done is amazin' Bailey. Today is goin' to be amazin' because of you and the hard work that you've put in. I honestly don't know where we'd be if it weren't for you. I'd probably just have a cookout and that is it."

"Thanks Grim. You know I'm always happy to help out. I did want to talk to you though." I say looking away from him.

"What's up crazy girl?"

"Um… today, can you leave Gage alone? I know that things have been pretty tense between you two since the twins' birthday party and I don't want anything to ruin today. It's been my decision to be with him and it's not anyone else's decision to have any input into who I'm with or what I'm doing. Everyone has made their feelings about Gage and I, and their feelings about me, quite fucking clear. But, it's no one's business but his and mine."

"Crazy girl, I promise I won't do, or say, anythin' to Gage today. But, you should know that if he hurts you, he *will* be gettin' an ass beatin'. I'm sure that it's not just from me either. You have to know that."

"I know. But I don't want anything to mess up today. You guys have worked too hard for this and I don't want to see it ruined."

Grim doesn't say anything else. We just continue pushing our carts and filling them with enough food to feed about three armies. It's funny how the other people are looking at us shopping. Grim is obviously wearing his cut and I'm just walking along next to him. Then you look in our carts and see piles of food that looks like we're buying the place out. It is quite funny if you think about it. A biker and a woman buying a ton of groceries like we buy this much food every day.

"How much more do you think we need? These carts are getting full. So, if we need much more, then I'll take this one up front and get a new cart." I say to Grim.

"I think that might be a good idea. I think we have enough meat and rolls. Sky's bringin' desserts and stuff so that's good. But I think we could do more chips and dip, drinks, meat and veggie trays. Maybe some fruit trays too. In case some people don't want to eat sweets, or let their kids eat them."

"Okay. I'll be right back."

After grabbing another cart and leaving the full one by the office, I go to find Grim. When I turn a corner, I almost laugh to myself. He's talking to some girl that's been at the club a few times lately. I've seen her there with one of the hang arounds. But, she's always looking to get the attention of the brothers, especially the brothers that hold a position. They can spot her type a mile away though and tend to stay away. Apparently Grim can't say the same thing. She's running her hand up and down his arm while her other hand is lying against his chest. I should be used to seeing this shit, but it still breaks my heart a little more every time I see it. One of these days I'll have to either get over him or seriously think about moving away. Gage has already told me that he'll make sure I have a job and stuff if I want to move closer to him. He knows the bullshit that's been happening where Grim is concerned, and that it's breaking me to see him fucking everything in sight. So, he's made it clear that I have a place to go if I can't handle it anymore. Plus, I think he knows that if I don't go there, I'll go back home. Dander Falls is only a few hours away. If I move back home, I'll be leaving the state. Hell, I'll be moving halfway across the country. It's definitely a move that my family doesn't want me to make, but if I have to I will. Everyone that knows anything about me knows that I will too.

Instead of interrupting their little whatever it is, I make my way to the deli to pick up the meat, veggie, and fruit trays. Thankfully they already have a bunch prepared, so I just scoop them up and make my way to get other things we need. Chips and dip are next on my list of things to get, then I get more soda, water, beer, and juice boxes. It doesn't take long to fill this cart up either. I'm still not sure where Grim is, so I decide to make my way up front to wait for him.

While I'm waiting, I decide to grab another cart to fill up with ice. We're going to need a ton of it so that we can fill the coolers and keep the food cold while we're waiting to cook it. I almost have the cart full of bags of ice when Grim walks towards me. He has a weird look on his face and I don't know what it means. What the fuck? I'm not the one being a male whore in the grocery store. But apparently I've done something he doesn't like. Too fucking bad!

"Are you ready to go?" I ask. "I think I got everything we talked about."

"Yep. Let's go."

We load almost everything up on the conveyer belt and I start loading it in the carts while Grim finishes unloading everything. The cashier calls for a stock boy to come help us while Grim is running his card to pay. I smile when I see the stock boy come over to us. He's looking at Grim with awe clearly written on his face. It's the same with all the teen boys in town. They all look at the club members with awe and reverence. It's like they can't wait until they're old enough to save money to buy a bike and join them. Or at least talk to one of them.

"Let's go." Grim says.

I walk out before them pushing two carts, leaving them each one cart a piece to push. Grim tries to catch up to me and take one of the carts, but I don't allow it. Ma always told me when I was growing up to never let a man do what I can do myself. There's nothing wrong with me pushing two carts. Even if I am pregnant, I won't break from doing it. We make it to my truck and I start to climb in the bed so that I can take bags and pile them in.

"Bailey, get down." Grim says, trying to pick me up and move me away from my truck.

"Fuck off Grim!" I say. "I'm fine and nothing's going to happen. Now start handing me the bags and stop trying to fucking cop a feel!"

The boy that's helping us starts laughing at our exchange until Grim looks at him. He quickly stops laughing and starts handing me bags to load up in the bed of the truck. If they hand me one that I plan on putting in the truck, I just set it aside until we're done. It doesn't take the three of us long to get everything loaded up. As I go to hop down, Grim grabs me by the hips and helps me down. Any other day, I'd be in heaven right now. But today, I'm not so sure. I lift my eyes to meet his and see what looks like a mixture of want and need on his face. He quickly lets go and blanks his face. I was probably just projecting my own desires on to him and seeing what I wanted to see. With as fast as he lets go of me, it's like I'm on fire and he doesn't want to touch me any longer than necessary.

I turn to ignore him and start putting the remaining bags in the back seat of the truck. Grim starts handing them to me so we can get done. As I turn to get in to leave, Grim calls out to me.

10

"Make sure the prospects unload everythin' when you get to the garage. Okay?"

"Whatever Grim. Do what you gotta do and I'll do what I gotta do. I'll see you whenever." I say getting in the truck and peeling away from him.

Once I get to the garage, Blade and a few other prospects meet me at the truck. I guess Grim called Blade after I left him. That just means that I can go to the bathroom and take these tests to figure out what's going on with me. Hopefully, Gage gets here early if I turn out to be pregnant. I don't want to talk to him with everyone around.

Finally, everything is set up, the guys are all here, and Sky helped finish with little things that needed to be done. I find a quiet corner and pull out my phone to text Gage.

Me: Are you getting here early? I need to talk to you. It's important!

I sit back and wait to hear back from him. From the tree I'm sitting under, I can watch everything going on around me. People are walking around making sure everything is where it should be. Cage and Joker are in the garage making sure everything is perfect. They're also keeping an eye on Sky and the kids. They don't really let any of them out of their sight. Grim's doing whatever he's doing. He's probably fucking some slut to christen the office right about now. Ma and Pops are just pulling in. I can see Ma making her way over to me as soon as she gets off Pop's bike. Just as she reaches me, my phone vibrates.

Gage: I'm almost there now. Where do you want to meet?

Me: At the house. No one's there and I need to get ready. Give me like ten minutes.

"Hi baby girl." Ma says pulling me up into a hug. She gives the best hugs and I've needed one all day. So, I snuggle in closer for a minute.

"Hi mom. Are you feeling better?" I ask.

"I am. My head still hurts a little, but at least I can stand up and look at the light now. It was a bad one today. What's wrong with you though? Why are you sitting over here all alone?"

"No reason. I just needed a quick break. But, I can see that everything's almost ready, so I'm going to go home for a little while. I'll see you when I get back?"

"Yep. We'll be here. I'm gonna help Sky keep an eye on the kids while the men are doing whatever they need to. I hope you feel better honey. Maybe you need to lie down for a little bit."

"We'll see. It's probably because I haven't eaten all day. I left the house early to shop and get over here. I'll grab something small to eat before I come back."

Ma

I watch my baby girl walk over to her truck and leave. Something is going on that's upsetting her. Like any nosy mother, I want to know what it is. She's breaking my heart knowing that she's hurting. It seems like she can't ever catch a break, but she's always the first one to step up and help everyone else out. If Grim hurt my baby girl, *again*, I will hurt his fucking ass. Anyone can see that he's in love with her, but he does nothing about it. We all know she loves him and seeing the way he acts indifferent towards her is slowly killing her.

As I walk back towards the garage, I see Joker coming over to me. He's got a shit eating grin on his face and that ever present faux hawk he wears. Today it's bright blue with a little bit of red at the tips. Jameson, his son, is also wearing his hair that way. He just doesn't have the color in it. Yet.

"How ya feelin' Ma?" He asks laughing. "Pops told me what the two of you did this mornin'."

"Well, can you blame me? Someone's gotta make that Pres of yours see that he's hurting my baby girl. I didn't raise her to be weak, but this situation is killing her. I'm not too far off from beating his ass! He's gonna make my baby leave one of these days. I know it and I'm not gonna let it fucking happen!"

"I know Ma. We won't let her go though. Not without a fight. It's almost like part of him doesn't think that Pops and I will be okay with him and Bay bein' together. But, it's their mess to sort out, yeah?"

"Fuck that! You saw her sitting alone over here, looking upset as hell. Now she's gone home and I don't know if, or when, she'll be back today. This day wouldn't even be happening if it weren't for your sister."

"I know Ma. If she's not back soon, I'll go get her. Maybe I'll talk to her and see if I can find out what's up." He says giving me a kiss on the cheek and going back to Sky and the kids.

I make my way over to Pops. He pulls me into his side and I snuggle in. Before all is said and done, I think we're all going to need some of his strength. Hopefully, Bailey won't break before the end. If she does, I don't know what will happen. She's been so strong for everyone around her for so long, that one of these days she's not gonna be able to keep it together. I just hope that she's not alone when that finally happens.

Bailey

I'm just getting out of the shower when I hear the rumble of a bike pulling up outside. I quickly send Gage a text telling him to come in my apartment entrance and I'll be out in a second. Rushing to my room, I get dressed and go out to meet him.

"Hey sweetheart. What's goin' on?" He asks me, pulling me in for a hug.

"We need to talk about something. Can we go to the pond?"

"I don't care babe."

I lead him out and we make our way to one of the benches around the pond. After sitting for a few minutes so I can figure out what I want to say to him, I turn to look at him.

"First and foremost, I need you to know that I didn't intend for this to happen. And, I'm not trying to trap you into something you don't want."

"Okay babe. Just tell me what's goin' on. You're fuckin' with my head right now." Gage says grabbing one of my hands in his.

"I'm pregnant." I say looking down and away from him.

"You're sure?"

"I took two tests shortly before I sent you the text. I've got a doctor's appointment this afternoon to make sure too. The only reason I'm getting in so quick there is because they had a cancellation. Otherwise who knows how long I'd have to wait to get in."

"Okay. Well, I wasn't expectin' this news today. I'm not sayin' that I think we should be together or anythin' like that. But, I think we'll make awesome parents and we'll make it work." He says kissing my temple and pulling me closer.

"You're not mad?" I ask him, completely shocked.

"No. I mean the timin' is off and shit, but I'm not mad. Just as long as I'm allowed to be in his or her life then I'm all good. I'm not goin' to be an absent dad like mine was. I mean, I won't be around every day or anythin' obviously if you're still livin' here. But, I'll be around as much as you let me. I mean, that is if you're keepin' the baby." He says, looking at me with a pleading look in his eyes.

"I'm not sure yet honestly. This is still so new that I haven't had enough time to process everything. As soon as I make a decision, I'll let you know. But, I think that if I decide to keep the baby then I should think about moving closer to you. There's really nothing here for me anymore. Ma and Pops obviously are. But Joker and

14

everyone else have their own lives now. Will you come to the appointment with me?"

"I'll be there babe."

"And I think you're right. I mean, I don't think we should be together just because of the baby. But, if we decide to be with someone seriously, I think we need to talk about it before the baby is brought into that mess. No one should be brought into their life if they're just a piece of ass or a fleeting romance."

"That sounds fine to me. Now, why don't you finish gettin' ready and we'll head over to the grand openin'." Gage says standing and leading me back to the house.

Pulling into the parking lot of the garage, I see that the grand opening is a success. There's a ton of people wandering around the place. Most of the guys are, of course, looking at the bikes in the garage. Joker and Cage are in their element talking about the thing they love the most, besides Sky and the kids.

Gage is right behind me as we make our way into the festivities. We'll only be able to stay for a little while before the appointment, but I'm glad I decided to come. Everyone is having a blast. Well, I don't know that I will after seeing Grim heading for us.

"Gage, it's good to see you here brother." He says, doing that man hug thing with him.

"Glad I could make the trip down. Looks like things are goin' good here man."

"It's been an amazin' turn out today. If it weren't for Bailey, I don't know how today would have turned out. She's wonderful and totally stepped up to make sure today was a great day." Grim says smiling at me.

"Gage, let's go get something to eat. We'll only have like an hour before we have to leave." I say starting to walk away from Grim. In turning my back on him, I completely miss the look of longing on his face.

We eat and mingle with everyone for a while before we take a look at some of the rides and stuff set up for kids. Ma tries to keep me in her sights while trying not to make it obvious. She's so funny. She wants me to grow up and be an adult, but wants to keep me close at the same time. I don't think she likes the fact that I've been fucking Gage either. It's not like she knows that's all we are. According to her, we're together and I don't have the heart to tell her any different.

"So, no one here knows?" Gage asks me.

"No. Well, Grim has an idea what's going on, but he doesn't know the results. Although, I'm sure he's figured it out by now."

"Just want to make sure before I say somethin' I shouldn't be sayin'. Is there any reason no one knows yet?"

"Not really. I kind of figured that you should be the first one to know. Plus, I didn't know what I'm going to do, so I don't see any point in telling anyone about it."

"You said you *didn't* know what you were goin' to do. Does that mean you know now?"

"Yeah. I don't think there's any way that I can go through with not havin' the baby. I mean it's a part of both of us and I can see that you really are happy about it. So, I kind of figure that we would keep it and figure everything out that we can before the baby's born."

"Babe, you just made me so happy! But, I don't want you to do somethin' that you don't want to do just to make me happy."

"Honestly, I'm not doing it for you. I mean, yeah, I figured your thoughts and feelings into it. But, I don't think I could live with myself if we don't keep the baby. Even if I had the baby, I couldn't go through with adoption because I doubt either one of us could trust someone enough with our child. Unless it was someone from the club. But, I want us to raise the baby together.

Not as a couple, just as parents. So, eventually, I'll be moving closer to you so that you can be there for the baby more often than once a week or something. Plus, it will allow you to go to doctor appointments with me. If you want to that is."

"Babe, let's get out of here and start headin' to the appointment. I'm sure we'll have a shit ton of paperwork to fill out and stuff before we even see the doctor."

We make our way back to my truck after he makes sure that he can leave his bike here until we're done. Ma wants to know where we're going and I just tell her we have something that needs to be taken care of. I'm sure she thinks I'm skipping out to go fuck him. But this is so much more important than fucking Gage. Finally, all the goodbyes are said and we can leave. I hand my keys over and let Gage drive my truck. This is unusual because I don't let anyone drive it but me. But, I'm getting nervous and feeling shaky. I don't want to crash on the way there.

It only takes about ten minutes to get to the doctor's office. He parks and we make our way inside. Gage is right, there's a ton of paperwork to fill out before we go back. I hand him over the part that he can fill out regarding his side of the family while I work on the rest. We no sooner get the paperwork filled out and a nurse is calling my name to go back. Gage gets up to come with me and I can see every female in here following him with their eyes. I just roll mine.

We get in the back and she tells me that I have to go pee in a cup and then she'll get my weight taken. In front of Gage. I quickly do my business and then go out to the scale. Gage turns his back to me while she's weighing me. How the fuck does he just know what I need and don't need? It's crazy as fuck that he just seems to know what I need from him.

"Okay. We're going in the last room on the left." The nurse says.

We follow her and go in the room. Gage sits in one of the chairs while I take a seat on the bed in the room. I know I'm gonna have to get partially undressed and on the bed, so I might as well just sit here now. The nurse asks me a bunch of questions and takes my paperwork, tells me to strip down, and that the doctor will be in shortly.

This time Gage doesn't turn away, he watches me undress and I can see the lust fill his eyes. Even though we have decided to back off on things, there's still a mutual desire between us. If I didn't desire him, I never would have fucked Gage to begin with. That's not why we decided to back off. The main reason I did is because I don't want to feel like I'm using him anymore. He deserves so much more than me trying to get my mind off of Grim. He has his own reasons that he hasn't shared with me. Maybe one day he will. But I know he's fighting his own demons from his past that he hasn't shared with anyone. Including me.

Once I put the stupid little paper things on and get back on the bed I drape the paper across my legs and lie back. I can see all sorts of naughty thoughts flashing through Gage's mind.

"Hey! My eyes are up here." I joke with him.

"I know. But, I can imagine all sorts of things to do with you lyin' there like that right now."

"I know you can. I can see your mind working from here." I laugh.

Gage has no chance to respond as there's a knock on the door and Doctor Bell comes in. She introduces herself to Gage and turns to me.

"Hi Bailey. I've been looking over your paperwork and your test results. You are definitely pregnant. After I get done with my exam, I'll get you a script for prenatal vitamins and then we'll see you again in a month. When was the date of your last period?"

"It was around five weeks ago. I'm not really sure things have been crazy for the past few months or so."

"Okay. Right now we'll put you around five weeks pregnant. When you come in next month, we'll have you

18

scheduled for an ultrasound too. This way we can get measurements and stuff to get a closer estimation as to when you're due. Actually, why don't I make a call down and see if anyone's available now? That way we don't have to wait and see if you can see what's growing in there. I'm mainly saying this because I see that twins run on your side Mr. Wilson."

"Yes, they do."

I didn't know that at all. These are all things that two people having a baby together should know about one another. Unfortunately, that's not the case with us. We're just gonna have to learn this crap about one another as time goes on.

Doctor Bell does the exam and tells me that she'll want to see me again in a month. She tells me to sit there and relax until the ultrasound tech come in and warns me that it will probably be an internal ultrasound because they don't think I'm that far along. I've seen shows where an internal one is done and I'm not looking forward to that at all. It always looks so uncomfortable and not something I ever wanted to have done to me.

Gage and I wait for about ten minutes before there's another knock on the door. This time it's the ultrasound tech wheeling the machine in the room with her. Gage moves over next to me on the bed so that he can see what's happening. The tech explains what she's going to do and then tells me that it will be an internal ultrasound. I groan and Gage laughs. Well, until he sees what she means by an internal one. Then he stares at me with wide eyes and an open mouth. It's actually kind of funny.

After a few minutes the screen goes from blank to filled with a picture. The tech is looking at things and taking measurements while we try to figure out what she's seeing with no success. To me it just looks like a kidney bean. After getting what she wants, the tech tells me that I'm about five weeks pregnant. She prints some pictures out and leaves the room. This time Gage doesn't watch me get dressed. He's too busy looking at the pictures in his hands. It's kind of cute.

As soon as I'm dressed and ready to go, I see Gage staring at my stomach. He's looking at me like he's trying to picture the baby and what it's going to look like when I get fat. It's kind of unnerving the way that he's looking at me.

"Yeah, Gage, we're really having a baby. You have the proof in your hands. Now, can you stop picturing me fat as fuck and move?" I ask getting annoyed.

"You're not gonna be fat babe. You're gonna be rounded with a baby. *My* baby. You're gonna look hot as fuck carrying him or her."

"Whatever. Are you ready to go now?"

"Yeah. Let's go make your next appointment so I know when it is."

We leave the doctor's office with Gage putting my next appointment in his phone so he doesn't forget it. Once we get down to my truck, he helps me get in and we head back to the garage so he can get his bike. He holds my hand while driving.

"Baby, are you gonna tell anyone now?" He asks, taking a glance in my direction.

"I don't know yet. I mean, let's wait until we get past the three-month mark, yeah? That's when they say it's safer to not worry about a miscarriage or something happening. Is that okay with you?"

"Whatever you want babe. I just hope you're not ashamed or somethin' to be havin' my baby instead of Grim's."

"Gage, don't ever fuckin' think that!" I yell at him. "Listen, I'm gonna be dumping a whole lot of shit on everyone all at once. I'm pregnant, I'm gonna be moving, and I won't be working at the garage anymore. That's a lot to drop on everyone at one time. Especially when I won't be living here anymore. You know how Ma and Pops are. They're going to be pissed that I'm moving closer to you and farther from them, with a baby. Plus, we aren't together so that's something else to take in."

"I understand that. I just hope that you don't come to regret these decisions you're makin'. That would kill me more than anythin' else." He says, kissing the back of my hand.

"Baby, I'm not ashamed of anything that I've done with you. Well, except for feeling like I was using you to get the fuck over Grim. That's something I'll always hate myself for. I'm just trying to think about everything and process this shit. There's a million things running through my mind right now." I say, looking at him so he can see the truth in my eyes.

"Alright babe. For now, I'll let it go. What are you doin' after I get dropped off?"

"Probably going down to the pond to think. Then I'll probably look online to see if I can find an apartment or something. Why, what are you thinking?"

"I was just gonna see if you want to watch a movie or somethin'. I'm probably not gonna head back until tomorrow."

"You can come home with me. We can veg out and talk some more."

"You head home and I'll stop and get dinner from that little diner in town and meet you there. Cheeseburger and fries for you?"

"Hell yeah! That sounds amazing. Will you grab me a chocolate shake too?" I ask, batting my eyelashes at him.

"Yeah. I can't wait until the cravings hit you. It's goin' to be funny as fuck seein' everythin' you're gonna wanna eat."

"Ha! Just think who I'm gonna be calling to go out in the middle of the night to get me that shit. I'll be closer to you and won't know anyone other than the guys from the club."

"Fuck! I didn't think of that. But, if my baby wants somethin' he or she will get it. I'll see ya soon babe."

"Yeah. Just come in the apartment when you get there. I'll leave the door unlocked. I'm gonna take a bath while I'm waiting."

Gage nods and heads over to his bike while I scoot over to the driver's side of my truck. Driving home, I think of all the changes that are going to be coming up. It's a lot for someone to go through. I just hope that everyone understands my decision to move closer to Gage. Well, I hope Ma and Pops understand. Everyone else can fuck themselves if they aren't happy with what I'm doing.

Chapter Two

A month later

Grim

I'M SITTING AT the bar, drinking a beer and thinking about Bailey. It's been a little over a month since I saw her standing in the pharmacy looking at pregnancy tests. She hasn't said anything to any of us, so I'm not sure what the hell's going on. I know that she and Gage left during the grand opening for Spinners, but neither one has said a fucking word. I'm guessing that she's pregnant though because I've seen her distracted and thinking about other things while she's at work.

As I'm sitting on the stool, I hear the outer door to the clubhouse open. I look in the mirror above the bar to see who's coming in. It's Bailey. She looks at me and stops in her tracks.

"Oh. I didn't think anyone would be here." She says.

"I was just takin' a break from paperwork. What's up?" I ask, turning to face her.

"I have to grab some work orders and other paperwork that got brought over here in the boxes. I'll get out of your way."

"You're not in my way crazy girl. Get what you need and do what you gotta do."

"Okay then, there's something I need to tell you." She says sliding on to a stool near me. "Um... I'm not going to be working at the garage that much longer. I'm going to look at apartments in the next few days. I just wanted you to hear it from me."

"What does lookin' at apartments have to do with not workin' at Spinners anymore? Why are you even lookin' for an apartment if you're livin' in the one at Sky's?" I ask her, getting confused.

"Um... Well, that's the thing. I'm not gonna be living at Sky's anymore. I'm moving to Dander Falls to be closer to Gage for the baby. He's made some calls for me to go look at a few places."

"I see. Well, what are you waitin' for then. If you want, you can consider today your last fuckin' day then. That way you can move even fuckin' sooner." I say getting mad that I won't be able to see Bailey anymore. This is not supposed to happen this way. She's supposed to be here with me.

"I'm sorry you feel that way Grim. It's not my fault my baby's father wants to be there for him or her. It's gonna be hard for Gage to be around for the baby if he has to drive here all the time to see it. I've made the decision to move closer and make it easier on him. It's not your decision to make or even fucking accept. You've had so many fuckin' chances to change shit and it's been your decision not to do anything about it. Grow the fuck up Logan! You can't keep me around, slowly killin' me, and then get pissed the fuck off because I'm moving away!"

Bailey turns on her heel and walks back to the office to get whatever paperwork she came here for. She knows I'm pissed that she's leaving, but she's right. I've had a million chances to be with her and I'm the one that fucked that up. I can still remember the first time she told me she loved me. She was sixteen and I was nearing twenty-five. She wasn't going to be around for my birthday, so she had talked me into taking her for a ride so she could take me out to dinner. Not that she really had to try too hard to get me to take her for a ride. We went for rides all the time.

I had just gotten to the clubhouse when Bailey had come barreling up to me wrapping her arms around me. I'm

not sure if something's wrong with her or what. And I don't get a chance to ask her.

"Can you take me for a ride Logan?" She looks up at me with a pleading look in her eyes.

"Sure babe. What's wrong? Is someone in there fuckin' with ya?"

"No. I'm just mad at Pops. He's not going to let me see you on your birthday. So, I want to take you out to dinner tonight to make up for it. Is that okay with you?"

"Sure crazy girl. Let's get goin'."

We make our way to my bike and I can't help but think something more is going on with her. But, I've known Bailey since she was a little girl in pig tails and I know she won't say anything until she wants to. I dig out the helmet I keep on my bike just for Bailey and hand it to her. She straps it on while I straddle the bike. I hold out my hand to her so she can climb on behind me. Once she's on, she scoots forward and wraps her body around mine.

"Don't go slow Logan. I want to go fast."

"We'll see pipsqueak." I say firing up my bike.

As we make our way out of town towards the diner I know Bailey loves, I feel the excitement radiating from her body. Shit's like this every time I give her a ride. She loves riding and she loves going fast. Joker and Pops would kill me if they knew how fast I drive with her on the back of my bike. I just can't ever seem to tell her no though.

Pulling into the diner, I let her off before I back into a spot. She's handing the helmet to me by the time I've shut the bike off. While I'm taking mine off, I see her shake her hair out and then smile up at me.

"You ready to go in now crazy girl?" I ask her smiling.

"Yeah. I'm starving!"

We head in and take our usual booth in the back. As soon as the waitress sees us, she grabs our drinks and heads over. I get a coffee and Bailey gets a chocolate *shake. The waitress asks us if we want our usual order of cheeseburger and fries before heading back to her other tables. It's funny that all we have to do is walk in this diner and they know what we want.*

"So, what's goin' on between you and Pops?" I ask Bailey while I get my coffee the way I like it

"He's just being pig headed as usual. I said that I wanted to do something for you for your birthday. I do something for you every year. Anyway, he said that I wasn't allowed near the clubhouse on your birthday, or for that weekend. So, I'm guessing that you're doing it up big this year huh?"

"I honestly have no clue what they have planned. I've heard some talk here and there, but that's it. But, if Pops said you can't be there, then you should probably listen to him. Apparently he knows what's goin' down." I say, sipping my coffee.

The waitress brings our food over and we take a break from talking so that we can devour it. It always amazes me to watch Bailey eat. She eats more than most men I know, and she's quick about it too. I guess growing up with a houseful of boys taught her that she had to eat her food quick so we wouldn't steal it from her.

"You wanna go for a ride to the lake when we're done?" I ask her. It's somewhere we often go, just the two of us.

"Sure. It should be quiet today since there's a little chill in the air."

We finish eating and Bailey beats me to the register to pay for our early dinner. I know she said she wanted to take me to dinner, but I was still planning on paying for it. She smiles at me because she knows where my mind was at. Hell, I didn't even get to leave a tip, she already left that too. What a crazy girl she is!

It takes us about ten minutes to get to our spot at the lake. Once again, Bailey has her body wrapped around me. She's the only female that's been on my bike and the only one I can ever see being on my bike. I don't

26

put random pussy on my girl, they're not worthy of riding on her. Bailey is something special though and anyone that meets her for a second knows that she's special.

We park in our usual spot and make our way to our rock. I sit down and Bailey climbs in front of me, just like always. To me, it's something that I don't even think about anymore. She always just sits in front of me like this and it feels right. Bailey sighs and leans into me further. It's like she has the weight of the world resting on her shoulders.

"What's the matter babe? I know from that sigh it's more than just disagreein' with Pops about my birthday. Talk to me." I ask her playing with a strand of her hair.

"Logan, things are changing so much, so fast. It's always been the guys not wanting me to tag along because I was girl. Now, it's because I'm only sixteen. I can't do anything that I want to. Pops doesn't even want me to get my license. Did you know that? No, I'm sure you didn't because you're just like Joker, Cage, and the others now. You always had time for me. But now, it's all about the club and the easy, random pussy you get."

"Crazy girl, it's because we're older than you. If we were the same age, things would probably be different."

"Don't lie Logan. Things are never going to be different. I'm young and viewed as Pops' daughter and Joker's little sister. I've loved you since I was twelve and you look at me as another brother. It's too much. I think Pops is right and I need to stay away from everything club related."

I don't even know what to say to what Bailey just said. She doesn't love me. She just sees me as someone that always allowed her to tag along because I couldn't stand to see the heartbroken look on her face. Bailey's too young to even know what love is. Shit, I'm almost twenty-five and I don't know what love is.

"Bay, you don't love me. You don't know what love is. I'm just the guy that can never tell you no. If you want *somethin', you know I'll give it to you. Please, don't confuse that with love. I don't want to see you hurt." I say, trying to make her understand that she doesn't love me.*

"That's bullshit Grim and you know it. You've always been more than just the guy that took pity on me. But, don't worry about me. You guys won't be seeing me anymore. Not at the clubhouse and not when any of you visit the house. I have a room that I spend most of my time in now anyway. I'll see you around Grim."

What the fuck? Not only is she calling me Grim and not Logan, but she's leaving me sitting here. Where the hell does she think she's fucking going? Bailey has never acted like this with me. And she's never left me sitting here alone because I pissed her off or upset her. Usually she would stomp her feet and start pouting until we talked it out. Apparently that's not happening this time. Fuck, I don't even know how she's getting home. We're at least an hour away driving, so it's going to take her forever to walk it.

I get up and go looking for her. There's one other spot we come to if this one's taken. Maybe she went there to pout or whatever. What I see when I get to our spot has me seeing red though. There's another guy wearing colors that aren't Wild Kings talking to her. What the fuck is she thinking? Well, if that's how she wants to play it, fuck her. She can find her own way home. Maybe I'll send Pops and Joker looking for her ass.

I'm still sitting here on my seat wondering where the hell Bailey is. She's been in the office for a while and it shouldn't be taking her this long to grab papers from a box that was right inside the door. So, I get up and go see what's going on. As soon as I round the corner, I stop dead in my tracks. Bailey's lying on the floor surrounded by a pool of blood. It's coming from the lower half of her.

"Bailey!" I yell running to her. "Crazy girl, wake the fuck up! Please baby!"

I get no response so I feel for a pulse. She has one, but it's weak as fuck. What the fuck is going on with her? I quickly pick her up and run to my truck with her. I lay her in the back seat and run to the driver's door. I shoot out a mass text to Gage, Joker, Cage, Pops, and Caydence telling them to meet me at the hospital really fucking quick. Throwing the truck in gear, I ram through the gate blocking the parking lot and make my way to the hospital, knowing that I can get her there faster than waiting on an ambulance. I do manage to call the hospital and warn them I'm coming though.

Squealing into the hospital parking lot, I pull right up to the doors and see a whole shit load of people running out the doors to get to Bailey. I'm grateful they're out here because I'm flipping the fuck out.

"What can you tell us sir?" A nurse asks me.

"She showed up lookin' for some paperwork and when she didn't come back out after I don't even know how long; I went searchin' for her. I found her lyin' on the floor in a pool of blood. She wasn't respondin' to me so I grabbed her and brought her here. I didn't want to wait for an ambulance because I knew I'd be faster."

"Okay sir. I'm gonna have you wait out here while we figure out what's going on. I'm sure that more people are gonna be showing up for her?"

"Yeah. I sent out a mass text when I was leaving. She's pregnant. I'm not sure how far along or anythin' though." I say sitting down because I feel like my legs can't hold my weight for another second.

The nurse disappears through the emergency room doors after telling me that she'll let me know what's going on as soon as they know something. Slouching down, I lay my head in my hands staring at my boots.

Until I hear a commotion coming through the door. It's either Gage arriving or everyone else. Looking up, I see Gage *and* everyone else.

"Grim, what the fuck is goin' on?" Pops asks me, concern lacing his voice and etched all over his face.

"It's Bailey. She was lookin' for papers that got sent to the clubhouse accidently for Spinners. When she didn't come back out, I went lookin' for her. I found her lyin' on the floor surrounded by a pool of blood." I tell everyone, but look at Gage.

"It's the baby?" He asks, sinking down into the closest chair.

"I think so." I tell him, putting my hand on his shoulder.

"What the fuck are you talkin' about? She's not pregnant!" Pops shouts.

"She is." Gage says. "We were waitin' until she hit the three-month mark to tell anyone. It was what she wanted."

Ma walks over and sits next to Gage, taking his hand in hers. There's tears shimmering in both their eyes as she starts whispering to him. She's trying to comfort him. I know she is. I'm sure she's upset as hell that she didn't know her daughter was pregnant, but that's not what she's focusing on right now. She's trying to make sure that Gage will be okay no matter what we find out. It's a good thing because Pops and Joker look like they're about ready to kill him for getting her pregnant. I've never seen Pops so pissed off before. His entire face is fire engine red and his veins are popping out all over the place. If he doesn't calm down, we might end up with him in a bed right next to Bailey.

It seems like we sit here for ages before the nurse comes back out with a doctor. He calls for Bailey's family and we all stand up. It doesn't even phase him, which is kind of surprising.

"Is the baby okay? Is Bailey okay?" Gage asks frantically.

"I'm sorry sir, but we couldn't save the baby. She suffered a miscarriage. Physically, she'll be fine. Emotionally and mentally, I don't think she's doing so good. We've given her a mild sedative so she can get some rest."

"Can we see her?" Ma asks, the tears streaming down her face now.

"You can go in two at a time." The doctor says before walking away.

Bailey

I'm lying in the hospital bed, trying to stay awake after getting shot up with a sedative. I guess I kind of flipped out when the doctor told me there was nothing they could do to save the baby. Even as they were asking me what happened, I couldn't answer them. The only thing I remember is arguing with Grim before I went to the office to find the papers I needed. As soon as I bent over, I felt this horrible pain shoot through my stomach. It came again and again, increasing in intensity each time. Finally, when I couldn't stand it anymore, I remember falling to the floor. Nothing after that though. They told me Grim was the one to bring me in.

"Babe, are you awake?" I hear Gage ask from the doorway.

"Gage, I'm so sorry!" I cry, refusing to turn over and look at him.

"You did nothin' wrong babe. This wasn't your fault. I know that if you could have prevented it, you would've done everythin' in your power to protect our baby. Obviously the cat's out of the bag now. I thought Joker and Pops were goin' to tear my head off when they found out."

"I'm sorry you had to deal with them on your own. I should have already told them about the baby so that they wouldn't be pissed at you. It's not like you were the only one there when I got pregnant, it took both of us. So, yes, I'm sorry you had to deal with them." I say finally turning over and looking at him.

"Babe, I'm sorry for what you just went through. Other than the obvious, how are you doin'?" He asks me.

"Not good Gage. It hurts so bad still and all I want to do right now is cry, scream, shout, and swear like a sailor."

"I know babe. What can I do for you?"

"I know this isn't gonna be a popular decision, but can I go back to Dander Falls with you? I just don't want to have to deal with everyone here. Plus, if I go home, there's the kids and Sky's pregnant and I don't think I can be around that right now. It's like she can carry a baby, not just a baby, but twins to term, and I can't make it over two months or so. What the fuck is wrong with me?" I ask, starting to cry all over again.

"I'll take you anywhere that you wanna go babe. If you want to go with me, I'll go rent a trailer for the bike and I'll drive your truck back home. Do you need me to pack a bag for you, or do you want Sky to do that for you?" Gage asks, taking my hand in his.

"If you can pack a bag for me, that'd be great. I really don't want Sky to have to pack my things for me. Just pack enough for a few weeks if that's okay. It'll give me time to think and figure out what I want, and need, to do. I'll figure out where I go from here. My truck should still be at the clubhouse. I'm guessing Grim brought me in his."

"Okay babe. I'll be back as soon as I can. I know Ma's chompin' at the bit to get in here to see you. I'll send her and Pops in now."

I roll back over so that I don't have to see the look of disappointment on my parents' faces as soon as they walk in the door. It'll be better if they just talk to my back or think I'm sleeping. But, if I know Ma, she'll walk right over to this side of the bed to see me. She's naturally a worry wart when it comes to me, even if she does encourage me to do what I want. This, though, will push her over the limit of shit she can tolerate.

"Baby girl, I'm so sorry." I hear my Pops' gruff voice.

He walks right over to the bed I'm lying in and turns me to face him before pulling me into a big bear hug. I love my dad's hugs. Most days I think they can heal whatever is making a person feel like shit. This is not one of those days though. I can feel the shoulder of my shirt getting wet, which means my dad is crying. I can't ever remember a day that I've seen him cry. Pissed, full of rage, angry, disappointed, happy as fuck. Yeah, I've seen all those emotions.

"Daddy, I'm gonna be okay." I say trying to soothe the big man.

"Bailey, I know you're gonna be fine. You're one of the strongest people I know, other than Ma. I'm sorry that you're goin' through this and that we weren't there for you when you found out. I'm pissed as fuck that it was with Gage though, and you know that."

"Daddy, there's nothing wrong with Gage. He's a great guy and has never treated me with anything other than respect."

"I know that baby girl. He's just not the guy I see you with. He's not in the same chapter as us, your family."

"That's enough Pops!" Ma speaks up. "Your daughter just suffered something extremely tragic. Gage is who she's with. It doesn't matter what you say. Now move your big ass so I can see my baby."

I can't help but laugh a little bit at Ma. She's so loving and knows when I'm being pushed to my limit. Ma's always been able to tell when I'm at my limit and shit's about to hit the fan. It's part of what makes me love her even more in times like this.

"Ma, I'm fine. Really." I say trying to convince her that I am fine. Even though that's the last thing I am right now.

"Hush baby girl! I know that you aren't fine, and that you're as far from fine as a person can get right now. But, we're here and we're going to help you get through this." She says pulling me in close.

"Actually, I guess I better just tell you this now." I say looking at a spot on the wall over my dad's shoulder. "I'm leaving with Gage as soon as I'm released. For the next few weeks or so, I'll be staying in Dander Falls with him. I just can't be around Skylar pregnant and the kids right now."

"Fine. But, you're not goin' with Gage." Dad says moving closer to me. "You can move back home until you know what you're goin' to do."

"No, daddy. I'm going with Gage and there's nothing you can do to stop me. I'm a grown woman for fucks sake."

"Alright you two. Now's not the time for you to be pissing and moaning to one another. Bailey, if that's what you feel you need to do, then I guess that's what you have to do. I'm not happy about it though. I think you need to be around your family during this."

"I know Ma. And I love you for that. But, I can't see everyone on a daily basis looking at me with pity. I can't see Skylar, who has already delivered two sets of twins and is pregnant again. I can't see the kids running around and happy. But most of all, I don't want to see Grim. I've been dying inside for a long time now watching him and the sluts. If I have to watch that shit now, it *will* break me. Losing this baby is already breaking me and making me question everything I've ever done. Everything I've ever known or thought about myself. I need space and time to figure out where I want to go from here. Hell, to figure out if I even still want to live here."

At my little speech, Pops doesn't say anything else to me. He turns on his heel and leaves the room. Ma looks at me with her face full of tears. She doesn't leave the room like Pops does, but her look of hurt and disappointment is almost worse than just leaving the room. My mom gives me a hug and kiss and then leaves the room.

Finally, alone, I roll over and let the tears stream down my face. I cry for hurting my family by leaving with Gage, I cry for hurting Gage by not being able to carry the baby to term, and I cry for losing the baby. Even though I wasn't sure at first about keeping the baby, I came to love the baby more than anything else in my life. Is this my punishment for not being sure in the beginning? Or is something really wrong with me and I'll never be able to have babies?

Pops

This has been one of the most fucked up days in a long time that I've had to face. First, I find out that my baby girl is pregnant. In the same breath as that, we find out that she's lost that baby. Then, she's leaving with Gage and going to stay in Dander Falls for however long. This is not what I envisioned for my baby girl. If she was going to be with anyone in the club at all, I would choose Grim for her. Not just because of the fact that I'm in his chapter, but because I know she's loved him for so long now. I know in my heart that he loves her too. He just won't man up and do anything about it.

Walking into the waiting room, I see my family sitting around waiting to see my baby girl. Grim is still sitting in the same spot. He hasn't moved since we arrived. The pain I see on his face shatters my heart even more. The only one that I don't see in here now is Gage. Apparently, he's doing what he has to do to take my baby girl away from us.

Joker, Cage, and Sky walk over to me. I can see that they're upset and want to know how Bailey's doing. Sky's been crying so I open my arms to her. She walks into my embrace and I hold her while I let everyone know what Bailey just informed us of.

"When Bailey gets released to go home, she won't be goin' back to the apartment. She's goin' to Dander Falls with Gage." I say looking around.

"What the fuck you talkin' 'bout?" Grim asks me finally moving.

"She can't be here right now. I hate that she's leavin' with him, but I can kind of understand why."

"Pops, you gotta do somethin'." Joker says. "She doesn't need to be goin' with him. We're her family and she needs to be here with us."

"You're not tellin' me anythin' I don't already know son. But, she wants to be with Gage right now. This loss isn't hers alone, but it's his too."

Grim gets up and walks to the doorway leading to the rooms in back. I can only hope that he's not too hard on Bailey. He looks devastated and I know how he gets at times when he's feeling more than he wants to. Heaven help him if he does decide to go off on her. I won't just hurt him, President or not, I'll fucking kill him! My baby girl has been through enough and doesn't need his shit piled on top.

Grim

Sitting in the waiting room while Gage and then Ma and Pops go in to see Bailey, I think about everything that has happened. Everything that I've done to hurt Bailey over the years. This has me knowing in my heart, even more, that Bailey is meant to be with me. I'm sorry that she's suffering through this loss, but to me it means that she's supposed to be with me. I don't need the loose pussy of the club girls anymore; all I need is her.

As soon as Pops announces that she's going back to Dander Falls with Gage, I feel the rage running through my body. She's not supposed to be leaving here, leaving me and her family. I can understand if she doesn't want to stay with Sky and the guys. But, she could stay with her parents, with me at the clubhouse, with Mackenzie, or Caydence and Irish. She doesn't need to go hours away and leave us all behind. If she does, I have the feeling that she won't be coming back home. Well, not for anything more than to grab her shit and leave us all behind.

Before I know what I'm doing, I feel myself walking through the doors to go see her. I pass Ma on my way back. She pulls me in for a hug and tells me not to lose my shit with Bailey. That I'll only push her farther away right now. I nod to her and continue making my way to her room. Once I get to her door, I stand there and take a few deep breaths trying to control my emotions before I walk in there. Finally, I walk in and see Bailey lying in the bed looking so tiny and fragile. She's got her back to me, but I can see her shoulders shaking as she cries. Now, I'm not pissed, I'm heartbroken. She's suffering and she's trying to do it alone. I know Bailey, and I know that she won't want us to feel sorry for her or to try to help her. My crazy girl always wants to be the one helping others out. She can't ever take the help for herself no matter what she's going through.

"I don't care if you try to ignore me Bay. You scared the livin' shit outta me earlier. And now I find out that you're goin' three hours away to be with Gage for a few weeks or whatever. If you need a place to stay, then stay with me." I say moving the chair closer and sitting down.

"And why would I do that Grim? Huh?"

"You don't have to run away to deal with your loss. Stay here with your family and friends. Who are you gonna have at Gage's clubhouse with all of us three plus hours away?"

"Don't you think that's the point of me goin' with him? I need to get away and figure things out for myself. I can't do it here with everyone up in my face. I'll have space at Gage's and I'll be able to think things through. Without everyone else's input."

"So, you're gonna leave everyone that cares about you to go with Gage? Why?"

"Because it was his child too! He's feeling just as much pain as I am right now. No one here understands it, but he does. He knows what I'm feeling and where I'm coming from right now. And I can't deal with all of the other hurt on top of this. Not right now."

"What other pain crazy girl? What are you talkin' about?" I ask her, leaning in closer.

"I've loved you forever Grim. If you don't know that by now, then you're fuckin' blind. I'm so tired of sitting there and watching you go off with whatever slut you have near you at that second and not being able to do anything about it. Do you know what my first thought was when I thought I might be pregnant? I wished it was your baby instead of Gage's. Now, it doesn't really matter. I'm so tired of hiding my feelings from you. Especially when you go all fucking psycho when I show up somewhere with Gage. You don't want me, but you don't want anyone else to have me either. I'm over it! All you see is Joker's little sister when you look at me. Or Pop's daughter. It's just gonna take some time to get over my feelings. And until I do, it's best that I not be around." The tears are streaming down her face now.

"Babe, please don't leave. I think we need to sit down and have a conversation one of these days. The way you think I feel isn't how it is." I start to say.

"I'm not dealing with this shit Grim. Let's just leave well enough alone. You're happy with your sluts and I'm not anywhere on your radar. I won't ever be to you what you are to me. It's time I accept it and move on. I just need to get away from seeing you all the time to be able to move on. Who knows, I might not even come back here for long. Maybe I'll decide that I like being closer to Gage's area and stay there. Or maybe I'll move back home. I know there's no club there now, but I still have friends there. Whatever I decide, it's my decision to make and no one will influence me or have any say in my decision other than myself. Please, can you just leave now? I want to be alone until I can leave here."

I sit in stunned silence for a few minutes, trying to take in everything that Bailey just said to me. All of a sudden it hits me. I've pushed her too far and she's finally had enough. Pops was wrong when he said I couldn't push her away from me. I just did. And she doesn't even know how I truly feel about her, how I've felt about her for so long now. It's my fault for not telling her and giving us the chance that we deserved. I thought I was protecting her. Now, it's my heart that's being ripped out and she'll be taking it with her when she goes. Even if she moves back home and never comes around again, she'll be carrying my heart with her until the day I take my last breath.

Finally, I get off my ass and leave the room. I don't say a word to anyone as I make my way back out to the waiting room. Hell, I don't even stop at the waiting room. I push my way through the door and leave the hospital. Instead of going back to the clubhouse though, I go to the apartment I have outside of town. There's alcohol there and I plan on doing nothing but getting drunk until I pass out. No one even knows that I have an apartment. I don't use it very often. In fact, the only things there are a bed, a couch, and alcohol.

Bailey

After Grim leaves, I hear more movement coming through the door. I just don't have anything else in me to roll over and see who it is. So, I stay facing the opposite wall and let the tears continue to go unchecked. Unfortunately, Sky, Joker, and Cage have other ideas.

Skylar is the first one I can see. She walks around the end of the hospital bed and right up to me. Sky sits carefully down on my bed and pulls me into her arms. I can feel the roundness of her belly and it makes me cry harder. This is not fair at all!

"Bailey, I'm so sorry!" She says into my hair. "I can't imagine what you're going through right now."

"I know you can't." I say looking at her. "You don't know what it's like to lose a baby. I mean you're on pregnancy number three and they've all gone to term pretty much. You know what it's like to hold that little bundle of love and joy, to protect that little person with everything you have. I'll never feel my belly getting big and round, holding my baby, or feel the baby move around inside of me while he or she grows." I say starting to cry even harder.

"Babe, I'm so sorry that you feel like that. You'll have more chances to experience all of that sometime." She says trying to comfort me.

"No, I won't!" I say forcefully. "There's only one man I want that with and it's never gonna happen. Please, I just want to be left alone. Can you guys leave and tell everyone else to leave too?"

"Sis, that's not gonna happen and you know it. There's a shit ton of people waitin' out there to make sure that you're goin' to be okay." Joker says looking down at me.

"Bailey, we love you and know that things feel like shit right now. But, don't push everyone away that loves you because you're hurtin'." Cage says leaning over to kiss my forehead.

"I'm not pushing everyone away. I need to get away and figure out what I want and need now. I was going to be moving to Dander Falls anyway. I mean Gage is there and I wanted to be closer so the baby could be near his or her father. So, it only makes sense that it's where I go now. I need time to heal and forget about certain things here for a while. I'll be back to see you guys and the kids. I just don't think I'll be around the club much anymore. It's my mess and it's my life to deal with. I've wanted a fairytale for so long that I finally know it's never going to happen. The three of you got your fairytale and found the love you deserve, but it's not in the cards for me. Now, I'm tired and I want to close my eyes until the doctor comes back in. As soon as I'm released, I'll be leaving with Gage. He's getting my stuff ready right now. I'll stay in contact with you guys. I love you all." I say, rolling over and burying my face.

All three of them kiss the top of my head and leave the room. Finally, I'm alone! My eyes close and I can feel myself drifting away.

When I open my eyes again, I expect to be alone in my room. I look over to see Gage sleeping uncomfortably in one of the chairs. Reaching out, I run my fingers through his hair. He slowly wakes up and moves closer to me.

"Hey baby." He says, his voice has that sleepy, husky sound to it.

"Hey." I say. "What time is it?"

"It's a little after six. You were out for a while. The doctor should be comin' back in soon. You were sleepin' when she came in the last time."

"Okay. Are they going to let me go home when she comes back?" I ask, wanting to leave.

"I think so."

Just then, there's a knock on the door and Doctor Bell peeks around the door.

"You're awake." She says entering. "How are you feeling?"

"I've been better, but the cramping in my stomach seems to be gone for now." I answer.

"Okay, that's good. I'm going to discharge you now. I'll be giving you a script for some medicine that I want you to take for the next few days. It will help slow down the bleeding that you're going to be experiencing."

"Sounds good doc." I say.

"You can get dressed now. When the nurse comes in with the papers for you to sign, she'll give you the first dose of it. Then she'll give you a bottle with your next dose until you can get to a pharmacy. If you have any problems, I want you to call my office and I'll get you in immediately. Do you have any questions for me?"

"Okay. I promise I'll call if anything comes up."

"I have a question that I think needs to be asked. Is Bailey goin' to be able to have kids in the future?" Gage asks.

"She'll be just fine to have kids. Sometimes women have miscarriages for no apparent reason at all. Bailey, you're young and healthy. There's no reason not to think that you'll be able to have kids and carry them to term in the future." Doctor Bell says reassuringly.

"Thank you." I say around the lump in my throat.

She leaves the room and I look to Gage. He stands up and hands me the bag he brought in with him. Then, he helps me out of the bed and helps me to the bathroom so that I can get changed. Once in the bathroom, I open the bag to see he put in sweats, a club shirt, underwear, my flip flops, and some pads. He surprises me again by making sure that I have exactly what I need when I need it.

It takes me a minute, but I finally get dressed and throw my hair up into a messy bun. Opening the door, I find Gage leaning against the wall waiting for me. He helps me over to the chair and as soon as I sit down, the nurse comes in. I sign the papers, take the pills, and get in the wheel chair that is wheeled in for me.

Gage wheels me out to my truck. As soon as he has me seated in the passenger seat, I see Grim pulling into the parking lot. He sees me in the truck and pulls into a spot. Gage is getting in the truck and I tell him to get out of there now. I know he's seen Grim pull in and knows that I want to leave without speaking to him. Right now, I just can't muster the strength to not spill my guts to Grim about how I feel and what I want from him. What I need from him. It's not going to happen and I need to let it go.

I look in my mirror and see Grim standing there with his hands shoved in his pockets and his head down.

It breaks my heart knowing that he's hurting and I want to take him in my arms and tell him everything is going to be okay. But I can't right now. Right now, I need to focus on me and getting over the pain of losing my baby.

"Baby, why don't you try to get some sleep? I'll wake you up when we get closer to the clubhouse." Gage says, looking in the rearview mirror.

"That sounds good. Thank you for taking me away. No one here is going to know what I'm feeling. But I know that you're hurting just as bad as I am."

"You're right, I am feelin' the loss. And together we'll get through this and move forward. It's not goin' to be overnight, but we *will* get through this."

I lean my head against the window and close my eyes. Just like in the hospital, I dream of a little baby in my arms. It's a little boy with blond hair and piercing blue eyes. He looks just like Gage and I quickly open my eyes up. I don't want to worry Gage, so I go through my bag and find my iPad and headphones. I turn on my music and the song playing is *Beam Me Up* by Pink. Once I make sure that the song is on repeat, I close my eyes again, letting the music lull me into a fitful sleep.

Chapter Three

Gage

AS I DRIVE towards Dander Falls, I look over at Bailey. She's got her headphones on and her eyes closed. I know she's sleeping based on the even rise and fall of her chest. But, she's crying in her sleep and I know she's dreaming of the baby. Dreaming of what could have been and what we're going to miss out on. I hurt even more because I know she's hurting so bad and blaming herself for it happening.

The closer I get to home, the more tense I can feel myself become. We're about a half hour from the clubhouse now and I can feel the tension ratcheting up even higher. No one in the club knows that Bailey was pregnant and that we were going to have a baby. The guys don't know that she was going to be moving here to be closer to me for the baby. If things were different, Bailey would make me an excellent old lady. But, with the things I've done, things I've seen, and the past I had growing up, I am not a man that deserves to have an old lady. The girls at the club are good enough for me. I get to scratch an itch when I have one without all of the commitments that come with an old lady.

I gently shake Bailey awake as we get closer to the clubhouse. She puts her iPad and headphones away in her bag and puts her hair back up into that messy bun thing she does. Then, she turns her sleep filled eyes to me and gives me a small smile.

"We're almost there baby." I say looking at her.

"Okay. I can't wait to get there. All I want is a bath and then a nice, warm bed to lay down in."

"Your wish is my command. Do you want somethin' to eat first?" I say grabbing her hand and kissing her knuckles.

"No. I don't feel like eating right now. Maybe in a little while. If I get hungry, I'll grab something at the clubhouse."

"Okay baby."

Bailey

As soon as we pull in to the parking lot of the club, I know that there's a party going on inside. Hell, not just inside, people are already spilling outside the clubhouse with drinks in their hands and the music is blaring. Right now I can hear *The House Rules* by Christian Kane. I look over to Gage and I can see that he's pissed that the guys are having a party right now.

"Babe, you can't be pissed. They don't know what happened or that you were bringing me back here afterwards." I say trying to calm him down.

"I know that they don't know about the baby. But, damn, they shouldn't be havin' a party right now. I was gone and they decide to fuckin' live it up!" Gage yells.

"It's fine. I'm just gonna go in to whatever room you have for me and rest. I'll put in my headphones and relax."

"Are you sure? I can make everyone leave if that's what you need."

"No. I'm not gonna disrupt what you guys have goin' on here. It will do nothing but make them hate the fact that I'm here."

We say nothing more as Gage parks my truck and calls over some prospects. The only one that I know is Shadow. He was here the last time I was here and he seems like a good guy. I think he'll make it far in the club. There are two new guys following him and you can tell just by looking at them that they haven't been here for that long. I'm guessing that they've been here around a few weeks' tops.

Gage talks to them and I can't hear what he's saying to them. But, I don't care. I can see Steel coming over to us along with Crash and Trojan. Crash and Trojan are my favorite guys here in this chapter. Steel was a nomad with Tank. When Tank decided that he wanted to settle down to one club, Steel did the same thing. For his own reasons, Steel chose to come to Gage's chapter instead of staying with Tank.

Steel picks me up in a huge hug and spins me around. He gives me a kiss on the cheek and passes me to Crash.

"Baby girl, it's so good to see you. But I gotta say, you look like shit. Is everythin' okay with you?" He asks me looking into my face trying to figure out what's going on.

"I'm fine babe. It's just been a really long and rough day today." I say. Thankfully, I took off the hospital bracelet and things before we made it here. I'm not ready to answer questions right now.

"Babe, I didn't think you were ever gonna come see us again." Trojan says pulling me into his arms.

"What the fuck? Why would you think that?" I ask getting confused.

"I know you were coolin' things off with Gage. Once that happened I knew you wouldn't spend time here. We miss you!"

"It's fine. I'll be stayin' here for a few weeks for now. So, you guys enjoy your party and I'll see you tomorrow."

I give Trojan a kiss and turn to face Gage. He's facing me and watching me interact with his brothers. Gage should know that I'm close to these guys. Well, some of them anyway. Gage grabs my arm and leads me into the clubhouse and down the hallway towards the room at the back. He opens a door that's between his room and Trojan's room.

Thankfully, there's a bathroom with a shower and tub in here so that I can take a relaxing bath before crawling into bed. Gage lets the prospect in with my bags and tells me that if I need anything to come get him.

"I'll be fine. Like I said, I'm gonna relax in a bath and then lay down." I say reassuring him that I'll be fine.

"Okay. Tomorrow, we'll go into town and get your medicine and talk if you want to."

"Sounds good. Thank you for bringing me here Gage. It means a lot to me."

Gage backs out of the door and I lock it behind him. I take some clothes in the bathroom and run the water as hot as I can stand it. While I'm waiting for the tub to fill, I start to set my bathroom things on the sink and fill the drawers. Gage grabbed everything out of my bathroom when he packed my bags for me. Once again he's come through for me.

It's been about a week and a half that I've been at Gage's clubhouse. I don't feel any better now than I did when I left the hospital. But, then again, I haven't really been dealing with it either. I don't have any more strength or fight in me to deal with the pain of losing the baby. When I get up in the morning, I grab a bottle from behind the bar and head back to my room. Gage has tried to get me to talk to him a few times and I just shut him down. Ma and Pops, Joker, Cage, Sky, Caydence, and Kenzie have tried getting a hold of me. Grim's even been trying to text and call me. They can all go fuck themselves as far as I'm concerned. I'm the one that suffered the loss and I'm gonna deal with it the way that I feel best. And right now, the way I feel like doing that is getting blasted off my ass every day so I don't have to deal with the pain. I don't have to think about what I'm never going to have. I don't have to think about losing something that was precious to me and Gage.

Just as I close my door, I hear my phone alerting me that someone sent me a text. Maybe it's someone other than Grim this time. But, I couldn't get that lucky.

Grim: How are you doin'? I miss you!

Me: Fuck off Grim. You don't miss me. You fucking miss everything I did to make your day easier. Now, you have to do that shit for yourself or get your slut of the fucking day, or second, to do it for you.

Grim: That's not true and you fuckin' know it! I miss seein' you every day. I miss you not takin' my shit. And most of all I miss not bein' able to look at you whenever the fuck I want to.

Me: Like I said, fuck off! I'm here and at this point I don't think I'm going to come back. I think I might even send prospects to get my shit for me. Maybe Crash and Trojan will help them. That's how much I don't even fucking want to see you!!!!!

I don't want to hear any response from him so I shut my phone off and throw it in my bag. The only thing I'm concerned with right now is finishing this bottle of Jack Daniels and getting another one.

Gage

It's been almost two weeks and I know that Bailey is going downhill fast. All she does is drink from the time she gets up until the time she goes to sleep. Most nights, she doesn't even sleep in her room anymore. She's taken to fucking my brothers and it's really starting to piss me off. I'm not pissed because of the fact that she's fucking my brothers. She can do whatever she wants to fucking do. What's pissing me off is she isn't dealing with the loss of our baby. I know for a fact that she's been with Steel, Fox, and Tech at this point.

On the rare nights she's in her room alone, I end up in there with her. She's crying and screaming in her sleep listening to this sad song over and over again. The only thing that gets her to stop is when I climb in bed with her and curl my body around hers. Then she only gets a fitful sleep at best. She can't continue on this way, and I think I'm gonna have to call either Grim or Ma and Pops to help me out here. Fuck, I can't even tell you when the last time she ate was. Even if one of us brings her a plate of food, we find it on the floor in the hallway. Still full of food.

Pulling out my phone, I decide to deal with the lesser of the two evils and call Grim. He answers almost immediately.

"What's up Gage?"

"I don't know what to do with Bailey anymore."

"What the fuck do you mean? What's goin' on over there?" Grim asks raising his voice.

"She won't talk or eat a thing. All she does is get up, grab a bottle of Jack from the bar, and go back to her room. Most nights she doesn't spend alone. When she does, I end up in her room holdin' her until she stops cryin' and screamin'. She's killin' herself Grim, and I can't get her to stop no matter what I do."

"Fuuuuuuuuuck!" Grim yells through the phone. "I knew she should have never fuckin' went with you. I can't get there until a few days from now. I've got shit to do here that I can't let someone else handle. There's no point in tellin' Pops unless you want to be put to ground."

"I was just callin' to let you know. I'm gonna figure out what to do to help her through this. I won't let her spiral any farther down. Don't come here just yet. I'll keep you updated."

"Fine. I want a fuckin' call every day about what's goin' on. I know she's still got her fire and spirit if the texts she sent to me are anythin' to go by." Grim says laughing a little bit.

"I'll call or text every day Grim. I'm gonna go drag her ass out of her room and get this shit fixed."

I hang up and turn to see Crash standing right behind me. He's staring at me trying to figure out what's going on with Bailey. I know Trojan and him are pissed as fuck with the way Bailey's acting. And, they're

49

worried as much as I am about her. Just looking at her you can see the weight she's lost. She's gonna make herself sick with the way she's drinking, and I can guarantee she's not taking her medicine. This can't fucking continue anymore!

"Pres, I wanna know what the fuck's goin' on. Somethin' isn't right with Bailey and she's killin' herself." Crash starts out, crossing his arms over his chest while Trojan walks up next to him.

"Fuck!" I yell. "Look, we didn't want to tell anyone, but obviously the secret's gotta come out now. Bailey was pregnant, and yes I was the dad. The night we showed up here, she had lost the baby. Since then, she's been on the downward spiral that you've been a witness to. She doesn't want to talk or anythin'. That ends today. I'm draggin' her ass out of here and we're gonna have it out." I tell them both.

"Fuck!" Trojan says looking down.

Crash just stands there not saying anything. He looks almost as defeated as I feel. But, with dealing with Bailey's downward spiral, I've had to put that shit on hold.

"What do you need us to do?" Crash asks.

"Nothin'. I'm gettin' her out of here for a while and we're gonna settle this shit tonight. She's had time to fuck off and now we're gonna deal with the problem at hand."

I don't say anything else to my two brothers as I walk away towards Bailey's room. When I get there, I don't even bother knocking. I go right in and drag her wasted ass to the shower. After shoving her in it, I turn on the straight cold water to sober her ass up.

Once she's through cursing and losing her shit, I pull her out and get her dressed. I then pull her out of her room and towards her truck. Bailey doesn't say a word the entire time. She knows how pissed off I am and figures she needs to shut her mouth. Getting in the truck, I pull out away from the clubhouse. I know where we're going to have this talk and we're not leaving there until I get her to open up and start dealing with the shit she's feeling.

Crash

I'm still reeling from the bomb that Gage just dropped on Trojan and me. I can't believe that they've been dealing with this, or not dealing in Bailey's case, all on their own. Gage hasn't been talking about anything to anyone. He's just been holding this shit in and trying to be there for her.

"What the fuck? I can't believe this shit." Trojan says.

"I know. We need to do somethin' for them." I say looking at him. "I'm gonna call Grim and see what he thinks. I've got an idea floatin' around."

"What's up brother?"

I let Trojan in on what's going through my mind and he likes the idea. We sit down in a quiet corner and shoo the club girls away while I place the call to Grim. He listens to my idea and agrees to help me on his end. Since Bailey will be going home eventually, we decide to put it in motion at the Clifton Falls clubhouse. Grim says he knows the perfect spot for it. After discussing a few more details, Grim says he'll keep in contact with Trojan or me and keep us in the loop. Before we hang up, he asks how Bailey seems today. I tell him honestly that Gage dragged her out of here a little while ago, but that she had been drinking until that point. He lets loose a few choice words and hangs up. Grim makes me promise to call him if Bailey doesn't chill the fuck out, his words not mine, before he hangs up.

Bailey

I know I've been on a destructive path the last few weeks, but what the fuck is Gage thinking? Can't he just let me live in this peaceful drunken bliss thing I have going on? Right now I sit in the truck and look out the window while Gage drives to wherever he's taking me. I know exactly where he's taking me after a short time. We're going to the lake. It's a spot we've been to a lot in the past.

"Okay Gage, let's get this the fuck over with. Obviously, you have somethin' shoved up your ass." I say, turning to face him as he parks and turns the truck off.

"Bay, you have to quit. You drinkin' all day and fuckin' random brothers isn't helpin' you deal with the loss of the baby. Come on, talk to me." He says pleading with me.

"I don't even know where to start Gage. I feel so empty, alone, afraid, and like I'm a failure. Not to mention like I've let you down. Why couldn't I carry our baby to term, but everyone else can? It's not fair! Is it because I didn't know if I wanted to keep him or her in the beginning? What the hell did I do so wrong that this happened to us?" I shout at him, starting to cry uncontrollably.

"Baby, you didn't do anythin' wrong. You heard Doc, it's somethin' that just happens sometimes. In our case, it probably just wasn't meant to be. I know that doesn't take any of the hurt or pain away, but we have to deal with this and not let it fester. The drinkin' is only goin' to dull the pain until you wake up with a hangover. Then everythin' is still gonna be there."

"I know it's still gonna be there. But, when I'm drunk, I don't feel anything. I can be numb and not have to think about all of the what-ifs or how I could have done things differently. I constantly blame myself for losin' the baby and making sure that something like that didn't happen."

"Baby, you couldn't have done anythin' to prevent it. You were doin' everythin' the doc told you to do and were figurin' things out that needed to be done. This is *not* your fault! Now, we both need to mourn instead of keepin' this shit inside. We will get through this by

52

talkin' about things we were plannin' for the baby and what we wanted to do. We will remember that we were goin' to be parents together every day."

"How do I think about the baby and not cry and get so sucked down in my grief that I can't breathe?"

"By talkin' about it instead of gettin' drunk and fuckin' every brother in sight. I don't care if you talk to me, Sky, Ma and Pops, or even Grim. You need to talk to someone about it. While I would love it to be me, I know it's not gonna be every time that you do come to me."

"I would talk to everyone, especially you, but not Grim. He doesn't deserve to be there. I'm done with his bullshit!" I say starting to get pissed off even more from just thinking about Grim.

"Bay, you know he loves you more than anythin' in this world. He's just worried about what will happen to you if he makes his feelins' known and makes you his old lady. There's not a single person on this Earth more important to him than you are." Gage says looking me straight in the eyes.

"Why are you taking his side? He doesn't feel anything for me. If he did he wouldn't constantly flaunt the club girls he fucks in my face." I whine.

"Do you ever wonder why he's with them? I mean yeah, it's a fucked up thing to do in front of you, but don't you ever think there's more to it than that?" Gage asks me.

"No. I know he'd rather have the easy pussy than take the time to be with someone that means anything to him. I don't have the strength to fight for him anymore. It's not worth it. And that hurts because before all of this, I thought I would fight for him until my last breath."

"Baby, you are one of the strongest people I know. Yeah, you've lost your way a little bit right now, but we'll get you back to feelin' somewhat normal. It's just gonna take some time. I don't think that you and Grim have had your time together though. Things are just gettin' started with him. And you'll fight with everythin' you have to make sure it lasts once you get together. I know you and I have been honored to get to spend time with you in more than just a club settin'."

"Gage, why couldn't things be different between us? You are like my perfect match." I ask him moving over to cuddle in to his side.

"Baby, if things were different, I would've made you my old lady in a heartbeat. You are exactly what a good old lady is and the brother that finally makes you his is goin' to do everythin' in his power to keep you. I know that man will be Grim. You do too, if you look in your heart."

Gage holds me close and we just sit there for a little while. For once, I'm glad that I don't feel numb. Yeah, I still feel the alcohol I drank at the clubhouse, but I can feel and think at the same time. I'm glad that Gage pulled me out of my head and dragged me out with him to talk.

I finally have the courage to tell him about the dreams that I've been having. They've all been about the baby and what he looked like. Some of them are about the baby watching over Gage and me. They all make me cry and I really don't want to talk about them, but I think I owe it to Gage to let him know that I'm pretty sure the baby was a boy.

"Can I tell you something without you thinking I'm crazy?" I ask him, looking away.

"You can always tell me anythin', babe." Gage says turning my face to look at him.

"I've been having dreams about the baby since I lost him. In my dreams, it's a boy and he's looking down on us. No matter how many dreams I have, the baby is always a boy. He's got your blond hair and blue eyes." I say shedding some tears as I'm talking to him.

"That doesn't make you sound crazy babe. It's probably somethin' in you tellin' you what the baby was so that you can do what you gotta do to try to move on. I'm not sayin' you're gonna forget about the baby, but eventually you will be able to go through the day without gettin' sad when you think about the baby. If it's a boy, and you wanna name him, then I'm all for it. You let me know." Gage says taking my hands in his.

"I kind of like the name Rhett. Or maybe Ryan."

"I like Ryan over Rhett babe."

"Then Ryan it is. Ryan Brock Wilson."

After talking for a little bit longer about random things, Gage tells me that we're going to get a tattoo in memory of the baby. He pulls out of the lake and we head to the club's tattoo studio. As soon as we get in there, we see Shadow sitting there waiting for some ink. He greets Gage in their man hug or whatever it is they do.

"You gettin' another tat Shadow?" Gage asks him.

"Yeah. I'm gettin' some new tribal around the verse on my chest."

"You know, you're not gonna have any room left for club colors if you keep goin' on the way you are."

"Oh, I have my back saved for that. Besides, I think this is my last tat for a while. I think I'm gonna move on to gettin' shit pierced next."

I just roll my eyes. These guys are always getting something tatted or pierced. I'm surprised any of them have any blank skin left at all. This includes the guys from Clifton Falls. It's almost like they have to get tatted and pierced in order to become a brother. I mean, my dad even still has his piercings. And I don't even know how many he has. I know he's got his ears and nipples pierced and that's enough for me to know. Anything else is just too much information for me to even contemplate knowing.

As I'm sitting here, I see a guy come out of one of the back rooms and look at Gage. He greets him in the same man hug thing that Shadow did and then steps back to introduce me.

"Bailey, this is Alex. Alex, this is Joker's sister Bailey."

Alex just grunts in my direction. I'm used to this so I just raise my head in response. Most of these guys don't say a whole lot and communicate to one another in grunts and nods. It must be another prerequisite for being in the club.

"What's up Gage? You here for more ink?"

"Yeah. Remember that piece I dropped off the other day? We're here to get that done today. Can you bring it out to show Bailey what I came up with?"

"Why don't you guys just come on back and I'll show her there. Then we can just get to work instead of walking back and forth. Shadow, Lennox should be back soon to start your work."

We follow Alex back to a room and he closes the door behind us. Once we're all seated, he pulls out a piece of paper and hands it over to me. As I look down at the little pair of angel wings with little tiny feet walking up between them, the tears start to well up in my eyes. I continue to look at the drawing and see the words 'Forever in our hearts and thoughts. You will be missed Baby Wilson.' I bring my head up to look at Gage.

"You drew this?"

"I did. When I couldn't sleep, it just came to me. So, I drew it up and kept at it until it was perfect. Do you like it?"

"I love it! It's absolutely perfect."

"Do you want to change the baby part?"

"No. I think that should just be for the two of us for right now. Everyone else can see Baby Wilson, but we'll know the other part."

"Okay. Do you wanna go first?"

I nod my head and start to remove my shirt. Gage and Alex just stare at me. Next I start to remove my bra.

"Um, babe. I'm all about you bein' naked, but what the hell are you doin'?" Gage asks.

"I want it on my ribs, right next to my heart. He can't tattoo there if my shirt and bra are on and in the way."

"Oh. Well, have at it then. Just make sure you keep yourself covered in case someone else walks in here."

Without any more talking, Alex makes the stencil and places it where I indicated I wanted it to go. After looking in the mirror, I tell him that it looks perfect. He gets started and I lay there with my eyes closed, feeling the pain of getting this tattoo. The pain soothes me in a way because I know that when all is said and done, this isn't going to be some random tattoo. This is a tattoo that I will carry with me in memory of our lost baby.

Once it's Gage's turn, I take his seat across the room and watch as he tells Alex that he wants his in the same place. I wasn't expecting that at all, but I like that he's doing this with me. It's something that we can do for our baby that no one else will ever be able to get. While sitting and waiting for Gage to be done, I pull out my phone and see that I have a ton of missed calls and texts from people back home. Grim has called a few times, yeah, not gonna call that fucker back. Joker, Cage, Sky, Ma and Pops, Caydence, and Kenzie have all called me or sent me messages. *Again.* I decide that I don't want to talk to anyone or deal with anyone's shit today and that I'll call Ma back tomorrow. Maybe by then I'll feel a little bit better and be able to handle a conversation with her.

Chapter Four

A few more weeks

Bailey

I'VE DECIDED THAT it's time to go home. I've talked to Gage about it and he agrees that it's the right decision. I can't hide out from my family forever. I need to go back and face reality and prove to myself that I can handle the loss without Gage and everyone else handling it for me. I need to know that I can handle being by myself and being around Sky and my nieces and nephew. Until I'm around the kids and Sky, I won't know how I'm gonna be able to deal with shit like that. The only thing that Gage doesn't know is that I still get drunk at night in my room. I don't sleep with his brothers, I just get drunk to try to sleep and not dream. When I wake up, I hide the bottles so that if anyone comes in my room they won't see them.

So, I've packed up my shit and the prospects have loaded it up in my truck for me. All that I'm waiting for is Gage and the rest of the guys I want to say goodbye to. I guess they had a meeting and they aren't out yet. In the meantime, I've sent a text to Ma letting her know that I'm gonna be hitting the road soon and that I'll let her know if I decide to stop anywhere along the way home and rest for the night.

I've talked to Ma and everyone on the phone more than I did when I first got here. Grim and I have even had conversations. He's been telling me more and more about how he wants things to go when I come home. Honestly, I would love to be with Grim and apparently he wants to give us a chance to work it out and be together. I'm just not going to come second place to his easy pussy. If he can't be faithful, then there's no point in trying. I haven't told him my thoughts on anything, I just listen to him talk about us and our future together. It's given me things to think about while I've been here. We're definitely going to be talking when I get home and see where things go.

After waiting for an hour and a half, the guys finally emerge from church. Gage is leading the pack as they all make their way to me. I suddenly feel this overwhelming urge to unpack my shit and stay here. It's not like these guys would force me to go back to Clifton Falls, they wouldn't. But, at the same time, I know it's time to go back to my family and let them help me finish healing and dealing with this loss. Besides, Ma would come here, skin me alive, and then drag me back with her. I don't need that shit either.

"There's been a change of plans apparently." Gage says, walking up to me.

"What do you mean a 'change of plans'?" I ask him, wondering what the hell is going on.

"Pops, Joker, and Grim want you to have an escort back home." Steel says, walking up and putting his arm around me. "Pops and Joker called this morning to let us know that we need to go there with you."

"What the fuck?" I yell at no one in particular. "I'm a grown ass woman and don't need bodyguards following me the fuck home!"

"Babe, it's not our call. They want it and we're gonna do it." Crash says walking up to me. "Now, let's get our asses on the fuckin' road and get you home. I don't want to face your Ma if we don't get in at a reasonable hour."

"Crash, it's like eight in the morning. The ride is only going to take us three to four hours to get there. If we stop and you guys decide to be the man whores you are, then we'll probably not get back at a reasonable hour."

"Hey!" Trojan says, coming up to me and picking me up as I wrap my legs around his waist. "If I'm gonna get a piece of ass on the way up there, it's only gonna be from you."

"Trojan, you know you couldn't handle me." I say kissing him, long and deep like a woman full of want and need. "Hell, it was all Gage could do to handle what I dished out."

All of the guys start laughing and bringing the good mood to the forefront. This is what I needed. I need one last laugh and good memory of my time here with these guys. I know once I get back home, I'm only gonna have limited contact with this part of my family. It's not fair, but I can't be in both places at once.

"Alright, let's get on the road. Bailey, you got all your shit?" Gage asks me.

"Yeah. Shadow already loaded it up in the truck and started it for me. I think he even went and filled the tank up for me too."

"Alright, let's ride!" Gage yells to everyone. "Babe, when Crash and I pull out, I want you to pull directly behind us. The rest of the guys will follow you. When we get on the highway, you'll probably have at least one guy on each side. Where they can ride like that anyway. Those guys will be Trojan and Fox."

"Gage, this isn't my first rodeo ya know." I say heading to my truck and getting in.

As soon as we all pull out, I crank up my music and start singing along to the cd while following Gage and Crash towards home. This is gonna be a long ride with a ton of time to think about everything that I need to worry about now. There's not gonna be any distractions to take my mind off Ryan, Grim, or what I wanna do. Gage told me last night that his offer of me moving to Dander Falls and living there is still open and always will be. Depending on what happens at home, I might just take him up on his offer. Time will tell.

We're finally back at the Clifton Falls clubhouse. On my drive here I've laughed, cried, gotten pissed off, and gone through a whole range of other emotions. I definitely had too much time on my own to think and let things get to me.

As soon as I park my truck at the end of the garage, away from where the guys park their bikes, my door is flung open. The first person I see is Ma. She's got tears in her eyes and she's pulling me out of the truck so she can hold me. I guess I didn't realize my Ma was so upset. Then again, if it wasn't about me or the baby in the last few weeks, I really didn't give a fuck. I know it sounds horrible and selfish, but that's the way it is. Even when I was on the phone with them, I still only half listened to what everyone was saying. They were all trying to tell me about the things going on here and if they tried bringing up the kids, I'd make excuses to get off the phone.

"My baby girl, you've finally come home!" Ma says wrapping her arms around me. "I've missed you so much. How are you feeling?"

"I'm doing okay Ma. I've missed you too. I'm so sorry that I had to get away for a while. It really wasn't my intention to be gone so long, but I kind of had a melt down for a while. Gage pulled my head out of my ass and told me to get my shit straight." I tell her looking over at him while he's talking to Grim and Crash.

When I took over at Gage, I notice that everyone from this chapter is standing in the parking lot. I also see the Phantom Bastards mixed in with everyone. What the fuck is going on? Looking at Gage, I notice that he looks just as confused as I do. I turn my head back to my Ma and I see the tears shimmering in her eyes. She just shakes her head at me and pushes me over towards Gage.

Grim lets out a whistle to get everyone's attention. Once he's sure he has it, he throws an arm around Gage and me.

"While you were at Gage's clubhouse, I got a call from Crash. He wanted to do somethin' for the two of you once he found out what happened. It hit us all hard, knowin' the two of you are goin' through somethin' that most of us know nothin' about. Anyway, he gave me his idea and we all pulled together to make it happen. So, you two need to follow us. But, there is no peekin'."

All of a sudden I feel a bandana being wrapped around my eyes. Then I feel my hand being put in Gage's and we're being led somewhere. At one point I think we go in the clubhouse and then out the back door but I can't be sure. So, I just follow along and think of what we could possibly be walking into.

I feel us being led up the slight incline at the back of the clubhouse, and all of sudden I think I know where we're being led to. There's this huge tree that I've always spent a lot of time at when I want to be alone. Everyone here knows that if I'm sitting under my tree, I'm not to be bothered. Even Ma and Pops know not to come near me when I'm up here. It means I'm at the end of my rope and I need to be alone to cool off or just think. It's my safe place where I can get away from everything and everyone.

All of a sudden we're stopped and I can feel everyone gathering around us. There's high emotions all around us, and I can hear the sniffling of people crying and trying not to. After a minute the bandanas are removed from our eyes and I see that we are at my tree. Unfortunately, there's a wall standing in front of us. Grim, Pops, Joker, Cage, Tank, Crash, Trojan, and Steel are standing there.

"I don't know what either one of you are goin' through." Crash starts. "But, I know how deeply you both feel and hold things in. So, I wasn't surprised that none of us in Gage's chapter knew about what was goin' on. And up until the loss, no one here knew either. But, that doesn't change the fact that you're family and you need us to give you our strength and shoulders to lean on. You also need a place where you can go to get away from everything when things get too hard to deal with. This is that place for you Bailey. And Gage when you're here, it's your place too. We've already got shit goin' at our club for you too."

"So, this is what Crash came up with. I hope that you both like it." Grim says and all the guys move to the side.

What I see absolutely takes my breath away and I can't stop the tears from falling down my face. There's now a bench sitting under my tree. In front of the bench is a headstone. In front of the headstone are tiny little flowers and off to the side are some balloons in various colors. On the headstone there are tiny feet on it walking away. Under the feet it says:

> *Taken too young before having a chance to grow and be loved*
> *Here lies the spirit of Baby Wilson*
> *May you watch over us and protect us until we meet again*
> *You will forever be loved and missed*

I can't believe that these guys did this for us. If I had to think of anything that they would have done, this would not even be on my mind. I'm not saying this because my family doesn't love us, but because this is so special and something for just Gage and I. It means so much to me. I look up at Gage and I can see the tears in his eyes and know that it means just as much to him. Turning to look at our loved ones, I take a deep breath.

"I can't believe you guys did this. It means more to me than you will ever know, and I'll never be able to tell you thank you enough." At this point I can't even talk anymore, the tears are just flowing down now.

Gage takes my hand and leads me over to sit on the bench. We sit there and stare at the headstone for what seems like hours. When I look up again, I see that everyone else has left us and headed back to the clubhouse.

"See babe, now you have somewhere to come and just sit with the baby. No one will come here without your permission. So, when you have a bad day, I want you to come out here and just be. I don't want you drinkin' and goin' back downhill like you did. Can you do that for me?"

"I can do that. I promise I won't go in that spiral again." I say and lay my head on his chest, knowing that I still drink at night to forget. It's hard enough to get through most days.

Gage wraps his arms around me and we just sit together. After a while, we decide to head back in to everyone. I don't know that I'm ready to face a ton of people, but they pulled together and did this amazing thing for us. So, I have to pull up my big girl panties and thank them properly.

As soon as we get in the clubhouse, I can sense that the atmosphere is subdued and mellow. There are still a ton of people here drinking and eating, but it's not a crazy ass party like it normally would be. Apparently everyone is treating this as a memorial service like they would if a brother or old lady had just passed away. This just puts me even more in awe at the fact that they aren't all using this as an excuse to party.

Gage and I come to the first group of people and we talk for a few minutes before moving on. There's a shit ton of people here and I'd like to talk to the ones that I know the most, but that's not an option. Everyone is here to support us and give us their strength when we need it the most. So, the only right thing to do is to thank them and spend some time with everyone that I can.

Grim

I'm sitting at a table with Joker, Cage, Sky, Ma, and Pops when I see Gage and Bailey come walking back inside. As soon as I see her, I want to go over and take her in my arms. But, I know that she needs to do whatever she's doing with Gage. If I know her, she'll want to personally thank everyone here but that's not gonna be possible. I know today has been emotionally draining on her. So, I just sit back and watch her while thinking over the conversations I had with Pops and Joker earlier today.

I called Pops into my office as soon as I knew he was here and I told him flat out that I was in love with Bailey and that I wanted to officially claim her. For the longest time he didn't say a single word to me. All he did was stare at me with this hard look on his face. Finally, he broke his silence.

"Grim, I respect you as my President. I've known for years how you've felt about my baby girl. Instead of mannin' up and claimin' her when you fell in love with her, you've pushed her away. If it wasn't the club girls here, it was strippers or random sluts at the bar. I've watched little pieces of her die a slow death watchin' this shit. I'm also not likin' the fact that you're older than her by more than a few years. However, I know my baby girl is crazy in love with you. So, I won't stand in your way. But, I will put you to ground if you fuckin' hurt her or make her leave us."

Pops didn't say another word about it. He got up from the chair and left my office. That honestly went better than I thought it would. I figured I was gonna get a fist to the face and a complete beat down for sure. So to say I was surprised he just walked out would be an understatement. One down, one to go.

A few hours later, I called Joker and told him we needed to talk. He told me to come over to his house, so I did. When I got there, we went down to the pond and sat on a bench. After what felt like an eternity, Joker started speaking.

"I know what this is about Grim. You are finally gonna claim Bay. Well, at least you want to. I'm not sure how she's gonna feel about that though. Not after everythin' you've done and after everythin' she's been goin' through now. Why now though?"

"You didn't find her bleedin' out and not respondin' to nothin' Levi. I did. When I saw her like that part of me died. Then she told me in the hospital that her first thought when she found out was that she wished she was pregnant with my baby. Then in the next breath she told me she was leavin' with Gage. My heart broke even more. When she was released and they were leavin', she wouldn't even look at me. It felt like my heart shattered in a million pieces. I'm done playin' the games and fuckin' random pussy. She's my world and my reason to live. I've been to the clinic and got tested to show her I'm clean. Fuck, I haven't even fucked anyone since I found her and took her to the hospital. I'm dead serious."

Joker took in everything I said to him for a little while. Finally, he spoke again.

"If you do this, you're done with the club girls, strippers, and any other random fuckin' pussy. This shit's for real, then you're gonna respect her, love her, and remain faithful to her. I don't care if you're one of my best friends and the Pres. If you fuck her over, I'll beat your fuckin' ass and then put you to ground. I won't think twice about it either. She's given up so much for you and you probably don't even realize it. I mean how many women do you know that would give up their entire life and everythin' they know to follow you here? Especially when they don't know what they are walkin' in to. My little sister is a fuckin' treasure and she deserves the world bein' given to her."

"If I hurt her, I won't even put up a fight. I can't live another moment without her. And you know I've never wanted an old lady. Especially her. I thought I was protectin' her by stayin' away and pushin' her away. It would kill me if some crazy fuck tried to use her to hurt

66

me, or the club. But, I can't fight this shit anymore. I've been goin' crazy since this happened and she's been gone. I give you my word as your Pres, your brother, and one of your best friends that I will give her the life she deserves. She's done more for me than any other person in my life. You can guarantee that I know everythin' she's done and everythin' she's given up for me."

With that, we stand up and Joker pulls me into a man hug before telling me that I'm gonna have one hell of a fight on my hands trying to win Bailey over. I am and I know it. It's gonna take everything I have in me to convince her that I'm serious and that I've loved her as long as I can remember.

I take another sip of the beer I've been nursing for the last hour and continue watching my crazy girl. Anyone that knows her knows that she's dead on her feet right now and can barely stand. I think Gage's arm around her is the only thing holding her up right now.

"My baby girl is dead on her feet." Ma says. "I'm gonna go see if she wants to go home with us."

"Ma, let me take care of her. I know she just got home and you wanna see her, take care of her, but please let me do this."

After looking at me through narrowed eyes, Ma finally agrees to let me take care of Bailey. I get up and head on over to where she's standing with Gage and a small group of people. Without saying a word, I pick her up and head up to my room. She looks up at me before laying her head on my chest and closing her eyes. At this rate she'll be passed out before we make it up the stairs. But I don't care. The only thing I care about is the fact that she's home and she's in my arms where she belongs. I feel like I can breathe easy now that she's in my arms.

My world has shifted and I feel right for the first time in a long time. Probably my whole life.

Ma

We all watch Grim take Bailey upstairs. I don't miss the fact that her head's laying on his chest and she's curled up into him. Pops told me about the talk he had with Grim, and I hope that he's finally done fucking around and is gonna do right by my baby girl.

"It's about fuckin' time!" I mumble.

Everyone at the table bursts out laughing. I guess I didn't say it quietly enough, oops.

"Ma, when are you gonna stop tryin' to play matchmaker? Bailey's not a little girl anymore and doesn't need you interferin' in her life." Joker says.

"You listen to me. I can still whoop your ass. Don't think that I won't. Or, just think about all the embarassin' things I could tell Sky here about you. I'm sure there's a ton of shit she would love to know about the two of you." I say looking directly in my son's eyes.

"Ma, why you gotta bring me into this? I didn't say a single word about anythin'." Cage asks, looking like a wounded puppy.

"It's only a matter of time before you open your mouth too. I know you both better than you know yourselves."

"Ma, I think we need to have a girl's day out and some conversation time alone." Sky says looking at me eagerly.

"We can arrange that. I've got so many stories to tell we might need a weekend away though." I say laughing as I think about everything these two have gotten up to growing up.

"Ma, I think that's enough." Pops says to me. "I think it's about time we head home. I know you're gonna be up early and back over here to see our baby girl. It's my alone time now."

With that Pops lifts me out of my chair and heads out to his bike. Yeah, my man still has it after all these years.

Chapter Five

Bailey

I SLOWLY WAKE up and I feel like I'm curled up with a furnace. Looking around, I see that I'm in Grim's room. Feeling tight arms wrapped around me and his legs tangled with mine, I should be surprised, but I'm not.

Rolling over, I look at Grim without having to hide what I'm feeling. In his sleep, he looks so peaceful. There isn't the constant worry on his face about running the club. His dark hair is a mess and some of it lays covering his face. I want to reach out and move it, but I don't want to wake him up. Once he wakes up, I know we're gonna have to talk and I don't wanna do that right now. I just want to lay here feeling safe and comfortable. I missed him so much while I was gone.

The blankets are down to Grim's waist and I spend time looking at the ink he has on his muscled upper body. There's tribal covering his arms. On his right side he has a smaller version of the club colors. He shifts and I see that he has a new tattoo covering his right side. I lean up so that I can try to get a better look at it, but his arm is in the way.

"Mornin' crazy girl." Grim says, startling me. "If you want to see it, roll me over."

"Um... I didn't mean to wake you up. I'm sorry." I say trying to roll out of his arms.

"You didn't wake me up. I was just layin' here lovin' the fact that you were in my arms. Here, I'll show you what it is."

Grim rolls over so I can see his side and lifts his arm up over his head. I gasp out as I take in his new tat. It's my name in scrolling lettering down his side. Surrounding it are vines and daisies. He knows they're one of my favorite flowers. I reach out and run my fingers down the tat and feel just how new it is.

"I can't believe you did this. Why would you put my name on you? I'm not your old lady, and you've made it painfully clear how you feel about that. Even though you've been telling me things have changed on the phone, I still don't understand why you'd get my name on you."

"I did it because you *are* mine, crazy girl. I've loved you since before I knew what love was and I've been pushin' you away because I thought I was protectin' you and tryin' to save you the pain of bein' with my stubborn ass. Over the years that love has grown from a crush to lovin' you more than anythin' else in this world. You are my world, and I don't know what I would do if somethin' ever happened to you. When you and Sky went through that bullshit, I felt like I couldn't breathe until I saw you. Then, with everythin' you've been goin' through, I felt like my world was crashin' and shatterin' around me knowin' you were hurtin' and I couldn't do anythin' to help you. When you left and refused to look at me, I felt like the light had been removed from my world. I can't breathe when you're not around. You are the air I breath and the light that shines on everythin' that's dark within me."

I look at Grim and don't know what to say to him. He's never given me the slightest hint that he thought of me as anything other than Levi's little sister. A pain in his ass that wanted to do everything the boys did and try to do it better than they did. Maybe today is the day we get everything in the open and lay it all out on the table. Our conversations on the phone were just that. I couldn't see what was in his eyes and know that he was being completely honest with me. That he wasn't just telling me what he was because of me leaving and not really having anything to do with him, or anyone else here. I mean, who is to say that he wasn't just saying all of that because he wanted me to come back and start doing everything I always have around here?

"Grim, I've loved you since I was twelve years old. That's eleven years of loving the biggest man whore I've ever met. I didn't love you because you let me follow you around when we were growing up, I loved you because of you. You've always been so strong, letting other people take your strength when they weren't strong enough to stand up for themselves. You are so responsible for everything and everyone around you. If someone is having a shit day, you know about it before anyone else does. When you need to step up you do. And when you feel that the other person needs to step up for themselves, you make sure you give them the nudge they need to do it. You're loyal to a fault and would never betray someone that you've given your loyalty to. How many times could you have told my parents or Joker about the baby? Yet you didn't. You let me have my time with my secret and tell them when I was ready to tell them. Even though that ended up being because of the loss." I take a breath and look up at Grim. "You've always tried to protect me. Other than fucking everything with a pussy. And I know you care about me. But caring about me isn't enough to make a relationship work. I want someone that's gonna love me and treat me like I'm the only one for them."

"Baby, it's always only been you. Yeah, I've fucked my share of women, but none of them were you. They were only fillers because I didn't think I deserved to have you. I wanted to protect you from someone usin' you to try to get to me. But, seein' you on the floor covered in blood and not wakin' up killed me. There wasn't anythin' I could do to save you. Then everythin' that happened in the hospital and when you left with Gage, broke my heart more than you'll ever know. You are one of the strongest people I know and to see you lifeless tore me into more pieces than I thought could ever be put back together. If somethin' were to happen to you, I don't think that I could still live. There would be nothin' left of me to go on."

I look up at Grim and tears are shining in my eyes. Looking in his eyes, I can see the truth of his words and I know that he means what he's saying.

"Crazy girl, it's never been a secret that I didn't want an old lady. Not because I didn't see what the love between a man and woman was like, because my parents loved each other fiercely. I didn't want to have the responsibility of lovin' someone enough that I put them in a vulnerable position because I'm the Pres of the club. I know we still have enemies and they'll use anythin' and anyone to get to me. When it comes to you, I don't ever want to feel like somethin' bad happened to you because you chose to love me. But, you deserve to be an old lady and not some casual fuck. You're strong, loyal, courageous, and know what it takes to be by my side. Bailey, you're one of the most beautiful people I know. It's not just the way you look; you have this light shining from you that pulls everyone in to you. You would give someone the clothes off your body if you thought they needed them. I love you crazy girl. I'll spend the rest of my life makin' up for the way I treated you and showin' you just how much you mean to me. Please, give me the chance to make you believe me."

Grim has moved and rolled over to face me. One hand is resting on my face, while the other one is holding my hip. He's never held me like this before. Sure, we've hugged and shit like that but it was always done in a way that a brother would hug his sister. The way he's holding me now is not in a brotherly manner. I want to believe him so bad it hurts. But I don't know if I can get over his man whore ways.

"Grim, you know I love you and I've wanted to be with you for longer than I care to think about. Or admit to you. But, there's things that I don't know if I can get over. It's more than just the sluts, strippers, and random women you've been with. You hide how you feel about a lot of things. And you've never fought for me. You've always fought your feelings for me and not taken a chance on what you wanted. How do I know that when shit gets hard and real between us, you're not just gonna cut and run? Because if we do this and get together, and then you decide it's too much, it *will* kill me inside and I won't be able to come back from it."

"Bailey, that won't happen. I've already talked to Pops and Joker about wantin' to claim you. Joker was easier than your Pops. He's not happy with the way I've handled things concernin' you at all. But, I know what will happen to me if I hurt you. I'm willin' to risk bein' put to ground if I hurt you. I will fight for you until the day I take my last breath. I'm not lettin' you go anywhere. I know it's not always gonna be good. There's gonna be days we want to kill one another, but that's what makes it fun. I promise you crazy girl there won't be any more girls, no more hidin' what I feel, and no more fuckin' off when it comes to you. But I need you to promise me somethin' too."

"What?" I ask, shocked that Grim just said he'd give up girls to be with me. That's not something I ever thought I'd hear come out of his mouth.

"I want you to promise that there won't be any more downward spirals from you. You got shit goin' through that pretty head of yours, then you need to talk it out. I don't care if it's me, Ma and Pops, Sky, Joker, Cage, or even a fuckin' prospect. You talk that shit out."

"I can't say that I'll always talk about things, but I can promise that I won't ever go on that downward spiral like I did again. If I feel myself getting to that point, I'll talk to someone. Even if I have to go to a professional and talk to someone. I didn't like myself like that, and I really didn't like drinking the way I was. I swear, I drank more in two days than you have since I've known you. It was bad Grim. Honestly, last night was the first night I haven't gotten drunk off my ass before going to bed. Even after the talk with Gage, I was still drinking every night and hiding the bottles and stuff so no one knew."

"I'm glad you didn't drink last night crazy girl. From now on, you need to stop the drinkin'. If you need to let loose and exhaust yourself for bed, we'll find other more enjoyable ways. I don't give a fuck if we spend a few hours in the gym and you beat the hell out of everythin' in sight. If we have to get more punching bags and things, we'll get them. No more drinkin'!"

I don't say anything in response to what Grim just told me. The truth needs to come out and if anything is gonna happen between us, we need to be honest with one another. I'm not saying I want to know club business, because I don't. If it's something Grim can share with me, then I'm all for it. But I know that almost everything that happens, I'm not gonna be allowed to know. Plus, I know that I have to stop the drinking. Working out and doing other enjoyable things before bed to make sure I can sleep is something I'm all for.

My thoughts are disrupted when Grim rolls himself on top of me and buries his face in my neck. All thoughts stop as I feel his lips and tongue on my neck, going up to my ear where he gently nips and sucks.

"Babe, I need you more than I need my next breath. Please, tell me you're on board with bein' my old lady. I want you in my life, my heart, my bed, and next to me through everythin' else. I want with you what I see Ma and Pops have, what Joker, Sky, and Cage have. In fact, I can't accept anythin' less than you ownin' my heart and me ownin' yours."

I look up into Grim's eyes and I can how deadly honest he's being. This is what I've wanted for so long now. I told myself when I was at Gage's club that I wasn't gonna feed into whatever Grim was gonna try to sell me, but I can't pass this up. Finally, my dream is coming true and I'd be stupid, regretful, and hate myself for not allowing this to happen.

"I'll give us what we both want Grim. But there's one condition that you have to agree to. You get one shot, and that's it. I hear about any other girls or find anything at all out, I'm gone. I know it's for life when you become an old lady and I accept that. In fact, I'd live the rest of my life as your old lady, but I can't accept being second fiddle to whatever the club girls think they have with you."

"Crazy girl, I'd give you the fuckin' world. So, I know you'll do what you have to do. But, I can promise you that there's not gonna be any other fuckin' girls. I finally have my piece of home in my bed and I'm not lettin' you the fuck go. That's a fuckin' promise!"

There's no need for me to respond to Grim. So, I wrap my arms around his neck and I bring his lips down to mine. Our kiss starts out slow and sweet. An exploration that only comes when you experience a first kiss with someone you love and care about enough to learn what they like, what they don't like, and what is going to make them happy.

All too soon the kiss turns into something more. Grim goes from soft and sweet to hard and demanding quicker than I can keep up. But, I want everything that he has to give me, so I change right along with him. He's building up a need in me so fast that I feel like I could cum just from kissing him alone. It's nothing like I've ever experienced before.

Pulling my mouth away, I moan and suck in a deep breath.

"Grim, I need more. I love kissing you, but I need more. Please..." I plead with him.

"You want more, crazy girl, I'll give you more. But when we're in here, or alone, it's not Grim. I want you to call me Logan. I need to hear my name fallin' from your lips."

Logan doesn't leave any more room for talking. He strips me of my shirt and shorts, leaving me only in my bra and panties. For the longest time, he does nothing but stare at me. I can feel his warm gaze travel from my face down to my toes and back up. Instead of feeling vulnerable like I would with anyone else, I feel safe and cherished. He's taking his time with the first look of me almost completely bared to him.

"Logan, please let me see you. You're looking your fill of me, and I want to look at you." I say, trying to rub my thighs together. No matter what Logan does to me, I can't help but be turned on more than I've ever been.

Logan quickly pulls the sheet off him and I see that he slept naked next to me last night. If I had known that, I probably wouldn't have lasted through our little talk. Holy shit! I've seen him without a shirt on plenty of times in my life. It's kind of hard not to when you're constantly around these guys. I knew that he had his tongue pierced, he's had that for a long time. As I let my gaze travel his body, I stop when I get down to his cock. It's long and thick, but not porn star proportions. He's got a Jacob's ladder piercing down almost the entire length. I feel the breath leave my lungs as I view perfection, at least in my eyes.

Grim

Finally, I have Bailey exactly where I want her. I can't help but stare at her toned body. She's lean, but with curves in all the right places. Up until losing the baby, Bailey was full of curves, but now she's lost more weight than she probably should have and so her body is smaller. After taking my fill of looking at her, I allow her the same with me. My heart starts racing as her gaze falls to my cock. There's never been a time that she's seen me naked. The one thing that I have done is make sure that I've never put her in the position that she would walk in on me fucking some slut. I couldn't do that to her. Even if I knew that I was hurting her just by being with them.

After a few minutes of letting her look at me, I decide that we've had enough time looking at each other. I can't wait for much longer to be buried deep inside her. It's like my life is finally starting after waiting for over ten years. Everything up until now has just been going through the motions and learning what I needed to know in order to make sure that I was going to please my crazy girl. Her pleasure means more to me than anything else.

I lower myself over the top of Bailey again and kiss, lick, and suck her neck, making my way down to her collarbone. At the same time, I run my hands over her silky smooth skin until I feel her tits in my hands. The perfect size for me, not too big or too small. Simply perfect. Moving my legs between hers, I spread her legs apart and move my mouth down to one of her nipples. I suck it in my mouth and nip it with my teeth. Bailey arches her back off the bed and moans. Just hearing her moans and feeling how responsive she is to me, I know I'm not gonna be able to take my time with her. I'm ready to cum now and I'm nowhere near inside her.

"Baby, I want to take my time with you, but I'm not gonna be able to this time. This time I need hard and fast. Tell me that's what you want, what you need right now."

"Logan, please. I need you so bad right now. You need to be in me. *Now!*" She pleads with me.

Before I can bury myself balls deep in her, I need to make sure she's ready for me. I slowly run my hand down her body and don't stop until I push a finger in her tight, wet pussy. She's so wet for me and I can't help the groan that leaves me. Knowing that she's more than ready for me, breaks the last strand of control I have left.

I lean back and kneel before her. Grabbing her hips, I pull Bailey up and close to me so I can thrust into her. There is no taking my time and making sure she can handle my size, I'm inside her in one thrust. Bailey lets out a moan and grabs the blankets beneath her, twisting them in her hands that has me stopping dead.

"Crazy girl, are you okay? Did I hurt you?" I ask, trying to control my breathing.

"Logan I'm gonna hurt you if you don't start moving right now. Please..." She begs.

Who am I to deny my woman anything? Without further thought, I begin to move inside her. "Fuck crazy girl! You're so tight."

I can feel every muscle ripple and contract within her. Using the barbells of my piercings, I make sure to rub over her g-spot with each and every thrust. I know I'm close as hell to cumming and I'm not gonna go without making sure she cums first.

I lean down and suck her nipple back in my mouth while I move my hand down her stomach until I reach her clit. Slowly rubbing circles around her clit, I continue to slam my hips into hers going harder and faster until Bailey's thrashing around on the bed. Her moans are coming louder and louder the faster and harder I go.

"Bailey, let go. I…need you…to…let…go. *Now!*" I growl out with each thrust, knowing I'm just seconds away from losing my shit.

She doesn't disappoint me. Bailey loses it like I've never seen another woman lose it before. I can feel her pussy clamp down on my cock like a vice and she drags her nails down my back. I'm sure there's going to be blood from her nails and I could give two shits about it. There is no holding back from my release now. Bailey screams out my name as I lose control and I follow her over the edge. Never in my life have I cum so long or so hard. I can feel myself losing my breath and I see an explosion behind my eyes. But, I continue thrusting in her as we both come back down to Earth.

"Holy fuck! I've never gotten off like that before." Bailey says.

"I haven't either." I tell her honestly. "That was the most intense experience I've ever had in my life crazy girl."

Bailey

Holy shit! No matter how many times I've dreamed of being with Logan, nothing prepared me for the love I felt pouring out of him. We might not have made love, but that doesn't mean that I couldn't still feel how he felt about me. In fact, I could feel it running down my legs as he pulled out of me.

"Logan! You didn't use a condom. What the fuck?" I practically shout. "Now, I have to go get my shit checked to make sure the walking petri dishes you've been with haven't fuckin' given me anything."

"Crazy girl, relax. I'm clean. The day you left the hospital, I got my shit checked. I haven't been with anyone else since you've been gone. Here."

Logan hands me a paper he picked up from off the stand by the bed. I look it over and realize that it's his test results. He is, in fact, clean. Well, that's a worry off my mind. But, I'm not on anything for birth control. Oh boy!

"Okay, I appreciate the fact that you did this. But there's more to worry about than just giving me something. I'm not on birth control Logan." I say, dropping my head into my hands.

"Hey, none of that. Crazy girl, whatever happens, we'll deal with it. I just couldn't have anythin' between us. If you want to start usin' condoms, fine. But, I told you I'm not goin' anywhere and I meant it."

"I just don't know if I can go through that again. I mean, what if I get pregnant again and the same thing happens? What if I'm just not meant to be a mom?"

"Crazy girl, we'll handle whatever happens. I think that what happened with the baby means that it just wasn't meant to be. No matter how much you wanted the baby and loved it already. Sometimes, it just isn't meant to be and that shit happens."

I can't even form any words to say to him right now. So, I get up and walk into his bathroom to clean up. I know that Ma and Pops are gonna be here soon to see me and I really want to spend some time with them. If I don't go out there, Ma will just hunt me down anyway.

It's not long before I feel Logan get in the shower with me. We quickly wash up and get dressed. Since I wasn't planning on being here, and my bags are still in my truck, I throw one of Logan's shirts on and a pair of his workout shorts. They're huge on me, but they tie so they'll work for now.

After I run a brush through my hair and throw it up in a messy bun, we make our way out to the main room. There's already a ton of people sitting there eating breakfast. I can see Joker and Cage sitting at a table, so I'm guessing that Sky's the one that made breakfast. I can see the kids with the guys at the table. All the breath leaves my chest as I look at the tight knit family sitting together enjoying one another.

Logan comes up behind me and wraps his arms around my middle. I lean my head back on his chest close my eyes.

"Babe, you're gonna have to see the kids some time. I'll be right here with you. Come on."

He leads me over to the table and I look down into the smiling faces of Reagan, Jameson, Haley, and Alana. Reagan is the first one to notice me. She throws down whatever book she was looking at and scrambles over Dec's lap.

"Auntie Bay!" I move away from Logan and brace myself for the impact of her hitting me with a huge hug.

"Hi sweetie!" I say, wrapping my arms around her tightly and burying my face in her neck and little curls.

"I missed you! Unc Grim said you had to leave for a little while. Daddy was real sad too."

"There were some things I had to help Gage with. But I'm home now and I'm gonna spend a few days doin' nothing but playing with you guys. How does that sound?" I ask her with my heart breaking a little at what I won't have with Ryan.

"Yay!"

At Reagan's excitement, the other kids start to join in and soon I find myself wrapped in four pairs of arms. The tears are getting close to making their way out of my eyes and down my face at the overwhelming sense of loss I feel. I'll never feel Ryan's little arms wrap around me, never see his excitement, or feel the overwhelming sense of love that's so pure from him. I look up at Levi and Dec and I can see the sadness in their eyes.

"Alright kids, let's go run some of that energy out, yeah?" Dec calls out to his children.

They unwrap from me and run over to him. The only thing stopping them is Sky coming out of the kitchen. They quickly give her a hug and continue following Dec out back to the play set that's been set up. Levi gets up from his seat and wraps his arms around me. He turns his head so that I'm the only one that can hear what he's gonna say.

"I know it's hard bein' around the kids right now. But, it will get easier. If you need to have some space from them, you've just gotta say the word. We'll help you get through this sis."

"It's fine. I have to get over this some time, right? Besides, I've missed them and maybe they'll help me start to move on."

I feel another set of arms wrap around me and I turn to see Sky has joined us. I kiss the top of her head and wrap my arms around her. I can feel the baby bump in between us and I look down. Well, I guess it can't be considered a baby bump anymore. She's blown up since I've been gone.

"Holy fuck!" I exclaim. "Are you sure there's only one baby in there Sky?"

"That's what they're sayin', but I'm not so sure. Not long to go now and we'll know for sure. I got about three months left. Every ultrasound we've had, we only see one baby, but I'm thinkin' there's at least two in there. If not more with the way I feel."

Levi stares at his woman and I start laughing my ass off. His face has gone pure white and he looks like he's gonna fall where he's standing. I start laughing so hard that my sides hurt and Logan walks over to see what the hell's going on.

"You okay brother?" I ask.

"What the fuck you talkin' 'bout Sky? Are you seriously sayin' there's more than one baby you're carryin'?"

"I don't know baby. I mean, sometimes one hides behind the other one. It's been known to happen that you're told you're havin' one and when you go into labor, there's more than one. We'll just have to wait and see on that day."

"You need to go lie down. Right now!" He says picking her up.

"Levi, I can fuckin' walk. And I don't wanna lie down. I'm fine!" Sky yells at him.

I can already tell it's going to be no use. He's gonna make her go up and rest now. Then I can see him running out to Dec and talk to him about this. It's actually hysterical when you think about it. The big, badass biker is gonna go take a nap with his woman and then go bitch because she's saying there's more than one baby in her. Then, I know he's gonna freak out over every little thing that happens until she goes into labor.

"Where's my little girl?" I hear Ma's voice ring out through the main room of the clubhouse bringing me out of my head.

"I'm right here Ma." I say making a bee line for her.

She wraps me up in her famous hug and kisses the side of my face. I just embrace her and let her hold me, knowing she needs this as much as I do right now. I've missed my mom and dad. Pops doesn't let her hog me for long though. He swoops in and moves Ma out of his way to pick me up and give me a bear hug, spinning me around like he used to when I was a little girl. This man has been my entire world and I can't believe that I thought I needed to leave them all. He would have given me everything that a daughter needs from her daddy to help me get through this.

"Daddy," I whisper into his ear. "I love you so much and missed you more than I can say."

"I know baby girl. But you're home now, where you belong. How are you doin' today?"

"I'm exhausted. Emotionally and physically. But, it's another day forward, yeah?"

"You keep movin' forward. If you have a bad day and need to blow off steam, you let us know and we'll figure it out, yeah? No drinkin' and no fuckin' random fuckwads."

I should've known he would've been told about that shit. But that's okay. I would've ended up telling him and Ma anyway. They know most everything about me and this wouldn't have been any different. One way or another, they would have known something happened at Gage's.

"I can promise you Pops, there will be no more random fuckwads." Grim says stepping up to us. "Isn't that right crazy girl?"

"That's right baby." I say moving closer to Grim.

"So, I see you moved forward then?" Pops asks.

"Daddy, please don't. You know this is who I've wanted for longer than I even knew."

"I know, and we've already talked about it baby girl. He knows the deal. I love you and only want you to be happy."

At that Grim whistles and gets everyone's attention. When he's sure he has it, he starts speaking.

"After talking to Pops, Joker, and of course Bailey, I'm announcin' that crazy girl is my old lady. So treat her with the respect she deserves and make sure everyone knows she's off limits, yeah?"

I bury my face in his chest while Ma wraps her little arms around both of us, kissing our heads. She's so happy. The rest of the crowd is cheering and murmurs of 'it's about time' are heard throughout the main room. Out of the corner of my eye, I can see a small smile on Gage's face. He knew it was always Grim. I hope that we can remain friends. I also see some of the club girls scowling and looking down right pissed. Too fucking bad! I don't share and Grim knows what will happen if he fucks around. Not only from me but from Pops and Joker too.

We sit down and one of the club girls brings over coffee and plates of food. I suddenly feel like I haven't eaten in about a month. Without caring about anything else, I tuck into the food and moan at the goodness of the eggs melting in my mouth. There's also bacon, home fries, and biscuits. Sky can definitely cook her ass off. One of these days she'll have to show me. I'm not a terrible cook, but there's always room for improvement. And Sky makes the best damn food I've ever had.

While we're eating, Ma asks us where we're gonna be staying. I look to Grim and he tells her that for now, we'll stay at the apartment at Sky's house. This is news to me, because I figured he'd want to stay here at the clubhouse. I'm glad that he doesn't want to stay here. Too much shit can happen when I'm not around. I know how the club girls are, they'll do whatever they can to start shit. Even if Grim doesn't do anything with them, they'll still make it seem like he is. It's the same thing Chrissy and Addison, who isn't a club girl, did to Sky when Joker and Cage went for her. I'm too drained and raw to deal with that shit right now.

Once we've finished eating breakfast and spent time with Ma and Pops, Logan leads me back to his room and starts to pack some of his shit. I sit on the bed and watch him. On one hand, I feel like this is moving real fast. It's only been a few hours since I decided to give him the chance he finally wanted. But, on the other hand, this has been ten years in the making. It feels like both of us were just biding our time to be together. Unfortunately, it took a tragedy to make Logan finally decide to quit wasting time and fucking around.

Chapter Six

Two weeks later

Grim

IT'S BEEN A few weeks since Bailey decided to give me a chance and be my old lady. I can't believe that she's finally mine! So far, things have been going great between us. We moved my shit into the apartment with her. There was no way I was gonna have us stay at the clubhouse. Right now, we need our own space to learn to live together without all the shit at the clubhouse. It's been peaceful at the apartment. The only thing I have left to give her is her rag, which I've already put in an order for. I'm just waiting for it to come in. Then we have to go get her tat.

First thing in the morning, Bailey gets up early and uses the gym Sky has in the basement. Some days Cage and Joker join her, but most days, it's just her. I give her this time to be alone and get her day started. There's still been a lot of nights she wakes me up dreaming of the baby. I know that's what she's dreaming of with the tears streaming down her face. She's called out the name Ryan a few times, so I'm thinking she thought the baby was a boy and they decided to name him Ryan. I'm also thinking that no one's supposed to know, so I keep that to myself.

Once she's done working out, we take a shower together and get ready to go to the garage. Our days are becoming a comfortable routine. Bailey's definitely getting back into the swing of things. Not only with our new relationship, but with work, family, and her friends. Every day I see a little of the old Bailey reemerging and my heart soars every time I see it.

It's also getting easier for her to be around the kids and Sky. Some days you can see the longing in her eyes when she's around them, but she pushes that shit down quick. Every day, I can see her spending more and more time with the four kids upstairs. Most days she tries to get them to come downstairs though. I think that has to do with the fact that some days it's too hard to be around the kids and Sky at the same time. But, no one says anything to her about it. It's like we're all just waiting for her to open up to us. We don't want to be the one to breach the dam and make things worse for her unintentionally.

This morning, Bay got up and changed to go workout like usual. But it's been almost two hours and she's not back yet. That's not like her. So, I push myself up out of bed and throw some shorts on before going to look for her. Maybe she went up for breakfast early. Instead, I find her sitting on the bike listening to *Broken* by Seether with tears streaming down her face. She's peddling the bike like she's trying to outrun a million ghosts.

"Crazy girl, what's wrong?" I ask heading over to her and shutting the bike down.

Bailey won't answer me, so I pick her up and carry her back into the apartment. I take her into the bedroom and lay her down on the bed. After quickly throwing on a tee shirt, I pick her back up and walk down to the pond with her. Maybe getting out of the house will help her be able to open up to me and talk about what's getting to her today.

As soon as we sit down, I position her in my lap so that she's facing me. She can still bury her head in my chest or neck, which is something she might need. I don't say anything, I just hold her and wait for her to talk to me. I've already asked her what was wrong and the last thing I want to do right now is push her and make her shut down.

"I'm so broken Logan. I can't get over the baby, and I pretend I'm happy every day. I'm so tired of pretending. I think you need to let me go and find someone that can truly support you."

"Bay, look at me." I say, waiting for her to pick her head up. "I know you feel broken right now and that you're never gonna be happy again. But, I don't think that's gonna be the case. I think, deep down, you don't feel like you should be able to move on and live your life because the baby doesn't get to live. You're wrong though. I know the baby wouldn't want you to suffer like this. He, or she, isn't sufferin', but you are. You're makin' yourself suffer because somethin' happened that was beyond your control. You'll get through this, and we'll all help you."

"Why would you waste time waiting for me to move forward from this though? You've got so much goin' on and I'm the last thing you need to be worried about. I'll be fine. You need to go to work. I think I'm gonna take today off and just be alone. Or maybe I'll call Caydence and Kenzie."

"I'm not wastin' my time crazy girl. I do have a lot goin' on, but none of that's more important than you. Ever! Even if you weren't havin' a hard time right now, you would still be more important than that shit. I'll go to work, if you promise to call the girls and not sit alone bein' upset and tryin' to fix somethin' that you can't control. Don't see the kids today, don't see Sky, just get out and do somethin' with the girls."

"I don't think I can stay here for much longer Logan. Seein' them every day is killin' me. Makin' me think about what would have been with the baby, if he'd lived. Sky is gettin' so big and I wonder what I would've looked like when I got further along. It's torture of the worst kind."

"I know baby. We'll get a place of our own. Hell, we can build a house in the big empty field between the clubhouse and here. If that's what you want that is. But, I can guarantee you that I'm not goin' anywhere. I told you, you are my world, and you're stuck with me until I leave this Earth. Now, let's get up and take a shower. I'll go to work and you'll spend the day with the girls. Tonight, if you want we can stay at the clubhouse and take a break from the kids and everythin' here."

"That sounds good. I'll meet you there when I get done with the girls. Maybe we'll go shopping or something."

We walk back up to the house and get in the shower. I can feel Bailey needs to have it proven to her how much I love her and that I'm not goin' anywhere. So, I'm gonna prove it to her the only way I can right now.

I gently push her against the side wall of the shower and push her legs apart with my knee. I slowly kiss her and then move my head down lower, making sure that I stop and pay attention to her nipples. I take one in my mouth and suck and bite down while pinching the other one with my thumb and forefinger. After spending time there, I begin to move lower again. My hands moving before my mouth. I get to her center and push two fingers inside her. Finally, my mouth moves to her clit and I suck it into my mouth. I gently bite down and then swirl my tongue around it. Looking up, I see Bailey throw her head back and a loud moan escapes her mouth. She looks down into my eyes and I'm captured, even if I wanted to I can't look away from her.

"Logan!" She moans out.

I can feel her starting to spasm around my fingers and I start moving them faster within her. My mouth starts moving faster over and around her clit, sucking it in my mouth and biting down on it. She's so close to cumming and I want to push her over the edge. So, with my other hand, I reach up and tweak her nipple. That's exactly what she needs to go over. Her inner muscles clamp down on my fingers, trying to suck them in and not let them go. I continue thrusting them in and out of her while she comes back down.

As I make my way back up her body, I can still feel her body shaking in the aftermath of her orgasm. I kiss the side of her neck and grab the body wash to wash my girl. She has other ideas and tries to move lower on me, running her hands all over me.

"No crazy girl. That was all for you. We'll do somethin' later and you can do whatever you want to me. But, this time was just about you."

"But..." She starts.

"No arguin'. There's times that I'm gonna take what I need and have to get you back later, if you don't get off. Not that it'll be often, I'll always make sure you get yours. This time, you needed to get off, and I can wait for my turn later. I'll have somethin' to think about the rest of the day." I say kissing her, taking her mind off whatever she wants to do to me.

"Okay baby. Let's get washed and get this day started." She says grabbing the soap, starting to wash my body.

Bailey

After Logan left to go to work, I called Caydence to have a girl's day out. Thankfully Kenzie was with her so I didn't have to make more than one phone call. I really wasn't in the mood to be on the phone today. Hell, I didn't even wanna have a girl's day out, but I knew it was better than sitting here in the apartment all alone. I knew that if I did that, Grim would be worried and he'd probably end up coming home from work. That's not what he needs to worry about. He needs to concentrate on making sure Spinners has no issues and that it's successful with the townspeople.

We agree that the girls would come pick me up in about an hour and we'd hit the mall to shop and then hit the spa for the total package. Kenzie was still debating getting herself waxed and she keeps chickening out. I've never done it, but I'd be down to do it if it meant that Kenzie would get over her fucking fear and take the leap. I plan on getting some shit at the mall specifically for Logan. Well, I'd be wearing it, and he'd reap the benefits of it.

Quickly getting dressed in a pair of tight jeans and one of Logan's tee shirts, I throw my hair up in a messy

90

bun and I'm ready to go. These days I'm more about comfort than about looking my best. Quite frankly, I don't give a rat's ass what anyone thinks of me. You don't like what I look like, don't fucking look! Logan doesn't give a shit what I look like, and neither does my family. They're the only ones that I care about what they think.

In no time at all, I hear the girls laughing and making their way into my apartment. As usual they're both dressed to kill and I look like a bum in comparison. Oh well. They stop laughing when they see me and both rush to give me a hug. I let them and quickly pull away.

"Alright, let's get out of here." I say grabbing my purse and sun glasses off the stand where I keep them.

"We can stay in if you want." Kenzie says.

"No!" I say too quickly. "I need to get out of the house today and not be anywhere around here. Let's go get some retail therapy."

"Alright. I'm down for that. Irish won't be, but that's okay. I'll make it up to him later." Caydence says, wiggling her eyebrows up and down.

We make our way out the door and I lock up behind us. I really want to include Sky in today's outing, but I can't deal with being in her presence after my break down. Caydence moves her car and we all pile in my truck to make our way into Benton Falls, where the mall is located. Plus, there's a new spa there where we can get everything else done. Too bad I didn't see Sky coming down the stairs as we were talking.

Skylar

I had the kids down for their naps and I decide to go down and check on Bailey. We haven't really seen her in a few weeks. Sure, she spends time with the kids, but they go down to her apartment. It's not the same. She used to spend hours up in the house playing with the kids, talking, and just hanging out. Ever since she came home, I've barely spent any time with her. I miss my friend!

As I make my way downstairs, I hear her talking to Caydence and Kenzie. When I hear her say that she doesn't want to be anywhere around here, my heart breaks. I can feel tears gathering in my eyes and I'm trying really hard not to let them fall. It's like she wants nothing to do with me anymore and I don't know what the hell I did to hurt her so bad.

Quietly I make my way back upstairs and shut the door. Turning on the music, I plop my ass on the couch and let the tears fall freely. I don't have many friends here to begin with, but I thought that Bailey was one. Apparently I was wrong about that. Especially considering that before everything happened, I would've been included in their girl's day out. Now, I'm not even a thought. I can feel all of my insecurities that I've fought hard to make disappear, surfacing.

I'm so deep in my own head that I don't hear anyone coming to the house. So I'm startled when I feel a hand on my shoulder. Looking up, I see Grim standing there with concern etched on his face.

"Sky, what's wrong? Is the baby okay? Is it Reagan?" He asks quickly.

"Oh, um…" I start, wiping the tears from my face. "I'm fine. Just one of those days, you know?"

"Sky, it's not one of those days. Somethin' happened. Now, you're either gonna tell me what it is, or I'm gonna call Cage and Joker."

"You don't play fair Grim."

"Babe, the kids aren't around, so I'm guessin' they're sleepin'. Now, I know that when the kids are sleepin', you crank the music just loud enough to not disturb them and bake your ass off. I walk in today, the music's playin' quietly and you're not in the kitchen. You're sittin' here cryin' your ass off. Now, I'm not gonna play fair when somethin' is eatin' at you."

"Fine. I don't know what I did wrong Grim. I mean, I've always been supportive of Bailey. Hell, I made sure that she made it out of that fucked up situation

92

better than what could have happened to her. And I wouldn't change that for anything in the world. I'd do it all over again in a heartbeat. I guess I just thought we were friends."

"What are you talkin' about?"

"Ever since she got back from Dander Falls, I've barely seen her. I know that you two are new and trying to navigate your relationship. She still hangs out with the kids, but it's always downstairs. In the past few weeks, I think I've seen her maybe twice. We live in the same building and she doesn't have a kitchen. Instead, you come up and take plates down to her. Yeah, I've noticed that Grim. So tell me what I did wrong? Or was I just being a fucking idiot thinking that we were friends? I went down to see her this morning, just to check on her, and I heard her talking to the girls saying she didn't want to be anywhere around here."

"Oh babe, it's not you. I promise you that. Bailey's fightin' some demons right now and she doesn't know how to deal with certain things. But, it's nothin' you did wrong. I know if she knew what you were feelin', and the fact that you were up here cryin', she would come talk to you and let you in." Grim says pulling me into his arms.

"No, she wouldn't Grim. Even though I know she's going through a hard time right now, I think that maybe it would be best if the two of you move somewhere else. I'm done feeling like I don't belong in my own home because she doesn't want to see me for whatever reason. I'm not going to continue to have the kids go downstairs to spend time with her. I've had enough and I'm putting my foot down. So, tell her that she can find somewhere to stay that isn't here. I'm done with everything!" I don't even wait for Grim to respond. I make my way upstairs so that I can calm down.

I've been doing so good when it comes to my insecurities and making progress standing up for myself. One statement from Bailey and I feel like I'm right back to where I started when I first met her. I'm not willing to slide backwards. I've got more to live for and more reasons than I've ever had to be happy and live life every day to its fullest. Bailey can become just a memory if she doesn't want to be in my life, I'm not going to waste any more tears on her. And I'm not going to try to be friends with someone that doesn't want my friendship. I don't care if she is my sister in law. Levi can see her and I'll do my own thing from now on.

Grim

I went home to pick up some shit I forgot to take to work with me. Knowing that Bailey was gone already, I chose to go into the main house. What I walked in on had me pissed the fuck off. Sky was sitting on her couch with the music softly playing and crying. I'm not talking hormonal tears from being pregnant. I'm talking about the tears of an ugly cry that is gonna be showing on her face for a while after she stops. What the fuck?

After talking to her, knowing all this shit stems from what's going on with Bailey, I can't help but feel for her. Bailey's shit isn't just affecting her. It's affecting the people she cares most about in this world. I know she loves Skylar like a sister, but she can't handle being in the same room with her right now because she's pregnant. Sky doesn't know this though because Bailey hasn't given her a chance. She hasn't given their friendship a chance because she's still too wrapped up in her guilt and pain to see she's causing those she cares about to feel pain too.

Once Sky walks away from me, I go downstairs and pick up the papers I need to take back to the garage. I'm still debating on whether or not I'm gonna tell Joker and Cage about what I walked in on when I pull back into Spinners. The one thing I do know is that I will be talking to Bailey when I see her later on tonight. She's gotta deal with this shit head on and let Sky in on what's going on in her head.

Even though I didn't want to go out, I ended up having a blast with the girls. The only dark spot on the day was that Skylar wasn't with us. Instead she's sitting home like she means nothing to me. I can feel the guilt weigh heavily on my mind about how I've been treating her. It's not something that I can control though. Seeing her pregnant brings all the pain, guilt, and confusion to the forefront and I don't know how to get past it. At this point, I don't know if I ever will.

We went to the mall and made our way to Victoria's Secret. Inside I bought a bunch of new bras and matching panties. I even bought a few corsets. They are pretty and sexy. I've worn them before under see-through shirts and love the way I look. So, I'm hoping Logan enjoys seeing them. After that, we went into a few of our favorite shops and I bought jeans, skirts, tees, dress shirts, and a few pairs of new shoes. Retail therapy is just what I needed.

After stopping at a cute little restaurant for lunch, where we had a few drinks, we made our way to the spa. We started with getting our nails done and then we got facials. Once all of that was done, we all went to get massages.

"I think I'm ready to get the waxing done now." Kenzie says, sounding muffled with her face buried in her massage table.

"You better be." I say lifting my head up. "I'm goin' first and then your ass is following me. I've never had it done either, so this should be quite the experience."

"Why would you do that?" Caydence asks me.

"Because we've been having this debate for so long now and I'm tired of her chickening out. So, I figured I'd go first and tell her how it feels and then she can go after me. How does that sound?"

"And you both can come in with me to make sure I don't chicken out." Kenzie replies.

"No offense, Kenzie, I love you like a sister. But, I don't need, or want, to see your lady bits." I say laughing.

"Whatever. I'm not askin' you to look at it. All I'm askin' is that you go in and hold my hand. You know, for moral support."

"I don't care what Bay says. I'll go in with you. Personally, I just wanna hear you scream out with pain." Caydence says, laughing her ass off.

We all start laughing at that. I try to tell her that it's not gonna be so bad, but I honestly don't know what it's gonna feel like. So, we just quiet down and finish our massages. I can feel the tension leaving my body as the masseuse works her magic. It's something I haven't felt since I lost the baby.

Finally, it's my time to go in and get waxed. I have a high threshold for pain, but I'm starting to wonder if this is gonna push me past my tolerance level. The lady that's gonna do it comes in and tells me to lie down on the table. She gets to work and the pain really isn't that bad. At least I don't think so. It doesn't take her long to do her thing and I'm told that I can get dressed. Thank God I won't have to shave for a while. In fact, I don't think I'm gonna go back to shaving. I think I'm gonna wax from now on.

Walking out, I tell Kenzie it's her turn. She walks in the room followed by Caydence. Telling them I'm not gonna go in, I go to the waiting area and sit in a plush chair. I pull out my phone and I see I have a text message from Logan. Wondering what's up, I check to see what's wrong.

Grim: We need to talk. It's important. Meet me at the garage when you're done.

I text him back asking him what's going on and then put my phone back in my purse. It doesn't take long for him to respond.

Grim: I walked in and saw somethin' today that I don't ever wanna see again. We need to talk and then you need to make shit right!

96

I can feel the anger he has pouring through the text message. What the fuck? I'm trying to wrack my brain to figure out what he's talking about, but I can't think of anything. What does he mean he walked in on something? I haven't hidden anything from him, and I know that he thinks I'm losing my mind over this shit, but I still don't have a clue.

Pretty soon, Kenzie and Caydence come walking out to the front room and pay for their services. I've already paid, so I stand by the door and wait for them. As soon as they turn and face me, I tell them we have to cut the day short so I can go meet Grim and find out what the fuck is going on. Caydence tries to respond but she's fighting her laughter off so I'm guessing that Kenzie went through with the waxing and was a screamer.

On the way back to get Caydence's car, we make plans to go out this coming weekend. They want to go to some new club that opened up on the outskirts of Clifton Falls. I didn't even know that a new club opened up. Apparently I'm more out of the loop than what I thought I was. Thankfully I bought a new dress today. It will be perfect for a night out dancing and drinking. My thoughts immediately turn to Sky and I wonder if we should invite her. But then I immediately push that thought away. She's pregnant and can't drink, so she probably won't have a good time. It'll be fine with just Caydence, Kenzie, and a few girls from the clubhouse.

After dropping them off, I turn around and make my way to Spinners. I really don't want to show my face there today, but I'm dying to know what has Logan so pissed off. As soon as I get there, I see Joker and Cage working on a customer's car. They stand up when they hear someone pull in and immediately turn away from me. What the fuck? I ignore that strangeness and park. Walking into the office, I say 'hi' to them and they completely ignore me. Now, I'm thoroughly confused.

I knock on the door and open it to find Grim sitting at his desk bent over looking at some papers. He looks up and sits up straight when he sees it's me entering. What he doesn't do is get up to hug or kiss me. So, I sit down in a chair across from the desk and wait for him to start talking. For the longest time, he does nothing but look at me.

"Crazy girl, I know you're all torn up about what happened with the baby. But you gotta stop the shit you're doin'." He starts. "I support you in whatever you think you need to do, but now it's time I step the fuck in and put my foot down."

"Logan, I have no idea what you're talking about. What did you walk in on today?"

"I forgot some paperwork at the apartment so I went back to get it. Knowin' that you had already left for whatever you decided to do today, I went in the main house. The kids were sleepin' and Sky was sittin' on the couch cryin' her fuckin' eyes out. When I finally got her talkin', she broke my heart. You've succeeded in pushin' her the fuck away completely. Skylar wants us to move out of the apartment downstairs now. She's not goin' to be sendin' the kids down there anymore either."

"What do you mean? I haven't pushed her away." I say, trying to tell myself that he's wrong.

"You have Bailey. That girl is absolutely heartbroken thinkin' you aren't her friend anymore. She's torturin' herself tryin' to figure out what she did wrong to make you hate her so much. It didn't help matters when she heard you tell the girls earlier that you couldn't be at the house. Or didn't want to be there. You've ripped her fuckin' heart out. How fucked up is that Bay? It's her fuckin' house and you've made her feel like she doesn't belong there!"

I can feel the anger, pain, and disappointment pouring off of him. At the same time, my heart is breaking because I know I caused this. I haven't let her in with what's going on with me, and I literally owe her my life. Now I know why Cage and Joker ignored me when I got here. Apparently, he told them what happened and I can't blame him at all. Sky doesn't deserve to feel like this at all.

"Well, what the fuck are you gonna do about it?" Grim asks me.

"I'm gonna go talk to her and make things right. I never meant to make her feel this way. I guess I was so wrapped up in my own grief and pain that I didn't think about what it was doin' to her. God, I'm so fucked up! I told you this morning I was broken and that you needed to get rid of me. Do you fuckin' believe me now? Look what I've done to this amazing woman. I made her cry and feel like shit because I can't handle the fact that she's pregnant. You can pack our shit up and move it wherever the fuck you want it!"

I don't let him say another word to me. Getting up, I walk out of the office and out to my truck. Somehow I have to fix this shit with Skylar. She doesn't deserve to feel like shit because of my drama and the way I feel. Instead of going to the house though, I make my way to Ma and Pops. If anyone can help me figure out how to fix this, Ma can.

It doesn't take me long to get to their house. As soon as I pull in, Ma opens the door and walks to the end of the porch. Almost immediately I burst into tears. She's never judged me, never acted like she was disappointed in me, and she's always been supportive in everything I've done or wanted to do. This time, I know that won't be the case. She loves Sky as much as she loves Joker and me. And, I've messed up royally this time. I don't even know if I'm gonna be able to fix it.

I get out of the truck and run into her arms. Ma holds me for the longest time before ushering me into the house. She leads me into the living room and sits me down on the couch. After making sure I'm sitting, she sits next to me, takes my hand in hers, and looks into my face.

"Baby girl, what's wrong?" She asks.

"I've messed up big time Ma." I say between sobs.

"I'm sure it can be fixed honey. There's never a situation too big or bad that can't be fixed with time, communication, and a little love. Now tell me what happened."

There's no holding back. I spill out every little detail about what I did to Skylar, how I've been feeling, telling Logan that I was too broken to be with him, and the fact that I can't get over losing the baby. Ma just sits there and listens to me pouring my heart out to her. She listens and holds my hand, knowing that I need the comfort and strength from her right now.

By the time I'm done pouring my heart out to her, I feel like a weight is starting to lift off my shoulders. But I also feel exhausted. So, I lay my head down in her lap and let my eyes drift close. She runs her fingers through my hair like she did when I was a little girl and something upset me. Before I know it, I'm falling asleep.

I don't know how long I was asleep for, but it must have been a few hours. The sky outside is darker, and I could smell dinner being cooked by Ma in the kitchen. I look over to my dad's chair and see him sitting there watching me.

"Hey dad!" I say sitting up.

"Baby girl, you've had a few people worried today. Disappearin' the way you did." He says coming over to sit next to me.

"What are you talking about? I saw the guys at Spinners earlier. I went out with Caydence and Kenzie for most of the day."

"I know that. But after whatever happened at Spinners, no one's heard from you. Look at your phone and I'm sure you'll see a shit ton of missed calls and messages."

I quickly pull my purse into my lap and start searching for my phone. Once I find it in this bag that I could probably fit a small child in, I unlock it and see that I do, in fact, have a ton of missed calls and messages. Most of them are from Logan. While I wasn't trying to punish him for the way he talked to me earlier, I'm not pissed that he couldn't get ahold of me either. Let his ass stew for a while longer. I don't give a fuck!

Without opening a single message, I quickly delete every message I'd ever gotten or sent. Maybe what I need to do is delete everything from my life and start over with a clean slate. I don't think as I start deleting everything from my phone period. Contacts, apps, even some pictures get deleted. My dad sits there staring at me like I'd grown two heads since I woke up. The only contacts I leave in my phone are my parents, Gage, the Dander Falls clubhouse phone number, Crash, and Trojan. Everyone else goes.

"Baby girl, what are you doin'?" Pops asks me as he watches me delete everything I used to hold so close to my heart.

"I guess it's time for a clean start. You know, time to move on with my life. I don't have time for people that are gonna bring me down. I need to start over with a clean slate and no one in it that doesn't need to be there anymore."

"I'm all for that baby girl. But I just watched you delete every family member you have from your phone, all your messages, and a shit ton of pictures that I know mean somethin' to you. Yet, you leave everyone in Dander Falls in your phone. Why is that?"

"Because only a few, Gage, Crash, and Trojan, know me there and I can be who I want to be. Yeah, they know about the baby, but they don't treat me like I'm gonna fuckin' break now. Everyone here does. Grim tore into me because of the way Sky feels I'm treating her. But how am I supposed to love her and spend time with her, knowing that she has what I want and can't have?

She's on her third pregnancy now and she has no problems other than some morning sickness. I can't even make it three months carrying a baby. What the fuck does that say about me daddy?"

"It says that nature decided that it wasn't the right time for you to have a baby. Maybe it says that Gage wasn't the right one to have a baby with. I don't know why it happened and no one does. I'm gonna tell you somethin' that not a lot of people know. Your Ma had a miscarriage before she got pregnant with you. A few of the brothers from that time know about it, but it's not somethin' that's talked about. Your Ma acted the same way you are now, and I didn't know if we were gonna make it through that."

"What are you talking about? I'm not acting like anything. All I'm doing is trying to get through each day as it comes."

"No you're not! You're tryin' to act like everythin's fine when you know it's not. You erasin' everyone from your phone is proof of that. I get what you're sayin' about it bein' hard to be around Skylar, but she doesn't know that's why your pushin' her away. Maybe it's time you sit down with her and let her know."

"I know I have to dad. But, I don't know how to explain it without makin' shit worse. I know Levi and Dec are pissed as fuck at me too. They proved that when they ignored me at Spinners earlier. But, I promise, I'll talk to her at some point."

"You're gonna do more than that. She's on her way over here now. I'm givin' you a protected place where no one else is gonna stick their fuckin' noses in, and you're gonna tell her what you just told me."

"Dad, how could you do this? I'm not ready to face her yet. Please, call her and tell her I left or something."

"You're my baby girl, and I love you. But this needs to be dealt with. You need to start dealin' with your grief and move past it. We'll help you any way we can, but this isn't somethin' you can hide from."

I get up and leave my dad sitting on the couch. Going into the kitchen, I prepare to tell Ma goodbye so I can leave before Sky gets here. Ma has other plans though. She tells me to wash my hands and help her finish making dinner. Tonight she's making spaghetti and meatballs, homemade meatballs. The meal is going to be complete with garlic bread and a fresh salad. So, I do what I was told and wash up to help her. I might just be a little bit afraid of my mom, not that I'd ever admit it though.

About halfway through preparing dinner, I hear a knock on the front door. My dad's booming steps can be heard walking to the door.

"Sky, it's so good to see you. I'm glad you could make it over." He says in greeting.

Fuck! I guess there's no backing out of having this talk with Sky now. My parents are completely unbelievable for pulling this shit. I was going to talk to her when I was ready for it emotionally. Obviously if I crash after just talking to Ma about it, I'm not ready yet. But, I guess we better get this over with.

Looking over my shoulder, I see Sky walking into the kitchen. I look at my dad and then my mom before motioning to the back door. Skylar is unsure about following me outside, I can see it in her body language and I can feel the tension in the air. Honestly, I hate myself for making her not want to be alone with me. The guys, Joker and Cage, have helped her so much since they've been together. Now, I've wiped all of her hard work away because I can't stand to be around her so happy, healthy, and pregnant.

"It's okay Sky. We're just gonna talk. There's some things that I need to clear up." I say pulling her in for a hug and pulling her outside with me.

We take a seat on the porch swing that's at the side of the huge back deck. After sitting down, I look at Sky for the longest time. I'm trying so hard to figure out how to tell her what's going on with me. I don't want to hurt her any more than I already have.

"First of all, I'm so sorry for making you feel our relationship isn't what you thought it was. That was never my intention and I feel guiltier than you can imagine." I start. "With that being said, it's so hard being around you right now. It's hard being around the kids, but with you it's worse."

"What did I do? I've talked to Karen and I can't figure it out." She asks, and I can see the tears pooling in her eyes already.

Pulling her in for a hug, I say "It's not you Sky. It's me. I'm so messed up right now. I've been acting like I'm okay and doing better about losing the baby. But, I'm not. It's so hard seeing you in love with two amazing guys. You have a houseful of beautiful, smart, and amazing children. If that's not bad enough, you're pregnant now. I just have a really hard time seeing you be able to carry babies to term when I can't. It's not just you either. I walk away from any pregnant woman I see now. Even though it's wrong, I feel like there's something so wrong with me that I can't do what you can. I can't be a true woman and give a man a baby."

By the time I'm done with my little statement, I'm bawling like a baby and Sky's pulling me into her arms. This is just the kind of person Sky is. Even after I treated her like shit and made her feel less than she ever should, she is comforting me when I need it. I really don't deserve her friendship.

"Bailey, why didn't you just tell me? I would do anything to make this easier on you. I just don't know how. You're so strong and I thought you were finally starting to move forward with your life. I mean, you and Grim are together, you've been going to work, having a girl's day out, and the kids have going down to spend time with you guys. It's on me for not thinking that you were having a hard time with this still. I'm sorry!"

"That's the thing Sky, it's not you or anything you did. Yeah, I've been doin' everything you just said. But, I've only been going through the motions. I haven't felt like doing a single one of those things. Half the people I'm around every day, Grim included, treat me like I'm gonna break at any second. And they're right. Today I was workin' out and *Broken* by Seether came on and I completely lost it. None of it's real, it's just me goin' through the motions and letting people see what they wanna see. I don't mean any of it."

"Not even Grim?"

"I don't know anymore. I mean I love him and he's my world, but I don't think I'm what he needs anymore. A big part of me wants to pack my shit and leave. The only place I can go where I know anyone is Dander Falls though. If I go there, it's gonna break Ma's heart and Pops will be pissed as fuck. I could go back home, but that's even farther away and I don't want to go back there. They'll try to make Gage's life a living hell for my decisions. It's not fair and I have nowhere to run."

"This is your home though. What if you talked to a grief counselor or something like that? Maybe that would help you start to move on." Sky says carefully.

"I don't know what talkin' to someone's gonna do to help me. When I was with Gage, after it happened, I went on a total downward spiral. I know that Grim and my Pops know about it, but I don't think anyone else does. Well, maybe Joker does. It was bad Sky. I was drinking from the time I got up until I passed the fuck out. Then I started fuckin' some of Gage's brothers. Even though I didn't really want to, I did it just to try to feel something. I'm sure it doesn't make any sense at all to you, but that's how it was." I stop and take a deep breath. "When I came back and saw what everyone had done for Gage and I, I was blown away. Grim and I talked the next day and we decided to try to be together. Well, the word try was never there. Anyway, it's been amazing. Better than I ever dreamed it would be with him. But, I'm so broken and not what he needs. I'm not the strong woman he needs at his side. For fucks sake, he's the President of the Wild Kings. I look at you and see everything you've overcome. The kidnapping, sending me away and getting it worse, Reagan's health problems, and taking on two old men. I wish I were as strong as you are. Then I look at me and see how I break down over a fuckin' song while I'm working out, see myself going through the motions and feeling nothing. That's not the type of woman that Grim needs by his side."

"Why don't you let him decide that? I mean, I'll go to counseling with you if you want me to. I'm not dealing with everything you are, but I'll be there to support you. If you wanna move to Dander Falls, then I'll support that decision too. I don't want you to go, but I'll support you all the way. One day, I hope that we'll get back to the way we were. I miss you and I love you like the sister I should have had growing up. And when I first started going to see Karen, I didn't think it was going to help me out either. But, it's good to get it all out. I don't know if you know, but I even told Cage and Joker every single thing about my past. We did it in Karen's office and once I was done talking, I felt like a huge weight had been lifted off of my shoulders. They know everything about me now and there's no judgement, just their love and support in doing what I have to do to get over shit."

"Sky, can you forgive me? I'll try to do better about bein' around you. There's no need for you to hide in your own home. And, I'll think about the counseling."

"Of course I forgive you. There's nothing to forgive. I just wish you could've talked to me about it."

With that, I wrap my arms around her and hug her for the longest time. So long that Ma opens the door and tells us that dinner's ready. After walking Sky to the door so she can go home with her family, I sit down to dinner with Ma and Pops. It's been a long time since I've had dinner with them, just the three of us. It's something I've missed and I need right now. Even if I am pissed at my

106

dad. He's just trying to protect me and help me start to finally heal.

It's been a few days since I started staying with my parents and talked to Skylar. I haven't been back to the apartment or talked to anyone. Well, anyone other than Skylar, Ma and Pops, and Caydence. Logan's been trying to get a hold of me, but I ignore him. I need to figure out what my next step is before I can talk to him.

After my parents left this morning, I plugged my iPod into the stereo to clean the house for them. Not that my mom doesn't do an amazing job, but I decide that I can help her out since I've been staying here. With the mood I'm in, I have three songs playing on repeat; *Never Let Her Go* by Florida Georgia Line, *Drink A Beer* by Luke Bryan, and *Let Me Go* by Christian Kane. I know, it's a confusing mix. But, I listen to all kinds of music. Like Skylar, I love music and I use it for whatever mood I'm in. Or to just keep in the background and distract me from life.

I'm so into cleaning, dusting all of mom's knick knacks that I don't hear the front door open up. Nothing clues me in until my music gets turned down so low that it's almost hard to hear it playing. Turning around, I'm face to face with Logan. I thought I was getting closer to being able to see him, but that's not true. It just makes me realize how much I miss and love him. even if he looks like shit. There's a week's worth of growth on his face, his clothes are a rumpled mess, and it doesn't look like he's slept since I last saw him. But, he still looks amazing to me.

"Grim, what are you doin' here?" I ask once I find my voice.

"Why wouldn't I fuckin' be here? This is where my woman's been hidin' out for the last week. Not answerin' my calls or messages. If it weren't for Pops and Ma, I wouldn't know where you were or how you were doin'. How fucked up is that? What's goin' through that pretty head of yours crazy girl?"

Hearing Logan call me crazy girl, like he's done forever, breaks something inside of me. All of a sudden I can't stop the laughter that bursts from me. I'm laughing hysterically and he's looking at me like I've lost my mind. If he only knew.

"What the fuck's so funny?" He asks, getting pissed.

"You callin' me crazy girl. If you only knew how right you are in calling me that." I say between my fits of laughter.

"If I only knew what? You're not crazy."

"I am though. Losing the baby, Ryan, broke me and I can't be fixed. I can't be put back together again, Grim. Don't you know that by now?" I ask, finally stopping my laughter.

"The fuck you talkin' about?"

"I'm not what you need. You need an old lady that's strong enough to be by your side during everything. I've come to realize that I'm not strong. I'm not the girl you need. You need to find someone like Sky. She's strong, loyal, fierce, and what a man like you needs." I say turning to move to the stereo to turn my music back up.

"Uh-uh baby. We're talkin' this shit out. I miss my girl and I want you to come home. We can work on whatever you need to work through, but we're gonna do it together. You are the exact person I need by my side. You say you're not strong, loyal, fierce, or what a man like me needs? Do I have to remind you of everythin' we've gotten up to growin' up? Or how about all the times you talked us into doin' shit we knew we were gonna get our asses punished for? What about, more

108

recently, talkin' about shit you didn't want to just to make sure that Sky would stop feelin' the way she was? You are everythin' you said Sky is and so much more. Baby, you are my entire world and I can't sleep, eat, or concentrate on anythin' knowin' that you're still fucked up over losin' Ryan. Let me in and help you. Don't run away and push us all away again Bay."

"You don't think I see the looks everyone gives me Grim? Everyone treats me with kid gloves and acts like I'm gonna fuckin' break at any second. I see pity in all their eyes because I went through something horrible. Well, I can't fuckin' deal with it and I'm goin' crazy trying to pretend everything's okay when it's not."

"That's why everyone's treatin' you like you're gonna fuckin' break Bailey. We all know that you're just goin' through the motions and that you're depressed as fuck. Anyone that knows you knows that you're sufferin' in silence and it's breakin' all of our fuckin' hearts. That's why you need to let someone in. If it's not gonna be us, then I think you need to talk to someone else that can help you. I know Sky mentioned that shit to you. It doesn't make you weak because you have to talk to someone, it means that you're strong enough to know that you can't help yourself and that you need help. You need to learn that it's okay to move forward with your life. I'm not goin' anywhere Bailey. You *are* my old lady, and that's not changin'. If you wanna stay at your parent's house, that's cool. Already talked to Pops about movin' my shit in with ya. So, you let me know what it's gonna be. And stop callin' me Grim!"

Without warning I burst into tears. I should've known that Logan wasn't gonna let me push him away. Even though I know I'm not what he needs, he's gonna stick by me until he realizes it. When he does, I don't know that I'll be strong enough to handle the loss. It's already so hard knowing he could walk out that door every morning and find someone that he thinks would fit him better than a depressed girl that doesn't believe in anything anymore.

Grim walks over to me and pulls me into his arms. He wraps me up tight and cradles my head against his chest. I can hear his heart beating strong and even. It's almost enough to lull me into a sleep. But, I can't allow that to happen. I need to decide what I'm gonna do. Apparently he's right, and so is Sky. I need to talk to someone about getting help. Especially considering I've been drinking in my room at my parent's house. They don't know since I lock myself away and hide the bottles where they won't find them. I can't keep putting my body through the binge drinking.

Picking me up, Logan takes me out to his truck and puts me in the passenger seat. Before the door closes, I hear him on the phone telling Blade to pick my truck up and bring it to the apartment. I guess we're going back home. It's probably time to stop hiding out anyway.

Grim

After a week of hearing nothing from Bailey, I'm done waiting for her to return. She needs to realize that I'm gonna have her back no matter what she needs to do. At this point, I completely agree with Sky that she needs to talk to someone that can help her. So, I quit what work I'm pretending to do at Spinners, and go to Ma and Pop's house. It's not like I could concentrate on work, or anything else right now anyway.

As soon as I pull up, I can hear the music coming through the windows. With it being so loud, I know Bailey won't hear me knock. So, I open the door and stare at her. She's wearing a pair of short cut offs that show just a peek of her ass cheeks and a Wild Kings tank top. Bailey's dancing to the music as she cleans Ma's knick knacks. I don't know how she can dance to the music she's listening to, but she is.

With our talk finished and Bailey crying, I put her in my truck and start driving towards the apartment. We aren't gonna stay at Ma and Pop's house. I can't fuck her there since it's their house. That's just disrespectful. After driving a few minutes, Bailey finally turns to me.

"I think you guys are right and I need to talk to someone. You have no idea how depressed and exhausted I am all the time. I don't care about anything anymore. That's why I know I'm not good enough to be by your side."

"Baby, you're more than good enough to be by my side. If anyone's not good enough, it's me. You know what I've done for the club and what I would do in a heartbeat to protect my family and especially you. I'm not a good guy, I don't have the name Grim for no reason. I'm thankful every day that you're in my life. Before it was a club member's daughter and sister, then it was tryin' to hide my feelin's for you, now it's as my old lady. Someday you're gonna see what I see when I look at you. You're gonna believe me when I tell you that I love you and that I got your back. You are my world and I'll do anythin' I can to help you through this. All you gotta do is say the word."

When I don't get a response from Bailey, I look over to see her sleeping. It's like as soon as she made the decision that she needed to talk to someone, the exhaustion took over and drained her. I run my fingers through her hair as I pull into the driveway. Joker and Cage are sitting out on the porch and they get up as I pull in.

Walking around to Bailey's door, I open it carefully and lift her into my arms. She's lost a ton of weight since losing the baby. If I'd been paying more attention to her, instead of just being happy that she finally agreed to look past everything I've done to her and be my old lady, I'd have seen it sooner. As soon as Joker sees her, he turns around and punches the truck they just bought Sky last year. She now has a huge dent in the side of it.

"Motherfucker!" He yells. "How did this shit get so bad with her and none of us fuckin' noticed it? She looks like death warmed over and she's not even wakin' up with you gettin' her out of the truck."

"Joker, she's gonna be fine. She finally agreed to go talk to someone. On the way over here she said she needed to talk to someone for help. So now we're gonna know to pay attention to shit with her and make sure that she's gettin' better. Now, help me get her inside. I'm gonna lay her down and start makin' calls to get her in somewhere as soon as possible."

"While you two are doin' that, I'll have Sky make her somethin' to eat. It'll be ready when she wakes up." Cage says walking back into the main house.

Joker and I get Bailey in the apartment and I take her into the bedroom. As soon as I turn to leave the room, Joker's pulling a chair in to sit vigil by the bedside. I leave him to it and walk to the living room to start making phone calls.

Chapter Seven

A few weeks later

Bailey

IT'S BEEN A few weeks since I started seeing a grief counselor. At first when I woke up and Logan told me he had an appointment for me, I was pissed as fuck. But the more I thought about it, the more I realized that he knew I would procrastinate making an appointment myself. Even though I know this is something that I desperately need to do, I would put it off until I couldn't afford to any longer. Everyone but me knew I was at that point, I just couldn't see it myself.

So far the counseling has been going good. The counselor he found is an older lady and she's suffered losing a baby. She knows what I'm going through and what I'm feeling inside. It also helps that she did the same things that I was doing. Pushing people away, pretending everything was fine when it wasn't, not wanting to be around other pregnant people, and going in a downward spiral. The talks that we have are amazing and she's really helping me work through some of my shit.

Logan has been amazing. He's there for me when I've broken down and cried my eyes out. When I need to talk, he's there to listen, and when I don't want to talk about it, he's there to take my mind off things. He can get very creative when he's trying to take my mind off things. We've been to a few parties at the clubhouse. Other than that we hang out at the apartment.

It's also been easier to be around Skylar. I still have days that it hurts to be around her, but they are getting farther and farther apart. We've been out a few times shopping for the new baby. The three of them decided that they didn't want to know what they were having this time, so we've been looking at gender neutral things. I thought I was gonna lose it the first time we went baby shopping, but I enjoyed myself and we had fun. It was great picking things out that the guys would flip over. It was also nice to hang out with Skylar the way that we used to and just be normal. Well, whatever normal is.

The girls and I have had a night out or two. With supervision of course. Our men won't let us go out without them around in one way or another. This caused a few fights between some of us but in the end we had a great time. Even if the guys don't come with us, they make sure that Blade, Crazy and Slim Jim come with us and watch us discreetly. Crazy and Slim Jim are two new prospects that Blade is showing the ropes to. I don't know how they're going to work out yet. Anyway, they make sure we have fun without getting too crazy and out of control. When they have to call our guys in, we know that we've gone too far. And yes, that has happened on more than one occasion.

I've also been spending time at my tree. Sometimes I just sit there and cry, other times I sit there and talk. When I talk, it's always about things that I would've done with the baby. Or it's about things my crazy family members have done. Instead of feeling sad when I come out here now, I feel kind of peaceful. The counselor has helped me see that I didn't do anything wrong and I need to quit blaming myself for losing the baby.

Today has been a great day. Logan woke me up in his own special way with his head buried between my legs. After making sure that we were both satisfied, we took a shower and got ready to go to work. Then we made our way up to have breakfast with Skylar, the guys, and the kids. I realize how much I missed all the craziness of the mornings around the house.

Now I'm sitting at work and the guys all decided that they were going to the diner for lunch today. Usually we just call and have something delivered, but today they want to get away for a little bit.

"You comin' with us sis?" Joker asks, walking up to my desk.

"No. I've gotta get caught up on this paperwork so that I can get to the inventory this afternoon. I've been slacking and need to get my ass caught back up so that I can feel like I'm pulling my weight again."

"I'll bring you somethin' back then baby." Grim says, coming up behind me and kissing my neck. "You can come with us you know. I don't think your boss will give a fuck."

"No. I need to do this shit. Inventory is gonna take all afternoon. I probably won't get done until late with it. So, the sooner I get this paperwork done, the sooner I can get started on the counting."

The guys start piling out and start their bikes. It's a sound that I always love hearing. Seeing all of the guys ride in formation is an amazing sight to witness. They all ride together as one, knowing what the other riders will do before it happens. It's the only way to ride in formation and not have a catastrophe happen. If you don't trust the guys you ride with, there's no point in riding together.

I've finally completed entering the paperwork into the computer and I stand to stretch. Looking at the clock, I figure the guys would have been back by now. They've been gone for just over an hour. Taking a drink of my water, I pick up the papers I need for inventory and make my way to the back room. Since no one's here, I decide to set up my iPod with the speaker Logan got me for work. *Breakdown* by Seether blares out. So, I make my way over to the back corner to start my counts. I need to make sure the counts are accurate so that the guys have everything they need without having to order it or go buy it from the local parts store and risk them not having it in stock. Once I'm done, I'll do any ordering that we need and make sure the companies get the order. It's not required of me, but it's something I do to make their job easier.

I'm about half way through my first shelf when I hear boots walking across the floor. I don't really pay attention, thinking that the guys are finally back from lunch. All of a sudden my head's ripped back by someone pulling my hair, hard.

"What the fuck?" I yell, trying to turn around.

"I don't know what the fuck you people think you're trying to fucking pull opening a garage when we already fucking have one. I'm telling you to fucking shut it down now!" A guy I've never seen before screams in my face. I can feel spit from him splatter on the side of my face and I have to resist the urge to throw up on him.

"I don't know who you are, but we have every right to have this garage. We went through all the proper channels and everything was approved. You don't have to worry about what we do here, we're not competition. We specialize mainly in custom work." I say trying to calm this guy down.

From the look of this guy, he's a mechanic. He's wearing dirty coveralls and there's grease under his nails. I knew there was a garage on the other side of town when we first thought about opening one. It never occurred to me that they wouldn't appreciate our business. I didn't lie when I said we mainly do custom jobs. Yeah, there's the odd customer that we get that wants something on their car or truck fixed. But, our main source of business is making custom bikes. I guess this guy wouldn't be happy knowing that we're thinking of expanding into doing custom car work, like rebuilding old muscle cars and then selling them.

"I'm not gonna fucking say it again. Close the fucking shop or you're gonna regret it." He yells into my face. Once again so close I can feel the spit hit me.

"Are you seriously threatening me right now motherfucker? You obviously don't know who the fuck I am." I ask him using my sleeve to wipe his nasty spit from the side of my face.

"I don't care about whatever gang you fucking belong to bitch. If you don't wanna start having accidents, shut this shit down. *Now!*"

"I'm not talking about the *club* asshole. I grew up with men and I could take your ass in a fucking heartbeat. You don't fucking scare me." I yell, getting pissed. No one threatens my family or me.

The guy doesn't say anything in return. But in the next instant, he flips his shit and starts flinging and throwing everything he can move. Once the parts are thrown all over the back room, he starts pushing the shelving units over. A few of the ones close to me barely miss hitting me and knocking me under them. I'm so stunned that I can't do anything but stand there in stunned silence. This guy must really not know who he's fucking with. What the fuck?

Before he leaves, the mechanic pushes me hard. I trip over some of the shelving units and land on my ass and wrist hard. I actually think I feel something break in my wrist I land so hard. But I won't let him know he hurt me. He'll probably get off on that shit. He quickly makes his retreat and I sit on my ass, holding my injured wrist in my hand, and look at the mess he made in less than five minutes. Thankfully the fucker didn't mess with my music. I know that's not important in the grand scheme of things, but that's where my mind went.

"Well, this shit ain't gonna clean itself up." I mutter as *Wild Wild Love* by Pitbull starts playing.

It's hard to pick this shit up when my wrist is killing me. It hurts to move any part of it and it's been steadily swelling since I landed on it. Right now it's huge and red. But, me being stubborn, I'm more concerned with cleaning up the mess that asshole made. I haven't even made a dent in it when I hear the guys return. I'd probably have more done, but I can't lift the shelves up one handed.

"Bailey, where you at baby?" Logan asks, yelling through the shop.

I try to make my way out to him so none of them see the mess. It's stupid, I know, since I can't lift anything heavy. Making my way to the door, I run into

Cage's chest and yelp as my hand gets crushed between us.

"What the fuck Bay?" He asks trying to look behind me. "What's goin' on?"

"Nothing. Let's go get back to work." I say, trying to turn him away from the doorway.

"You're hidin' somethin'. What the fuck is it?" Cage asks pushing me out of the way after seeing my wrist.

Making his way into the backroom, Joker and Logan round the corner. Their eyes immediately zero in on my injury and they rush to my side. Logan gently lifts my arm away from my body so he can get a better look at it as Joker makes his way to the backroom.

"Sis, what the fuck happened? Did you decide to trash this fuckin' place?" Joker yells out.

"What's he talkin' 'bout crazy girl? What the fuck happened while we were gone?" He asks, still holding my arm.

"Some guy showed up and decided that he'd warn me to shut Spinners the fuck down. Apparently he's not happy we opened a garage up. After threatening me that if we didn't close up shop we'd start experiencing 'accidents', he trashed the backroom."

"Okay, but how did you get hurt? This isn't a fuckin' sprain or somethin' that's gonna fuckin' bruise baby. Your wrist is fuckin' broke."

"Um…" I start.

"Did he put his fuckin' hands on you Bay?" Logan asks getting pissed. I can see the rage boiling through him.

"He pushed me right before he left. I fell over some of the shelving units he shoved down. I know I felt something break when I landed, but I was tryin' to get shit cleaned up."

Logan lets go of my arm and makes his way into the backroom. I can hear the cussing and things flying and crashing from where I'm standing. Hearing more bikes, I turn to see Tank and my dad pulling in. Great, I bet Joker called them. Pops quickly parks and runs over to me. He goes to pull me in for a hug, but notices my wrist at the last second.

"What the fuck?" He yells. "What the fuck is goin' on here?"

Joker and Grim come back out and retell what I told them. I can see the veins in Pops' head and neck start to bulge out. This isn't a good fucking sign at all. He's barely restraining the anger he has rolling through him. I know what those veins mean, and it's not gonna end good for someone.

"Who is this fucker that put his hands on my fuckin' little girl? And where the fuck were all of you?"

"We were at lunch dad." Joker says. "As for the dead man walkin', Bay said he looked like a mechanic."

"Fuck!" Pops yells.

Logan pulls out his phone while standing behind me. "Blade I need you to bring me a fuckin' cage to Spinners. I gotta get my girl to the hospital. Then get the rest of the guys here and start cleanin' up the backroom."

After listening to Blade's response, he hangs up and wraps his arm around my shoulders. None of us say anything for a little bit. Cage comes out with a bag of ice and gently puts it on my wrist. I know that I should've already had ice on it, but I was more concerned about the mess being cleared up so the guys wouldn't find out anything happened.

Within a few minutes, Blade is pulling in driving Grim's truck. He loads me up inside, still holding the ice on my wrist, and jumps in the driver's seat. I see Pops, Cage, and Joker jumping on their bikes to follow us to the hospital. This is not how I imagined today turning out at fucking all.

Pops

As soon as Joker called me, I knew something was wrong. I just didn't know that some motherfucker put their hands on my little girl. Apparently some dumb fuck has a death wish, putting his hands on my baby.

Joker, Cage, and I follow Grim taking Bailey to the hospital. My poor girl has been through so much shit the last few months. She's just starting to get her head straightened back out, and this shit happens. Why the fuck would they leave her at the garage alone? The guys never all go to lunch away from the shop at the same time. Someone's gonna fuckin' answer some questions when we get there. Especially when Ma shows up!

Within a few minutes we pull up to the emergency room doors and park. We all make a circle around Bailey leading her through the doors. No one else is gonna fucking get to her on my watch. That's for fucking sure! I'm staring down the other three men as Bailey lifts her gaze to me. Instantly my eyes soften as I take in my baby girl. I move the other guys away and put my arms around her, being careful not to hit her wrist or that side of her body.

"My girl needs a doctor." Grim says to the nurse sitting at the desk.

"What's going on?" She asks looking up.

"Someone attacked my daughter, and I'm pretty sure her wrist is broken. Get someone out here for her. *Now!*" I yell.

The nurse scrambles up from the desk and takes Bailey with her. She probably just wants to get away from the four of us. I know you can see the rage burning through me, and Grim isn't looking much better. Joker and Cage look the calmest out of the four of us, but I know they're just as filled with rage as we are. They just know how to hide that shit better. Well, until it comes to Sky and the kids they do.

"Now, my daughter is bein' looked at in a fuckin' hospital. I wanna know what made all of you decide to go to lunch away from the garage at the same time and leave her the fuck alone. Whose head am I bashin' the fuck in for leavin' her?"

"Dad, we all decided to go. We tried to get her to go with us, but she wouldn't have it. She said she was gonna finish up the paperwork and then start inventory. Bay said she hasn't been pullin' her weight at the shop the last few months and she refused to go." Joker started. "We haven't had any issues at all since we opened. None of us thought anythin' would happen to her, otherwise we wouldn't have left her."

"That's not good enough son! Someone should have fuckin' stayed behind with her. Grim, she's your old lady now. You should have stayed with her. What the fuck were you thinkin'?"

"I wasn't Pops. We were starvin' and decided to go to the diner. I should've gotten our lunch and made my way back to the shop. Instead, I stayed to eat with the guys. Bailey's been doin' so much better and I didn't want her to feel crowded by havin' me there. It won't fuckin' happen again!"

"I know it won't. As of now, if my daughter's at Spinners, I'm at fuckin' Spinners. And I'm tellin' you right now, you better be doin' somethin' at home to make sure no motherfucker gets her there too. Otherwise, you have a new fuckin' houseguest."

None of the guys say anything more. I sit down and wait for Ma to show up. No sooner do I sit down and she comes running in the hospital. Standing back up, I pull her into my arms and bury my face in her neck. Her pulse is racing and she's shaking from head to toe. I know she's just trying not to cry. She's trying to be strong and not break down in front of Bailey. If I know her, she'll be back with our daughter in about thirty seconds.

"Where is she? Where's my baby?" She asks, looking back and forth between all of us.

"She's in back Ma." Joker answers her. "We haven't heard anythin' yet. Don't even know if she's seen anyone."

"What the hell? I'll get the fucking answers if you guys can't be man enough to find out."

With that she takes off and forces her way back to her daughter. Yeah, my woman's a monster when it comes to her kids and grandbabies. She makes me proud when she pulls this shit. Putting us in our place and getting what she wants in the span of thirty seconds or less.

Grim

I can't believe how bad we fucked up today. This shit should have never happened. Especially not to Bailey. My girl's been through so much shit and this is high on the list of shit that she didn't need to go through. Fuck! I should've stayed behind or made sure she went with us to the diner. Hell, the least I could've done is made Blade come to the shop and help her while we were gone.

I sit down in a chair and put my head in my hands. At this point, I don't think I'll ever get things right with her. She deserves someone so much better for her than me, but I'm a selfish bastard and I'm not letting her go. I'll just have to step the fuck up and be better. She'll never be left alone again!

Pulling out my phone, I type out a message to Tank and Glock. I want them at the apartment wiring up a security system on the whole fucking house. The cost doesn't matter to me; I want it done now. Our women, and the kids, are gonna be protected at all times. I'm not stupid enough to believe that at least one of us are gonna be at the house with them every day all day long. That's just not possible. So, the security system will help give us a piece of mind.

Glock messages me back that they're on it. That's one less thing I have to worry about. About the same time Glock messages me back, Bailey and Ma come walking through the doors. Bailey has a blue cast on her arm and a prescription in her hand. Fuck! I get up and make my way over to her. She looks up at me with love shining bright in her eyes.

"Baby, are you ready to go home?" I ask, pulling her into me.

"Yeah. We just gotta get this script filled and then we can go."

"Baby girl, how are ya feelin'?" Pops asks, walking up to us.

"I'm fine dad. It was a clean break. So, I'm in a cast for a few weeks and then possibly have to have physical therapy. We won't know that until the cast comes off."

A growl bursts out of me. I can't stand to know that she has to go through all this shit. All because we got too relaxed and didn't think anything like this would ever fucking happen. Our being too relaxed stops right fucking now. I'm gonna end up calling church for later on today, after I get Bailey settled in at home. Then we're gonna get this shit sorted the fuck out.

After finally making our way out of the hospital, I drive to the pharmacy and run her prescription in. When I get back out to the truck, we decide to head over to the diner to get a bite to eat before heading home.

"What do you want to eat crazy girl?" I ask settling in the booth she chose.

"I'm thinking a giant burger with fries and a chocolate milk shake. That sounds really good right about now."

I start laughing and go to the counter to order our food. Bailey's order actually does sound good so I order the same thing for myself. Making my way back to our table, I watch her. She's so resilient and has no clue that she's as strong as she is. Other women that went through the same thing she did today wouldn't be so calm and ready to eat half a cow. My girl can handle herself.

"Are you okay Logan?" She asks me as I walk up to her.

"Other than bein' pissed as fuck this happened to you, I'm okay. Why do you ask?"

"Well, I was trying to make sure that nothing happened. But it was like a switch just flipped with this guy and the next thing I know the backroom is trashed and I'm landing on my ass. I couldn't even move to stop him I was so shocked that he was going off like that. I'm sorry."

"Crazy girl, you got nothin' to be sorry for. I'm glad you didn't try to stop him. I can't imagine what he would've done to you if you had. I'm the one that needs to apologize for leavin' you alone. This wouldn't have happened if I stayed behind. It won't happen again!"

Bailey goes to say something but I shut her up by kissing her. There's nothing she can say to me right now to convince me that this didn't happen because we got too lax in thinking no one was gonna do anything to us. For fucks sake, the Soulless Bastards are still out there and we have no idea where they are or what their next move is gonna be. Later tonight, at church, I'm making sure that everyone knows we have to step back up and keep an eye out better than what we have been. Security measures are gonna need to be stepped up and I want eyes on things all day and night. Nothing like this is gonna happen again to anyone. Especially our women!

After we eat, we head back to the pharmacy to pick up Bailey's medicine so we can get home. Glock and Tank should be there by now starting to set up the new security measures at the house. But, my plan is to get Bailey inside and get her settled either in bed or watching a movie. I don't want her to think about anything that happened today, even though I know that she's gonna be thinking about nothing else. My hope is that a movie will help take her mind off of it though.

Bailey

As we pull into the driveway, I see two bikes parked outside. Upon closer inspection, I see it's Glock and Tank. I wonder what the hell they're doing here. As far as I know, no one's home. Skylar took the kids over to Ma and Pops today to visit with Ma. But, that could've changed with what happened at the garage.

"What are they doin' here?" I ask.

"I had them come over to install a security system here. Joker and Cage have been talkin' about it for a while but things kept comin' up and we all just kind of forgot about it. So, Glock and Tank are doin' it now."

"Oh. Well, that's good that the kids and her will be protected. I mean when the guys aren't here."

"Baby, this shit's for you too. I want to know that if I can't be here, you'll be okay. Yeah, it's good for the kids and Sky. But, you're my main concern and you're the only one that I'm concerned about right now."

"Logan, it happened and it's over with now. Some asshole just got pissed because he thinks we're gonna take his business away. That's not our intention, and it never was. I think when he sees that he's still got his fair share of customers he'll calm down and this will go away." I start. "Think about it. This is a small town and he probably just thought that he'd have to close his business, which has probably been in his family for years, just because we decided that we wanted to open a garage. To him, it doesn't matter that we cater to a different type of customer right now. We're new and people are gonna wanna see what we're about. I'm not worried about it and you guys shouldn't be either. Now, I don't wanna talk about this crap anymore. It's over and I just want to curl up in your arms and relax. Do you think we could do that?"

"Yeah, we can do that. Let's get inside and we'll get settled in on the couch and watch a movie. Does that sound good to you? I'll even let you pick the movie."

I nod my head and we get out of the truck. Making our way inside the apartment, I wave to Glock and Tank. Once we're inside, I make my way to the bedroom and grab one of Logan's tee shirts to wear. Knowing that the guys are outside, I decide to put on a pair of shorts to wear. At least until they're gone. Logan would flip his shit if I went out in the living room wearing nothing more than a tee shirt. Especially when I can hear voices coming from out there.

Walking over to the couch, Glock meets me before I sit down and carefully pulls me in for a hug. After kissing the top of my head, he asks me how I'm doing.

"I'm doin' good. It's just been a long day and I'm ready to relax. What are you guys doin'?"

"We're just finishin' up with the security system before headin' back to the clubhouse. Then of course there's the trip to Mystic." Tank says giving me a hug.

"A night out spent watching sluts dance naked so you get all turned on only to be turned down. Sounds like my kind of night boys." I say teasing them.

"What the fuck you talkin' 'bout?" Glock asks me. "Who the fuck you think is gettin' turned down?"

"Well, you two of course. I mean, I know I would turn you down so quick your heads would spin."

"Grim, is she for fuckin' real?" Tank asks. "Sweetheart, I get more pussy than any of these fuckers combined. There's no way I'm gettin' turned down. That's a fuckin' fact!"

"I know it is Tank. It's just so fun to get you boys worked up. Now, I know you're gonna work even harder to make sure you don't strike out." I say laughing.

The three guys just stand there looking at me for a few minutes before they join in on my laughter. It feels good to act semi-normal around them again. It's something I've missed more than I realized. Hopefully this means that I'm starting to finally put my pain behind me. Although I know this doesn't mean, in any way, that I'm not gonna have hard days. I just hope that the good days start outnumbering the bad ones.

Finally, after talking to the guys for a while longer, they leave and it's just Logan and me. We get settled in on the couch after he went upstairs to make some popcorn and get us some drinks. I have water down here, but we wanted some soda. Plus, I had him sneak me down some of Sky's fudge. It's amazing and if I could eat it every day without getting a fat ass, I would. I picked a comedy to watch and as we settled in to watch, Logan pulls me onto his lap so I was resting with my head in his lap. He starts running his fingers through my hair. I love when he does this and he knows it. When my man starts running his fingers through my hair, he knows it relaxes me and starts to put me to sleep. Apparently, I'm not gonna watch the movie, I'll be asleep in about five minutes or less. That's fine because I'm sure there's gonna be church and he's just hanging out with me until I fall asleep so he can go.

Chapter Eight

About a month later

Bailey

AS MORE TIME has gone by, I've become more relaxed and I am starting to get back to myself again. Thankfully I didn't have to have to cast on for six weeks. The doctor took it off a few days ago and said that I can resume all activities. There was no other damage to my arm than it just getting broke so I don't have to have physical therapy at this point.

It doesn't feel like I have to make myself get out of bed every morning. It's been amazing to fall asleep in Logan's arms every night and wake in them every morning. Well, just wake up in the same bed with him. The only time he doesn't wake me up is when I wake up early to work out before we make our way to Spinners.

This morning happens to be one of those mornings. I've been working out for about an hour when *Like A Wrecking Ball* by Eric Church is turned down. Turning around on the treadmill, I see Logan making his way to me. So, I turn the speed of the treadmill down and start my cool down so that I can give him a kiss.

"Mornin' crazy girl! How long have you been in here?" He asks me, sitting on the weight bench the guys bought a few weeks ago.

"A while. I woke up and wanted to get a good workout in before we got ready for the day. I was gonna wake you up but I know you've had a lot going on so I decided against it."

"You could have. Remember, I'll sleep when I'm dead."

Instead of responding to that remark, I just glare at Logan. He knows that I hate him talking shit like that. It has nothing to do with losing the baby anymore, it has to do with losing him. Even though the club doesn't do shit that it used to, there's still a dangerous element with the protection runs they do for other people. Plus, we still have the Soulless Bastards out there somewhere and we don't know what is going on with them. Or when they're going to come back for round two.

As soon as I complete my cool down, I get off the treadmill and make my way over to the bike. Logan watches me the entire time I'm moving from place to place. I guess he didn't come in to work out. He's still just sitting there watching. Sometimes he does this. There's a weight room with a boxing ring at the clubhouse and I know that's where he likes working out. Most of the guys work out there. I know the reason for this is because they like to get in the ring and take their frustrations out on one another.

"So, I was thinkin' about somethin'." He says as I get into my groove on the bike.

"Logan, just spit it out and let me know." I respond more harshly then I intended to.

"Well, I was thinkin' that since the club owns the field in between the clubhouse and here that maybe we could build a house in it. That way we're still close to Sky, the guys, and the kids. Plus, we're still close to the clubhouse. It's just somethin' I've been thinkin' about." He says looking at me.

This is the first time I've ever seen Logan look as though he's unsure of himself. Usually he's so confident that it annoys me to no end. I don't know why he wouldn't be that way when talking about building a house, hell a future, together now. Unless he thinks that I won't go for it. But that's crazy! If he thought that, he would just tell me that we're building a house together and that's the end of it. He must really be unsure of what I'll think right now. So, I get off the bike and make my way over to him.

"Baby, you know I love you right?" I ask him, settling myself in on his lap.

"Yeah. I love you too."

"So, why are you acting so weird about this?"

"Because I don't want to push you. I know that things have been gettin' better every day for you, but this needs to go at your pace. You know if it were up to me, I'd just be sayin' we're buildin' a house. Hell, it'd probably already be built and I'd just move your shit in."

"There's the Logan I know and love. Yes, I want to build a house with you. We need our own space and its time that we have it. I'm ready to take that step with you. I think I was ready when I was little. You're the one that's been draggin' ass here!" I say kissing him.

"Well, if that's what you want, then we'll start plannin' it now." Logan says laughing and pulling me tighter to him. "I just wanted to make sure that you were ready to leave here and not seem like I was forcin' the decision on you."

"Babe, I'm doing fine. You don't have to be scared to talk about something that you want. If I don't want to do it, then I won't. You should know this by now. So, how much input am I gonna have in this new house of ours?"

"You can have all of the say as far as I'm concerned." He says standing up and starting towards the apartment. "There's only one thing that I want in the house."

"Oh yeah? What's that?" I ask him.

"A huge ass master bedroom so that we can have a huge ass bed to roll around in." Logan says, giving me a wicked grin.

"Oh! I like the sound of that. Maybe I'll make sure that there's enough room to put a swing in too."

Logan stops and looks at me like I'm crazy. Maybe he doesn't want something like that. I've never used one during sex, but maybe it's something that I'd like to try out. But, if Logan doesn't want something like that then I'm not gonna push for it.

"Are you serious right now babe?"

"Absolutely! Never used one, but it sounds fun."

"Alright then. Hell, if you want to make a fuckin' playroom then go ahead. I don't give a fuck."

Okay then. Now my mind starts wondering about if I can find enough things I'd like to try using to warrant an entire playroom being made into the plans of our house. I know that Logan has dabbled in bondage and shit like that, but I never have. He looks at me and I must have a look on my face because I'm thinking about what I could buy to put in there.

"If you don't want a playroom, don't worry about it crazy girl. Whatever you want."

"No, it's not that. I was actually just thinking about different things that we could get to put in there. I mean, I know that you've dabbled in some stuff but I never have. I wouldn't know the first thing to buy for a playroom."

"If you want a playroom, then we'll have one. Once the house gets closer to completion, we'll go shoppin' together and pick things out. It's not a big deal."

I don't respond as Logan enters the bathroom. He sets me down on the counter while he starts the shower. While waiting for the temperature to even out and become the right temp, I start stripping. Since Logan's back is to me he has no idea that I'm now sitting here naked. As soon as he turns back around, I grip the waist band of his gym shorts and pull them out over his hard length before they drop to the floor.

I slide down off the counter and land on my knees in front of him. Thankfully my clothes landed there so I have a little bit of padding against the tiles. Looking up at Logan from beneath my lashes, I open my mouth so that I can take as much of his length into my mouth as possible. As soon as my lips close over him, I hear a hiss leave his mouth. Since my hair is up, I can feel him taking it down so that he can shove his fingers in it in a tight grasp. Logan doesn't just use my hair to control the speed and tempo when I'm giving him a blowjob. He likes to make sure that it's out of my face so he can see me when I'm going down on him. When I asked him about it before, he told me that he loves to look in my eyes when we're doing anything sexual. That way he knows without a doubt if I like something that he's doing to me or not. Even if I can't tell him what I like, or don't like, my eyes tell him for me.

"Crazy girl, this is not what I was expectin'. But, I'm not gonna turn it down. *Ever!*" Logan growls out.

The only thing I can get out is a moan around his hard cock. I know that he loves when I do this because the vibrations add to the sensations I make him feel. I've just started and I can already feel the tremors wracking his body, I can already feel the wetness pooling between my legs. So, I move one of my hands down lower towards my center so that I can relieve some of the tension I feel in my body.

"No!" Logan says. "The only things goin' near that pussy belong to me. You will not touch yourself Bay. That's my pussy and it will receive pleasure from me only."

Moaning again, I move my hand back up and rest it on his thigh so that he knows I'm not going to touch myself. Logan starts to push my head faster and faster. Thankfully he knows that I have a horrible gag reflex so he just puts enough pressure on my head to make me aware that he wants me to speed up. At the same time, I increase the speed of my hand at the bottom of his cock. All too soon he's pulling me off of him.

"I'm not gonna cum in your mouth today. The only place I'm gonna cum is in you crazy girl."

Logan lifts me up and leads me into the shower. It's not exactly a huge shower, but we've learned to make do with the limited space we have. After stepping in behind me, Logan uses his hand to push on my back so that I bend over in front of him. I grab onto my ankles and trust him not to let me fall or bang my head off of the end of the tub.

"Crazy girl, this is gonna be hard and fast. We need to get a move on if we're gonna have breakfast."

"Then get goin' stud." I say back.

Logan's answer is to enter me in one smooth, hard thrust. He doesn't give me even a second to become used to his length. Instead, he just continues on a punishing rhythm so that we can each find our release. Knowing that I didn't have a warm up like he did, Logan reaches around me and uses his fingers to pinch my clit. At the same time, he bites down on my shoulder and my neck before peppering kisses all over my neck, shoulders, and back. He knows exactly what I need to find my release right along with him.

"Babe, I'm getting close." I moan out.

Logan only increases his tempo. I can feel his movements becoming erratic, faster, and harder. This means that he's close and he's gonna step up his game to make sure that I find mine right along with him.

"Crazy girl, I need you to let go. If you don't you're gonna be disappointed." He growls out.

On top of his fast pace, bites, and pinching my clit, Logan's words are all I need to let go. Screaming out his name, I find my release as I feel him start to find his within me. Usually he pulls out, but this time he didn't. As we both try to catch our breath, Logan pulls me closer to his chest and holds me as we come back down. He rubs my back and holds me until he knows that my breathing is slower and I am steady on my feet.

"Babe, you didn't pull out this time. Again." I say burying my head in his chest.

"Crazy girl, look at me." He says, waiting until I turn my face up to him. "I know I didn't pull out. I told you before that we'll handle anythin' that comes our way. That includes you gettin' pregnant."

"Babe, I don't know if I'm ready to go through that again. Besides, I don't even know if I can get pregnant again. I know the doctor said I should have no problems, but I can't help but wonder. Maybe I should go get on the pill or something so that we don't have to worry about that right now. We can revisit the topic in a little while."

Logan just kisses my forehead and brushes my wet hair out of my face. He turns me back around and I can feel him begin to wash my hair. I love it when he takes care of me. When it comes to having a baby with him, it's all I used to dream of. Now, I just don't want to disappoint him if I can't get pregnant. Hell, what if I can't carry any child to term. I can't handle the fact that I may not be able to give Logan something he wants so bad. Before, he would always say that he didn't ever want to have kids. However, he could never hide the longing on his face whenever he's around kids.

"You do what you feel you have to do crazy girl. I'll support you no matter what decision you make. If you want to wait and let nature take its course, we'll do that. If you wanna go get on birth control, make the appointment and I'll take you. Or, we could just use condoms and I'll go buy the entire damn store out of them. I'd love to have kids with you, but it's your decision."

"Logan, I love you. I want nothing more than to have your babies. But, what if I can't? What if there's something wrong with me and I just can't give you that?"

"Then we'll deal with it. We can adopt, find a surrogate, do whatever we have to in order to make it happen."

"That's why I love you so much. You want to give me whatever I want. Even if I can't physically handle it. Logan, you are the strength that I need to hold me up when nothing else in this world can. And, I know that you've been going up to my tree and to Ryan's headstone. Want to tell me what you do up there?"

"I tell him how amazin' his mom's doin' these days. You've made such an improvement and I'm so impressed by it. I tell him how much I love you and how complete you make me feel. Then I tell him that I will always make sure that you always remember him and that we'll make sure that any other kids we have will know about him and how important he was to you and Gage. Which means that he's important to me."

I'm so floored by what Logan just told me that I have no words to respond to him. The more time I spend with him, the more time we talk, I fall more and more in love with this man. He doesn't have to go to my spot and sit where they made the memorial for Ryan, he doesn't have to tell me what he does when he's up there. I was just curious. But, the love I feel from him rivals anything I've ever felt in my life. There's not even enough words to describe what I feel for him. I hope that my actions show him how much he means to me.

Grim

I honestly thought that when I brought up wanting to build a home with Bailey, she would balk at the idea and not want to leave the apartment. It doesn't matter to me one way or another really. But, I want us to have our own home and be able to build our life in our own space. Thankfully she wants that as much as I do. Maybe we can finally start to move on and build our future.

After we got done in the shower, I knew that I should have talked to Bailey more about the whole kid thing. I want to watch her get round with my baby and know without a doubt that we're making a family together. The way that it's supposed to be. I can definitely understand where she's coming from, and I know that her not wanting to talk about babies and get pregnant has more to do with just losing Ryan. If I know her like I think I do, she's worried about disappointing me if she can't carry the baby long enough to deliver safely. Honestly, I don't give a fuck how we have kids. I just know that sooner rather than later, I want to have kids with her.

Once we finally make our way up to breakfast, I send a message to Tank to get a hold of Rage. He's a prospect that had to go away for a little while. A few months ago, he got word that his ex had gone psychotic and went to his mom's house. While she was there, she beat the hell out of his mom because she didn't believe her when she told her he moved. His daughter witnessed the entire thing. So, he just got back to town with his little girl. I have yet to talk to him. This morning, I want a sit down to see where his head's at and to get his help on building the house. He's done construction most of his life and I want him to get back in the swing of things if he's ready.

"Mornin' guys." Cage greets us as we enter the kitchen.

"Mornin." We both respond.

"Everyone else should be down shortly. They were gettin' the kids up so I came down to start breakfast for everyone before we go to work."

"I'll help." Bailey says moving to the fridge.

"It's all good Bay. You just sit tight and I'll have it done shortly. Reagan wanted pancakes this morning, so that's what we're having."

As Cage starts pulling the griddle out and getting things around, Bailey starts setting the table. I sit on my ass and watch her movements. The entire time, I'm imagining her in our home doing the same thing. I can't wait until we can start building it.

"When you guys go to the shop this mornin', I'm gonna head over to the clubhouse for a little while. Rage got in last night and I need to see where his head's at. Plus, I want to see his baby girl and make sure she's okay too. I do need to talk to Sky and Bailey about somethin' though."

Cage and Bailey just look at me as I get up from the stool at the island. Grabbing Bailey's hand, I move us through the house and upstairs. We can hear Sky and Joker talkin' to the kids. Thankfully they're in separate rooms so that we can talk.

"Sky, where you at?" I ask.

"In the nursery Grim."

Walking in the nursery, we see Sky sitting on the floor with the babies in front of her. She's just finished changing them and now she's getting ready to dress them. Bailey immediately sits down to help her. For a minute all I can do is stand there and stare at her. She's going to make such an amazing mom one day.

"What can I do for you Grim?" Sky asks, breaking me out of my thoughts.

"Well, Bay and I talked this morning and we've decided to build a house in the field that you like to use to run away."

"OH MY GOD!" Skylar screams excitedly. "I'm so happy for you."

Bailey leans into the hug Sky wrapped her up in and grins up at me. This is her letting me know that we've made the right decision. So, I step back and wait until they're done so that I can finish talking to Sky.

"Sky," I finally say. "I need to talk to you about somethin'. And I need all of your attention."

"What's going on Grim?" Sky asks me finally turning and looking at me.

"Well, I have a prospect that just came back to town. He has a little girl that's around the same age as Reagan. I was wonderin' if, when we move out, if he can use the apartment. I know it's not ideal since it doesn't have two bedrooms. But, I want to make sure that he's in a good spot and that he has somewhere to call home for her."

"Absolutely!" Sky immediately answers. "We can expand down there or something to make another bedroom. If I have to, I'll have a building made for the gym equipment and we can expand into that room. That way a kitchen can be added if he doesn't want to come upstairs to eat."

"Are you sure?" Bailey asks her. "I know Logan doesn't want to put you out or anything like that."

"Who the fuck is Logan?" Sky asks, looking confused.

"I am." I answer smiling down at her.

"Oh. I never knew what your real name was. I'm sorry. But, no one's putting me out. I want to help out. Especially if he has kids. Make sure to let him know that I can watch her while he's doing club stuff too."

"I will sweetheart. I'm sure bein' here will help him. She's been livin' with his ex up until recently. I haven't seen him yet, so I'm not sure how he's doin' with everythin'."

We make our way down to breakfast with Bailey and Sky carrying the girls downstairs. Joker already made his way down with the other two kids. I can hear them squealing at whatever the guys are doing. Oh man, what we walk into has Sky wanting to scream bloody murder. Cage apparently thought it was a good idea to let Reagan and Jameson help him make the pancakes. They've gotten batter all over the kitchen. I mean, it's even on the ceiling. Someone's in trouble when Sky gets her hands on them.

"What the hell is going on in here?" Sky yells as she's putting one of the girls in her high chair.

"The kids wanted to help make breakfast for you." Joker says trying to kiss Sky.

"No! Levi, you can't kiss your way out of this one. How the hell did it get on the ceiling?"

"I was tryin' to flip the pancake in the air to make the kids laugh. I guess I got a little carried away baby girl." Cage says with laughter in his eyes.

"I'm not cleaning this fucking mess up. You two are before you go to work." Sky says.

Sky sits down at the table and starts getting Alana and Haley's breakfast around. Without worrying about the guys eating, she makes their plates of pancakes and then makes a plate for Reagan and Jameson. I'm thinking that we're on our own for food today. That's okay. I'll eat when I get to the clubhouse and I'll make sure that Blade takes a plate over to Bailey.

I lean in to Bailey and give her a kiss before I make my way to the clubhouse. As I'm going out the door, I can hear Cage and Joker trying to get back on Sky's good side. I don't think that's gonna happen any time soon. Bailey can be heard laughing her ass off. God, I missed that sound and I cherish it now every time I hear it.

Walking into the clubhouse, I can hear the giggles of a little girl. Must be Rage and his daughter are up eating breakfast. The first thing I notice is the wide smile on Rage's face. It's so good to see him smile. I know when he left, we ended up having to patch up more than one hole in the wall at the old clubhouse and the rage was showing on his face. The rage isn't so unusual, but that day it was nothing like I had ever seen before.

Rage looks up as I make my way over to him. He stands up and greets me in a man hug before saying, "Mornin' Pres."

"Mornin'. Welcome home. Do you two mind if I pull up a chair?" I ask, looking down at his daughter.

"No. Pres, this is my daughter Kasey. Kasey, can you say 'hi' to Grim?" He asks.

"Hi!" Kasey smiles at me before turning back to her plate.

"Hey beautiful! Is the food good?"

"Yes sir." She answers.

"So, how are you doin' Rage?"

"I'm doin' okay. As good as can be expected with everythin' goin' on."

"Are you ready to get back to work?"

"I'm more than ready. I mean, I have a few things to figure out with Kasey and where we're gonna stay. But, yeah, I'm ready."

"Well, I think I have a solution or two to help you out. You've heard Cage and Joker got an old lady?"

"I did. How are they all doin'?"

"They're good. The guys will be over later to see you. Or you can stop by Spinners since you haven't seen it yet. Now, about the rest of your worries. Sky inherited a house when her grandma passed away. An apartment was built in the basement. Right now it only has one bedroom, but the rest of the basement is a gym. Since Bailey and I are gonna need your services to build our house in the field, Sky said you could move into the apartment. She's also willin' to move the gym into a separate buildin' and add rooms onto the apartment. It's simple right now with just a living room, bathroom, and one bedroom. We usually just go upstairs with them for breakfast and dinner. But, she's willin' to move everythin' and add a second bedroom and a kitchen if you don't want to go upstairs."

"First of all, it's about time you and Bailey got together. Pres, are you for real right now? I mean I haven't even had a chance to think about all that stuff. Let alone buy Kasey everythin' she needs right now."

"Well, we're gonna take the worry away for you. You'll love Sky. And trust me when I say that you'll want to go upstairs for as many meals as you can. Ask anyone here about Sky's cookin'."

"I don't even know what to say right now Pres. Why would she be willin' to do that when she has no clue who I am?"

"Rage, that's just who she is. When the guys were first startin' to get to know her, her demented ex kidnapped her and Bailey. She made sure that Bailey got out and got tortured more because of it. Then she went into labor early because that skank Chrissy pushed her into the pool table at her baby shower. Plus, you have a little girl. Right now there's four kids runnin' around there and at least one more comin' soon. She's more than happy to watch Kasey for you too. She's the same age as her little girl Reagan."

"Holy fuck! Is everyone okay?"

"Yeah. When I left this mornin' she was chewin' Cage and Joker a new one. There's still a shit ton of stuff you don't know about, especially concernin' Bailey, but there's time to fill you all in on that. All that matters right now is you settlin' in with this beauty here."

"She's stayin' in my room with me. But, I don't want her here longer than I have to. With everythin' the boys do here, I don't want her seein' shit she doesn't need to."

"I hear ya. Let me talk to Bay and see what she thinks about movin' in here for now so we can get Kasey out of here. I really don't think she'll mind."

"Thanks. I'll be over in a little while to check out Spinners. Is it okay if I bring Kasey? I don't want to just leave her here with someone yet."

"Absolutely. She can see Bay while we talk. Plus, I'm sure she's gonna want to talk to you about the house."

"Sounds good. I'll see ya in a few."

Parking at Spinners, I take a second to look at what we've accomplished. I used to dream of owning a garage, but with the club the way it was, I never thought that dream would be a reality. Thanks to Bailey, it's not only a reality, but I can feel that it's gonna be a successful reality. Without her, I don't think Spinners would be real right now. I wouldn't have known the first thing to do as far as opening this up. She made sure we had all the right permits, went in front of whoever was needed to start building, and made sure that the grand opening was a huge success. The only black spot in the whole thing was the guy that came in and hurt her and trashed the backroom. He'll be dealt with though.

I can hear Pops barking out orders from the parking lot. I guess he was serious about being here whenever crazy girl is. That's fine by me. He's just another set of eyes on her. Tank and Glock will be here later to upgrade the security system. There will be cameras installed in every possible spot so that no corner is left uncovered. No one will ever get in here without one of us seeing it again.

"Pops, you know that we'll be fine. We're building a house between the clubhouse and Sky's house. We're not leaving."

"Still, I want to make sure that you're ready for that step baby girl. You're my only daughter and you've had one hell of a fucked up time lately. I know you're doin' better, but I don't want him pushin' you."

"I'm not fuckin' pushin' anythin' on her Pops. If she says she's ready and wants to do this, then we're gonna do this. Now, you can accept it or not, but it is happenin'" I growl to him.

"Grim, I'm just makin' sure she's okay. I know how pushy you can be. You're not gonna steam roll over her."

"That's why I left everythin' up to her old man. The house and everythin' is gonna be just the way my crazy girl wants it to be. Speakin' of which, Rage will be over in a little while with his daughter to talk to you about it." I say looking at Bay.

"Okay. I've already got a list of what I want in the house and how I want things set up. It's gonna be two story, if that's okay with you. Plus, I'm thinkin' a finished basement."

"Whatever you want. You tell me what you need and we'll get it done."

"Sounds good babe."

"Pops, why don't you go make yourself useful and see if the guys need help." I say turning to Pops.

142

"Fine. Bay, I won't be far away."

Once he makes his way into the garage, I pull Bailey into my arms and give her the kiss I didn't get to give her when I left. "I missed you crazy girl. Did the guys get back on Sky's good side?"

"Nope. She's standing her ground." She says, laughing her ass off.

"Well, I need to talk to you. I spoke to Rage this mornin'. He needs to move out of the clubhouse now. He's got Kasey stayin' there with him and is worried about her seein' things she don't need to."

"Oh my god! I didn't know she was here already. When we get done here today, we'll pack our shit and move into your room at the clubhouse. She doesn't need to be there. Hopefully he can move out tonight and have her in a good place."

"You're fuckin' amazin'!" I tell her. "If you wanna leave after he gets here, that's fine by me. I'll get out as early as I can and meet you there to finish."

"Okay babe."

Rage

I can't believe how much has changed since I left to go take care of my business. My ex, Charlene, had taken my baby girl away from me and wouldn't let me know where she was so I could see her. I missed so much of Kasey's life and there was nothing I could do about it. When I wasn't need at the clubhouse, I was out searching for her.

Finally, after years of searching and coming up with nothing, my mom called me and told me that Charlene was there threatening to kill her if I didn't show up. Apparently, Char was high as a kite and driving with my daughter in her car. Then she pulls a gun on my mom. It took me a few hours to get there and what I walked into had me seeing red. There was no way that Char was walking out of there alive.

Kasey was a filthy mess. It looked like she hadn't been bathed in months. Her long brown hair was a matted mess. Instead of having the bright eyes of a child, her eyes were dull and she didn't look at anyone. Her clothes were about two sizes too small and that's saying something since she is just a tiny little thing.

My mom was tied to a chair and gagged. There were bruises and cuts all over her. I knew without a doubt that she had put up a fight. And she ended up paying for it with her life. But not before Char paid for it with hers. As soon as the funeral services were over, I packed what little Kasey had up, rented a truck and a trailer, and came home.

"Daddy! Daddy!" Kasey yells excitedly. "Ride?"

I look up and see that Kasey is looking at a swing set in the back yard of the clubhouse. That was never here before. Must be a new addition. I've noticed a lot of those.

"Yeah baby. But only for a little bit. We've gotta take a ride to town soon."

"Okay."

I push Kasey on the swing set for a little bit before deciding enough time has passed and I should get down to Spinners. It's not like I don't know where it is. This town is small and I passed it on my way in. So, I load Kasey up in the truck I still have and we make our way into town. I'm hoping that the welcome home I received from Grim is the same I receive from the rest of the brothers. I know that I'm not a patched in member yet, but I don't want to have to start all over again.

"Rage!" I hear being yelled as soon as I go to pull Kasey out of the truck. "It's so good to see you man. Welcome home!"

"Hey Cage! It's good to be home." I say walking over to him with Kasey walking behind my legs.

"Who's this little darlin'?" Joker asks.

"Guys, this is Kasey. Kasey, this is Joker and Cage. Can you say 'hi'?"

"Hi." She says, burying her face in the bag of my legs. So, I turn around and swing her up into my arms.

144

"Well, I'm gonna go see Bailey and Grim. Are they in the office?"

"Yeah. I think Pops is in there too." Cage answers.

"Thanks guys. I'll see ya 'round."

Leaving the guys, I make my way into the office area. I can hear Bailey and Grim talking and laughing. I'm happy they finally got their shit together. Knocking on the office door, I wait until I hear Grim tell me to come in.

"Rage, it's good to see you again." Bailey says getting up and walking over to give me a hug. "I'm glad you're back."

"Thanks Bay. It's good to be home again. I missed you guys. Bay, this is my daughter Kasey."

"Oh, look at you precious. You are adorable. I'm Bailey, but you can call me Bay."

"Hi." I hear Kasey's muffled reply.

"So, Grim mentioned that you guys were goin' to build a house and that I would want to talk to you about it."

"Absolutely. He's left me in charge of everything. I'm excited. Especially now that I know you're gonna be the one to build it."

"Thanks. So, what did you have in mind?"

"Well, downstairs I want an open floor plan. I also want a finished basement that we can use as a gym. Upstairs I want five bedrooms for when we go on lockdown or have other chapters here for a while. I also want an outdoor party area. Plus, I want a finished attic. If you just make sure it's finished, I'll take care of the rest in that room." Bailey says looking at Grim.

"Okay. Let me draw up some plans tonight and I'll get with you in the next few days."

"That sounds good. In the meantime, I'm gonna get out of here so that I can start packing the apartment up. We're gonna try to get you out of the clubhouse tonight. You don't have to worry about a bed for Kasey. I bought two toddlers beds when Sky was in the hospital. So, I'll leave one in the bedroom for you."

"I can't thank you all enough. Especially to Skylar for openin' her home up to someone she don't even know. I'll continue to make sure that I'm available to the club as much as I can with Kasey. I know you said that Skylar would babysit, but I kind of have to hear it with my own ears. Not tryin' to disrespect anyone, I just need to hear it from her."

"No disrespect. I know the guys have been missin' you. Plus, we already decided in church that we're not gonna count the time you spent away against you. We're gonna act like you've been here the entire time. Even got two new prospects. Your year's almost up and I can't wait to patch you in. The same goes for Blade. He should've already patched in, but we didn't have anyone else to help with the new prospects, so he said he'd wait."

There's no way to respond to that. I'm so blown away by this club right now, and I know I've truly made the right decision as far as bringing Kasey home. I can't live without the club, and there's definitely no way in hell that I can live without Kasey in my life.

Bailey

After meeting with Grim and Rage earlier, I made my way to the apartment so that I could start packing. Even though I had a lot of crap here, I still had more in a storage unit. That would stay there until the house was done. Most of it was decoration shit anyway and pictures. Cage and Joker had loaded the back of my truck with boxes a little while ago so that I could pack without having to go searching for boxes at the stores in town.

Pulling in, I see Sky and the kids under the canopy the guys set up for Reagan. She's doing so much better and hasn't had a seizure in such a long time. Sky's still a nervous wreck about it though. Since we don't know what her triggers are, she could still have one at any point in time. I wave and make my way over to them for a few minutes. I'm really gonna miss seeing them whenever the hell I want to.

"Hey! How was work today?" Sky asks setting Haley down.

"It was the same old thing. Rage came in though and we had a talk. Logan had already told him about staying in the apartment, I told him that I'd leave one of the toddler beds for his daughter Kasey to sleep in."

"I can't wait to meet her! Him too obviously, but you know I'm all about the kids." She says looking at her four playing in the shaded area.

"Well, as much as I'd love to spend the day with you guys out here, I've gotta get packing. He's staying at the clubhouse until I can get my stuff out of here."

"Do you need some help?"

"No. You guys stay out here and enjoy the day. I'd rather the kids be able to play and breathe instead of being cooped up inside." I say turning to go inside.

Stopping by my truck, I grab an armful of boxes to take with me. I'm pretty sure that I still have packing tape in here somewhere. Hopefully I can find it. Otherwise, I'll have to go steal Skylar's from upstairs.

As soon as I find the packing tape, in the bathroom no less, I turn on music and get packing. The first room I work in is the living room. It's not like I have a lot in here. Plus, I plan on leaving the t.v. and couch for Rage. I'm not sure what he has and what he doesn't, so at least he can have this. So, I really only have to pack the few decorations I have hanging on the wall, my pictures, and my candles. Yeah, can't have a room without candles in it. They are one of my favorite things in the world.

In just under an hour, I have the living room and the bathroom packed up. I've decided to leave everything that I have for the kids here for Kasey. Rage said that he needed stuff for her and I'm not going to need it at the clubhouse, so he can have it. Just as I'm finishing up in the bathroom, I hear Logan pull in. He walks through the door as I place the last box from the bathroom by the door.

"Hey crazy girl!" He says giving me a kiss. "Damn, you've been busy this afternoon!"

"Yeah. Well, it really hasn't been that long babe. It's only been like an hour. Remember, most of my stuff is still in storage?"

"Yeah. I remember the ten trucks it took to get your shit here."

"It wasn't ten asshole! Anyway, I'm just getting ready to pack up the bedroom. I was thinking about leaving the bed here for Rage. I don't know what he has."

"Let me ask him real quick and I'll let you know."

While Logan is texting Rage, I move into the bedroom to start emptying the closet of all my clothes and shoes. He comes in while I'm sitting on the floor packing my shoes up. After staring at me for a minute, he joins me on the floor and pulls one of my stripper heels out of the box.

"Why haven't I ever seen you wear these crazy girl?"

"Because I just bought them. What did Rage say?"

"He'd appreciate the bed if we don't need it."

"No, we don't. It's too big for your room at the clubhouse. So, it might as well get some use by him."

"What do you need me to do?"

"Well, you can start loading the truck up, or you can start packing up my dresser while I get the closet done."

"I'll load the truck up." He says getting up and walking out to the living room.

"Pussy!" I call to his retreating back.

"Who you callin' a pussy sis?" Joker asks coming in my room.

"Logan. I told him he could pack my dresser and he chose to go load the truck up." I say laughing.

"Yeah, can't blame him there."

"It's not like he hasn't seen my underwear Levi. What's the big fucking deal?"

"Maybe he doesn't wanna find any toys you may be hidin'."

"No, those are by the bed."

With that, Levi walks away groaning. I can hear Cage and Logan laughing at him from here. Must be they heard our conversation. After deciding that I don't want to pack my clothes in boxes, I put them in the laundry baskets I have at the back of my closet. Too bad I have more clothes than I do room to put them in those.

"Crazy girl, you almost done in here?" Logan asks coming back in my room.

"No. I still have to finish the closet and then pack my dresser up. Unfortunately, I can't leave that for Rage. I need it at the clubhouse."

"It's fine. The guys and I will take the dresser out to the truck now. We'll just leave the clothes in the drawers and put them in the backseat of Joker's truck."

"Okay. I gotta figure out how to pack the rest of my clothes. I don't want to pack them in boxes, but I don't think I have a choice now."

It only takes me about ten minutes to finish packing the closet up. Yeah, I have a crap ton of clothes. I don't know where Logan's clothes in his closet are going to go because I have that many. It's insane! I guess we'll figure that out in a little while.

"Babe, I'm done. Just need to get these boxes loaded up." I call out.

"Okay. I'll be there in a minute. Rage just pulled up so I'm gonna take him to meet Sky and the kids."

"Alright. I'll start loading this stuff up. Where's it goin'?"

"Sky's SUV."

Grabbing up two of the boxes, I make my way out to the SUV. One of the guys backed it up to the doors. Placing the boxes in the back, I go to get the remaining ones while they're upstairs. By the time I'm done, Logan is leading Rage and Kasey downstairs to show him the apartment.

"Hey Rage." I greet them. "How are things?"

"Good. I can't thank you guys enough for this."

"Well, I wasn't sure what you had, so I'm leaving the furniture and t.v. in here. There's stuff in the bathroom for Kasey that I bought for the monsters upstairs. Plus, there's the beds in the bedroom."

"Thanks. I would have been fine sleepin' on the couch."

"You don't have to. Besides, I'm sure that Kasey is gonna want her daddy close for the first few days or so. Being in a new place and all."

"Yeah. This definitely makes things easier."

"Okay. Well, I'm gonna head over to the clubhouse then. Oh, Rage, I wanted to talk to you about adding an office to the downstairs of the house. I know I want an open floor plan, but that wouldn't be able to be open. I want to make sure that Grim has somewhere in case he needs to conduct business at home."

"Okay. That's not a problem. I can put that room in a corner or somethin'. That way it can have walls and the rest can be open."

"Thanks. I can't wait to see what you come up with." I say kissing Logan. "I'll see you guys later then. Bye Kasey."

Chapter Nine

Grim

IT'S BEEN A few weeks and life's been steady. I thought it was gonna be rough staying at the clubhouse with Bailey, but it's been fine. We spend time with the guys in the common room most nights before locking ourselves away for the night. She still goes over to spend time with Sky and the kids during the day at some point. I knew it was gonna be hard for her to leave the kids, but Rage needs space for Kasey away from the clubhouse.

The garage has been busy too. So, we've been staying open a little later than we originally wanted to. On top of our customers, Cage and Joker have been working on building two custom bikes. So, they're usually the last to leave and the first to show up. But, they're just about done with them. I think they'll finish them up today. They have a light schedule today, so I know they'll be working on them.

Bailey woke up early this morning and went to get breakfast at Sky's before going to work. Plus, she wanted to see the progress that Rage has made on the building going on over there. As soon as that's done, he's starting our house. Well, he'll be over there working on it. Some guys have already started building it without him there all the time. He only checks in every day so that he can add the room on to the apartment. The building for the workout equipment didn't take him long at all. He had that shit done in a few days. I guess it helps when you have twenty guys from the clubhouse, including the visiting brothers, working on it. Plus, Skylar didn't want anything outrageous. Just four walls, electric, and lights.

"Pres, you in there?" I hear a knock at my door.

"Yeah. What's up?"

"Went by the garage on my way here this mornin'." Pops says after coming in.

"Okay."

"There was a note on the fence outside." He says handing me the crumpled paper.

"What the fuck is this shit? Did you talk to Tank or Glock about pullin' up the camera feeds?"

"Not yet. Goin' there now. I wanted to get you that first. I'm not wantin' baby girl there today."

"I agree. I think she should take the day off and help Sky. She's there now. Why don't you go let her know while I get on this?"

"Yep." Pops says leaving.

Making my way out of our room, I look for Tank. I know that Glock's probably still sleeping. He was drunk as fuck last night. Something's eating away at him, I just don't know what it is. Going into the common room, I find Tank sitting at a table with breakfast in front of him and a club girl under the table on her knees. I just shake my head and smirk.

"Tank, I don't mean to interrupt the company you have, but we need to talk."

"What's wrong?" He asks, pushing the slut off his dick and putting it away. "Get lost."

After watching her walk away, I push the paper across the table to him."

"'This is your last warning to close shop and move on. No one wants you here. If you don't close within 24 hours, you'll leave us no choice but to make you leave.'" He reads aloud. "What the fuck is this shit?"

"Pops brought it to me before goin' over to tell Bay to take the day off. I want you to pull up the camera feed to see if we can find out who did this shit."

"On it. You want me to call you, or are you gonna wait around?"

"Call me. Or better yet, come over to the garage when you find somethin'. I'm gonna go fill Cage and Joker in on what happened."

"Got it Pres."

After Tank disappears to do his thing, I go grab my cut so I can get over to Spinners. I don't know what the

152

fuck is going on, but I think some prospects better go over to Sky's. If the girls and kids are there, then we need more guys there. I know Rage is there and probably Blade, but Slim Jim and Crazy can make their way over too. So, on my way out, I relieve them of their cleaning duties and tell them to go watch over everyone at the house. Then, I send a message to Blade and Rage about them making their way there. Rage can be in the house and the rest of the guys can walk the perimeter.

As soon as I pull into Spinners, I go in search of Cage and Joker. They need to know what's going on and that the prospects are at their house watching over our girls and the kids. I hear them in the last bay where they've been working on the custom builds. I knew they'd be here early again today. It's just them. They want to get the bikes finished so that we can display them.

"Guys, you talked to Pops in the last little while?" I ask, walking up to them.

"No. Why? Where's Bay?" Joker asks me.

"He went by on his way to the clubhouse this mornin' and found this on the fence. I got Tank pullin' security footage to see what he can find out now." I say handing the paper over to them.

I watch their faces as they read the note that was attached to the fence. Cage's face turns to one filled with rage, and Joker stands still and bunches the note up in his fist. He's better at blanking his face out than Cage is sometimes. But, if I know Joker, and I do, I know that same rage is filling his veins and running rampant right now.

"This why my sister ain't here?" He asks me.

"Yeah. She's at your house with Sky. Pops went over and told her to take the day off and stick close to Sky. I know Rage is goin' to be there all day workin' and that Blade is helpin' him. Before I left the clubhouse, I also sent Slim Jim and Crazy over there."

"What we gonna do about it?" Cage asks me.

"I'm thinkin' that we're closin' for the day and tryin' to figure out who's fuckin' with us. At this point, I'm not sure that it's the mechanic that fucked Bailey up. If it is him, he ain't workin' alone. So, we'll stay until Tank gets here with info and then we're out." I say looking at both men. "Let's get these bikes finished. Tell me what you need me to do to make that happen."

For the next hour the three of us work to finish the bikes. Just as Cage and I finish working on the one he started, Tank pulls in. Joker just finished the wiring on his bike, so it's done. Now, we have to fill fluids and start 'em up. But, I'm not worried about that. Right now, we need to figure out what the fuck's going on.

"Tell me you got somethin' Tank."

"Not really. Whoever put the note here, knew about the camera's. So, it's either an inside job, or they've been watchin' the place. Glock and I did this shit at night so no one knows where every camera is. Especially the ones watchin' the front. But, the person that put the note here, knew where every camera out front is."

"Fuck!" Cage roars.

"Alright. Let's lock this place up and get home. Well, I'll be goin' to your house since crazy girl's there. Tank, you can follow or go back to the clubhouse until we call church in a little while."

"I'll follow. I wanna see how Rage is makin' out." He answers and starts closing the bay doors.

I go through and make sure that the office doors are locked and everything is shut off in there. The guys clean their tools up and make sure the bay doors are locked before we head to our bikes. After making sure that the gate is secure, we make our way to the house.

The sight that greets me when we pull up warms my chest and I can feel the smile covering my face. Bailey is sitting in one of the swings with either Alana or Haley in her arms. She's swinging just enough to make sure the little one can go to sleep. Kasey is sitting in the swing next to her reading a story to Bailey and the little one. We all just sit on our bikes and watch the scene for a minute before getting off. Cage, Joker, and Tank all head inside while I make my way over to Bailey and the girls. Kasey looks up at me and I can see her eyes widen.

"Hey Kasey. How you doin' today?" I ask her.

"Good. Reading to Bay." She answers.

"That's good darlin'. How are you crazy girl?" I ask looking down at her.

"I'm fine. Why you guys here now? The garage closed?"

"Yeah. Pops explain it to you?"

"Yeah. He's around here somewhere. I think he started helping Rage."

"Okay. Slim Jim and Crazy make their way over here?"

"Yeah. Slim is on the other side of the house and Crazy is over this way somewhere. He's been tryin' to stay close but not too close. Kasey still isn't used to all the guys yet."

"I can tell. She'll get there though. I think we need to do somethin' to get her close to some of the guys. Maybe a small party here or somethin'? Kind of a welcome home thing."

"Okay. I'll get with Sky and plan something. Maybe we'll get Reagan and Kasey here to help us plan this one."

Kasey starts clapping her hands together softly since the little one is almost asleep. The book she was trying to read is forgotten as she rushes towards the house to tell her dad about the party. So, I take her vacated swing and watch Bailey. She looks so good with a baby in her arms. I hope that one day she can get comfortable enough to have kids. Bailey is a natural when it comes to kids and taking care of them. She has so much love to give and it will be wasted if she can't get past her doubts about having our own kids.

"So, I gotta take off in a bit. We gotta meet about this and figure out who's doin' this shit. Speakin' of which, I gotta go see what Tank was able to find on the security footage. He already told us, but I want to see it with my own eyes." I say leaning down to kiss her.

"Okay babe. I'll see you later on then. Maybe I'll stay here and have dinner with Sky and the kids. I don't really feel like having dinner with a bunch of skanks that are pissed as fuck you aren't available anymore."

"They givin' you problems crazy girl?"

"No. I just don't want to be near them. I'd rather eat with the kids and Sky. I'll just be back when you let me know you're done with the meetin'."

"Sounds good babe. Maybe I'll just come back here and have dinner with you guys if we're not late. If you come back to the clubhouse before I get done, text me and let me know. I'm not makin' the guys keep phones out of the meetin' today. With not knowing what's goin' on, I want everyone available at any given moment right now."

"'Kay. I'll see you later."

Bailey

After Logan goes inside, I continue sitting on the swing with Alana in my arms. She was fussy earlier and Sky couldn't get her to calm down, so I brought her out here to swing. Kasey decided to follow me out after making sure Rage didn't mind. She's such a cute little girl. Carrying a book with her, she sits down next to me and tries to read it. I help her with the words she doesn't know only when she asks me for help. Kasey's an independent little thing and I know that unless she asks for help, she's not gonna appreciate someone giving it to her. I was the same way at her age.

Alana finally calmed down as I was swinging her. So, I made her more comfortable by laying her across my chest and cradling her close to me. She's tired and fighting it so hard, but she can't compete against the swing, and a set of boobs. No baby can. That's where Logan finds us when the guys pull in. Joker and Cage wave over their shoulders as they make their way inside to find Sky. One of them will be out shortly. They can't stand to have one of the kids out of their eye sight for too long. It doesn't matter if brothers, or prospects, are standing guard. It's not them, so they'll be out shortly. I'm guessing it will be Joker since I'm the one that has Alana.

Since Kasey and Logan have left Alana and me alone, I stop swinging and sit there watching Alana sleep. On one hand it breaks my heart that I'll never experience this with Ryan. But, on the other one, I'm glad that I've healed enough that I get to spend time with my nieces and nephew without feeling like I can't breathe. Maybe Logan's right about us having kids. I know it will absolutely destroy me if I can't carry another baby to term, but the doctor did say that she didn't see any reason why I would have the same results if I do get pregnant again. I'm not saying that I want to have a baby right now. Our house isn't done and I'm not sharing a room at the clubhouse with a baby if we're not on lockdown. I guess I'll have to continue to weigh my options and see what happens.

"Hey sis. What you thinkin' about out here so hard?" Levi asks me, quietly sitting down in the swing next to me.

"About how I'm happy that I'm healed enough to enjoy doing this with the kids. But at the same time, how I won't get to experience this with Ryan."

"How do you know you were havin' a boy?"

"Just a feeling. I've dreamed about him ever since I lost him Levi. I know I sound crazy saying that, but I have."

"You don't sound crazy. I believe that you've dreamed about him. We've never talked about him. The day it happened, I was so shocked when Grim said that he was pretty sure you were havin' a miscarriage. Then I was pissed as fuck because you were pregnant by Gage. I mean, what the fuck? When I thought about why I was pissed, it was because I knew that you would be leavin' us if you hadn't lost the baby. Nothin' about Gage and you pissed me off unless he hurt you. I understood why you were with him. I just didn't want to lose you. For a while there we all lost you. And it scared the ever lovin' shit out of me because no one knew how to reach you in whatever place you had gone to. I don't ever wanna have to watch you go through that shit again."

"I'm sorry Levi. I was so far down in my own despair that I couldn't think about anyone else. It took a lot for Gage to reach me while I was still there. And I was on a bad downward spiral. I'm glad that none of you were around when I was there."

"Now, I wish I would've been there. But, on the same hand I probably would've killed someone if I was there. But, to see you sittin' here with Alana, I know that someday, you're gonna make one hell of a mama. I just hope that you don't rule that out when the time comes. You and Grim are gonna be awesome parents to some lucky kid."

"We've talked about it. Since it happened, I honestly haven't wanted to have to kids. But, sitting here with Alana and having time to think, I think I've changed my mind about it. I'm just so scared about it Levi. What happens if I can't carry a baby to term? It gutted me when I lost Ryan, and I know it gutted Gage. What happens to Logan if the same thing happens? Will he be able to handle it? Will he leave me because I can't give him kids? What if something's wrong with me?"

"Sis, there's nothin' wrong with you. I know without a doubt, Grim will handle whatever happens. He'll be by your side and the two of you will make it through. If you can't have kids the traditional way, you know Grim will do whatever it takes to make sure that you have them. There's always other options available to you and you know it. Grim loves you enough to take that chance with you. So, yeah, I think he's strong enough to handle whatever this ride you're on together throws at you. But you have to be just as strong. I know you're a badass and you're strong as fuck. You just need to believe it."

Before I can respond, I see the guys walk out of the house and head towards their bikes. Logan walks over to me and gives me a quick kiss before they leave and I head back inside with a still sleeping Alana. Sky's already starting dinner, so I lay Alana down and help her cook for everyone. She's cooking enough to feed an army so I'm guessing the guys will be here for dinner, plus Rage and Kasey. It's a comfortable routine helping Sky out when she's making dinner.

Grim

After meeting and going over the information that Tank found, we've decided to keep an eye on the other garage in town to see if they make any more moves. I'm still not convinced that mechanic is working alone, but I can't prove that. I'm sure the Soulless Bastards are still in the area, but no one's seen them either. My gut tells me that we haven't heard the last of them though.

Once the meeting was concluded, most of us made our way to Sky's house for dinner. I just want to get with Bailey and have her in my sights. It's killed me today not being near her or knowing that she was where I know she's safe.

Dinner is a rambunctious affair. The kids are all going crazy with all of us there. They don't know who to turn to for attention. Kasey is sticking close to her dad, Alana has not allowed Bailey to leave her sight, Reagan is all over Cage when we walk in the door, and Jameson, is right by Joker. It seems like Haley is the only one that hasn't decided to cling to one of us since she was born. But, she's so laid back and relaxed that it doesn't surprise me. She just kind of goes with the flow. Currently I'm sitting next to Bay on the couch, balancing my plate on one knee and Haley on the other. We're enjoying all of the chaos going on around us, knowing that soon we can escape to our room at the clubhouse. I wouldn't change it for anything in the world.

Shortly after we all get done eating, and helping Sky clean up, we head back to the clubhouse to have a drink before we turn in for the night. I'm not sure what happened today, but for some reason she seems lighter. Maybe spending the day with Alana has been a good thing for her. It wasn't her watching, and playing with all of the kids, it was one-on-one time with her and Alana. Other than the little amount of time Kasey was with her. I wonder what the change is.

After we make it to our room, I can tell that Bailey's tired as fuck. She's not used to taking care of kids all day long anymore. So, I pull her down in bed next to me and just hold her. If she wants to tell me what the change is, she will. I'm not gonna pressure her into telling me, I'm just gonna enjoy the feeling. Once we get comfortable, I put a movie on the t.v. until I feel her relax enough to fall asleep. Then I turn it off and lay there in the dark listening to her even breaths.

"This better be important." I growl into the phone, sleep making me sound even grumpier.

"Grim, you need to get to Spinners. Now!" I hear Tank yell into the phone, completely waking me up.

"What's goin' on?"

"Spinners is on fire! Get here now!" He tells me hanging up.

Bolting up, I get out of bed and throw my clothes from the day before back on. Looking at the clock, I see that it's only 2:30 in the morning. Bailey turns over and looks up at me. I can tell that she knows something is going on, but she knows not to ask me questions.

"I'll explain once I know what's goin' on crazy girl. I gotta get to Spinners." I say before dropping a kiss on her forehead and running out of the room.

It takes me no time at all to get there considering I broke every rule of the road imaginable. This fire just took everything up to a whole new level. When we find the douchebag that is fucking with us, he's gonna learn how I got the name Grim. I haven't let that side of me surface in a long time, but I will now. What the fuck would have happened if Bailey had been there and we lost her because she couldn't get out? These motherfuckers are gonna fucking pay!

As soon as I drop the kickstand on my bike, Tank is all over me. The cops won't let him get close since the garage is in my name. Just as I'm about to walk over to the cops on the scene, I hear the rest of the guys pulling up. Tank must have alerted everyone. It's good that he did so we don't have to relay what is going on multiple times.

"Pres, what the fuck?" Glock asks coming over to me.

"I don't know who's doin' this, but this is too much. We'll discuss it when I find out what the cops and firemen are sayin'."

Joker, Cage, and I walk over to the nearest cop to find out what's going on. Just as we make it up to him, I hear Cage shout obscenities over all of the noise. Following his line of vision, I see that the two custom bikes they had just finished for a rally are completely destroyed. Now I know that Cage and Joker are gonna be ready to fuck some people up. They have put their blood, sweat, and tears into those builds. It has taken them weeks to finish them. Looks like we'll all have to pull together and help them build two new ones because the rally is in another few weeks. We need them for the focal point in our booth to help get word out about Spinners.

"Officer, I'm Logan Elliott. I own Spinners. This is Dec and Levi, my mechanics. Do you guys have any idea yet what started the fire?"

"Captain Bly. We're not completely sure at this point, but I think it started at that end of the garage." He says pointing to the end where the custom bikes were sitting.

"Does anyone know how it started? I mean the garage hasn't been open that long so I doubt it was faulty wiring or anything like that."

"You'll have to wait for the fire chief. His name's Black. As soon as he gets a chance, he'll talk to you."

"Thank you Captain Bly." I say, shaking my head as we make our way back to the group of the guys.

They're all standing there watching the firemen work at putting out the fire. By the looks of it, it's gonna take a while. But, we'll stand here until it's out and Chief Black can talk to us. The looks on the guys faces range from pure rage to confusion to looks of venom rolling through their veins. These guys are ready to go to battle to get these attacks to stop. Turning my head, I see Pops standing there with his arms folded across his chest. He looks at me and I can see the same thoughts rolling through his mind that I had concerning Bailey being there and this happening. He's definitely ready to bash some fucking heads together and take care of business. Not only does his daughter, his baby girl, work here, but his son works here too. Honestly, he considers all of us his kids though. So, he'd lose a shit ton of family if we'd been here. He'd probably lose Ma too, because she wouldn't be able to survive anything happening to any of us.

"Listen up." I say looking at my brothers, "They don't know what started it at this point, but they think it started on the end Joker and Cage used to build the custom bikes. We have to wait for any more information to come from Chief Black of the fire department. Tank, can you pull anythin' up on the security feed?"

"I don't know what we're gonna be able to use Pres, but I can go back to the clubhouse and work on it."

"Good. Why don't you and Glock do that? The rest of you, other than Joker, Cage and Pops, I want you to spread out and canvas the area. I'm bettin' the ones that started this shit are gonna wanna watch the show and enjoy their handy work."

162

Everyone scatters. The four of us stand here and watch the firemen try to put out the fire. It seems like every time they get a handle on it, the wind shifts and the flames flare back up. I already know that it's gonna be a total loss. My main concern is the vehicles in there that belong to customers. This is definitely not the way to keep customers at a new business. Hopefully they'll understand. Although, I'm sure they will because the vehicles that we have here at this point in time actually belong to people that Sky grew up around. I'm hoping that they'll take the insurance money that I'm going to be giving them to cover the cost of getting new vehicles. Plus, I already plan on letting them use cars that we have sitting at the clubhouse instead of having to try to rent cars until I can get the insurance company to cover the costs of the fire. This is such a clusterfuck of epic proportions.

"Grim, you know we have to handle this now, right?" Pops asks me.

"Yeah. I'm thinkin' that the mechanic definitely found some help to go this big."

"What are you thinkin'?" Cage asks me.

"I'm thinkin' they got in touch with the Soulless Bastards. Some local mechanic isn't gonna have the knowledge to start this kind of destruction."

"I agree with you." Pops says. "They've had a hard on for us since we didn't turn Sky over to them. I know they didn't go back to the hole they crawled out of."

"We'll wait to get any information that we can from everyone and then we'll go to church to come up with a game plan. For now, I want everyone to be on guard. When it comes to Bailey and Sky, I want no less than three guys on them at all times. Everyone's gonna have to take shifts."

"Should we put them on lockdown?" Pops asks. "If it is the Soulless Bastards, then Sky might be in danger. If, by some chance, it is just that guy that came here, then

Bailey could be in danger. Bailey already lives at the clubhouse for now, but Sky and the kids don't."

"I think that's a good idea Pops. I know it's gonna be crowded with all of you there, but I think it's for the best." I say, looking at Cage and Joker.

"I'll call her and then Rage. Rage can help her get the kids around and then make sure they make it to the clubhouse. Besides, Kasey's upstairs sleepin' in Reagan's room tonight." Joker says.

We all make the necessary calls and then continue waiting for the fire chief to make his way over to us. After about three more hours, they finally get the last of the fire put out. It's a total mess.

"Chief Black." I say, extending my hand to the fire chief. "I'm Logan Elliott, the owner. These are my mechanics Dec, Levi, and Pops."

"We can't be sure at this point in time exactly what happened here. But at this point, it's starting to look like someone set some small explosives on each end of the building and along the back wall. Do you know who might have done this?"

"No. I mean there was an issue with a local mechanic a few weeks ago, but we haven't heard anythin' else from him."

"A local mechanic?" Captain Bly asks.

"Yeah. We all went to lunch and my girl, who works in the office was left here alone. She was goin' to do inventory. When we got back, the backroom was completely trashed. He told her that we better close or else. Somethin' along those lines anyway. Since then, we haven't heard from him."

"Did you report this?" Captain Bly asks.

"No. We thought it was a one and done occurrence. So, we just cleaned it up and went about our business." I tell him.

"Okay. Well, I'll head over to Fred's and question them when they open. I'll see if they know anything about what happened here this morning."

"Thank you Captain." I say turning back to the fire chief.

"Why don't you guys go home and get some rest. It's still too hot to go anywhere near there. We'll get together in a while and see if we can find out any more information. Here's my card. Call me when you get up and we'll make arrangements to meet back here."

"Sounds good." I tell him, shaking his hand.

Once the fire chief and Captain have walked away, I turn to my guys and we head to our bikes. Instead of the guys going to their homes, we all make our way to the clubhouse. I'm sure that Ma's there by now if she knows what's going on. Fuck, we did not need this shit right now.

As soon as we pull in, Bailey, Sky, and Ma come running out the front door. Well, Sky goes as fast as her pregnancy will allow her to. Each woman heads straight for her man, or men, to be reassured that we are fine. Bailey pulls me into her arms and doesn't want to let go. I can tell by how tight she's holding me.

"Crazy girl, I'm fine. We're all fine. Now, let's get back inside so I can call church and get back to you."

"Grim, don't do this shit to me. I can't handle the thought of losing you." She says.

"Bay, we're fine. Now let us go to church and then I'm yours the rest of the day. Does that sound good?"

"Yeah. Kasey's waiting for me anyway."

I follow her inside and head straight for the meeting room. Most of the guys are already in there with the exception of Joker, Cage, and Pops. They come walking in a minute or two after I take my seat. Quickly taking their seats, I call the meeting to order.

"Now, you all know that a local mechanic came to the garage a while ago, threatened Bailey, and ended up breakin' her arm. This mornin' Pops was on his way here and saw a note on the fence. He brought it to me this mornin' and Tank pulled video footage but got jack shit. Now, Spinners is burnt to the fuckin' ground. There was no savin' it. At this point, the fire chief thinks it might be caused by several small explosives. One on each side and a few on the back wall. Tank and Glock, did you find anythin' on the footage this time?"

Tank and Glock stand up with weary expressions on their faces. "We didn't get much. Like earlier, whoever did it knew where the cameras were. But, check this shit out." Glock says.

Glock makes his way over to the screen we have set up along one wall for when we need to pull up information on the computer. After messing around to find what he's looking for, Glock stands back and we watch the video start playing on the screen. A few minutes after it starts, there's two guys creeping around the shop. One of them goes to one side and the other one goes to the other side. When the camera view switches, one of the guys is wearing a Soulless Bastards cut. The other guy is wearing a coat with the decal of the local garage. Motherfucker! I knew he was working with those Bastards.

"Alright guys, this just means we have more than one guy on our radar now. We can't make out which Bastard that is from a view of the back, but you can definitely see the cut. Right now our priority will be the asshat from the garage. We get him and then we'll make him squeal like a fuckin' pig!"

A round of cheers goes up around the table. There isn't a single guy sitting here at this table that doesn't want revenge against these assholes. Especially the four of us that are directly involved in this shit. Two old ladies have already been targets of these guys. Now, we need to end it before they start going after more old ladies and other members of our families.

"I hate to say this, but I think we need to call a soft lockdown. I want all families here, if anyone leaves, you guys included, there will be at least four of you. No one is to leave this clubhouse alone. So, everyone go make your calls and do what you have to in order to get your family here. Someone needs to go with the prospects and make sure the club girls make it to the safe house. Which prospects are we gonna leave there with them?"

All the guys look around at one another. We have two prospects that are experienced, Blade and Rage, and two new ones. I'm not sure that the new guys are experienced enough to stay at the safe house, but I don't trust the old ladies with anyone other than full patch brothers, Rage, and Blade. Rage also has Kasey and we have to think about that.

"I say you send Slim Jim and Crazy. They're the two new guys and they need to fuckin' prove themselves. If they can't handle babysittin' a bunch of fuckin' sluts then we know they don't deserve to be here." Joker speaks up.

"I think that I have to agree with Joker." Irish speaks up.

"I agree. All in favor, say 'yay'." I say, looking around the table.

One by one, every member sitting here agrees to send the two new guys to babysit. It's gonna be a long fucking day. There's a crap ton of stuff to do before the rest of the family members get here. Rooms need to be cleaned out, food needs to be gathered. Extra clothes and other supplies need to be bought. But, it's all in the name of keeping every one of my brothers and their loved ones safe.

"Alright, meetin' adjourned. Make your calls and get your loved ones. Get your asses back here as soon as fuckin' possible. And remember, no one leaves this fuckin' place alone." I say, banging the gavel down.

Everyone leaves the room and goes about their business. The guys are breaking into groups that they know they usually do this shit with. I'm busy scanning the room for any sight of Bailey. Finally, I spot her sitting in the corner with Sky, the kids, and Ma. So, I quickly make my way over to her.

"Hey crazy girl. We need to talk." I say pulling her up from her seat. Kasey quickly scoots into her empty seat to remain close to her.

"What's goin' on babe?" Bailey asks me.

"We're goin' on a soft lockdown. I need your help gettin' shit together and ready for the families comin' in."

"What do you mean by soft lockdown?"

"We can leave, but with four patches with you. There is no debatin' this shit. Especially when it comes to you, Sky, and the kids."

"Why are we so special?" She asks, looking confused as hell.

"Because there was a fire at Spinners this mornin'. That's where I was. It's a total loss. What I'm about to tell you, stays with you, yeah?"

"Absolutely babe."

"We caught two guys on camera. One is a Soulless Bastard and the other one is the mechanic that fucked with you."

"Oh my God!" She says turning into me. "Tell me what you need and I'll get it done."

"You're gonna go with me, Joker, Cage, and Pops shoppin'. We gotta make it fuckin' fast as fuck. Groceries and other essentials that people are gonna need."

"Okay. I'll get a list goin' while you do what you gotta do."

"Thanks crazy girl. I love you."

"I love you too babe. I'll see you soon." Bailey says heading off to start her lists.

Bailey

As soon as I leave Logan to make my list, I head into the kitchen to make a list for groceries. I'm about halfway through the pantry when I feel someone watching me. Turning around, I see Chrissy standing there. What the fuck is she doing here? She disappeared after the shit with Skylar and making her go into labor early.

"What the fuck you want bitch?" I growl out, storming towards her.

"Just a friendly heads up that you won't get out of this shit. Grim must be stupid as fuck bringin' everyone in for a lockdown. You think that isn't gonna play right into their hands?" She says with a dirty ass smirk on her face.

"What are you talking about? Whose hands is that playing into?" I ask, moving closer to her.

"Don't worry about it. Just know that you've been warned. Now run along and warn everyone like we both know your snitchin' ass is gonna do. By the way, how's my man doin'?"

"Your 'man' is sitting with his wife right now, and their kids. So, I'd say he's doin' pretty fuckin' good. He'll be doin' better once we know you're put to ground."

"Yeah, like he's gonna allow that shit to happen. He loves me and everyone here fuckin' knows it. My job here is done, you've been warned."

I don't know how the fuck that bitch keeps getting in here, but I'm gonna find out. Following the way she went, I creep to the back door and see her fucking with one of the prospects as he opens the back gate for her. Once she's through, she hops on the back of a fucking bike and they take off. Before the prospect can see me, I slide to the side of the door where I can still see out. As soon as he turns around, I can see that it's Crazy. What the fuck?

Quickly I make my way back to the kitchen to finish making my lists and have Logan meet me in here. Sending him a text, I go back to making a list of food we need to feed everyone. I need to warn him about Chrissy being in here, what she said to me, and that Crazy was the one helping her in and out of here now. I'm not sure how she got in here before, but she was definitely getting help now.

"What's goin' on crazy girl?" Logan asks, walking up to me.

"I need to tell you something, and I need you to keep your cool about it right now. Especially with all the families coming in."

"Okay. You're kind of fuckin' with me right now Bay. So, just tell me what you gotta say."

"I was in here making my lists and I could feel someone standing behind me. It was Chrissy. She knows we're goin' on lockdown, not that it's a soft lockdown, and said that you're playing right into 'their' hands. She refused to tell me who they are, though. When I followed her back out, I saw Crazy helping her at the back gate. Plus, she was spouting all sorts of shit about Dec and him lovin' her and them being together and shit."

"Fuck! We really don't need this shit right now. That's all she said?"

"Yeah. I made sure that neither one of them saw me when I was seeing how she was getting in and out of here. I know he didn't help her when she attacked Sky at the baby shower. But, now she's got Crazy helping her and I don't know why."

"Okay baby. I'll get with the rest of the guys and we'll get it taken care of. You finish your lists and come find me, yeah?"

"Yeah. You go take care of what you gotta take care of."

Grim

After talking to Bailey, I make my way out and gather up all the guys for a quick church relating to Chrissy and Crazy. I don't know what the fuck is going on, but she won't get in here again. Crazy isn't going to be as lucky as Chrissy will right now though. Well, she'll be lucky if Bailey doesn't get a hold of her.

"What's goin' on Pres?" Irish asks me once we're all sitting down.

"We got a situation, and things have to change. Crazy girl was in the kitchen to make her food list. All of a sudden she felt someone there and it was Chrissy. She told her that by goin' on lockdown we were playin' right into their hands. Don't know who they are though. Then she started talkin' shit about Cage lovin' her and them bein' together when this shit was done." I have to pause because I know that Cage is gonna lose his shit.

"What the fuck? Why hasn't that bitch been put to ground yet?" He explodes.

"We're gettin' to that. First, she had some help gettin' in and out this time. Crazy helped that bitch. Crazy girl followed her when she left and saw Crazy helpin' her out the back gate. He was supposed to be goin' to the safe house with the girls. What we gonna do?"

"He goes to fuckin' ground!" Pops explodes, standing up and sending his chair flying. "He's helpin' that bitch fuck with my daughters. I'm tired of them bein' the ones that get fucked up. He goes to ground now!"

I sit there and wait to see what the rest of the guys say. If it were just up to me, I would completely agree with him. But, I have to let my brothers have their say too. However, other than a nodding of heads, no one says a fucking word.

"What about a different plan?" I ask. "We don't know if the Soulless Bastards are workin' with anyone else. Right? I say we let him go to the safe house with the girls and Slim Jim and see what he does. Instead of just havin' those two up there though, we send a full patch in with them. A single full patch."

There's a few murmurs around the table. Especially from the single guys. Irish is the first one to raise his hand like we're in fucking school or some shit still.

"I'm all for helpin' out and goin' with them." He says.

"Unfortunately, that won't be happenin'. It won't be anyone from this chapter. I want him to put his fuckin' guard down and spill what the fuck is goin' on. Steel is almost here. I say we send him and Wood from the Phantom Bastards up there with them. Not sure about Wood, but I know Steel can keep it in his pants when it comes to shit like this. Besides, you're not fuckin' single Irish. I'm not havin' you leave Caydence here alone."

I can see the rage and veins popping out on Pops head and neck. He's not happy with this plan. Really, I'm not either, but I'm thinking that this might be the only way that we're going to be able to get the information that we need to learn what the end game is and who all the players are.

"Pops, I know you're not happy. But we need this information. As soon as it's done, you, Cage, and Joker get to do your damage to him. Now, we need to decide what the fuck we're gonna do about fuckin' Chrissy. She's not goin' away and not givin' up."

"Honestly, I know we don't put bitches to ground. But it needs to happen to her." Glock speaks up. "She's not gonna give Cage up and whatever delusional dream life she has with him. So, someone needs to put her to ground."

As soon as Glock is finished speaking, everyone around the table starts cheering because he's right. This has been going on for long enough and we've given her multiple opportunities to stop her shit. Instead she's getting bolder and even worse than she was before. Chrissy is getting almost desperate in her attempts to get to Cage.

"Everyone in favor say 'yay'."

Everyone around the table says 'yay' and I bang the gavel. "Alright, crazy girl should be just about done. But I want Pops, Tank, myself, Blade, and Irish with us to go shoppin'. I know it's no one's favorite job, but we gotta get this shit for lockdown. Cage and Joker, you need to stay with Sky and the kids so that's what you two are doin'. On the way, I'll ride in the cage with Bay and make the calls to the Phantom Bastards and Gage. I want at least a few members from them here. If we're playin' right into their hands, then I want extra bodies here."

We all pile out of the room and I immediately go to find Bailey. Hopefully she's done with making her lists because I know we're gonna need a whole shitload of stuff for this lockdown. Especially with extra bodies coming here. Fuck!

Chapter Ten

Later that day

Grim

WE ALL MADE it through shopping and back to the clubhouse. The prospects, Slim Jim and Crazy, are just waiting on Steel and Wood to get here so they can head up to the safe house with the club girls and the girls from the strip club. Right now I have them lugging all the crap we just bought inside and to the rooms it goes in so the old ladies can work on putting it away.

"Pres, Steel just sent a text and said he's about a half hour out. Knowing how he drives though, I'm gonna give him about ten to fifteen minutes." Joker says, walking back in the main room.

"Okay. Make sure the prospects are done and ready to go when they get here. I'm gonna go make some more calls to see exactly how many guys are coming from the Phantoms."

"I'm on it."

After making my way into my office, I slump down in my chair and take a minute to just breathe. There's so much that needs to be done from protecting everyone, finding out what the hell Crazy is doing, figuring out what happened at Spinners, rebuilding the garage, building the house with Bailey, and making sure everyone has what they need during this lockdown. Some days I hate the fact that I'm the President of this club, but on the other hand, I wouldn't change it for the world. So, I best get back to it.

Picking up the phone I call Slim, the President of the Phantom Bastards. "Hey Slim, how are things goin'?" I ask when he answers the phone.

"Good here. How are things there?"

"A little crazy at the moment. I know Wood is comin' down, how many others are you sendin' with him?" I ask, while looking at the paperwork on my desk.

"I've got him, Des, Hitter, and Whino comin' your way."

"Sounds good. I've got Wood goin' with Steel and two prospects up to the safe house with the club girls and strippers. I'll fill him and Steel in before they go."

"What's up Grim? More goin' on than you first thought?"

"Yeah. We got someone helpin' an ex club girl get in and out when she's been banned. He's goin' up to the safe house. We're gonna have Steel and Wood watch him while they're up there."

"That's shitty man! You think he's workin' for another club, or just the girl?"

"I'm not sure at this point. That's what we're gonna find out. I'll let you go do what you gotta do and I'll talk to you later on."

"If you need more guys, let me know and I'll see what I can do." Slim says, getting ready to hang up.

"I will. I'm hopin' with your guys, my guys, and Gage's guys we'll be fine though."

I no sooner hang up with Slim and there's a knock on my door. Peeking his head in, I see Steel and motion for him to come in. Behind him is Wood. Must be the rest of the guys are mingling or getting their stuff set up in rooms Bailey and Skylar are putting them in. I know that Joker would've told these two I need to see them though.

"Guys, good to see you. I just wish it were under better circumstances." I say while they sit down.

"Joker said you needed to talk to us as soon as we pulled up." Steel says, leaning back in the chair.

"Yeah. I got a little project for the two of you. I need you to go to the safe house with Slim Jim, Crazy, and the girls. I don't care if you get your dick wet, but I need you to be focused on the job at hand first and foremost."

"What job is that?" Wood asks.

"That crazy bitch Chrissy made her way back in here again today and cornered Bailey in the kitchen.

When she left, Bay watched her leave and Crazy was the one to help her leave at least. I'm sure he helped her in here too. Anyway, we need to know if he makes any calls or anythin' while you guys are up there. We need to know what the hell his game is."

"You got it. When we find out, what do you want us to do?" Steel asks.

"I want you to call either Joker or myself. We'll decide what to do when we know what the hell is goin' on."

"Alright. When do we leave?" Wood asks, standing up and stretching.

"They just went to pick the girls up in the van. So, as soon as they get back you guys are ridin' out. You two on your bikes and them in the van with the girls." I tell them, leaning back in my chair and putting my feet up on the desk.

"Okay. I'm gonna go sit down for a minute while we wait for them then. We'll make sure we find out what's going on for you." Wood says, leaving the room followed by Steel.

For a minute I sit here and close my eyes and relax. All I want to do is find Bailey and bury myself balls deep in her. I don't want to think about what's going on around me or everything that I have to do. I just want to be with her and forget for a little while.

Bailey

Almost as soon as we walked in the door from shopping, Logan made his way into his office and I haven't seen him since. I know that he's done talking to Steel and Wood, but he hasn't made an appearance yet. So, I think I'll go find him and see if he's okay. Making my way through the men, women, and children, I knock on his office door. Even after waiting a minute there's no answer, so I quietly peek my head in to see if he's okay. He's sitting back in his chair with his feet up on his desk, his eyes are closed, and there are wrinkles lining his forehead. Even when he's relaxing these days, he doesn't fully relax. There's always a ton of things running through his mind. But, I have my ways of making sure that he can take a little bit of time away from all the business he needs to get done.

Quietly walking over to him, I bend down and kiss his lips softly. I can feel his grin as soon as our lips touch. Logan's not one to let me have control for long so I know it's only a matter of time before he will turn our kiss into something more. This isn't about that though, this is all for him. I can get mine later on.

Breaking away, I grab his legs and swing them down off of his desk. Logan just eyes my movements, probably wondering what I'm doing. Without missing a beat, I rub him through his jeans, not letting my intentions known to him just yet.

"Just relax baby and let me do my thing." I whisper in his ear before nipping it and kissing down his neck.

After taking his shirt off I use one hand to undo his belt before starting in on his button and zipper. The entire time Logan's doing nothing but watching me. Finally, I get his cock out and start to stroke him up and down while leaning back in for a kiss. Logan, being who he is, tries to grab control of the kiss, but this is all for him and I'm not having any of it.

"Uh uh. This is all about you. So, for once, you're gonna let go and take what I give you." I tell him, moving away from his lips and down his body.

I lick and kiss my way down his flat stomach until I get to my intended target. Opening my mouth, I swirl my tongue around the head before taking as much of him into my mouth as I can. I can hear the hiss leave his mouth as I go lower and lower on him while hollowing out my cheeks. There's no way I can take all of him in my mouth so I change my position a little bit so that I can use both of my hands. One I use to stroke the length that I can't take in my mouth. With my other hand, I grab his balls and begin to gently roll them. I know what he likes and he knows to let me know when he needs more.

"Fuck Bailey!" Logan grits out between clenched teeth.

Moaning, I make sure to start sucking just a little bit harder as I increase the speed of my head bobbing up and down on him. Logan thrusts his hands in my hair after removing my hair tie so that he can increase the pace and let me know exactly how fast he wants me to go. He quickly starts losing control and his hips start thrusting up, forcing just that much more of his cock in my mouth.

"Crazy girl, I'm close."

Logan's letting me know because he thinks I'm gonna stop. Not this time though. He's the one that needs to relax and get his mind off of all the crap he's got going on right now. So, I pick the pace up even faster and swirl my tongue around the length that I have in my mouth. As I come back up, I suck even harder and start rolling his balls just a little bit faster.

"Bailey! Fuck! Swallow it all crazy girl."

As soon as Logan finishes saying that I can feel him start to swell in my mouth before shooting streams of cum down my throat. I can't get enough of him so I know I won't have a problem swallowing every drop he gives me. Once he's done, I slowly pull him out of my mouth and tuck him back in his pants.

"What was that for crazy girl?" He asks me, his breathing is hard and fast still.

"I know you need to relax and get your mind off shit for a little while. So, I thought I'd distract you from business for a while."

"You can distract me anytime you want to!"

"Okay. Well, I'm gonna go see if Skylar needs help in the kitchen. I'll see you when dinner's ready babe."

Without waiting for his response, I give him a kiss on the cheek and make my way back out into the clubhouse. The common room is full of people from this chapter, guys from the Phantom Bastards, and guys from Gage's chapter. I smile and say hi to the ones I know as I make my way in the kitchen.

"Sky, I'm here for whatever you need." I say, walking through the door.

"Thanks hun. I'm just making meatloaf, potatoes, and a vegetable I think. Maybe some homemade biscuits."

"Well, point me in the direction of what you need me to do and I'll start it." I say washing my hands and looking for the towel.

"Why don't you start peeling the potatoes?" She asks, just as Joker walks through the doorway.

"Hey baby." He says pulling her into him. "I was gonna see if you needed any help, but I see Bailey's here."

"I know what kind of help you wanted to give and it wouldn't be helping get food ready." Sky says laughing. "But, you can still help me since you're here."

I laugh as I hear Joker groan. "Baby, maybe I should make sure Cage doesn't need help with the kids."

"Nope, you're not getting out of it now. You're gonna help in here. Ma and Pops can help him if he needs it. Now, get the stuff out for the meatloaf and start it while I get the biscuits going."

My brother doesn't want to piss his woman off and get cut off, again, so he does as she asks. He's going to complain and groan the entire time, but he'll get over it. Or he won't get any of Skylar.

With the three of us working together, it doesn't take long at all to get things going and in the oven. Joker gives Sky a kiss and then practically runs out of the kitchen. I'm sure he's tired of all the gossip he's been hearing from the two of us. He probably knows more now about the guys and the club girls they're fucking than he wants to know. Summer and Storm can finish helping Skylar in the kitchen. I need to make sure that everyone has everything they need. Plus, I want to make sure that Logan's out of his office and relaxing with the guys for a while.

Walking into the common room, I see him sitting with Cage, Joker, Trojan, and Crash. I wasn't expecting the two of them here, but I'm glad to see them. Eventually I'll say hi, but they need their man time and I've got other things I could be doing. Like making sure everything we bought was put away. If not, I'll be busy for a while!

Grim

After Bailey surprised me earlier with an amazing blowjob, I decided that she was right and I needed to relax for a while. So, I decided to go out and have a drink with the guys that were here still. I know that Wood, Steel, the prospects, and girls are on their way to the safe house. Steel's going to text me when they get there so I know they made it without anything happening on the way up there.

I see Cage, Joker, Trojan and Crash sitting at a table so I nod to Summer to bring me a beer and head their way. Pulling over a chair, I sit between Crash and Cage and wait for my drink.

"Where you been hidin'?" Trojan asks me.

"I was in the office. Paperwork can wait though. There's enough shit goin' on that I can put that off for a little while. Steel's gonna call when they get there."

"Well, we're just here waitin' for the food to get done. And Joker's joined us since he's done playin' kitchen bitch!" Crash jokes.

"Hey, if you had Skylar, you'd play kitchen bitch for her in a fuckin' heartbeat." Joker says.

"I'm sure I would. But, so far, I haven't found anyone to hand my balls to on a silver platter." Trojan says, adding his two cents.

"You know you're not gonna be happy in a one on one arrangement." I say.

We all know that Crash and Trojan are Dander Falls' Joker and Cage. They like being with the women together and you can find both in one of their rooms at any given time. A lot of outsiders don't know it, but we all do. Eventually they'll find what they're looking for and it will be one woman to share forever. That's their story to tell though.

"Where's crazy girl?" I ask no one in particular.

"She just poked her head out of the kitchen and then disappeared. So, I'm not sure what she's doin'." Cage says. "Maybe she's pullin' a Ma and won't rest until she knows everyone has everythin' they need."

I can absolutely see her doing that. She's going to work herself to death to make sure that everyone is comfortable in this lockdown. Later on I'll just have to make sure that I return the favor to her and make sure she's relaxing. Gives me something to look forward to.

"How are you gonna handle her appointments?" Joker asks me.

"I'm gonna take her with a few of you guys. I know she has one comin' up in a day or two."

"She gettin' help?" Crash asks me, turning serious.

"Yeah. She finally broke down and told me she needed it. So, she's been seein' someone for a little bit now. It's been helpin' her a lot."

"I'm glad." Trojan says. "We were all worried about her for a while there. It was bad."

"I'm just happy that Gage pulled her out of it. And, I'm glad that none of us witnessed it. I would've killed anyone that touched her!" I say.

We all just sit back and enjoy a few beers while we wait for Skylar to tell us that dinner's ready. I don't see Summer behind the bar right now so I'm sure that she's helping Sky in the kitchen if Bailey is doing other things. I'm glad that Summer and Storm are here and they didn't go to the safe house. Even though they're club girls, they know how to act when the women and kids are around. They don't dress skanky and they respect everyone in the club. Those two are the only ones that I will ever consider staying here in a lockdown.

Steel

After making it to the safe house, I need to stretch the hell out and take a shower. Maybe when things quiet down and I know that motherfucker Crazy is down for the count, I'll go see one of the girls. But, first and foremost is finding out what the hell is going on with Crazy so I can let Grim know. I nod my head to Wood so that we can go have a conversation to make a plan as to how we're going to make sure we have an eye on him at all times.

"Let's go inside and make sure it's all clear before anyone goes in." I say to him.

"Sounds good." He says before turning to everyone. "We're goin' in first and then we'll let you know if it's clear."

We make our way in and go room by room making sure that no one's in here and that nothing's going to catch us off guard. Once we're done we let the girls, Crazy, and Slim Jim in to pick their rooms. Most of the girls are going to be sharing rooms so that each of us guys have our own room. Wood and I will be on the ground floor with most of the girl's upstairs. We pick rooms that have an adjoining door so that we can talk about the situation without anyone overhearing us. Or seeing us walk back and forth into one another's room.

"Okay. So, we need to figure out how we're gonna keep an eye on this prick at all times." I start out.

"If you're sleepin', in the shower, doin' what you gotta do to relieve stress, or whatever else I'm on him. If I am then you're on him. How's that sound? As far as I go, I can just act like I'm gettin' to know him since I haven't been to Clifton Falls since he showed up. I don't know if you've seen him before."

"Nope. Can't say that I have. The only two I know are Blade and Rage. I know Rage just got back with his kid."

"Okay. You go clean up and I'll start talkin' to him. When you're done let me know and I'll jump in the shower real quick. When everyone else goes to bed, we'll meet in your room to discuss what we learned throughout the day."

"Alright then. I'll see you in a few."

Making my way into the shower in my room, I strip and leave my clothes where they land. I'll pick them up once I'm clean. I'm happy that I got picked for this part of Grim's lockdown. I'd rather be here than in a clubhouse full of families. Not just because of the fact that the club girls are here, but being around the families makes me miss what I used to have and want more with every passing day. I quickly shove those thoughts aside and do my business so I can get back on Crazy duty.

After dressing I make my way out to the living room where I see Crazy sitting watching t.v. Wood leaves to go take his shower as I head to grab a beer for us before sitting in one of the chairs.

"Want a beer kid?" I ask Crazy.

"Sure. Thanks."

"So, how long you been a prospect for Grim? I haven't seen you around on my other trips to that clubhouse."

"Not long. I've been there around a month or so."

"Makes sense I haven't seen you then. I haven't been around there longer than that. How you likin' it there?"

"I like it." Crazy says before his phone rings. "I gotta take this outside. I'll be back in."

"No problem man." I say, looking like I'm getting settled in my chair to watch whatever program he has on.

After seeing him pace back and forth on the porch, for a few seconds Crazy looks up to see what I'm doing. I see Wood coming back out and I motion him to wait a second. He backs up around the corner so Crazy can't see him. So, I have to get up and look like I'm going to the bathroom.

"He's outside on his phone. Go out the back door and sneak around to see what you can hear. I have to go back in the living room so he doesn't think anythin's up." I say, starting back towards the chair and my beer.

I grab the remote on my way back through so I can change off the program he was watching. I'm not sure what the hell it is, but anything is better than that. So, I go to my back up and put on porn. I'm in a houseful of easy women so what the hell. It's not long before I hear the click from the back door shutting and see Wood enter the living room. He nods his head to me telling me he got something already.

"You're watchin' porn already man?" He asks me sitting down.

"Yeah. Nothin' else on. Porn's always good to watch. We got the girls here so why the fuck not?" I say, grinning at him like I don't have a care in the world.

"True. I think I might have to get a taste of new before I head back home."

"Yeah? Anyone catch your eye?" I ask, making mundane conversation because I honestly don't give a fuck if one has or not.

"Naw. I'll just pick one later when things get settled." He says going to grab a beer.

"You okay?" I ask Crazy, who's just come back in looking wild eyed and pissed the fuck off.

"Yeah. Girl problems you know?"

"That's why I don't got one. Too much fuckin' drama and games." Wood says sitting back down.

"I hear you. I'm about ready to get rid of this one. Always naggin' my ass about somethin'. Well, I'm gonna go shower. I'll see ya later on." Crazy says passing Slim Jim in the hallway.

Wood and I get up and walk to our rooms so we can meet in one. I make my way to his so that I can find out what he overheard and decide if I need to call Grim and let him know we have proof of something. He's watching out through a small opening in his door to see where Slim Jim is before shutting it all the way and heading in to the bathroom.

"What did you hear?" I ask.

"He was definitely talkin' to Bull and he's not happy with Crazy. Bull wanted him at the clubhouse to let someone in during the middle of the night. I'm guessin' it wasn't that bitch this time."

"How do you know it was Bull?" I ask, wondering how the hell he heard that from around the corner of the house.

"The dumb fucker had the phone on speaker once he walked off the porch so he could find his cigarettes. I'd never be that fuckin' dumb if I was doin' whatever the fuck he is. I'm thinkin' they had him plant himself there, or they got to him after he was a hang around." Wood says. "What do we do now?"

"I'm callin' Grim to let him know we already found shit out and see what he wants to do. I'll let you know as soon as I talk to him and we'll go from there." I say making my way back to my room.

Pulling out my phone I go in the bathroom so I know he won't hear me. I'm not really all that worried though. If he's dumb enough to put his phone on speaker, Crazy probably has no clue that anyone's even on to him. He's in for a fucking surprise though because I know Grim's gonna be happy that we already found shit out, but he's gonna be pissed as fuck Crazy is trying to fuck the club over.

"This better be fuckin' good!" Grim yells through the phone. Oops I guess I interrupted him and Bailey.

"We already found out he's workin' with Bull and the Soulless Bastards." I say.

Grim starts whispering and I can tell he's moving away from Bailey and somewhere more private. "How?"

"He got a call and Wood went out the back door and heard the conversation. Dumbass put his phone on speaker so Wood heard a lot. Bull's pissed he's not at the clubhouse to let someone in during the middle of the night. Probably in an hour or so."

"Okay. I'll get everyone up here to be on guard. We'll send the women and children down in the basement to the backroom there. I'm gonna call Gage and have him come pick up my package and deliver it to me. He'll call when he's on the way." Grim says, hanging up.

Going back in to Wood's room I tell him what Grim said and tell him I'm going to go find a girl for a while until Gage gets here. He says he'll keep watch and if there's time he'll get a girl after I do.

Grim

Steel has the worst fucking timing ever! I was balls deep in Bailey when he called with the news about Crazy. So, I quickly call Gage to get him to go pick Crazy up and leave another guy at the safe house. Then I get Bailey to help me get all the women and children downstairs in the spare room in the basement before I call church.

When I make my way into church, I see a bunch of men disgruntled and pissed I woke them up or took them from their old ladies. No one says a word as I walk to the head of the table though. They know from the look on my face, I'm just as pissed for the interruption as they are. This is the last place I want to be right now.

"Alright, I know you're all pissed as fuck right now. But, I got word from Steel about Crazy. He's definitely workin' with Bull and the Soulless Bastards. Bull called him and was pissed because he's at the safe house and not here to let someone in. I'm guessin' they were gonna ambush us in the middle of the night."

"What the fuck? That fucker's dead!" Cage yells, slamming his hand down on the table. "Our old lady and kids are here. All the families are here!"

"I know. Which is why I woke your asses up. We're on guard as of now. No one is gettin' in here. I want all of you in two or three man teams around the perimeter. Gage and some guys are on their way to get Crazy and then he'll bring him here. Then the fun begins. Now, get in your teams and get outside. Joker, Cage, and Pops you need to find other partners just in case. I'm not gonna lose anyone, but the four of us aren't gonna partner up just as precaution."

Everyone moves quickly to get in teams and get outside after grabbing their gear. I grab Irish to work with. We're the last two out to make sure that everyone has what they need. If anyone is light on anything, we'll provide it. Finally, we can go outside and make our way to the farthest point of the fence line. Bull will more than likely come in through the back somehow if he's gonna still come in here tonight. We'll be ready for his ass!

Gage messaged me about an hour ago to let me know he's almost here with Crazy. We've been up for almost twelve hours watching the perimeter of the clubhouse. Summer and Storm were the only two to leave the basement and that was only to get things to make sandwiches for everyone and get drinks.

I pull almost everyone out to the front so we can at least watch the gate while I'm talking to the guys. "Gage will be here within fifteen minutes. Cage, Joker, Pops, Glock, Blade, Rage, Crash, and Trojan you're with me. The rest of you get new partners, grab a quick coffee, and get the fuck back out here. We're gonna break this fucker and find out what's goin' on."

As soon as I'm done talking, I make my way inside for a coffee and to make sure I have everything ready. We're gonna need to get the women and kids upstairs before Gage gets here. I guess they'll all have to go to the game room. Blade and Rage will be on them while we're downstairs.

"Guys, the women and kids are in the game room. Rage and Blade you're on them. The rest of us need to get everythin' ready downstairs. I'll get Bailey, Ma, and Skylar to help get everyone moved."

Rage and Blade make their way, with coffee cups in hand, to the game room to clear it before everyone gets in there. Cage, Joker, and I make our way down to move everyone as quick as we can. We open the door to the room to see total chaos. Kids are running everywhere, women are talking in small groups, and Skylar, Bailey, and Ma are with the babies. Looks like we get to help take my nieces and nephew upstairs since they bombard us all and wrap themselves around our legs.

"What's going on baby?" Skylar asks.

"We need to move you guys upstairs. Rage and Blade are gonna stay with you." Cage answers, pulling her in for a kiss.

"Okay." Bailey says. "Everyone settle down and listen up. We're moving back upstairs now. Follow Grim and he'll lead us to the room we're going in. Let's all line up now."

Picking Alana up, I grab Bailey and pull her into me. "Thank you baby. I'll be back to you as soon as I can."

"You do what you gotta do big guy and I'll see you when you're done."

"We're finishin' what was started last night crazy girl. When I'm done, you're not leavin' the room for a few fuckin' days so get your time in with the girls while you can."

"As much as I love the sound of that, you got other things to do baby. We both know it and I'll take my time when I get it."

I pull her in for a kiss and lead the way upstairs. Bailey waits until she's the last one and comes up with

Kasey. As soon as the doors to the game room are shut, I make my way back downstairs to get this shit over with.

Shortly after I get in the room, you can hear a commotion coming down the stairs. Cage runs upstairs to help Gage bring Crazy down while Joker gets the straps ready to tie his ass up. I just lean against the wall waiting for Crazy to fully realize what's coming to him.

"Grim!" Crazy yells. "You gotta tell them to let me go. I haven't done a fuckin' thing wrong!"

"Shut the fuck up prospect!" Pops yells. "You know what the fuck you did and now you're gonna fuckin' pay. The only thing you should be worried about is how easy this is gonna be on you."

"Grim, I don't know what he's talkin' about. I swear!" Crazy tries again to get out of the situation he finds himself in now.

I don't say anything until he's tied down to the chair and struggling to get up. "Now, are you gonna answer our fuckin' questions?" I ask.

"Anythin'!" Crazy says, still trying to figure out what we know.

"How's Bull doin'?" I ask and Crazy immediately shuts up. "Oh, you didn't think we knew you were workin' with his ass?"

Now Crazy's tune changes and he's not saying a word. "Must be we hit the nail on the head, boys." I say.

"How long you been with Bull's club?" Cage asks.

Crazy stays quiet so I nod to Cage to let him loose. He's about ready to snap and I'm gonna let him. "Just leave the head alone. I want to make sure he can still talk."

Cage lands punches to both of his sides in quick succession. Then he pulls out his knife. Crazy loses it about this time and pisses himself. He's heard the damage Cage can create with his knife. He's not as good as Blade is, but he's damn close.

"I ain't tellin' you fuckers anythin'." Crazy spits out. "I can't believe that Bull thought it was gonna be hard to get to you pussy whipped bastards!"

"That's where you're wrong, motherfucker!" Cage yells in his face. "I'd die to protect my brothers. But you threaten my woman and kids and you're already buried, you just don't know it yet."

"You gonna talk before he starts cuttin' fingers off?" I ask.

"Fuck you!"

With a nod, Joker grabs Crazy's right hand and Cage starts cutting his fingers off. Crazy only makes it through the first one before he loses consciousness. Pops grabs the hose and starts spraying him down with freezing cold water until Crazy starts sputtering.

"Wanna try again?" I ask.

"Fuck off! You're goin' down and I'm gonna laugh my ass off as I watch!"

"Do another one Cage."

Joker adjusts his hold and Cage goes for another finger. Not wanting to miss their chance, Crash and Trojan land a few punches to make sure he doesn't pass out again. I just stand in front of him with my arms crossed, waiting for him to break. He's weak so it won't be much longer.

"Fine, I'll talk!" Crazy screams out through the pain he's in.

"What does Bull want?"

"That bitch Skylar. She was promised to him and her sister is long gone. That bitch didn't make it an hour with us."

"So, you're part of the Soulless Bastards? Let me guess, you help get Skylar and you get your top rocker?" I ask him, walking up closer to him.

"Yeah. I help Chrissy get in and I was supposed to help Bull and the guys get in last night until you sent my ass to the safe house. Now, they're gonna wait until I get back and let me know when to let them in."

"Well, looks like Bull's gonna be pissed again because your ass is goin' down and won't be makin' that call. We'll be sure to let him know it only took two fingers gone before you caved, you weak piece of shit. Cage and Joker have your fun and end this fucker." I say, walking out and heading to my office. "Make sure Pops gets his time in too."

Now, I gotta call Bull and let him know we know he wants Skylar and that his fucking piece of shit is buried. Not what I wanted to do, but we'll take his ass out one way or another. I guess another church is gonna be called so we can make the call and figure out where to go from here. I just need one of the guys to bring me the crap Crazy had in his pockets. Then I can get this shit taken care of once and for all. The only thing I have left to do now, is decide when we make our move. I think for right now, we'll just sit tight and monitor how many times Bull tries to get ahold of Crazy.

Chapter Eleven

A few weeks later

Bailey

WE HAVEN'T HEARD anything from the Soulless Bastards, or anyone else for a few weeks. So, Logan has decided that we can go out and do something. Just the girls with one prospect. I have just the thing to do. Rage has our house almost done, and I want to go furniture shopping. Logan and I both have enough furniture to fill the house, but I want us to start out fresh. When I ran the idea by Logan, he agreed with me. So, Caydence, Kenzie, Skylar, and I are going out shopping today. Not our usual type, but we only have to take Blade with us, so we're not arguing. Besides Logan is busy trying to get the garage back up and running. It's almost been rebuilt so he's chomping at the bit. You can get things accomplished pretty quickly when you have guys working on it from three different chapters. So, he's consumed with getting it finished and running again.

"Let's go girls!" I call out to Caydence and Kenzie.

"We're coming!" Kenzie hollers back.

"You're slower than Sky. At least she has a reason to be moving slow. What the fuck's your excuse?"

"Hey!" Sky pipes up from next to me.

"Sorry. But, you know I'm right."

After another ten minutes, we're finally ready to head out. I've been waiting to get on the road for an hour now. Logan told me last night we could go out today and I've been more than ready.

The first shop we hit is the furniture store downtown. I've been in here before and already picked out a few things that I like. There's an awesome bookshelf that I absolutely love. I know Logan wants a big ass t.v and there's a stand that would go perfectly around it. Another thing that I picked out was a huge wrap around couch that I fell in love with. It's almost like

Sky's but on the one end it has a recliner, which I know Logan will love. The only thing that we really look at in the furniture store are beds. I left mine for Rage to use and I'm not bringing Logan's into our new home.

"What size bed you looking for girl?" Kenzie asks me.

"I think that I want a king."

"Gotta have room to roll around. Right girl?" Kenzie says, wiggling her eyebrows up and down.

"You guys! Let's go look before you get us kicked out of here." Sky says. "I can already tell you're both in a mood and it might not end well for us."

We all start laughing loudly. The salesman comes over looking at us. He looks like a guy that wouldn't know how to have fun if it bit him in the ass. So, I sober up and tell him what I want. While I'm listing everything off, he looks at me like I don't have a pot to fucking piss in.

"Is there a fuckin' problem here?" I ask him.

"That's quite the list of furniture and I know that the "garage" you had isn't running right now." He says, actually putting the word garage in quotation marks.

"How fuckin' dare you. Just because Spinners isn't running right now has nothing to do with me buying furniture. I have fucking money and probably more than you do, you fuckin' piss ant!" I yell at him, letting my bitch flag fly.

"Maybe you should spend that money in another location. I don't think it's any good here." He says, turning his back on me.

"Oh really! I have more pull in this fucking town than you do. I want your fucking boss out here. Now!"

The girls try to calm me down while I wait for a manager to make their way over to us. I see a lady making her way over to us and I just get the feeling that she's not gonna be any more help than the asshat of a salesman was. Just fucking great!

"Can I help you ladies?" She asks, practically sticking her nose up in the air.

"Yeah, I wanna buy furniture and your salesman told me to take my money elsewhere." I tell her.

"I think that might be a good idea. You've been here less than ten minutes and already have caused multiple scenes."

"What are you talkin' about?" Caydence speaks up.

"You're pulling all attention to you and it's not needed."

"Listen Blaire." Skylar says. "She has money and she wants to buy furniture. Her money is no different than yours. Are you gonna help her or not?"

"No, I'm not. Quite frankly, I'm surprised that you've thrown yourself in with this crowd Skylar. What would your grandmother think of you?"

"Oh hell no!" Skylar yells. "You don't ever talk about my grandma. You're just a stuck up bitch that's probably fuckin' that salesman because your husband's gettin' it from every other woman in town. And I know you try to fuck anyone with a cock! So, we'll take our money elsewhere. But, you can rest assured that I will be talkin' to Marian about this shit. Not only is she your mother, but you know she will tell everyone about what happened here today."

"You have no right. We have the right to refuse any sale we deem necessary."

"You're right, you do. But, we were doing nothing wrong and we're going to take our hard earned money to another establishment that will make a killing on the amount of furniture Bailey is planning on buying. You know, enough to outfit an entire house." Skylar continues on.

At this information, Blaire's face pales. Yeah, she thought I was only gonna purchase one small thing or something. Too bad she just lost out on one hell of a sale. So, we turn on our heels and leave the store. Blade witnessed the entire exchange, so I'm sure that it's only gonna be a matter of time before Logan, Dec, and Levi hear about it.

"Alright girls, I guess we're going to Phantom Bastards territory. Let me text Logan so he can give them a heads up." I tell the girls. "Actually, I'll just have Blade get a hold of him."

I make my way over to Blade and tell him about the change in plans. He immediately calls Logan and tells him what our plans are now. It's not necessary, but I know that Logan would want to let them know we're gonna be there. If nothing else, they'll send another prospect out to help Blade watch over us so nothing happens to us in their territory. That's just the way that Slim, the president, is. Plus, he's friends with Pops so he'll really want to make sure that nothing happens to Sky or me.

It takes us about an hour to find the furniture store once we get to Benton Falls. As soon as we pull in to the parking lot, I smile because I see a prospect and Slim sitting there waiting for us. I pull in as close to them as I can before we all pile out.

"Slim, it's good to see you again." I tell him, giving him a hug.

"You too sweetness. Grim called me to tell me you were gonna be here. So, I want to make sure that ya'll aren't treated the same way. Let's go in so I can have some words with the salesman and then I'll leave ya be. Blade, this is Boy Scout. He's with you for the day."

"Thanks Slim." Blade says after giving him that man hug thing.

The rest of us make our way in the store while Blade and Boy Scout get to know one another. I'm actually kind of glad when I walk in the store and see that they have a much better selection of furniture. Not only do they have all the pieces I already picked out, they have other ones that I might like even better. We might be here a while, so I feel bad for Sky. Maybe she can sit down somewhere while we're here.

"Alright Bailey, you're good to shop until you can't anymore. This is Louis and he'll help you guys out with whatever you need." Slim tells me.

"Thank you so much. It's nice to meet you Louis. Um, just so I know now, do you have some place that my friend can sit if she needs to?" I ask pointing to Sky.

"Absolutely. If you need to sit down honey, you just plop your ass where you want." He says smiling at us all.

"You guys don't need me anymore, so I'll leave ya to it. If you need anythin' else, let me know." Slim says giving me a hug and kiss before leaving.

"What are you looking for today honey?" Louis asks me.

"Actually I'm looking to fill a house. My old man and I are building a home and it's almost done. But, I decided that I want all new for our beginning. There are a few pieces that I had picked out at a different store, but I'd like to look around for a little bit if that's okay."

"Absolutely! When you're ready, you just let me know and we'll get you taken care of."

Once Louis walks away, we make our way over to the beds to start with. Immediately I see a king size sleigh bed with matching dressers and night stands. Instantly I'm in love with the set and I know Logan will like it too. Next we move on to the bookshelves and entertainment centers. I don't see one better than the center I had already picked out, so I make note of the same one and pick out two bookshelves that go with it. Our next stop is living room furniture. There's a similar wrap around couch that's an upgrade from the one I originally picked out. It's leather and has a recliner at both ends. It also has a stand that is leather on it to match. This set is something that Logan will definitely like. So, I quickly snap a picture of it and send it to him. Not even a minute later I get a response from him telling me to tell them to wrap it up.

I get Louis as soon as I'm sure that I have all of the furniture that I want. He has no problem helping me and assures me that he will make sure that all of the furniture I want will be removed and stored until we're ready to move it in to the house. Plus, there's not gonna be any fees added on for delivery. I'm so glad that we got to come here to shop instead.

Our next stop is a general store that has everything else we'll need for the house. I quickly grab enough stuff to fill both our bathrooms, the kitchen, Logan's office, the gym, the extra bedrooms, and decorations. Needless to say, I've put a huge dent in my savings account. But, I don't care about that shit. It's the start to the future for Logan and me and I really can't put a price on it. The only thing that I'm not buying is a sound system, stuff we need for the outdoor party area, and stuff for our playroom. Logan and I'll do that together.

"Sky, I'm sure you're getting hungry. Let's find somewhere to eat before we make our way home." I say as we're making our way back out to my truck.

"Yeah. That sounds good."

"Let me talk to Boy Scout and see what he recommends." I tell the girls after unlocking the truck so they can get in as I make my way over to him and Blade.

Boy Scout tells me to follow him and he'll get us to a diner a few blocks over. He assures me that it's a hometown diner and that it's where they all eat. Plus, there's no alcohol served there so we don't have to worry about any of us drinking when Sky can't drink. That's being saved for when she can go out with us and live it up.

When we pull up, I see what he means about it being a hometown diner. It actually looks a lot like the diner back home. I see the sign and the place is called Rosie's. That's it. I bet Rosie is the owner and she's lived in Benton Falls all her life. But, those are the kinds of places I love. More than likely all of the food is homemade and the food all comes from local farmers and things.

I park the truck and we all get out. Boy Scout leads us in and as soon as I get inside and get a whiff of all of the smells that are mouth-watering good, I feel like I'm going to throw up. Quickly covering my mouth. I run to the bathroom before I make a mess all over the floor. I'm not sure what the hell's going on and why I'm feeling like this. The only thing I can think of is that this is the same way I was when I pregnant with Ryan. My mind starts whirling all over the place and I feel like I'm going crazy with worry and doubt.

After I get done throwing up what little there was left in my stomach, I use toilet paper to wipe my mouth off before going to wash my hands. Before I can get out of the stall though, I see a hand come under the door handing me a pregnancy test. Without saying a word, I use it and stay in the stall until I get the results. I don't need an audience while I wait to find out what's wrong.

Once the allotted time is over, I look at the test and see two pink lines. The tears immediately start streaming down my face and I feel like I can't breathe. My only concern right now is getting out of this place and hiding away from the world. I really don't know if I want this to happen, but I know I have to leave the stall and face the girls. The last thing I want is for them to be worried about me.

They must know that I'm gonna need them because Sky, Caydence, and Kenzie are waiting for me. One look at my face and a look at the test has all of them wrapping their arms around me. Sky has tears running down her face and I know that she knows I'm on the fence about having kids now. Before there wasn't a doubt in my mind that one day I wanted to have kids, and that I wanted that with Logan. Now, I'm already so worried that I'm gonna lose this baby too. That's the last thing that Logan needs to deal with. Hell, I wouldn't wish that kind of loss on my worst enemy.

"Alright. Let's go out and see if we can get some food in your stomach. Then we'll listen while you vent and we'll work through everything going through your head right now." Sky says.

"I don't know what's going through it." I say between sobs. "I can't go through that again and I don't want to put Logan through it either."

"We'll figure something out Bay. Let's go before we have Blade and Boy Scout in here with us to find out what's going on." Kenzie says taking charge.

She's right. I don't need those two getting all up in my business. The first person, other than these girls of course, who needs to know about this is Logan. Until I figure this out though, I'm not sure when I'm gonna tell him. Or how I'm gonna tell him. When I used to dream about having kids with him, I always thought of cute ways to tell him the news. Now, I know as soon as he looks at me, he's gonna know something's going on. That's just how he is.

Making our way back to the tables, Kenzie picks one and we all sit down. Blade and Boy Scout sit close, but not close enough that we can't have a private conversation. They'll make good additions to each chapter when they get patched in. I can tell just by the way they've been with us today. Well, Blade I know better, but Boy Scout is just as good as Blade.

"Okay Bay, let's see if we can figure out something for you to eat." Sky says. "I know with just about every pregnancy I've had it's been all about comfort food. Do you wanna try some soup and a grilled cheese or something like that?"

"Maybe some soup and French fries I think." I respond.

An older lady comes over to take our order. She reminds me of Ma and I instantly like her. Especially after she looks at me.

"Honey, I know just what you need to eat right now. You let me take care of your order and sit tight. All of you sit tight and I'll be back with some iced tea for ya'll."

We all just look at each other until Caydence speaks up. "She didn't even ask if we knew what we wanted to eat. What kind of place is this?"

"She'll bring you exactly what you want to eat. Rosie's good like that." Boy Scout tells us.

So we all settle in and resume our conversation. "I want to know what's going through your head Bay." Kenzie says.

"I don't know. It's all so jumbled and one scenario is running right after another."

"What's the main one going through your mind right now though?" Caydence speaks up.

"That the same thing is gonna happen again and I'm not gonna survive it. You guys don't know what it's like to go through that."

Caydence gets a weird look on her face and goes quiet. What the hell? Has she lost a baby? Why don't I know this?

"What about after that?" Sky asks.

"That if I do lose the baby, I'm also gonna lose Logan. That he's not gonna be happy at all about the baby."

"Okay. Well, what did the doctor tell you when you were in the hospital?"

"She said that I shouldn't have any problems if, and when, I decided to get pregnant again. Doctor Bell seemed to think that it was like a one-time occurrence or something."

"Okay. That's good news then. You should be concentrating on that instead of stressing yourself out thinking about the worst possible scenario happening again." Sky says. "I've seen the way that Grim looks at you when you're at the house with Alana and the rest of the kids. There's no way he's not gonna be happy about this."

"What are you talking about Sky?" I ask confused as hell.

"When you were outside on the swing with Alana and Kasey was with you, Grim stood back for a while and watched you holding her cradled to your chest. Then he got this longing look on his face when the three of you were sitting there on the swing set. He wants a family with you Bay. There's no question about it."

"Yeah, I've seen the looks he's been giving you at the clubhouse when you've been hanging out with the kids. That man seriously wants you pregnant. He sees nothing else when you're holding a baby."

"Why haven't I seen this?" I ask, just as Rosie returns to the table.

"Here you go ladies. Tea all around and tomato soup and French fries for you honey. For the little mama here, soup and a grilled cheese. And cheeseburgers and French fries for the two of you. I'll bring out dessert when you're done with this."

For the next few minutes, we all remain quiet and stuff our faces with food. I'm glad that Rosie knew what to bring me because the soup and fries are already starting to calm my stomach. Hopefully I won't be sick again today and it's just going to be a minor case of morning sickness like the beginning of my last pregnancy. I don't know what I'll do if I can't eat and get really sick this time.

"When are you gonna tell Grim?" Caydence asks me as we're getting done with our food.

"I don't know. On one hand I want a minute to think about everything. But, I know him. He's gonna know something's wrong as soon as he sees me."

"You gotta tell him babe. This isn't something you can keep from him until you're comfortable with it." Kenzie says.

"Besides, we'll be with you every step of the way. No matter what happens!" Caydence says.

At this point our conversation is interrupted by Rosie bringing our dessert over. Once again, she not only knows exactly what we want, she knows that we all wanted some. Rosie is amazing and it's awesome that she knows what her customers want before they want it. Unless she isn't like that with everyone. I haven't really been paying attention with the news that I just got. All I know is that I'll have to remember this place for when I come to this area again.

"I appreciate you guys, but I need to figure this shit out on my own. Then I'll talk to Logan about it."

"We understand. Just don't shut us out again. We feel like we just got you back." Caydence says.

As soon as we finish our desserts, I grab Rosie's attention so that we can get the bill. When she gets over to us, she tells us that Boy Scout already covered our bill. I'm not sure why he paid for our lunch but I'm not gonna bitch about it. So I turn around and thank him before we gather our shit to go home.

Once we get back to the clubhouse, I walk away from the girls and go around the outside of the building to go to my tree. Unfortunately, Gage is already sitting there. I don't want to interrupt him, so I decide to go for a walk to think.

"Bay, you don't gotta leave. Come join me." Gage calls out to my retreating back.

Turning around, I walk up to him. Sitting down, I look at him and he immediately knows something's wrong. But, he gives me a few minutes before he says anything to me.

"What's wrong sweetheart?"

"Nothing. I just wanted to come sit here for a while. Everything good with you? I can leave if you want me to."

"You can't lie for shit Bay. It's written all over your face that somethin's up. Talk to me."

"I'm pregnant." Is the only thing I say.

"Are you okay?"

"No." I say as the tears start once again. "I don't know what to do. How am I gonna tell Grim? What am I gonna do if I lose this baby? I'm not strong enough to go through that again Gage."

"Yeah, you are. I know without a doubt that Grim will be fuckin' ecstatic. He's wanted to be with you for as long as I've known you guys. What's really goin' on?"

"I don't know if I can do this Gage. I feel like I'm replacing Ryan. And I don't want to feel like that."

"Oh babe. You're not replacin' Ryan. He would want you to move on and make a family out of love. I'm sure he's sittin' up there and he's happy as fuck. Even though he's not here, he's a big brother and he'll watch over this new baby with everythin' in him." Gage tells me, wrapping me in his arms.

"You're not mad at me?"

"No Bay, I'm not. I always knew I was never gonna be the one for you. It's always been Grim. He's your world and the air you breathe. You're the same for him. Now, I know that you might not feel ready to do this and risk goin' through that shit again, but you're gonna make a great mom and Grim's gonna be there every step of the way. Not to mention that your family is here and you're not movin' away. I'll always be here for you, you know that. But, you need to enjoy this with Grim."

"Do you really think Ryan would be okay with this? I mean it's only been a little while."

"He really would babe. Now, you need to go find Grim and let him in on the news that he's gonna be a daddy."

"I can't go in there right now. I don't wanna face everyone. Pops is here, I saw his bike. If I see him first, he'll demand to know what's wrong. So, for now I think I'll just sit here."

"Why don't I go get him and send him out here to you? That way you can have privacy and I'll make sure that no one comes out here."

"Don't you think that's disrespecting Ryan though. Talking to Grim here?"

"No. I think talkin' to him here will give you the strength you need to get everythin' out that you need to."

Without another word, Gage gives me a kiss on my forehead and walks to the clubhouse. I just sit here, tears still streaming down my face, waiting for Logan to show up. My mind is still going a million miles a minute with every fear, hope, and dream about creating a family with Logan. Nothing could be more perfect than creating one with the man that I love and need. He's been my rock for longer than I can remember and the one person in my life that has always been there for me and had my back.

"Crazy girl, what's goin' on? Gage told me to come talk to you." Logan asks sitting down next to me. "Did you enjoy shoppin' today?"

I can't even bring myself to say anything to him yet. So, I dig in my bag and pull out the box with the pregnancy test. He just looks at me for a minute before he pulls the test out. Once he can see the screen, he just stares at it.

"Babe, you're gonna need to tell me what's goin' on. I have no clue what I'm lookin' at right now."

"I'm pregnant."

"Are you serious?"

"Yeah. Boy Scout took us to a diner and as soon as we got inside, I had to rush to the bathroom. When I was done throwing up, one of the girls handed me that under the door."

"Okay. Well, I'm happy as fuck that we're gonna have a baby. But, I know that you've got a shit ton of stuff rollin' through your head right now. So, let's have it." He says, moving even closer to me.

"I don't even know where to begin. There's just so much shit. The main one is that I'm gonna lose this baby too and then I'll lose you because I can't give you this."

"I already told you that if we can't have kids the normal way, then we'll do whatever we have to. So, we'll just take it a day at a time and make sure that we follow every single order the doctor gives you. Crazy girl, we'll get through this and at the end, we'll have a beautiful baby to make our family even bigger. This is goin' to be an amazin' journey we're about to begin."

"Okay. I also feel like I'm trying to replace Ryan. It hasn't been that long and now I'm pregnant again. It's not like we've used protection, but I feel like I'm trying to replace what I didn't get to experience the first time."

"That's not what's happenin'. You're right, we haven't used protection. And I told you the other day that if you wanted to get on birth control, I was gonna support you. Well, we didn't get to that point. So, now there's a new life growin' in you. It's not to replace Ryan at all. Maybe, this is somethin' you need to go through with to make yourself believe that losin' Ryan wasn't your fault. I'm sure he's lookin' down right now and he's gonna be by your side every step of the way to make sure that you don't go through that shit again. Maybe that's why you lost him, so that you'd have a guardian angel watchin' over you and any child that we have. Please crazy girl, stop feelin' like that."

"It's not gonna be easy to stop worrying and thinking that shit Logan. I'm probably gonna feel like this for a long time to come. But, I'll talk to my counselor about it and get her take on it. I know she's got kids. Just do me a favor please?"

"Anythin' you want crazy girl. You know I would move heaven and earth to give you whatever you want and need."

"Don't tell anyone yet. Too many people know as it is. I don't want anyone to know until I'm ready."

"Okay. We'll keep it mum for right now. First thing in the mornin' though, we need to make a doctor's appointment. That's one of the only things that's gonna help ease your mind."

"As soon as we wake up we'll call. I'm gonna go in and get ready for bed. I know it's early as fuck, but I just wanna be alone, or with you, and not around everyone right now."

"Okay crazy girl. We'll go hang out in the room and just relax."

Grim

Today Bailey both made me the happiest man in the world and tore my heart out. I'm so fucking excited hearing that she's growing a little us in her belly. But, at the same time, it's gonna be so hard on her. We're gonna have to keep a close eye on her during this pregnancy. Just to make sure that she's eating, resting, and doing everything the doctor says she needs to do. There is no way in hell that I'm gonna let her go through everything she's been dealing with since she lost Ryan.

I'm so excited that I want to run in the clubhouse and yell at the top of my lungs that I'm gonna be a daddy. But, I'm going to respect her wishes and wait to tell anyone until she's ready. Part of it, I'm sure, is because she doesn't want to disappoint more than just me if she has another miscarriage. I really hate that she feels like this.

One way or another, I'm gonna make sure that she knows every day that we're not replacing Ryan. As soon as we move into our home, I'm gonna make sure that his ultrasound pictures go up somewhere in the house. I don't give a flying fuck if it's only in our bedroom. They will be up.

"Crazy girl, when this baby is born, we're gonna make sure that we talk about Ryan every single fuckin' day. No, he may not have been born, but he was real and they're gonna know that they have an older brother that's gonna be lookin' down on them every fuckin' day of their life."

"We don't have to do that Logan."

"Yeah, we do. This child won't be your first child. Ryan was your first child and this new baby is gonna fuckin' know it."

"I love you so much. How do you know the exact thing to say to me, exactly when I need to hear it?"

"Crazy girl, I'm just tellin' you what's gonna happen. Now, let's get inside, get a bunch of junk food, or somethin' you can tolerate eatin', get some drinks, and watch some movies. How does that sound?"

"It sounds good. Why don't you raid the kitchen and I'll go get changed?"

After kissing her, I make my way into the kitchen to see Gage. He's standing with his back to me and slumped over. I'm guessing that he knows what's going on and it's messing with him. I don't know what to do about that shit. The last thing I want is for him to be hurting over this.

"Gage, how you doin'?"

"I'm good man. Everythin' good with you two?"

"Yeah. I'm sorry man. I'm sure this is bringin' up all sorts of shit for you."

"It is. But, I'll be fine. It's just hittin' me hard right now. But, I want her happy."

"I don't know if that's gonna happen any time soon. Listen, she doesn't want anyone to know about it right now. Like with your baby, she wants to wait until she hits a certain point before we start tellin' people."

"It's good man. My lips are sealed. I'm not gonna say anythin' and go against what she wants."

The entire time we've been talking, I've been gathering shit for our night in. Not knowing what Bailey's gonna want, I just grab a little bit of everything. Plus, I grab soda, tea, and bottled water.

"Well, she wants to stay in the room the rest of the night. So, you guys enjoy the party and I'll see you tomorrow before you leave."

"Yeah man."

Making my way upstairs, I hope that Bailey is done crying. I'm sure it can't be good for the baby. But, I'm not gonna stop her so that she holds everything in either because that will be worse. Maybe I can talk her into making an extra appointment with her counselor this week. I think she needs it with finding out she's pregnant. As soon as I open the door to our room, I see Bailey curled up under the covers. She's sound asleep. Oh well, she needs the rest. I'll go back down to the party for a while and talk to the guys until they all find someone for the night.

Chapter Twelve

Grim

I DON'T KNOW what time I ended up falling asleep next to Bailey, but I wake up in the middle of the night to my phone ringing from somewhere in the room. My only thought was getting back to my crazy girl so we could wrap around one another and veg out in front of a movie to take her mind off all the things running through her head about being pregnant. But, when I walked back through the door to our room she was already passed out. So, I went to see the guys for a while before climbing in bed with her.

"Yeah." I say finally finding my phone.

"It's time Pres." I hear Joker's voice say.

"Time for what?" I ask still more than half asleep.

"We're takin' Sky to the hospital. The baby is ready to meet everyone." He says, excitement lacing his voice.

"Alright. I'll get your sister up and we'll be on our way there. Congrats man!"

Joker doesn't respond. He's already hung up and I don't even know if he heard what I said to him. The poor guy is probably freaking the fuck out right now. Hell, when our little one is born, I don't know that I'm gonna be able to make a single call to anyone. I sure as fuck hope someone else is around to make sure that my brothers, and Bailey's family, know to get to the hospital.

"Crazy girl, time to get up." I say, gently shaking her. "You're goin' to be an auntie again in just a little bit."

"Huh?" She asks, rolling her back to me.

"Bay, we gotta get up. The guys are takin' Sky to the hospital."

These seem to be the magic words since Bailey jumps up and starts to get out of bed. Unfortunately, she must move too fast or something because in the next instant she's running to the bathroom and slamming the door. Putting my head to it, I hear her getting sick. So I make my way in to support her. I rub her back and hold her hair out of her face until she feels good enough to get up.

"You okay crazy girl?" I ask.

"Yeah. It's just something that happens because I'm pregnant. Get used to it babe."

"Crazy girl, I'll be here to hold your hair, rub your back, go out all hours of the night, and whatever else you need me to do for you. I'm all in and I'll be here every step of the way."

"I know babe. Now, let's get ready so that we can go meet our new niece or nephew." She says getting excited.

It's kind of surprising that she's excited to see the new babies with everything flying through her head right now. But, we'll see how she is when we get to the hospital. I'll support her no matter what. If she wants to leave, we'll leave and see the baby at a different point in time when Bailey feels comfortable enough to handle it. I know that Sky and the guys will understand and support Bailey's decision.

Since it's the middle of the night, I decide that we're gonna take the truck even though I see the rest of the guys that are at the clubhouse loading up on their bikes. There's no way in hell I'm putting Bailey on the back of my bike right now. She's already worried as fuck about the baby and I'm not gonna do anything unnecessary that could harm the baby. If I have to drive a cage for now when she's with me, I have no fucking problem with that. Bailey and my baby are more important than whether or not I get to ride my bike. There's plenty of time to do that when I go on runs or out with the guys.

Leading the rest of the guys to the hospital, we make it there in about ten minutes. I can see Bailey getting nervous and anxious about being here. And why we're here. I'm beginning to wish that we didn't come and I explained that to Joker when he called. But, then I might have slipped up and told him what's going on now. Bailey being pissed the fuck off at me is the last thing I want. Not only because I hate her being pissed at me but also because she doesn't need the stress.

Once we get up to the maternity ward, the nurse at the desk tells us it's still gonna be a little bit so two people at a time can go in as long as Sky doesn't have a problem with it.

"Crazy girl, do you wanna go in?" I ask her, taking her hand in mine.

"I don't know. I want to see Sky, but I don't know if I can handle going in there."

"I'm sure she understands. How about I go in and let her know we're here and that you might be in later?"

"Thanks babe. I'll be here waiting for you."

Bailey

As soon as Logan disappears through the doors to Sky's room, I start to feel like the walls are closing in on me. Maybe I should've stayed at the clubhouse and let him come alone. I thought I could handle it when he first woke me up, but being here is making it a reality. One that I can't handle. So, I make my way back downstairs and go outside.

I quickly find a bench and park my ass trying to drag breath in my lungs. This is definitely hitting me harder than I thought it would. Maybe it wouldn't be as bad if I weren't pregnant right now. I just don't know.

I'm so in my own head, that I don't notice anyone sitting down next to me. Not a good thing when we don't know what the Soulless Bastards are up to. But, I can't help myself right now. Thankfully it's only Tank.

"Hey sweetheart. You doin' okay?" He asks me.

"No, I'm really not. I thought I could do this, but I can't. There's something going on that I think is making it harder on me right now." I tell him, leaning in closer just for comfort.

"Did you know that I lost a baby a few years ago?"

"No. What happened?"

Tank doesn't say anything for a little while. Just when I go to tell him that he doesn't have to share his story with me, he continues.

"He was still born. Apparently his mom was doin' drugs and I didn't catch it. We named him Dean Roman Hendersen and he's buried by my grandma back home. It's not ideal since I can't be there as much now, but I wouldn't change bein' here for the world. That's why you've seen me up visitin' your baby. In a way, I feel closer to Dean. Not a lot of people know about it because I was tryin' to keep her out of the club. I thought I was protectin' her. So, I've carried the burden by myself for a long time."

"What happened to his mom?"

"She overdosed not long after he was born."

"Tank, I'm so sorry!"

"Not tellin' you this for your pity or anythin'. Just lettin' you know that I get where you're comin' from. It's not a good thing to go through when it's a miscarriage, but it's a whole different game all together when you can hold that baby in your hands and see them. I'm not sayin' that you aren't sufferin' and shouldn't be depressed, it's just different. I held him so long that they had to physically restrain me when they had to take him. When he was buried, it was only me, my mom, and my grandpa. I didn't want anyone else there. So, other than you and maybe one or two brothers, no one knows."

"I'll take it to my grave, Tank. You don't have to worry about that. I'm glad that you can go to Ryan's spot and feel close to Dean."

"It was a boy?" He asks me.

"I've had dreams about it being a boy. So, Gage and I decided that we were gonna go with it."

"If you had dreams, then I'm pretty sure it's what you think. Babe, I'm gonna go back in so Grim don't get frantic. Blade's out here somewhere and he'll be watchin' out for ya. You take all the time you need and I'll make sure Grim leaves you be for now."

"I just need to catch my breath and then I'll be in. Can I ask you a question before you go back in?"

"Absolutely."

"What do you think when it comes to having other kids? I mean do you want to take the chance to have other kids?"

"Absolutely. I mean if I found someone that I could see myself wantin' to spend my life with, then I'd have kids. As long as she wants to that is."

"You don't feel like you'd be betraying Dean's memory by having other kids?"

"Nope. I'll make sure that any other kids I have in the future know about Dean. He'll always be my first born and the big brother of any other kids I have. So, no I absolutely don't think I'd be betrayin' his memory in the least. He'll still remain a part of my family by rememberin' him and thinkin' about what I would've done with him. I'll always imagine him when I do anythin' with my kids in the future. Why?"

"Take it to your grave?" I ask.

"Anythin' you tell me I'll take to the grave."

"I just found out I'm pregnant. A big part of me thinks I'm betraying Ryan and his memory."

"Honey, that's not the truth at all. Would that be the case if he survived and you didn't have a miscarriage?"

"No."

"Exactly! I don't care if he's not here with you, he's still your first born and will always be a part of you. When your kids get old enough, make sure they know that. Show them your tree and explain why it's important to you. They'll get it."

"How do you always know the right thing to say to people? Especially us women of the club."

"Because I've been through a lot more than most of the guys in the club. So, when you women go through somethin', I've probably already dealt with somethin' similar. If you don't have any more questions, I'll head back in and make sure Grim knows you're okay."

"I'm good. Thank you."

After Tank leaves, I spot Blade a little bit away standing guard. So, I sit back and just breathe. I try to blank out everything in my mind so that I can go see Sky. It's important that she knows I'm here to support them. Even though I know she'll understand if I can't stay in the room, she needs to know I'm here. With my decision made, I make my way back inside and up to see my girl and brothers. Yeah, even though Cage isn't a brother by blood, he's still my brother. Always has been.

As soon as I get back up to the maternity ward, I bypass everyone and don't say a word. I need to get in there before I talk myself out of it again. I know Logan won't follow me if Tank's talked to him. Besides, I'm sure he knows this is gonna be hard on me. Sky knows it too, and they both know why it's even harder right now.

"Hey sis. How you doin'?" I ask, walking in the room.

"Good. This one's bein' stubborn like their daddy though. They want to be born, but now that we're here nothing. So, they're gonna induce me in a little bit."

"Where are the kids?"

"At Ma and Pop's house. They're gonna bring them over when the baby's born." Joker answers me, coming over and wrapping his arm around me.

"I can go sit with them for a while and let them come here. If you want that is."

"No. I know why you wanna leave, but you don't need to do that. It's up to you though." Cage says, giving me a hug.

"It's okay. I'll let them come over and someone can call me when you want me to bring them back. I'll just have to take Sky's SUV so I can fit them all in. The guys can stay here and I'll grab a quick nap while they're out and then we'll be back."

"Okay sis."

"Bay, please. You have a lot going on right now. If you don't want to do this, you don't have to. We all understand what you're going through. Well, I do more than them, but it's okay."

"I want to do this. Please, let me. It's one way I can support you since it's a little too much for me to be here."

"Okay. We'll have Grim call you when everything's done. After that, you decide when you want to come back and if you want to come in."

I don't say anything to them, I just make my way out. Stopping by Logan, I let him know what the plan is now. He tells me that he'll go with me, but I tell him no. I just want to be alone with the kids until we need to head back. When Logan goes to give me the keys to his truck, I tell him I'm taking Skylar's SUV so I have room for the kids.

At Ma and Pops, I go in to see my dad sitting on the couch with Jameson sleeping on his lap. The girls must be in the bedroom with Ma. He looks up and sees me standing there after taking a picture of them on my phone. Pops smiles this cheesy grin and goes back to watching t.v. I know that he's waiting for me to sit down and tell him what's wrong, but I can't. It's important that I know things are gonna be different this time around before anyone else knows. But, then again, I know Pops was hurt the last time when he didn't know. What the fuck am I supposed to do?

"I know you got shit brewin' over there baby girl. Come talk to me." Pops says, patting the couch beside him.

"I told Logan I wasn't gonna say anything yet dad."

"Say anythin' 'bout what? Is somethin' wrong with you?"

"Not in a medical sense dad. I'm pregnant." I say looking down at my hands.

For a minute he doesn't say anything to me. He just looks at me, trying to read what's going through my head right now. It's just something my dad can do when it comes to me. I'm an open book when my dad looks at me and something's wrong with me.

"How are you feelin' 'bout that?"

"I've got so much shit running through my head right now dad. What happens if I can't carry this one again? Is Logan gonna leave me if that happens? Am I betraying Ryan's memory by being pregnant right now?"

"Baby girl, none of that's right. I know this is hard for you, but it will get better. Grim ain't gonna leave you if the same thing happens. He's gonna stay by your side no matter what happens. But, I think you're gonna find that nothin' will happen this time. And by Ryan, I'm assumin' you mean the baby you lost?"

"Yeah. I think it was gonna be a boy. So, we named him Ryan."

"Okay. Well, I don't think you're betrayin' nothin' about his memory. He'll always be loved in your heart. That's where you'll keep him alive. When the time's right, you'll tell your little ones about him and they'll help you keep his memory alive."

"That's what I was told earlier too. I want to be happy about this, I really do. But, I'm so scared that something's wrong with me."

"Baby, you know about your mom's miscarriage. She went through the same feelin's but you're here. If you need to talk, you talk. I don't give a fuck who you talk to, but you talk."

"Okay dad. I'll try to be happy about this and try to stop being scared about it. I'm gonna talk to my counselor about it too. I know she's had kids after she lost her baby."

"That's a good idea. Now, why are you here and not at the hospital with everyone else?"

"I just can't be there. So, I actually came so that you and Ma can go there. It's better for you guys to be there than me. I'm gonna bring the kids over when the baby's here."

"Okay baby girl. I'll go get your mom and we'll head out."

Once Ma and Pops leave, I lay down on the couch with Jameson. He doesn't even stir as I move him to curl in front of me. I turn down the volume on the t.v. and I pass out. Thankfully the monitor is sitting on the table so I'll be able to hear the girls if they wake up. I hope that I won't dream of Ryan, but with everything going on, I know that's probably not gonna happen.

I'm walking through a field of wild flowers down to a stream. The sun is shining and there's a slight wind blowing through my hair to keep the heat from being oppressive. As soon as I get to the stream and put my toes in the cool water, I hear someone coming up behind me. But, I don't turn around to see who it is because I already know. It's Ryan.

"Hi mama." I hear his little voice come from my side.

"Hey baby boy. How are you today?" I ask him, smiling down at his little face.

"Mama, I love you!"

"I love you with all my heart."

"I know you're gonna have a new baby to love too."

"I am. I'm so sorry baby boy. I didn't mean for this to happen. You're so important to me and I don't ever want to forget you."

"You won't mama. I'll always be there with you, Grim, and new babies. I'll always be with you no matter where you go."

"But I don't want to hurt you if this baby makes it."

"This baby will make it mama. They're strong enough to make it. I wasn't. But, I'm glad that I didn't. Now I get to watch over all of you and protect you."

We sit together at the stream for a while just watching it flow by us. Ryan points out the frogs, little minnows, and other animals around us. Because it's a dream, they don't run away scared. Instead, they join us and sit still surrounding us.

"Mama, it's time for you to go now. But, I'll see you again soon. Tell daddy I love him and I'll visit him soon too. I love you to the moon and back."

"I love you to the moon and back too. But, I don't want to go yet. I'm not ready."

"You are mama. This little one needs you to go back and stop being afraid. Don't hurt this baby because of me. I want this for you mama. Please, for me, go back and be happy."

"Only for you Ryan. If this is what you truly want, I will for you."

"It is mama!"

I wake up with a start. Jameson is staring at me with his little hand on my cheek. The girls are starting to stir in the bedroom. So, I take a minute to think about the dream I just had. Maybe I can get through this pregnancy to the other side. If my dream is right, I should listen to what everyone's been telling me. Ryan was a horrible experience and I don't want to go through that again. But, it doesn't mean that it's gonna happen this time. Maybe Ryan was right and he's gonna help me make sure that it doesn't happen this time. I have a doctor's appointment next week and we're gonna talk to the doctor about everything going through my head. I can't think about that now because one of the girls is starting to get restless and probably wants her breakfast.

Jameson walks into the bedroom with me to get the girls. He's still the little protector to them. Now, it's even worse since Alana and Haley are starting to walk and get into things. He follows them around and makes sure that they don't get hurt. Reagan has also started following them around making sure they don't get hurt, but she's not as bad about it as he is. I can already see him joining the club when he gets old enough to do it. Whether anyone wants to admit it or not, he's already following in the footsteps of Cage and Joker.

Just as I'm getting the kids dressed after feeding them, my phone rings in the living room. Jameson runs out to get it for me without me having to ask him. I can't believe this kid is only four. He acts so much older than that. Bringing it into me, I see that it's Logan calling me.

"Hello."

"Hey crazy girl. How you doin'?"

"I'm good. I'm real good babe."

"Okay. Well, Sky's askin' for you. Are you gonna be on your way soon?"

"Yeah. I'm just getting the kids dressed and then we can leave. Will you have someone meet me outside to help get them all in?"

"Yeah. Text me when you pull in and let me know where you park so I can meet you."

"One of the prospects will be fine babe. You don't have to come down."

"I want to crazy girl. Maybe I want some lovin' before we come inside."

"Alright. I'll let you know when I get there."

"I love you."

"I love you too." I say, hanging up to finish with the kids.

The last thing I do before we walk out the door is give Reagan her medicine. That's something that I absolutely can't forget to do, and I never would. Once we're all in the SUV, I turn on the music and we head to the hospital. As soon as I pull in I text Logan and tell him I'm there and that we're parked almost right by the entrance. Thank God I was able to get a close parking spot!

He comes walking around the building from where I saw Blade standing earlier when I was out here. Blade and he must have been walking around the perimeter to make sure that no one from the Soulless Bastards was here to fuck anything up.

"Hey crazy girl! I missed you. You sure you're okay?" He asks, opening my door for me.

"Yeah. I had an amazing dream and I think I'm ready to do this. I'm ready to have a baby with you and start building our family."

For a little while, Logan just looks at me. Finally, I can see the smile light up his face. I know he was worried about how I was going to be through this pregnancy. Weird or not, my dream helped ease some of the fear that I've had since finding out I was pregnant. Not that I've known for long. But, I'll take it so I can get through this journey that I know we're about to have. It's going to be such a ride, and I know it's worth the pain I went through with Ryan.

"I'm happy that you've found some peace crazy girl. You'll have to tell me what that dream was about later. Now, let's get in there before Sky kills someone."

"She that bad?" I ask, trying not to laugh.

"She just wants all of her family together. Apparently, besides wanting her kids with her, she has an announcement to make."

"Well, let's go then."

Logan takes Alana and Haley while I hold the hands of Jameson and Reagan. We make our way upstairs to see everyone waiting in the waiting room for us. Ma and Pops come over to help with the kids as we make our way into Skylar's room.

As soon as I walk in, I'm shocked as hell. Not only is there one bassinet sitting by her bed, there are two. Both have babies in them wrapped in little blue blankets. Apparently my brother has super sperm too. This is quite the shock to me so I can't imagine what they're thinking. Instead of one new addition to the family, there's two.

"Hey guys!" Sky says.

"Hey mama!" I say. "What's goin' on here?"

"Oh, you know. Your brother has super sperm too. Apparently the second little guy decided that he wanted us all to be surprised so he stayed hidden when it was time for ultrasounds and listening to the heartbeat. We never heard two because he was always laying directly behind his brother."

I make my way over to the bassinets to get my first look at my nephews. They are so cute! Their little faces are all scrunched up as they sleep. But, Levi walks over to me and hands me one of the babies. I sit down and pull his little hat back to see a head full of hair. Right now it's so blond that it's almost white. The same way that Levi's hair was when he was born. No doubt these are his little boys then I guess. I'm happy because I know that he struggled with the fact that Alana and Haley were fathered by Dec. He tried not to let it show, but I know my brother and I know I'm not the only one that noticed it. Dec noticed it, and I know that Pops had a talk about it with him.

"One thing is for certain. Sky, you make some gorgeous babies. I can't give any credit to these two cavemen because Jameson and Reagan are gorgeous too. So, it's all you as far as I'm concerned." I tell her.

"Thanks. Now, we have an announcement to make. So, is everyone in here that needs to be in here?"

"I think so baby girl. The only one missin' is Tank. He'll be in in just a second. He had to finish up a phone call real quick. Let me go take a look and see if he's almost done."

Logan comes over to me and looks down at me holding this new baby in my arms. I know he can't wait until the day comes that I'm sitting and holding our baby. It's always been a dream of his to have kids. Even when he would say that he didn't want an old lady or kids, I always knew he was full of shit. He's not as good at hiding some things as he is others. For example, right now, he's got a dreamy look on his face and his eyes have gone soft. It's cute to see him when he's like this because he looks so hard so often because of his job.

"Alright baby girl, everyone that needs to be in here is here now." Cage says walking back in.

"Okay. The first thing we're going to do is announce their names. We kind of had one boy's name picked out, but it took us a second to pick a name for the second little guy. So, their names are Kyle Logan and Brandon Jackson." Sky says, looking right at Logan.

No one says anything for a minute. Everyone is looking at Logan to see what he's gonna do. I look up and see that his eyes are still soft and there's a slight sheen to them. So, I reach up and grab his hand.

"I don't know what to say guys. But, it's an honor to know that you've used my name for one of your boys. I love you all!"

"There wasn't even a question Pres. You've been there for us in more than one way whenever we've needed somethin'." Joker tells him. "Now, we have another announcement to make. We've decided that we're gonna have one ceremony and have the kids baptized. Grim and sis we would like you to be Kyle and Brandon's god-parents."

Both of us look at them with shock written all over our faces. But, you can see that we're both honored as hell that they're trusting us to be god-parents to two of their children.

"I don't know what to say." I start. "But, I'm thankful that you trust us enough with your children to give us this."

"There's nothin' about trust sis. This is about you lovin' on our kids like you do and bein' there for whatever we need without a hesitation. There was never any question about it."

"For Reagan and Jameson, we've chosen Irish and Caydence to be their god-parents." Cage says.

"You for real?" Irish asks.

"Absolutely. You know you've been there when we needed you. Caydence has watched them more times than I can count the last little while. Reagan and Jameson love you both as much as the rest of us." Sky says.

"It's an honor guys." Caydence speaks up.

"Now, for Alana and Haley, we would be honored if Tank and Kenzie would be their god-parents." Sky says. "Tank, you've been there to help me so many times when I couldn't open up to anyone else. Kenzie, you've taken on a load of shit when I needed help and didn't want to ask for it. Instead you just bulldozed your way in and knew that I needed someone there to help."

"We'll do it!" Kenzie says for both of them, excitement lacing her voice.

As Sky and Cage made their announcements of their choices of god-parents, I start to feel extremely bad that I haven't been there for Sky and my family like I should have been. I know that I've been dealing with a lot of things, but that's no excuse. It should have been me that was there helping out with whatever Sky needed. Logan can feel me getting upset so he takes the baby from me and I make my way out of the room. I head in

223

the opposite direction of the waiting room until I find an empty room at the end of the hall. It must be a waiting room for if a mom has to have a C-section or something.

"What's goin' on Bay?" Cage asks, coming in behind me. "You looked happy and then all of a sudden that changed."

"I've failed you all Cage. I don't deserve to be Kyle and Brandon's godmother. Please, choose someone else."

"What the fuck you talkin' about? Of course you deserve it. How the fuck have you failed anyone?"

"I haven't been there for any of you. I've been so far in my own head and depression that I let you all do shit without any help from me."

"That don't mean you failed any one of us. You've been dealin' with some heavy shit babe. Not a single one of us blames you or got pissed because they had to step in to help anyone else. You need a break just as much as the rest of us, if not more."

"But it's my family and Caydence, Kenzie, and whoever else shouldn't have needed to step in for me."

"Babe, we're all a family. Like I said, you needed the break and you got it. If you feel the way you do, then you change it. If you're not ready, then you stay on break and take care of you. We're not goin' anywhere. Everyone will still be there when you're ready to join in again. But, you've done more than enough with helpin' with the kids and shit. More than a lot of other women would have done after goin' through the shit you've been dealin' with."

"I don't know if I'm ready Dec, but I'll try harder to be there for you guys. I promise you that. Maybe I can stay in the last bedroom to help you guys out for a while. Logan won't like it, but you guys are important too."

"If you *and* Logan wanna stay at the house, let us know and we'll get it ready for you guys. We're sure as fuck not gonna have a problem with it. But, you know he's not gonna let you out of his sight. Now, I'm gonna head back in there. You come back in when you're ready, yeah?"

"Thanks Dec. I'll be there in a minute. Let Logan know I'm good please?"

Dec nods his head to me and heads back to his family. I continue sitting there for a few more minutes composing myself before I head back in. Almost everyone has cleared out except for Ma and Pops, Tank, and Logan. The rest of them have either gone back to the waiting room or left the hospital all together. Not surprising since a lot of the guys don't like being in them. But for family, they'll show up.

Once I make my way back into Sky's room, I see that all of the guys are gone. The only one left in her room is Ma. She's getting her cuddles in with new babies. One of the things that make her life happier than I've ever seen her. If Pops could've given her a hundred kids, he would have. Now, she makes due with her grandbabies.

"Hey baby. You doing okay?" Ma asks me.

"Yeah. I just needed a minute by myself. But, since Sky and daddy know, I need to tell you something."

"What's the matter?"

"Nothing's wrong Ma. We just found out I'm pregnant. I'm scared as fuck and Logan's trying to help me through that. I have a doctor's appointment next week and we're going to make sure to talk to the doctor about all of my concerns. I'm also scheduling extra time with my counselor this week. I just wanted you to know. But, we're keeping it mum for right now. I don't want a lot of people knowing in case something happens."

My mom doesn't say anything to me for a long while. She stands there holding the baby, staring at me. Finally, she hands Sky her son and makes a beeline for me. Wrapping me firmly in her arms, she starts crying.

"Ma, it's okay. Why are you crying?" I ask confused. I thought she'd be happy about it.

"Baby, it's all good. These are happy tears. My only concern is everything you're going through right now. There's only so much that Logan and your counselor can do. The rest is all up to you."

"I know Ma. And I was real confused until I had a dream at your house. To me, it felt like I was replacin' Ryan. That's not something I ever want to do. But, I've talked to Logan, Gage, and Tank. They couldn't get through until I had my dream. It's gonna be okay."

"I don't understand. Who's Ryan? What dream?" Ma asks me, sitting down in a chair and pulling me with her to sit down next to her.

"Not the way I wanted to get into this. After I lost the baby, I kept having dreams that it was a boy. Gage and I decided to name him Ryan. Anyway, at your house, I had a dream that I was sitting with him. He told me he was good with me having more babies that I wouldn't ever forget him or the memory of what could have been with him. He said he's watching over all of us and protecting us. He's gonna make sure that nothing happens this time."

Ma and Skylar are both silent, and I can't look at either one of them. I don't want to see them looking at me like I'm crazy. It sounds weird and I know this. Logan and Gage are really the only two that know about the dreams and I really didn't want to share that shit with anyone else. But, I guess I don't have choice in the matter now.

"Please keep that shit to yourselves. I'm sure you guys think I'm crazy and I don't need everyone else to think that too." I say, still not picking my head up to look at them.

"Bay, I don't think you're crazy. When I was in the hospital after all that shit happened with Damon, I knew I was pregnant before I even woke up. I could hear little voices calling for their mama and when I went to find them, it was twins. I couldn't see what they were or anything like that. But, it was right after that I woke up.

226

Then the guys told me I was pregnant. When we had the ultrasound, it was twins. So, no, I don't think you're crazy. I fully believe that you dream of Ryan and that you're able to talk to him."

"Baby, I don't think you're crazy either. Even if I hadn't gone through what you went through, I would still believe you. But, I did go through it and I felt the same way about replacing that baby when we found out I was pregnant with you. I started having dreams and the baby telling me that it was okay I was gonna have another baby. They were fine with it and told me, same as you, that they would watch over us and make sure we were always protected. I haven't ever told that to anyone. Not even your daddy. So, I think you need to go with that and listen to what your baby is telling you."

"I'm really tryin' here Ma. But, I still have my doubts and I still can't help but feel like we're replacing him. It's so hard. I want to be happy with Logan about this baby, but I don't know what to do to make myself that way."

"You'll find it...." Ma starts.

Before she could get anymore out, I had to run to the bathroom to throw up. I was hoping it wasn't gonna happen, but I guess it's a good thing I just told Ma so she's not freaking out. Unfortunately, the guys choose this moment to walk back in the room. Since I shut the door, I was hoping that no one would hear me. But, since Logan came back in with them, he immediately made his way to the bathroom to rub my back and hold my hair back. I'm so glad that he remembered to shut the door since we weren't at the clubhouse, in our room, and alone.

"Crazy girl, I'm so sorry that you're goin' through this. If I could do somethin' to help you I would. I hate seein' you sick. Is it gonna get better soon?"

"I don't know. Sometimes women suffer the entire pregnancy with morning sickness. At times it's not bad, but other women also suffer really bad. I mean bad to the

227

point that they have to be admitted to the hospital. I don't know which way it's gonna go honestly."

"Well, when you feel up to it, we'll go back to the clubhouse and relax. Just us."

We waited for a few minutes to make sure that I wasn't gonna be sick again and then we left. Joker and Cage were looking at me trying to figure out what was going on when we were saying goodbye. I didn't have it in me to explain it to them that I was pregnant. They would find out when the rest of the extended family did. More people already knew then I wanted. So, I just want to relax until we can get to the doctor's office next week and talk to them. Even though there's gonna be a ton of shit to do in between then and now. There's work, counseling, baptism and party for Sky's kids. For now, I'm just worried about laying in Logan's arms and not thinking about anything.

Chapter Thirteen

A few days later

Grim

THE BABIES HAVE come home. We've stayed over in the guest room a few days and I've been amazed to see the way Joker, Cage, and Sky work together. Not a single one of the kids is left out of anything. Little Jameson is even more overprotective over all of the kids than he was when Alana and Haley came home. It's awesome to see him want to take care of all the kids and make sure that everyone's fine. So, the few times we haven't been able to find him, he's been in Kyle and Brandon's room sitting between the two cribs watching over the sleeping babies.

We've been through the baptism ceremony. Now we're back at Sky's house to get changed to go down to the pond for the party. Bailey and I are in the guest room to change and finish getting ready. All of a sudden she falls to the floor and starts crying her eyes out.

"Crazy girl, what's wrong?" I ask, sinking down to the floor to pull her in my lap.

"Logan, I'm so scared. We don't know how far along I am and I'm scared as fuck that I'm gonna lose this baby too. I can't go through that again and I don't want to disappoint you."

"Crazy girl, I've already told you that we'll get through it together if anythin' like that happens. Now, even if somethin' were to happen, I would not be disappointed at all. The only thing that I'll be concerned about is you. I know that you can't go through that shit again. You were broken when you lost Ryan. If it were to happen again, it would kill you. So, we're gonna take it a day at a time, keep you as relaxed as possible, and we're gonna talk to the doctor and follow everythin' she tells us to do."

Just as she goes to answer me, she jumps up and runs to the bathroom. Over the past few days her morning sickness is getting worse. I don't know if it's normal and I don't know who to ask about it. So, like I do every time, I go in and rub her back while holding her hair back from her face. Then I know we're gonna lie down for a little while because she doesn't feel like doing anything when she leaves the bathroom after getting sick. I pick her up and carry her into the guest room and we lay down on the bed over the covers. Even if she passes out, I know I won't so I just lay down and hold her until she wakes up.

After laying there a little while, I hear voices coming upstairs. From the sounds of it, I'm sure it's Joker and Cage. So, I slide out from under Bay and make sure she's still sleeping before I go to the door. There's no way in hell I'm gonna let anyone wake her up. She needs to rest so that for a little while she's not thinking about everything that can go wrong. It's not good for her and it can't be good for the baby.

"Hey guys. Why aren't you out with everyone?" I ask, shutting the door behind me and moving down the hallway a little.

"We were just comin' to find you guys. Didn't want Sky walkin' in if you were fuckin' my sister. Not that I really want to think about that either." Joker says.

"No. She got sick and now she's relaxin'. I was just layin' with her so she wouldn't be alone."

"She was sick at the hospital too. Is everythin' okay with her?" Cage asks.

"Yeah. She'll be fine. Crazy girl just needs to rest for a little while and we'll make our way down to the pond. Just make sure everyone knows so no one else comes up here."

"And you won't tell us what's goin' on?" Joker asks, concern etched on his face.

"Crazy girl doesn't want anyone to know yet. She'll let ya know when she's ready. For now, just trust that she'll be okay." I say looking at both of them. "I'll say I'm concerned that she's gettin' worse as far as bein' sick, but we'll deal with it."

"Alright. We'll let you get back to her and see you when you get down to the pond."

Cage and Joker head back outside and I go back in the spare room. Bailey is still sleeping but she's curled in a fetal position now. There's no way for me to get back in bed without disturbing her, so I settle in a chair in the corner and wait for her to wake up.

Bailey

I slowly stretch as I feel myself waking up. I'm expecting to feel Logan somewhere near me, but he's nowhere to be found. So, I slowly open my eyes and see him sitting in a corner chair. He's just looking to see what I'm going to do, if I'm going to rush to the bathroom to be sick again. But, thankfully, I don't feel like I'm going to again.

"Hey babe! What are you doing over there?" I ask.

"I got up so Cage and Joker wouldn't wake you up and you were layin' in a fetal position when I got back in here. Didn't wanna disturb you so I sat over here. You ready to get around to go to the pond?" He says. "Plus, Gage called. He's havin' some trouble at the strip club and wants to know if you can go there to help him out for a little while? I'm not crazy about the idea, but if you want to go, then I'm behind you."

"Yeah. I think I'm gonna take a quick shower. You gonna join? What kind of trouble is he having?"

"He can't keep a manager in there to save his life. They either steal, let the girls do what they want, try to pimp the girls out, or let them use drugs in the club. He wants you to go and get the paperwork straightened out and help him train a new manager. I think we need to talk though. Cage and Joker are really concerned about you. They wanna know what's goin' on, but I didn't tell them." Logan says, following me into the bathroom.

"I know we should let certain people know, but I don't know if I'm ready for that. Ma and Pops already know. Plus, the girls know since they were with me. But, if you feel like we need to let certain people know now, then I'm okay with it. By, the way, I'll go help him out. It shouldn't take me that long to get things back in order there."

"Thank you crazy girl. I'm not sayin' we gotta tell everyone right now. Just the people that are goin' to be watchin' you or hang out with you. I'm thinkin' like Blade, Rage, your brother, and Cage. Anyone else is up to you. Maybe now we should tell Crash and Trojan too. If you're gonna be there then they need to know."

"Okay. But that's it for right now. I don't want the whole world knowing."

"Now, let's get washed up so we can head out to join everyone."

After taking a shower, we get dressed so that we can make our way to the pond. The closer we get, the noisier it is. I can already hear the kids squealing and laughing in the water. There's music playing, and everyone seems to be having a good time. The sight that greets me when we get to the clearing is one that I love seeing. All of my family is gathered together to celebrate and have fun. There's no drama, no running off somewhere, and no one bitching at someone else over some stupid bullshit.

"There's my baby girl." Pops says, coming over to hug me.

"Hey daddy!"

"I was gettin' worried baby. Are you okay?" He asks.

"Yeah. I was sick a little while ago so I took a nap. I'll just hang out and stay as far away from the grill as I can."

"You do what you gotta do and we'll make sure you're taken care of. Sit and relax."

"I think I'm gonna get in the water for a little while. I want to play with the kids and try to get some sun." I say kissing Logan on the cheek and heading to the building to leave my dress and grab a towel.

Unfortunately, I can't get in the building and out with no one stopping me. Joker comes up and wraps his arms around me. After a minute, he pulls back and just looks at me trying to make sure that I'm okay.

"Levi, I'm fine. I'll explain what's going on later. I don't want a lot of people knowing right now. So, when people start to go home, I'll let those that need to know in on the secret."

"Are you sure? Do we need to get you to the hospital?" He asks me.

"No. I'm fine. You'll understand when I explain it later. Now, I wanna get in the water with the kids before they get out. I love you Levi!"

"Love you too sis."

Finally, I make my way into the pond and immediately go over to the kids with Sky, Cage, and Kenzie. Jameson is staying close, but he's kind of doing his own thing so I swim over to him.

"Hey buddy!" I say once I'm close to him.

"Auntie Bay!" He says, coming over and wrapping his little arms around me.

"You gonna swim with me?"

"Yeah. We race!"

"Okay."

Jameson tells me where we're racing to and then sets off across the pond. His little arms, covered in floaties, are going a hundred miles an hour trying to get across faster than me while I'm just casually swimming behind him. I make sure to stay close enough to him so that I can get to him if something happens, but that's it. As soon as he gets close to shore on the other side of the pond, Jameson starts yelling and hollering because he beat me. Everyone is laughing with him. I smile and pick him up swinging him around in celebration.

"Way to go buddy!" Logan says coming over to us. "You beat auntie Bailey!"

"Yeah! It was awesome!" Jameson says, a huge grin on his little face.

We all swim for a little while until the food is done cooking. I take Jameson and Reagan over to fix their plates while Cage, Joker, and Sky are taking care of the other four kids. When we get their plates done, I lead them over to sit with Ma and Pops before sitting down myself. Logan follows behind us and hands me a plate loaded up with food. Sitting down, I smile up at him because he knows it's way too much food for me to eat. On a normal day, I wouldn't eat this much. Now that I'm pregnant, I don't eat all that much. Instead I eat smaller meals, but more per day. It's the only way that I can keep stuff down without getting sick. That would kind of defeat the purpose.

Once I'm done eating, I hand my plate over to Logan and get up. I see Sky has the boys in their car seats, so I walk over and peak down at them. One of the boys, I'm pretty sure it's Kyle, is just kind of laying there, not sleeping. So, I pick him up and make my way back over to my seat. Sky and her men watch me but don't say a single word. At this point, I think they're just happy that I'm willing to spend time with any of the kids.

Ma

As we're all sitting around in different areas of the pond, I watch my baby girl get up and make her way over to Sky and the boys. She doesn't say anything to anyone though. I wonder what she's up to. It's not like her to not say anything to anyone these days.

Bailey has made so much progress since starting to see her counselor. I'm more amazed every day at the things she's getting back into doing. Now, I hope that she can make it through this pregnancy without losing more of herself. Or having it set her back to a shell of her former self again.

To my surprise, I see her pick one of the baby boys up out of his car seat and make her way back over to her chair by Logan. This is kind of a shock since she hasn't really gone out of her way to hold any of the kids. I mean if she's helping Sky out, she'll hold the babies, Alana, or Haley. But not just out of the blue on her own like she just did. I can only hope that means that she's doing better than we thought she was.

Logan goes over to take care of their trash and Tank stops him to talk for a few minutes. That doesn't mean that his eyes are ever off of my baby girl for long though. He's constantly looking over at her with soft eyes and a dreamy look on his face. I'm guessing that he's thinking of what Bay will be like with their own baby in her arms.

"Would you look at that Ma?" Pops asks, coming up and wrapping his arm around me.

"She looks so peaceful and content right now. It's like she's in her own little world holding that baby."

"It's a look that looks good on her. I'm guessin' she told you the news?"

"Yeah. In the hospital room shortly before she and Logan left. I hope that she decides to let other people know soon. I don't think it's safe for certain people that are going to be around her not to know."

"I agree with you. But, it's their decision. We can't force them to do what we want. It doesn't matter how much you meddle Ma, they need to do what they feel is best."

I don't say anything back to Pops. So, I just lean into him and watch Logan and my baby girl. She's going to be such a good mom. I just hope she can get over her loss in order to embrace motherhood. Just like I know Logan is going to be an amazing father. He has so much love to give and I know Bailey and this baby are going to make him realize that fact sooner rather than later. If he hasn't already realized it.

Bailey

It's been a fun day. I haven't been sick since earlier this afternoon, thank God. For most of the day I've been in a lounge chair holding Kyle and relaxing. I've noticed Ma and Pops watching me and trying not to let on that they're doing it. Until I see them watching Logan. Looking out of the corner of my eye, I see him watching me with Kyle. He's got this soft look in his eyes and his entire face is relaxed. It's not Logan with the weight of running the club and various businesses on his shoulders. This is a man that's relaxed, spending the day with his family, and imagining me with our baby. God, I love him looking relaxed and peaceful! I hope I can see that look every day for the rest of our lives.

"Crazy girl, you still gonna make that announcement tonight?" Logan asks me, sitting on the side of my lounge chair.

"Yeah. I think it's important that the people that are going to be spending time with me know. When some of these bodies clear out and it's just the important ones left, I'll let them know."

"I love you Bay. I can't wait to see you holdin' our baby in your arms." He says leaning over to kiss me.

"I know babe. We'll find out next week how much longer you gotta wait to see that happen."

"I'm gonna go help the guys get things set up for the bon-fire to be lit. Jameson wants to go gather more wood and find sticks to roast the marshmallows Ma brought."

"I'm fine here. You go do men things and I'll watch that ass!" I say, wiggling my eyebrows at him.

"You're perfect! You know that right? Cause I think I'm supposed to be the one tellin' you that I'm gonna watch your ass."

"I'm sittin' on my ass so you can't say that. So, I figured I'd watch your ass instead."

Logan laughs as he walks away. True to my word, I watch his ass. Once he's made it a fair distance away, I see him turn his head to look back at me before shaking his ass. I can't help but start to laugh my ass off. In the process I manage to wake Kyle up. So I get up and make my way over to Skylar with him so that she can feed him before he wakes his brother up.

Without having the baby, I make my way over to where the bon-fire is going to be so that I can get a seat before everyone else makes their way over. I'm sitting on the opposite side of the fire so that I can watch everyone. Yes, I'm sitting alone and away from all the activity but I'm not doing it because I'm pulling away from them. I'm watching my family interact with one another. It amazes me every day that I get to be a part of this world and have all these people as my family. Just because they aren't blood doesn't mean they are any less important to me. I would give my life for each and every one of them.

"Hey sweetheart!" Pops says walking up to sit with me. "What are ya doin' over here alone?"

"I'm just watching everyone. Kind of reflecting on everything that I have in my life, and what I almost lost when I went on that downward spiral."

"Baby girl, you are so much stronger than you realize. It's still gonna take some time, but you will learn to breathe again. Grim, us, and everyone here will help you. But, I have to say that I enjoyed watchin' you holdin' that baby earlier. Hell, a few weeks ago, you wouldn't have been in the same room as him. Now, you're walkin' up and just takin' him away from his mama. Which is a bold move in itself!"

I can't help but laugh. He's absolutely right. Between Sky, Levi, and Dec no one gets close to those kids. But I just walk up and steal a baby away from Sky without anyone batting an eyelash. I think they know that I needed it today. Today I needed to be able to hold my nephew and not have any interruptions and just be.

"Daddy, do you think I'm gonna be okay with my own baby? That when Logan's not home, I'll be able to handle it with no help?"

"Baby, I know without a shadow of a doubt that you'll make an excellent mother. You give so much of yourself to everyone around you without thinkin' twice about what you have to do, or what you want to do, that I know this baby is goin' to be loved more than any other baby in this world. It's goin' to be rough and there are gonna be days you wanna rip your hair out, but you'll be more than fine. Those are the days that you'll give more of yourself and that will be more rewardin' because they are the hardest. Besides, you're never gonna be alone. I know Ma isn't gonna be able to get enough and she's gonna drive you bat shit crazy with the attention."

"But that's the thing daddy. I don't wanna have to depend on Ma helping me. I want to be able to make it through those rough days on my own."

"And you will baby. But, you also have an entire family to help you when you need a break. Even if it's just to go for a walk alone or take a bubble bath. All you're gonna have to do is make a call and you'll have any one of us there for you."

"Thank you daddy. Now, I want a hug. I miss my hugs from you." I say standing up.

"Anytime you need a hug baby, just give me one. You'll always be my little girl and I'll always do anythin' I can to help you. Even if it's just a hug."

I wrap my arms around my dad's middle and close my eyes. Immediately I'm transported back to being a little girl when one of his hugs could heal any pain I had. Knowing that without a doubt my dad loved me and would support me no matter what. Other than starting my own club. But that's a topic for another day.

"Looks like they're gettin' ready to start the fire." My dad says, letting go to sit back down. "People are leavin' too."

"That's good. I'm telling the people that need to know about the baby tonight. Logan and I talked and we decided that the ones that are gonna be around me the most need to know the situation in case anything happens."

"That's a good idea. I don't want anythin' to happen because someone didn't know. Ma and I were just talkin' about that earlier."

I smile at my dad and wait for everyone to gather around the fire. After the kids have their s'mores made and settle down a little, I'm going to let everyone know. With Logan at my side, I know that we'll make it through this. No matter what happens, I was being ridiculous thinking that he would leave me if anything happened to the baby. We'll be grief stricken, but we'll make it through it together and with the help of our family.

"Everythin' okay crazy girl?" Logan asks, pulling me up from my chair to sit down.

"Yeah. Just thinking about everything and talking with my dad. Once the kids settle down, I'll let everyone know."

"Okay. I'm right here and I'm not goin' anywhere."

"I know. I want to apologize for thinking that you would leave if something happens with this baby. My emotions are all over the place at times and I take it out on you. I'm sorry."

"There's nothin' to be sorry for. I know you're still dealin' with everythin', just don't shut me out."

"I won't."

"Auntie Bay! Auntie Bay!" Jameson yells, running up behind us.

"What sweetheart?"

"I need your help with the smarshmallow. Daddy was helping and it's in the fire now."

Jameson's face is crumpled up in annoyance that his dad lost his marshmallow in the fire and I can't help but laugh. He tries to be so grown up and wants to do everything his own way already. Hearing me laugh, he stomps his foot.

"Not funny Auntie Bay."

"I'm sorry honey. How did your dad manage to let it fall?"

"He's trying to help Reagan too."

"I see. Well then, let's go roast you some smarshmallows." I say, getting up to help him.

As soon as we make our way to the bag of marshmallows, I look at Levi. He shrugs his shoulders at me and turns back to help Reagan with her marshmallow. Dec is helping the girls next to him trying to hide his laughter and failing miserably at it. Turning my attention back to Jameson, I listen as he explains to me what we have to do. This kid is too funny. But, I listen to him like I've never roasted marshmallows before and we successfully make his s'mores so he can sit by his parents and munch away.

"Guys, I need to tell you something." I say to everyone once I take my place back on Logan's lap.

Everyone stops talking and looks at me. I turn my attention to Levi because I know he's been worried as hell about me. So, tonight I'm going to set his mind at ease. At least that's what I hope I'm going to accomplish.

"Levi, I know that you've been worried about me. There's nothing wrong with me. The only reason I've been sick is because I'm pregnant."

Levi stands up after setting Reagan on the ground next to Dec and comes over to me. He pulls me up off Logan's lap and pulls me in for a big hug. I can feel the tension ease from him and I feel bad that he's been that worried and I didn't tell him sooner.

"I'm sorry brother. If I'd known that you were that worried I would have told you sooner." I say burying my head in his chest.

"Are you okay with this sis?" He asks me, pulling back to look me in the eyes.

"I'm getting there. It's still a bit of a struggle, but I'm gonna be okay."

"Then I'm happy for you guys." Levi says letting me go back to Logan. "I'm gonna be an uncle!"

We all start laughing and celebrating the news. All the guys give me a hug and the girls move closer to me. Logan gets his turn with the man hugs and kisses from the girls on his cheek. I can tell by the looks on their faces that they're relieved that we decided to announce this tonight. Not a single one of us wants to keep anything away from one another, but they were respecting my wishes and keeping it to themselves. I couldn't love this group of people more.

For the next hour or so we all sit around talking and laughing. The kids are slowly falling asleep. So, we all decide to help Rage, Sky, Levi, and Dec take them up to the house before we all leave. Logan and Pops stay and put the fire out before heading up to the house. Today was definitely a good day.

Chapter Fourteen

Bailey

FINALLY, THE DAY has arrived that we go to the doctors. I'm so nervous because I don't want to get bad news. At the same time, I'm so excited to find out how far along I am. Plus, I really want to talk to Doctor Bell before I go see my counselor again. That way we can talk about the information that she gives me.

Last week I went to counseling and we had a long talk about me feeling like I was replacing Ryan. She completely understood where I was coming from and told me she felt the same way that I do. For the most part, I'm trying to let it go and think that we're adding to our family instead of replacing him. The most important thing that we talked about though was the fact that I'm worried about how I'm going to be once the baby is born. Some days I'm so nervous that I'm going to sleep through him or her waking up, not be able to calm them down when they're upset, or that I'm going to lose my mind if I don't know what to do in situations. She reassured me that most new mothers have the same worries. It's not just women that have lost a child that feel the way that I do. That actually was a relief to know that this is actually a common feeling.

"Crazy girl, you about ready to head out?" Logan asks me coming into the bedroom.

"Yeah. I just have to get my purse and I'll be ready. Are we takin' the truck?"

"Yeah. I think we need to add ridin' on the bike to our list of questions. I'm completely against you ridin' on the bike, but I know you love it. If it were up to me, we'd take a cage everywhere we go."

"I know. And I'm beginning to think that's the best way to go. I don't want anything to happen."

"Alright. Let's roll!"

We make our way to his truck and head into town. Once we're in the office I get the necessary paperwork and we begin to fill it out. Logan lets me do it and just tells me what I need to write for his side. He does enough paperwork and I don't mind filling the whole thing out. Shortly after we're done with it, I get called in by a nurse and she leads me through everything I need to do before going into a room. Logan is by my side the entire time.

"Doctor Bell will be in shortly. I know that she's planning on having an ultrasound tech come in too. She wants to make sure that you're completely relaxed and she thinks you seeing the baby will help make that happen." The nurse says before leaving the room.

I strip down and take a seat on the exam table. Unlike Gage, Logan pulls his chair right up next to the table and reaches for my hand. I'm glad that he's choosing to sit next to me instead of on the other side of the room. He has the ability to relax me and take away some of my anxiety. Just as I feel some of the tension release from my shoulders, there's a soft knock on the door before Doctor Bell comes in.

"It's so good to see you Bailey." She says, coming right over to me.

"You too doc. Logan, this is Doctor Bell. Doc, this is the baby daddy." I introduce them trying to bring some humor into the room.

They both start laughing at me as they shake hands. "It's good to meet you doc." Logan says.

"Same to you. Alright, let's get this show on the road. I see on your paperwork that you're not sure when your last period was."

"No. I never did get right after the miscarriage. I could go a month or so with nothing. So, I'm not sure."

"That's fine. How have you been doing since that happened?"

"It was really rough for a while. But, I'm seeing a counselor now and my family has been wonderful. It's just since finding out about being pregnant again, things have surfaced that I'm trying really hard to deal with. We have some things we want to talk to you about though."

"Good. Let's do the exam and we'll talk while we wait for the ultrasound tech to get in here. How does that sound?"

"That sounds good."

Doctor Bell does what she has to do and then she pulls out a stool so that we can talk.

"Okay. What is the thing that concerns you the most about being pregnant again Bailey?"

"That I'm going to have another miscarriage." I answer immediately.

"That's really normal. But, I honestly don't think that you have anything to worry about. The most important thing is that you keep your stress level down and not hold things in. It's very important for you to talk things out."

"I've been trying to open up more and more. Mainly though, it's been with the counselor I'm seeing. Logan found me a good one. She's actually suffered through a miscarriage and went on to have children afterwards."

"Logan that was a really good move to make." Doctor Bell says. "It's important that Bailey has someone to talk to that's actually suffered through what she has. Is there anything that you're concerned about?"

"Thank you." He says. "My main concern is not knowin' how to help her. I mean she's the one goin' through everythin'. Plus, I don't like that it seems her mornin' sickness is gettin' worse."

"Unfortunately morning sickness is a part of the process. If it gets to the point that you can't keep anything down though, I need you to call me. Then we'll have to figure out something to make sure that you can keep things in. Logan, the most important thing you can do is just be there for her. At this point, there's not going to be much for you to do. So, if you see her getting stressed out, find something to help her relax and get out of whatever situation she's in that's stressing her out."

"I can do that."

"Alright. The ultrasound tech should be here soon. Bailey, make sure you stay relaxed, take your vitamins, and rest when you get tired. Don't push yourself! I also want you to call me if you think anything at all doesn't seem right. We'll bring you right in and see what's going on. It doesn't matter to me if you're here every day."

"Thank you Doctor Bell. I really appreciate it!"

"You're welcome. I'll see you again in a month."

We tell her goodbye and sit back to wait for the ultrasound tech to come in. Logan continues to hold my hand while watching me closely. I know that he thinks I'm still hiding how I'm feeling from him, but I'm not. I'm actually getting used to the idea that we're bringing a new baby into the world. Which is actually helping me relax and not stress about replacing Ryan or failing as a mom. But, that could change any day. I feel like my emotions are all over the place and that it's only going to get worse before it gets better.

Grim

I think that the doctor helped reassure us that things weren't going to go wrong with this pregnancy. All that matters to me though is that Bailey feels the same way. She needs to relax and I'm going to do whatever I have to in order to ensure that happens.

"How are you feelin' crazy girl? Did doc help reassure you at all?"

"Yeah, I think she did. I don't think I have to worry about having a miscarriage as much as I have been. But, it's always going to be on my mind. You know that."

"Yeah, crazy girl I do. But, we'll get through it and come out on the other side stronger and parents to an amazin' little person."

"I love you so much." Bailey says with tears in her eyes. For once I'm pretty sure they're happy tears.

Before I can respond there's a knock on the door. Turning I see a lady in scrubs push in a machine. I don't know what this is all supposed to do, but if my girl feels even a little bit better about seeing the baby then I'm all for it.

The technician goes over some technical things that I don't understand at all. Bailey seems to know what she's talking about with words like internal and things. *What the fuck does that mean?* As I sit here and watch what's going on, I see her pull some sort of wand looking thing out. I don't think I want to know what that's all about.

"Alright. Let's see what we can see and hear. Are you guys ready?"

"Yes." Bailey says.

In the next instant I see the tech put a condom on the wand looking thing, add some lube or something like that to it, and then start to insert it in Bailey. *What the fuck?* I look over at Bailey and she squeezes my hand.

"Babe, they don't know how far along I am. This ensures that we'll be able to see what's going on. It's okay."

"If you say so. I'm not likin' things bein' shoved up you though."

"Calm down caveman!"

As I'm thinking of a response to that, I hear this sound fill the little room. Quickly I look over at my girl to see a huge smile lighting up her face.

"This is the heartbeat you're hearing dad. It sounds strong."

What? We can actually hear our baby's heartbeat? That's the best thing I've ever heard in my life. Bailey is so happy that she has tears streaming down her face. Now I know she's crying happy tears.

"Alright. Let's see how far along you are now."

While she's doing whatever it is she's doing, I'm looking at the screen trying to figure out what the hell I'm looking at. Whatever it is looks nothing like a baby to me. It's weird. Bailey's entranced by whatever she sees on the screen. That's good enough for me. If she's convinced that's a baby, then I'm all for it.

"I'm gonna say that you're around nine weeks pregnant." She says looking at us. "I'm done now, so I'll take a few pictures and you guys can be on your way."

"Thank you." Bailey says still lying on the table.

After a few minutes the technician hands me a few pictures and leaves the room. Bailey sits up and gets off the bed so she can get dressed again. I remain sitting looking at the pictures she handed me. No matter how long I look at these I know that I'm not gonna see a baby here. Maybe the next time I will.

"Let's go make my next appointment and get out of here." Bailey says pulling me out of my daze.

"Okay crazy girl."

We head out to the window at reception and she waits until the lady opens the window. As Bailey's talking to her, I pull out my phone and see that Tank, Cage, and Joker have been blowing my phone up. They knew we were coming here today so I don't know why the hell they're trying to get a hold of me so bad.

"Crazy girl, I don't know what's goin' on but I think we need to get to the clubhouse. The guys have been blowin' my phone up while we were in there."

"Okay babe."

Bailey grabs her appointment card and we head out. Now I'm really curious as to what the hell's going on. Things have been really quiet lately, and we've all been waiting for things to blow up in our faces since the fire at Spinners. Maybe it has something to do with that. It's a good thing that it won't take us long to get back to the clubhouse.

Chapter Fifteen

Grim

AS SOON AS we pull up to the clubhouse, I see a lot of bikes that do not belong here. I wonder who the fuck it is. I help Bailey out of the truck and we make our way inside. She's holding onto me as I fling open the door, ready to smash some heads together. Once we're inside, I see a bunch of guys from the Soulless Bastards sitting around the common room. They look like they don't have a care in the world, drinking our alcohol and relaxing in our house. My guys are all standing around the room. You can see the tension in their bodies from across the room.

"Crazy girl, I need you to get to the game room. If you find any women wandering around on your way, take them with you." I tell her before kissing her forehead.

"Okay baby."

I stand in my spot until I see Bailey disappear down the hallway leading towards the game room. Then I make my way over to Bull, who's sitting at the bar trying to laugh and talk with Tank. Yeah, that's not gonna fucking happen. Tank looks like he's ready to rip Bull's head off and laugh while he's doing it.

"I don't know why the fuck you think you can walk into our house with no warnin', but I'm glad you're here. You can tell me which of these motherfuckers helped torch Spinners. I want him and I fuckin' want him now!" I yell, getting right up in his face.

"Relax. I've already delivered that piece of shit to your boys. I don't know where they took him, but he's in your custody. The rest of us had nothin' to do with that shit."

"I don't buy that for a second. Tank, what do you have to say about that?"

"We got him Pres. He's where he belongs right now. Blade is standin' guard with Rage."

I look over my shoulder to see the rest of my guys nodding their heads. Cage and Joker look like they can't wait to get their hands on the fucker that cost us everything with that garage. Turning back to Bull, I crack my neck trying to relax a little bit. And to think today started out so good with the doctor's appointment.

"Then what the fuck do you want Bull?" I ask, grabbing the beer that Slim Jim set on the bar for me.

"We had some local guys come to us recently. They want us to run the Kings out of Clifton Falls for good."

"Okay. So, why are you here tellin' us? I would think you'd be down to help them."

"Cause I want nothin' to do with it. My guys and I are happy where we're at. We don't want nothin' here."

"Yeah? Where ya been hidin'?"

I can see some of the Soulless Bastards tensing up. Looks like they're ready for a fight. But, I know my guys will rip them to shreds. No one comes in our house and treats us with disrespect. And as far as we all knew, they were heading back to wherever the hell they came from when the deal over Sky was done. Apparently that's not what went down though. It's not like we didn't know that though.

"We've been a few counties over on the opposite side of the Phantoms and your other chapter. We're lookin' at settin' up shop over there. Just tryin' to get a feel for the town and shit."

"Is that right? Well, it's the first I've heard of it. And I know that Slim and Gage know nothin' about you stayin' around this area."

"We're not sure what we're doin' yet, so we didn't make any calls." Bull says, getting pissed at me calling him out on that shit.

"It doesn't matter. You know that you need to let any local clubs know that you're even thinkin' that shit. Hell, it's disrespectful that you didn't at least let us know you were gonna be that close and you fuckin' know it.

Now, thanks for the heads up about the locals, but I think it's time you fuckin' get your guys and get the fuck off my property. Now!" I yell, letting him know that I'm tired of looking at him and his so-called club.

"Yeah. We're out. Have fun takin' out the trash too. You're welcome by the way. Where's that little thing I was supposed to take with us the last time? I haven't seen her around here."

I don't even bother responding to that. Looking over, I can see a bunch of brothers surrounding Cage, Joker, and Pops so they don't lose their heads. He knows that he's being disrespectful and that he's worn out his welcome with us. Looking around, I know my guys are itching for a fight. They've been wanting to get their hands on these fuckers since the shit went down with them demanding we hand Sky over to them. These fuckers would have broken her and not thought twice about it. That's just the type of club they are. Women mean absolutely nothing to them.

"Church. Now!" I call out to my guys. "Slim Jim, I want you to make sure that the women stay where they are and don't come out. We don't know where these guys are going or what their next step is gonna be."

"Yeah Pres." He says, coming from behind the bar.

As the guys all pile into the room for church, I debate going to see Bailey. I know she's gonna be worried and wondering what the fuck is going on. But right now I think it's more important to try to think of a way to let the community know that we're not going anywhere. It's not our intention to bring trouble to Clifton Falls. We want to be here and there are ways that we can make sure that they know we're willing to help this community out. It might be a close-knit farm town, but there are still people in need.

Walking into church, I take my seat and call it to order. "Alright guys. I think we need to come up with ways to let everyone in town know that we're here to stay and that we have no problem helpin' locals out with what they need. Let's hear some ideas about how to achieve that shit."

"I know the Phantoms have toy drives." Glock speaks up. "I mean they have a center that helps out kids in the foster care system and that's where the toys and shit go."

"I know another club farther south also helps out members of the community with anythin' they need. I mean if someone needs a roof and can't afford it, they do it for free. Someone needs groceries, a ride to appointments and shit, anythin' at all like that, they provide the means for people to have what they need." Irish pipes up.

"That all sounds great. But we don't have a center like the Phantoms do." I say.

"Well, why can't we build one and run it?" Pops asks. "I know that Ma, Bailey, and Sky would love somethin' like that."

"I don't have a problem doin' that. All in favor?" I ask.

I hear 'yay' all around the table. Slamming the gavel down, I announce that it's passed. Rage is going to have his hands full with projects around here I'm guessing. It'll be good for him though. He likes to work and he'll do an awesome job with the work he does. He's not one to allow his crew to cut corners and do a shit job on any project they take on.

"Alright. We can also work on settin' up a toy drive if no one opposes the idea. But, I want somethin' to raise money for the town now."

"Why don't we do a carnival? We can either do it here at the clubhouse or look into renting somewhere to put it on." Cage throws his idea out.

"What do you think we'd have at it?" I ask.

"We can do games and rides, raffles, a bike show, demolition derby. Hell, we can even put a concert on." Joker says, getting excited about the idea.

"That sounds good. All in favor of havin' the carnival and a toy drive?"

Once again, I hear 'yay' all around the table. I think that we've made some progress today. Now, we just have to work out the details of everything to make sure that it's successful. Plus, we need to look into things in town to determine where the proceeds can go and do the most good. Hopefully, this is going to help us get in the good graces of the town and show them that we're not a bad bunch of guys. They just need to get to know us and not run scared because they don't know anything about us and what we stand for. Now I think it's time to pay our little friend in the basement a visit.

"Guys, let's go have some fun! Everyone down to the basement." I say standing up.

We all make our way down to the basement and I see Blade and Rage standing against the wall on either side of the door where the bastard that helped blow Spinners up is locked in. They're not talking or anything. I think they're having too much fun listening to him whine and beg to be let out. I look at Rage and tell him that we need to talk later and then we head in the room.

"So, you're the fucker that burned our garage down?" I ask him.

"No, I swear it wasn't me!" He says. "Please, let me go and I'll tell you everythin' I know about the Soulless Bastards!"

"I don't know. Guys, do you believe him?"

After hearing a chorus of no's, I turn into him throwing my fist in his face. He crumples to the floor. I immediately proceed to kick him in the ribs a few times before I squat down and get in his face.

"I'm sure that you're the one that helped that other guy torch our garage. Now, I'm not sure why you did it, or what you gained out of it. I don't really give a fuck. My guys are gonna spend some quality time with you though. So, please feel free to spill your guts while you still can."

Standing up, I make my way over to lean against the wall. Joker and Cage make their way over to the guy on the floor. Cage pulls him up and rips his cut off him and throws it to the ground. He holds him while Joker gets some shots in on him. Next, Joker takes Cage's place so that he can take his shots in.

"You asshole! Not only did you torch our garage, you torched customer's property, and destroyed our custom bikes for a show comin' up. That's our work and time that we spent away from our family. Our kids didn't get to see as much of us because of those builds and our work. You destroyed everythin' and for what? A few dollars in your pocket."

Cage doesn't let him answer. He immediately lands a punch to his nose and I can hear the bones breaking from across the room. I know that he's nowhere near done with this ass though. Cage continues to pound the guy until he's breathing heavy. Then he steps back to allow someone else to do their damage to him. Tank is the next to step up. He doesn't hesitate to go to town on the guy, who's now laying on the floor. One by one the guys all take their turn. The last one to go is Irish. We usually save him for last because he lives for this shit. Irish is our go to guy when dealing with motherfuckers that want to cross us.

"I'm gonna head out guys." I say looking around. "Irish, do your worst and deal with it when you're done. Or have Slim Jim and Blade deal with him. But, I want one of you to go with them."

Everyone nods their head as I leave the room. I've watched enough and I don't need to see anymore. All I want is to go have a beer and think about something else. Like getting my hands on the other dumbass that decided to cross us.

Bailey

As I make my way into the game room, I see that everyone that's usually here is already in here. One of the other guys must have already told them to come in here. There's one girl in here that I've never seen before though. Looking at her you can tell that she's pregnant. So, I make my way over to her to see who the hell she is.

"Hey!" I say walking up. "I haven't seen you around here before."

"I was here about eight months ago. My name's Vicky."

"Oh. You were only here one time or something?"

"Yeah. Well, I spent a weekend here before I left. I didn't want to be in the way of whatever was goin' on with the baby daddy."

"What do you mean? Who's the baby's dad?" I ask her thoroughly confused as to what the fuck she's talking about.

"The President, Grim." She says, looking me in the eyes.

All of a sudden it feels like my world is collapsing. I know that we weren't together at that point in time. But, he's going to have two babies running around. One just sooner than ours. After excusing myself, I make my way out to the tree and sit. I know that I'm crying because I can feel tears running down my face. Inside though is another story. I feel numb.

I know that I need to give him space to get to know this woman and let her in so he can be a part of his baby's life. But, this is my home and I'm not going anywhere. Well, I will be for a few weeks or so to help Gage out. He called a few days ago and asked if I could go help out at the strip club. The guys don't have time to manage it and the girl they had doing it left one night and they haven't heard from her since. So, they need someone in there to help until he can hire someone. This will be the perfect time for Logan to do what he needs to do and figure things out without me in the way.

Knowing that I have a solid plan in my head, I head back inside and directly up to our room to wait for him to show up after he handles business. In the meantime, I'll pack my bags and get ready to go. I know I'm not leaving until tomorrow or the day after, but I want to be ready to go.

With nothing to do now but wait, I decide to lay down and take a little nap. All of a sudden I'm exhausted beyond belief.

Grim

After talking with the guys in church, the only thing I want to do is find Bailey and relax. We were going to go veg out in the room and watch movies or something, but I'm thinking we need to take a ride now. Cage and Joker have told me about where they take Skylar to the waterfalls and I'm thinking that we need to go there for a while. Some peace and quiet is needed right now.

As soon as I walk out of the meeting room, I'm met with some woman that I've never seen before. She sidles up to me and tries rubbing herself against my chest. I stop dead in my tracks and push her away. Since I can see that she's pregnant, I make sure that I hang on to her arm so she doesn't fall or get hurt in any other way.

"I don't know who you think you are, but you can back the fuck off right now." I growl out.

"You don't remember me?" She asks, trying to push up on me again.

"No, I don't. You obviously got a man somewhere, so go find him."

"The baby is yours Grim. I was here about eight months ago for a weekend. One we spent in your bed."

"What's your name?" I ask her, trying to rack my brain for any memory of her and searching for Bailey at the same time.

"Vicky." Is her only response. "We need to talk about the baby."

"Go sit at a table over there and I'll be right there." I say going in search of Bailey. I hope to hell she hasn't seen this woman claiming to have my baby growing in her.

She's not in the common room or the kitchen, so I open the back door to see if she's at her tree. Nope. Maybe she went to lay down. So, I make my way to our room and I find her sitting on the bed surrounded by her luggage. Tomorrow is the day that she's most likely leaving so it makes sense she's packing some things up.

"Hey crazy girl." I say, moving over to sit by her on the bed. "Are you takin' enough stuff with you?"

"Well, we don't know how long I'll be gone. So, I don't know how much crap I'll need."

She still has yet to look at me, so I gently cup her chin and tilt her head up so I can look her in the eyes. "I take it you talked to that woman?"

"Yeah. I saw her in the game room and talked to her. So, I guess you have some things to talk about with her and figure out."

"I guess so. I don't remember her at all Bay. She's waitin' downstairs for me now so we can talk. But, I had to find you first. What's goin' through your mind crazy girl?"

"I'm thinking that it's a good thing that I'm going to Gage's clubhouse for a while. That way you guys can figure out things without trying to take my feelings into consideration. You have to think of that baby and only that baby Logan."

"I know I have to think about that baby. But, I also have to think of you and our baby too. Some way I'll figure somethin' out. You and our little peanut won't be left out at all. I don't have to have anythin' to do with this woman, other than conversations about the baby. If it's even mine!" I say, standing up and running my hands through my hair.

"You use the time I'm away to get to know her, figure things out, see what you both want and need. I'll be back when I'm done with the job."

"I don't want you to go at all. I didn't before this shit, and now I really don't."

"I said I would go and I'm not gonna back out now Logan. It's a job, the guys will be there to make sure nothing happens to the baby, I'll have Dr. Bell recommend a good doctor closer there in case I need to go to one, and when I find a new manager I'll come home to you."

"I love you so much crazy girl." I say kneeling in front of her and grabbing her hands in mine.

"I love you too. Now, go out and talk to her. See what she has to say."

The last thing I want to do right now is go talk to some bitch that says she's having my kid, but I know I have to find out what's going on. So, I make my way back out to the common room so that I can get this over with and spend the rest of the night wrapped around Bailey. Vicky is sitting at a table in the corner, alone, with the rest of the guys trying to figure out what's going on. Before I make my way over to her, I stop at the bar and Blade hands me a beer. I don't pay attention to anyone else as I weave through the tables to get to her.

"So, Vicky, how am I supposed to believe that this baby is mine?" I start out.

"Well, I understand that you don't believe me. I'd think there was something wrong with you if you did believe me right away. I was here for a party with one of my friends that usually comes out for them. We were drinking pretty heavily and ended up fucking all over the clubhouse. Like I said, we really didn't leave your bed once we got in it until the weekend was over. Apparently at least one of those times there wasn't a condom used."

"Why did it take you this long to come tell me? I mean I don't even know how far along you are." I say, staring at her stomach.

"I honestly didn't know if I was going to keep the baby. Then it got to the point that I couldn't terminate the pregnancy and so I started debating even telling you about her. Now, I just figured that you have the right to know that you're gonna have a daughter."

"What do you really want? This sounds really fuckin' suspicious to me." I ask, getting more pissed.

"I don't want anything. Like I said, I thought you should know and decide what you wanna do." She says, batting her eye lashes at me with a little pout on her lips.

"Well, if I'm the dad, then I'm gonna be there for my kid. If not, then you're gonna go through hell for bringin' shit to my door. Where the fuck are you stayin'?"

"Well, I just got in town, so I'm staying at the hotel coming into town."

"Let me guess, no long term plans either."

"Nope. I'm gonna be looking for a job and apartment today. I don't know who will hire someone about to pop out a kid, but I'll find something."

"I need time to wrap my head around this clusterfuck. You can get your shit and I'll have a prospect find you a room here for now."

After saying my peace, I grab Rage and Blade and tell them to follow her to the hotel. I want to know if she's meeting anyone there and if this is legit. There were a few nights I got drunk enough to black out, but something about this doesn't ring true to me. Not with the Soulless Bastards showing up here earlier. They head out to the cage, so that they can make her believe they're there to help her out if she needs it. Before I head back to Bailey, I have one more call to make so that I can make sure everything is ready for tomorrow. Bailey leaving is the last thing I want right now, but maybe she's right. I need to know what the hell is going on and figure out if this kid is mine. Now, I have to get to know this bitch in case we have to have some sort of co-parenting relationship for the kid.

"Gage, what's goin' on?" I ask when he answers the phone.

"Not much man. I'm happy as hell Bailey's comin' to help figure this clusterfuck out. These girls are about on my last damn nerve and I'm ready to fire all their asses and close shop. I don't have time for this."

"You got somethin' else goin' on I don't know about?" I ask, hoping there's nothing else landing in our laps right now.

"No, just runnin' everythin' and tryin' to stay on top of what's goin' on at the strip club. Davina really screwed everythin' up before she left."

"Who's comin' to follow crazy girl back there?"

"Crash, Trojan, and Shadow. You need more? Cause they already pulled out."

"No. There's some shit goin' on here now and I'm glad those three are the ones comin' to get her."

"What's wrong?"

"Some chick showed up today, after the Soulless Bastards made an appearance, claimin' she's havin' my kid in about a month or so."

"Fuck!" Gage starts out. "How's Bailey dealin' with it?"

"I don't know. She says her leavin' to help you out is good so that this Vicky bitch and I can figure out what's gonna happen when the baby gets here. I don't remember her at all and I'm doubtin' the baby's mine."

"Get the test done then." Is Gage's only response.

"Oh, it's gettin' done as soon as fuckin' possible. Just, take care of my girl while she's there man. She's gettin' a doctor lined up just in case there. Make sure my girl takes care of herself."

"She will. I was gonna put her up in an apartment, but I'm puttin' her back in a room at the clubhouse. That way there's always eyes on her. Crash, Trojan, and Steel are gonna be at the strip club with her whenever she's there, and they all know she's top priority no matter what goes on there."

"Alright. I'll talk to you later." I say hanging up without waiting for any response from him.

Now, it's time to spend what's left of today with Bailey. I don't give a fuck what's going on, we're locking ourselves away and not coming out until she has to leave. Maybe I'll take her out and get the hell away from here for a while. For some reason, I don't want her in the same place as this Vicky bitch. I don't trust her as far as I can throw her ass!

"Crazy girl, where you at?" I ask, walking in our room.

"Bathroom." She calls back weakly.

Quickly crossing the room, I open the door and see her on the floor in front of the toilet. "I'm sorry I wasn't here crazy girl."

"It's fine. You have things you need to do. I'm just gonna go lie down for a while."

"Nope. My shit's done. I'll lay down with you and we'll relax until you leave tomorrow. Consider my schedule cleared."

"Okay babe. I just want to rest for a little while. Then we can eat."

By the time Bailey's head hits the pillow, she's practically out. This morning sickness is taking its toll on her and I know I need to tell Crash and Trojan to make sure they keep an eye on it. She's not gonna like them watching her like a hawk, but I could give two fucks.

Bailey

After waking up on Logan's chest, I slide out of bed and brush my teeth, run a brush through my hair and wake him up. I don't want to because he needs to rest, but I know he'll be pissed if I don't. So, I straddle his thighs and start kissing his neck. I make my way from his neck to his nipples, biting down on them just enough to cause the pain I know he likes. Before I make it too much farther, I can feel his hand come up to my hair. He gathers it in his fist and pulls it to one side so he can watch me.

"Nice way to wake up crazy girl." He says, his voice still laced with sleep.

Instead of responding, I make my way down his washboard abs. The lower I move my body, the more the sheet moves with me. He went to bed naked, as usual, so all I have to do is open my mouth and take him in. Using one hand, I stroke what I can't fit in my mouth while I move the other one lower to roll his balls in my hand. Logan uses his hand in my hair to guide me to what he wants as usual. I love him going for his and if he needs to guide me, I'm all for it.

"Crazy girl, come up here. I want my breakfast." Logan says, trying to grab me under my armpits.

"Nope." I say going back to swallowing his cock.

"I'm not askin' crazy girl. Not sayin' you have to stop either, I want that pussy though."

I don't give him what he wants still. If he wants it bad enough, he knows how to take it. I'm not going to give him everything he wants on a silver platter, that's not me and he knows that. After another minute or so Logan sits up as much as he can and grabs my hips. He turns me around and rips my underwear off of me. Before I can gasp, his mouth is on me and he's going to town on my pussy, licking me from my slit up to my clit. He bites down on my clit as I take as much of him in my mouth as I can and moan around his shaft. Swirling my tongue around him, I can feel his hips starting to thrust up so I take just a little bit more of him. Knowing that he's close, Logan starts working even harder to get me off. At the same time, I start grinding myself on his face so that I can get mine.

"Not in your mouth baby. I want this sweet pussy wrapped around my cock." Logan says, dropping his hips so his cock leaves my mouth.

Turning around, I place myself on all fours so that he can take me from behind. Within seconds, I can feel him behind me lining his cock up with my opening before he thrusts in as deep as he can go. I moan and push back against him. Slowly, he pulls out before thrusting back inside again. He always starts out slow to tease me, so I lower my upper half to the bed and move a hand underneath me so I can play with my clit while he teases.

"You're killin' me crazy girl. Don't think I don't know what you're doin'."

"Harder Logan!"

Logan doesn't disappoint. His hips start thrusting harder and faster. There's no way I can stop the moans leaving my mouth at this point. I know he's getting closer by the frantic pace he's starting to move in, along with adding the rotation of his hips.

"I'm close crazy girl." He says on a moan.

Leaning over me, Logan uses one hand to pinch and pull my nipple while he kisses and bites where my neck and shoulder meet. He knows that gets me every fucking time. I start thrusting back into him harder, meeting him and grinding my ass into him. I'm so close I just need that one little push to get me over the edge. Logan must sense this because he pushes my hand out of the way and pinches down on my clit as he thrusts into me.

"Oh God! Logan!" I scream out.

As I go flying with a hard orgasm, Logan thrusts a few more times before I feel him still behind me and hear his roar of release. Coming back down, we collapse on our sides and he rubs my side. Now, instead of getting up, all I want to do is go back to sleep. Hell, I don't even know what time it is.

"Let's get cleaned up." Logan says, pulling me up and leading me into the bathroom once we both catch our breath.

Starting the shower, I pull my shirt over my head and stand watching him. He makes sure of the temperature before leading me in. I stand under the water while he grabs my shampoo to wash my hair. I love when he washes me. Usually we get dirty again before we get out, but I know it won't be the case this time. So, once he's done washing me, I'll wash him and then get ready to hit the road. Because if I know him, there's going to be a few guys from Gage's chapter coming to pick me up and follow me there. It's how he always is.

"I'm gonna get dressed and meet you out there." Logan says drying off real quick.

"Okay. I'll text you when I'm done dressing so you can send Blade up to get my bags. What the fuck time is it anyway?" I ask.

"It's about ten in the mornin'. We slept all night and didn't get a chance to do anythin' else."

"I'm sorry babe. I know you wanted to relax since I'm leaving today."

"Obviously you needed the rest. I'm not worried about it crazy girl. We'll do somethin' when you get home. Or I'll come visit while you're there."

"There's no time for you to come down. You don't know what's gonna pop up here. Besides, I don't know how busy I'll be there getting everything in order."

"We'll see." Is all he says before leaving the room. Damn, I wish I could just throw some clothes on and not worry about my hair or anything else like guys!

Chapter Sixteen

Bailey

I'VE BEEN IN Dander Falls for about two days now and I'm tired of everything already. I left Logan in a pissed off mood since I walked in the common room and Vicky was hanging all over him. Apparently she has some sort of right to him because she's pregnant. When he walked me out to my truck, she was leveling me with a nasty look. What's that saying, if looks could kill? Yeah, I'd be a goner for sure. Her entire face changed when she thought he was going to turn and look at her though. He's right and something's not right there.

Yesterday, I didn't show my face at the strip club. I wanted to see everyone and just relax after the drive in. Crash and Trojan made sure we stopped more than normal to make sure I was okay, but it's still a long drive when you feel sick. Shadow ended up putting his bike in the trailer Logan made us take and drove my truck more than half way here. So, as soon as I walked in the office today, I was ready to throw everything out.

Davina, the last manager, had no concept of paperwork, cleaning, filing, or making sure the money count was right. How the hell did she last so long here? The desk was piled high everywhere with trash, papers, condoms, money, and I can't even tell you what else. I think I threw a pair of underwear, or two, off the mix of papers. A shower is definitely going to be needed before all is said and done here.

"How's it goin' Bay?" Gage asks, walking in the office.

"I need a fucking hazmat team in here! There's fucking dirty ass underwear on the desk!" I shriek at him. Yeah, I'm at my damn limit just in the office.

"You tell me what you want to do first and we'll get it done."

"I want all the girls in here in an hour. Before then, I want the club doc in here so we can get things set up." I say sitting in the chair next to him.

"For what?"

"Drug tests, STD, and pregnancy tests. If they're using, they're gone. No questions asked and no second chances. You have to stick to this Gage."

"I'm not the one runnin' this show. You are until we can hire someone."

"Then get it set up. I want Fox in here too. He needs to set up an accounting program so we can start getting rid of all this paperwork. I don't know what's been entered, what hasn't, what's been paid, or anything else. How the hell did you guys not see this before she took off?"

"Honestly, it's all on me. I didn't make the time to pay more attention. I've had a lot goin' on and it's no excuse. I'll get the girls now. Crash and Trojan are sittin' at the bar. They'll do whatever you need." Gage says standing up and kissing me on the forehead before leaving.

I stay sitting and lean my head on my knees for a minute. The last thing I need is to be sick right now, and I can feel it coming. Thankfully there's a bathroom in the office that I just make it to before losing my breakfast.

"Bay, you okay sweetheart?" Trojan asks through the door.

"Give me a minute. I'll be fine."

I don't hear anything else, but I know he's still by the door. He'll wait there in case I need help. Finally, there's nothing left for me to throw up so I get up, wash my hands and splash some cold water on my face. Making my way out of the bathroom, I leave the office with Trojan following me and go into the bar.

Crash is sitting at the bar waiting for me with a cold beer in his hands. He looks up and drains the rest of it before hugging me. I can see the concern etched on his face and I don't know how to reassure him that I'm fine.

"Crash, it's fine. I'm pregnant so I get sick. Now, I want to move some tables around before Doc gets here. The girls are going to be tested for everything today. If they fail the drug tests, they're gone no second chances."

"Alright babe. We'll move the tables for ya and you do what you gotta do."

"I told Gage that I want Fox in here to set up accounts on the computer so we can get rid of most of the paperwork in the office. Can one of you call him and get him down here now. Tell him I just need him to set it up, I'll put all the information in myself."

"You got it sweetheart." Trojan says.

We all get to work doing the tasks that need to be done so we can get the girls tested. Doc shows up after a little bit and sets everything he needs up. Trojan and Crash are gonna help make sure that no one tries to use anything to pass their drug test. I'm going to be running back and forth between the girls and Fox. After that, I'm done for today.

I make my way behind the bar to grab a drink just as I hear the front door open up. Already the girls are bitching and whining because they have to be here so early. Too damn bad! They want to keep their job, they'll do what I tell them to. The guys might be lenient with them, but that's not what they're gonna get from me.

"You want to keep your jobs, you're gonna suck it up and quit bitching!" I yell over them. "I'm the manager for now and you *will* listen to what I say or you're out on your ass. No questions and no second chances."

"Who the fuck are you?" A dark haired girl asks, showing her attitude in front of the rest of the girls.

"I'm Grim's old lady. I'm the one that is running the Kitty Kat Lounge for the foreseeable future for my man and for my friend, Gage. Any more fucking questions?" I stare at her for a minute. "No, good. Now, everyone line up in front of the first table. It's testing day bitches!"

They all groan and moan. A few of them look downright scared. Looking down the line, I see Addison standing there. Fuck! I didn't know she was stripping here. Oh well, she's not gonna be treated any different than the rest of the girls. Even if she's the only one not complaining.

Doc goes through what's gonna happen and what he needs the girls to do before starting. While he's doing his first exam, Crash takes a few girls to the bathroom so they can piss in the cup. The door remains open and he stands guard to make sure they're not trying to pull any fast ones.

In order to take care of all of the girls, it takes about an hour and a half. As soon as they're done, they sit and wait to find out what's happening next. Doc pulled me into the office soon after he was done doing his thing to tell me what results he had already.

"You've got a mess Bailey. There's five girls that tested positive for drugs and two more are pregnant. I don't know what your game plan is, but here's the names of those results." He says handing me a piece of paper.

"Fuck! Okay. Thank you for coming in on such short notice Doc. Gage will take care of the fees."

Doc leaves the office and I slam the door behind him. What the fuck am I supposed to do with this shit? Now I'm gonna have to fire seven girls and replace them before we can open the fucking doors again. I'm not going to make Addison, Harley, Alyssa, and Kaitlyn perform all night long. I want at least three or four more girls to make it through one night. The guys are just gonna have to suck it up until I can hire more bodies.

Walking out into the bar, I call the girls to attention so that I can break the news. Calling the ones up that need to be fired, I line them all up in front of everyone. Is doing it this way being a bitch? Probably. The rest of the girls are gonna know not to fuck up while I'm in charge though. So, I don't give a shit if they hate me or not.

"Do you girls know why you're standing here and the rest are still sitting down?" I ask, looking at all of them.

"No. We gettin' raises or something?" The bitch with an attitude from earlier asks with a smirk.

"Fuck no! You are the lucky ones that are being fired right now. Collect your purses, or whatever else you got, and get the fuck out."

"You can't do that!" She shrieks. "The guys won't let you get rid of me. I'm the biggest earner here."

"They will let me let you go. They don't want a coke head on their stage. So, get out."

Trojan and Crash pull her back from me when she goes to attack my ass for being fired. They don't let her collect anything belonging to her, they just drag her ass out of there. The rest of the girls being let go run to get their things and leave on their own before the guys come back in. As soon as they're out the door, I sit down by the remaining girls.

"Okay. If I catch you using anything, pimping yourself out, or anything else that's going to hurt this strip club, or the Wild Kings, you are gone. No second chances here girls. We need to get this place back in shape and running the way it needs to be ran. Are you still with me?" I ask, looking at each of them.

They all say 'yeah' and wait to hear what else I'm going to say. "Great! Now, tonight and for the time being we're gonna have to shut the doors. I'm not gonna run you girls ragged because we don't have enough strippers to get through one night, let alone a week. If you know of anyone that's looking, let me know and we'll get them in here. I'm gonna talk to Gage and see if the boys know anyone too. I know you all live in the house the Wild Kings own but I want cell phone numbers. If I call, you better answer."

Each girl grabs a pen and napkin from the tables to write their numbers down for me. Harley stands up telling me she knows a few girls she can get in here to audition or whatever I'm looking to do before leaving with a promise to be back in a little while with them. Addison hands me the napkin and sits back down. Alyssa and Kaitlyn give me their napkins and walk out the door. So, I look at Addison to see what she's gonna run her mouth about.

"Bailey, I'm happy here. I know I messed up real bad with Skylar and the way I went on about Joker."

"I'm not here for that Addison. Gage said he needed help and I came to help out. I'm not gonna go easy on you because you're Irish's sister. I don't know what the hell happened to you, and I'm not gonna be your new BFF. If you want my respect, you're gonna bust your ass and do your job."

"That's why I'm still here. What do you need me to do until we open back up?" She asks, looking down at her lap.

"Right now, I'm going back in the office with Fox to see what he's doing. If you want you can move the tables back and start cleaning. I want everything clean. Harley can help when she comes back. Make sure the coolers are stocked too. If the guys find out there's gonna be auditions today, they're gonna show up."

Making my way into the office, I call Gage to let him know what happened and see if he can get some more girls in to audition this afternoon. He says he's on it and if I need anything else to call. Fox is almost done setting up the new accounting system for me so that I can get to work on that. So, I take a minute to call Grim and see what's going on back home.

"Hey crazy girl. How are things there?" He asks, answering on the first ring.

"This is a mess! I just let go of seven girls for drugs and pregnancies."

"Damn! Is that all?"

"No. I was cleaning the damn desk off and found everything from condoms to dirty fuckin' underwear. How are things there?"

"The same. I have no time to breathe and I'm worried about you bein' so far away. How are you feelin'?"

"The same as I was back home. But, I gotta get things done, so I'm pushing through. How's Vicky?"

"A pain in my fuckin' ass. She's actin' like she's the queen of the club because she says she's havin' my kid. It's only been a few days and everyone's ready to boot her ass out."

"I'm sorry. I'm glad I'm not there then because that's the last thing I need to deal with."

"I know. I miss you so much! I'm thinkin' I might make a trip there and leave in an hour or so."

"I'll be busy baby. Auditions are today and I've got all this information to put in as soon as Fox is done with the new accounting system. Stay and do what you have to do with Vicky and the club. I'll call you later."

"Bay, if I want to make the trip, I'm makin' the damn trip. Gage might need help with somethin' and I'll be there for that too."

"And I'm sayin' you don't trust Vicky so keep an eye on her and find out her game plan. I love you and I'll see you soon enough baby."

"Why do you always know what I need to do? Fine, I'll stay, but you better call me later. I love you too."

Hanging up I sit down and let Fox explain everything he needs to so I can get down to business until the girls come in. Crash hung signs up about auditions starting in a few hours. Trojan went to get us all some lunch. Now, we wait for the girls and hope that we get some good ones in.

I've been sitting here through five auditions so far and they sucked. These girls didn't know a stripper pole from a light post. All they did was shake their body in a way that looked like they were having seizures and then run off stage. The guys that are here couldn't stop their laughing if I paid them to.

"Okay, Maddison, you're up." I call out.

This tiny girl that looks no more than sixteen walks up on stage and waits for *S & M* by Rhianna to start playing. At first I don't pay any attention to the stage because I'm sure she's going to be just as bad as the rest have been. When the guys don't start laughing though, I raise my eyes and see that this girl knows what she's doing. Not one of the guys is talking, laughing, or drinking. They are all entranced by the way she's moving to the song. Frankly, so am I. Maddison doesn't even look like she knows we're all sitting out here watching her.

"This one Bailey. She's good." Crash says from next to me adjusting himself.

"I agree. We've only got about five more girls here. So, let's hope that they're even half as good as Maddison is. Make sure she doesn't leave when she's done."

"You got it boss lady. On to the next."

Vicky

Why the hell couldn't I have hooked up with the Wild Kings in the first place? They are so different from what I'm used to. But, I have a job to do that my life depends on so I better do it right.

It's been easy to sneak around the clubhouse without Bailey here. I know she and Grim are staying here, so I know she'd be all over me snooping. Now, I just wait until the guys get drunk or disappear for a while doing whatever it is they do. Grim hasn't really been an issue either. I haven't seen his ass hardly at all since I got here. How the hell am I gonna get close to him if he's never around?

"Give me breakfast!" I snap at the woman in the kitchen.

'Um… okay." She responds.

"Now!" I shriek in her face as someone walks around the corner.

"I don't know who the fuck you think you are, but you're not gonna talk to my woman like that again." One of the sexiest men I've ever seen says before pushing past me. "You okay baby girl?"

"I'm good. I'll be done in a minute. She can get her own plate and I'll bring these out for you guys and the kids." She answers before kissing him like she's starving for him.

I just stand there and watch thinking that she's still getting my breakfast. I'm certainly not getting my own shit. Perks of being knocked up by the President. She'll take care of the man she probably spent the night with when she's done feeding me. If I decide that I don't need her to do anything else for me.

"Now, I want eggs, toast, juice, and bacon." I say, turning my attention to her again.

"So get it. I'm not a club girl, I'm an old lady. The VP and Sergeant at Arms old lady, bitch. You want something you get it yourself. As far as I'm concerned, you're lower than a club girl and can serve your damn self!" She says before leaving me alone in the kitchen.

Great! Guess I just met Skylar. I guess I'll see what else I can get to eat real quick before I do some more snooping. Or find Grim. I'm sure he can entertain me for a while. Looking around, I don't see anything that I want to eat, so Grim it is.

He was easier to find than I thought. In the main room, he's sitting at a table with kids, Skylar, and her men. So, I make my way over to them and try to sit on his lap. There's no more chairs and he can hold me. It's time I cozy up to him and make him forget all about Bailey. She's not a real old lady if she can't even stay here at the first sign of something not going right. Biker Princess indeed has to run and lick her wounds over losing her man to me.

"Get the fuck off me!" Grim yells before I'm even fully in his lap. "I don't know what game you're playin' but you *aren't* my old lady. You are only here so that I can find out if the kid is mine and then you're gone. If you're not eatin' then I suggest you find somethin' to do."

"We need to talk about the baby and I have an appointment this afternoon. You're coming right?" I say, batting my eyelashes at him.

"What time is it?" He growls out.

"It's at one. I'm establishing with this doctor so I don't know how long it's gonna take."

"Fine. We can talk on the way. Now, disappear. I'm busy."

Turning on my heel, I make it look like I'm going back to my room. Instead I turn in the room that I know is Grim's office. Looking around to make sure no one's coming, I open the door and squeeze through before shutting it and locking it. Grim's desk is the most organized I've ever seen a desk before. It certainly doesn't have things all over it looking like the man actually does something. So, I quickly go through the drawers and look around to see what I can find. There's nothing but a ton of invoices and customer lists for garages. No gun running or drug running information here. Not that I really thought there would be.

Hearing a noise outside the door, I run into what I'm guessing is the bathroom before the office door opens. This is perfect because I can hear about any meeting he has with anyone and maybe I can find out where Bailey is if he talks to her. Closing the bathroom door all but an inch or so, I can see that he's on the phone talking about leaving to go somewhere and helping Gage. I don't know who that is, but I'm betting that's where Bailey is. Looks like I just got my first bit of information to send back.

Chapter Seventeen

Grim

SITTING IN MY office, I'm so confused. Bailey is down with Gage helping out there and all I want to do is be with her. I hate that she's out of my sight in case something happens. She's right though, I need to figure out what's going on with this bitch here. Something's not right. First she treats Sky like a club whore and then she tries to sit on my lap. Not gonna happen.

Soon, I'm pulled out of my head with a knock on the door. It's then I notice the bathroom. The door's not quite shut all the way and I can see a shadow moving around in there. I'm gonna bet it's that bitch. Opening the door, I see Pops and Joker standing there. Without being obvious I make a motion toward the bathroom and tell them to be quiet.

"What's up guys?" I ask, heading back to the desk.

"Just wonderin' if you heard from my daughter." Pops said.

"Yeah, she's gettin' ready to head back home to meet with Shelby and help her out." I say, raising my eyebrows and looking at them.

"Good. Is anyone goin' with her?" Joker asks.

"No. She wanted to go alone. Shelby doesn't want a lot of people there all up in her business."

"Let's head out then Pops. I told you she was okay." Joker says standing.

"I'm not happy about the fuckin' situation at all. You know someone should be with her in case somethin' happens to her." Pops says, playing along making it known that he's not happy. Hell, I'd love to show her that there's dissention in the club and see what Vicky does with that information.

"Pops, let's go get a beer and calm down for a bit. Then we'll go see the kids. They miss their Papa." Joker says, trying to get him to leave the room.

"Come on Pops. I'm ready for a beer already."

The three of us make it sound like we're leaving the room when in reality we're gonna catch this bitch in my office. It doesn't take long for her to appear either. She glances up and sees the three of us standing there with our arms crossed over our chests.

"Find anythin' good?" I ask her.

"I don't know what you're talking about. I had to go to the bathroom and got lost in the maze of halls."

"You know where your room is and you have a bathroom in there. You won't find anythin' at all here. So, what were you lookin' for?" Joker asks.

"I got lost!" Vicky screams. "Leave me the fuck alone. Grim, I'm ready to fuckin' go when you are."

"I'm ready alright. Joker and Pops, talk to Blade, Tank, and Glock. This bitch is gonna have escorts at all times around here. I don't know what she's tryin' to pull, but she doesn't go anywhere without a shadow. Plus, I want someone outside her door around the clock when she's in there."

"You can't do that!" She screams again.

"I can and will do that. You're in my clubhouse and what I say goes. Get your shit and get in the car. Have Rage take my truck over to your house Joker. There's no need for it to be here since Bay's gone."

Pulling Vicky behind me, I lead her to her car so that we can get to this damn doctor's appointment. Then, I'm going to find out what the hell's going on around here when we get back. I'm not gonna wait for her to mess up, we're gonna get down to business now and I'm going to figure out who she's working for, or with.

"So, what do you think we should do with the nursery?" Vicky asks me, like she wasn't just caught in my office.

"I don't care what you do with your nursery. Bailey and I will have our own for when the kid comes to our house."

"You honestly think I'll let someone else raise my daughter? Especially someone like her."

"You really have no choice in the matter. Bailey is my old lady and you're not even a memory. So, if this kid is mine, then they will be stayin' with us whenever I get a chance to spend with them."

"It's a fucking girl Grim. Call her a she or whatever and quit referring to her as kid!"

"Tell me who you're workin' with Vicky and we'll get this done and over with now."

"I don't know what you mean. I'm not working with anyone. If Bailey is your old lady where the hell is she? I haven't seen her around since the day I arrived."

"That doesn't concern you. She and I have nothin' to do with you. All I'm doin' with you is takin' you to an appointment and then finding out with a paternity test if this kid is mine. If it is, then I'll be a dad. If not, you've got some explainin' to do." I tell her, pulling into the doctor's office.

"I just know that an old lady's place is by her man's side. Not off somewhere else away from her man and the club."

"Like I said, it doesn't concern you."

"You will be mine again Grim. The sooner you realize that, the better off you'll be."

This woman is fucking delusional! I'm not going to be anything with her at all, ever. Now, I really can't believe that I ever hooked up with her. I may have chosen every piece of easy pussy around, but I still had standards and crazy wasn't on that list.

"I won't ever be yours. Now, let's get this damn appointment done so I can take care of things that matter to me."

"Nice. Saying this baby doesn't matter to you. That's real nice Grim." Vicky says before leaving me standing there alone.

Maybe I have overstepped the boundary on this one, but damn she's making me think more and more this baby isn't mine. It's a gut feeling I got when she first told me and the way she's acting is justifying it more and more every day. She wants to try to take Bailey's place and that's never gonna happen.

"Look, I'm sorry okay. I don't know what to do here, but I know that you're pushin' somethin' that isn't gonna happen. I have one old lady and that's all I'm ever gonna have. I'm not steppin' out on her and you don't have a place in my life as anythin' more than possibly my daughter's mom. You got that?" I ask, catching up to her.

"We'll see." Is her response.

Going in to the office, we don't wait very long before she's called back. The doctor exams her and I just sit in a chair against the wall listening to everything Doctor Bell has to say. Basically, Vicky will be coming back once a week until she goes into labor, which could happen any time now. I have to ask my question now before this bitch makes it seem like more is going on here than what really is.

"So, doc, as soon as possible I want a paternity test done. Can you arrange that for me?"

"I can. We can get a sample as soon as the baby's born from the umbilical cord. Then I can call as soon as we get the results back." She says looking at me. "How's my other patient doing?"

"I'd actually like a minute if you can spare it without other ears listenin'."

"Let's go to my office, or you can call in a few hours so I can get to my next patient."

"I'll call you later then."

Vicky gets off the table and we go make her next appointment. She tries to grab my hand and I wrench it away from her. Apparently she's not gonna be giving this shit up any time soon. I'll just have to make sure that I'm not alone with her and that she's got that guard on her at all times.

"You're really not going to let this go without a damn paternity test are you?" Vicky asks nervously.

"No, I'm not. You think I'm just gonna take your word for it when you show up the same day as the Soulless Bastards? I'm not dumb, you're workin' for them aren't you?"

Vicky doesn't respond. Instead she looks around the parking lot almost like she's expecting someone to be there watching us. So, I start looking around to see if I can see anyone watching us. I don't see anyone, but now my guard's up. We need to get back to the clubhouse now and I'm pulling her into church to find out what's going on. Sending out a mass text, the guys should all be there when I get back.

"You ready to talk now?" I ask her.

"I-I don't know what you're talking about." She tries again.

"Yeah, you do. Look, if you tell us what's goin' on, we can help you and figure out the best way to protect you and the baby. If not, then we'll only protect that baby you're carryin'."

"Fine. Let's just get back and I'll tell you everything. I never wanted to go along with this shit to begin with." Vicky says, and I can finally see the crack in her armor.

Once we pull into the clubhouse, I see all the guys' bikes parked. Quickly making our way in to the meeting room, I pull Vicky in and sit her down in a chair against the wall for now. Everyone is looking at me like I'm crazy for bringing her in here.

"I can see you're all wonderin' why she's in here. She's goin' to tell us what she's really doin' here and then we're gonna figure out what to do with her. Vicky, you can begin now." I say, leaning back in my seat.

"I am pregnant, but Grim's not the father. Bull is." Vicky says wringing her hands together. "I've been his old lady for a while now and I was ecstatic when I got pregnant, Bull was not. He was pissed because I wouldn't get an abortion. Then when everything started going down with Skylar and Kelsey, he figured he could use the pregnancy to his advantage."

"What do you mean 'when all this started with Skylar and Kelsey'?" Cage asks, looking like he's ready to jump out of his seat.

"Bull didn't want to take Kelsey in place of Skylar. He couldn't stand that bitch when Damon brought her to the clubhouse. She was dead in less than an hour of being there. He wants Skylar and he's using me to figure out the best way to get to her. Getting Bailey too is just a bonus. So, I was supposed to come here and convince you that I was pregnant by you, get you under my spell, and then feed them information when you guys were going to be gone and where the girls would be. I'm so sorry. I didn't know what else to do."

"Have you told them anythin' yet?" I ask her.

"No. I haven't found anything out to tell him. Bull's been blowing up my phone since I got here and I haven't answered it yet." She says, looking me dead in my eyes so I know she's telling me the truth.

"Okay. What do you want now? What are you hopin' to gain from this?"

"I just want to leave. It's not good there at all. All they do is drink, use drugs they're supposed to be selling, and beat their women. All I want is to disappear and forget all about the assholes."

"What about the baby?" Irish asks.

"I don't know. I know I'm not in a place to raise a baby. I guess I'll look into adoption."

"Give us a minute. I'll have Blade sit with you so I know you're not makin' any calls. When we decide on your fate, we'll let you know." I tell her walking her to the door and motioning for Blade to get Vicky to a table and sit with her.

"Okay guys, what do we do now?" I ask, taking my seat at the head of the table again.

"First of all, I want the baby if she's serious about givin' it up." Irish says. "Caydence and I can't have kids and that's somethin' she wants more than anythin' on this Earth. So, if she's serious, we'll be takin' that baby."

We all just sit there speechless for a minute at his news. Why the hell haven't they talked to us about this before now? Every person in this club would've helped figure out a way to give them a baby. Hell, most of the women that have been associated with the club would help out in a heartbeat to make their dream of a family a reality.

"Okay brother. We'll figure out how to make that happen for you. Next time, you fuckin' come to us if you got shit goin' on. You got me?" I tell him.

"Caydence didn't want anyone knowin'. Especially after Bailey losin' the baby. We've lost so many through miscarriages and Caydence is givin' up on her dreams. I can't let her do that if I have a way to make it happen for her."

"Now, what are we gonna do about Vicky?" Pops says. "That bitch was gonna help take my daughters and she has to fuckin' pay!"

"Pops, I get you're pissed, the same as the rest of us. But, she's been used as a pawn by Bull and his club. I say, if she really wants to disappear then we make it happen for her. Once that baby is born, we make sure she disappears. Until that time, she's guarded every fuckin' second of every day. One prospect and one brother at least."

"You sure about that?" Joker asks. "What about Skylar and Bailey? How are we gonna keep them protected?"

"Skylar won't be allowed here for right now. I don't want her anywhere near Vicky. For now, you guys stay on her like white on rice. Don't let her out of your sight. Bailey's with Gage, so I'll call and make sure they step up security on her there. As soon as Vicky can travel, she's gone. I don't care where she goes. We'll give her enough money to get set up somewhere new and wash our hands of her."

There's grumbling from around the table and I know my decision isn't a popular one. But, we don't hurt women if we don't have to and I'm not gonna start with Vicky. As long as she disappears and stays gone, then we're good. All that's left is to figure out what to do about Bull and his club. I motion for Glock to bring Vicky back in so we can tell her what was decided. She enters and takes the same chair I put her in before.

"Are you serious about wantin' to give the baby up?" Irish asks.

"Yeah. I just can't bring a baby into my life right now when I don't know where I'm going or what I'm going to do next."

"I want the baby then. As soon as it's born, my old lady and I will take it. No questions asked or anythin'." He states, leaving no room for argument.

"Are you sure? I mean what about Bull?"

"You let us worry about him. But, you don't ever get to come back and try to lay a claim. Your name won't even be on the birth certificate."

"And you'll take care of her as if she were your own flesh and blood? Just because I can't raise her doesn't mean I don't care."

"We will cherish her and treat her as our own. You agree not to come back and not to tell Bull where she is?" Irish asks, looking more confident.

"Yeah. I want nothing more to do with him or his club. He's running it into the ground. So, what happens to me?"

"You stay here, guarded, until you give birth. As soon as you can travel, we'll get you out of here and you disappear. We'll also give you enough money to set yourself up. Think of it as havin' your bills paid for bein' a surrogate or somethin'. You ever show your face again or we find out you told Bull anythin', you will regret it. Do you understand?"

"I understand. Can I go to my room now please?"

I nod and Glock walks out with her and Blade follows them. Looks like they're the first two on watch. Now, I need to call Gage and Bailey. I'm not keeping this from her no matter what anyone wants or thinks. She needs to know to be vigilant while she's not around here.

"I'm callin' Gage and Bailey. I don't know if they're at the Kitty Kat or not, but I know Bailey just fired a bunch of girls and was doin' auditions for new ones." I tell the guys still sitting around the table. "We're gonna have to figure out when to have Rage on Vicky duty since he's got Kasey to think about. Maybe durin' the day he can watch over her startin' tomorrow. The rest of you figure it out amongst yourselves for now."

While everyone is leaving I make my calls. I'm calling Gage first since he's gonna have to have time to figure out who's on my girl. If I have to, I'll take my ass there to watch her. But, I think Pops and Ma might be up for taking a vacation. I'll have to bring that up to him and let Gage know he might be heading that way.

Once I'm done talking to Gage, I call my crazy girl. I need to hear her voice and see how our baby is. Gage already told me she's working on putting information in the computer and that Addison is helping her out. That surprises me, but I'm happy she's not doing it all alone. Maybe they won't have to hire someone to manage the Kitty Kat and can have Bailey train Addison instead.

"Crazy girl, I miss you like hell." I say as soon as Bailey answers the phone.

"I miss you too babe. What are you doing?"

"Sittin' here. Just got done with an emergency church. Listen, Gage is gonna be uppin' security for you. Vicky isn't havin' my baby, she's havin' Bull's. He sent her in here to spy so he can get his hands on Sky. She opened up today and told us what's goin' on."

"Okay. I can handle the extra security. Other than that, you okay?"

"Just missin' you crazy girl. I want you here with me so bad. But, Gage said that Addison's helpin' you out.

Maybe you can train her instead of them hirin' someone else."

"She has been a huge help. The girls I just hired are being trained by her right now. She's showing them some new dance moves and things. But, she has been helping me with the paperwork end of it too. Maybe she would make a good manager. I'll talk to Gage about it."

"How's our baby doin'?"

"Okay for now. I have a doctor's appointment next week. I don't know if it'll be here or there though."

"I hope like hell it's here. Either way I'm gonna be there. How's the mornin' sickness?"

"It's been there still, but I don't have time to rest afterwards. So, I've just been pushing through it. Besides, I don't have your arms to curl up in when I need to. I'm hoping to be done this week so I can get home."

"You need to rest, you fuckin' rest Bay! Doctor Bell said not to overdo shit and that's what you're doin' down there isn't it? Fuck! I knew lettin' you go was a bad idea."

"You didn't let me go anywhere babe. I was always gonna come help out. All I've been doing is sitting at my desk, putting numbers in a computer for fuck's sake, Logan! I'm eating, sleeping at night, and drinking plenty. I'm fine."

"Bay, I'm sorry. I'm just goin' crazy without you here."

"I know. I miss you too. Now, I love you, but I have to get back to work. I'll talk to you later."

"Love you too baby. I'll call you when I go to bed."

After hanging up, I make sure that Vicky is being watched before I go talk to Pops about going to Dander Falls. Ma will definitely keep an eye on Bailey since I'm not there to do it. Damn, can anything go right today?

Bailey

I love talking to Logan on the phone, but damn that man can piss me off like no other. Addison heard the last part of our conversation, and she's been laughing her ass off ever since. She loves seeing the guys put in their place. I sit and look at her for a few seconds as she grabs a drink so she can cool down after dancing with the new girls. We're opening back up tonight so they've been putting in extra time.

"What? Do I have something on my face?" Addison asks sitting down next to me.

"No. Grim just brought up a good point and I'm thinking about it is all. Let me ask you a question."

"Go ahead."

"Do you like stripping? I mean, if you could do something else and stay with the club, would you do it?"

"Yeah. I don't like dancing, but I had to do something. I mean, I know why I had to leave you guys and I'm happier here than I was there. Besides, Blaze doesn't like me dancing anyway." She says, blushing.

"What's going on with the two of you?"

"Nothing really. I mean not a lot can happen when he's always on the go. So, we talk on the phone and he stops in if he's close by. But, he can't change who he is and I would never ask him to do that."

"Well, why don't you go with him on the road then?"

"He hasn't mentioned it and I'm not going to. If he wanted me with him, he'd let me know. Until he does, which I doubt will happen, I'm content with what we have."

"Well, I have a proposition for you. I still have to talk to Gage about it, but I don't see a problem. How would you like to be manager here? Then, you're still working for the club and get the protection and shit, but you're not stripping."

"Are you serious? I'd love it!" Addison says, getting up and dancing around.

"What's goin' on in here?" Gage asks, coming to the door.

"I was just telling Addison about an idea I had. Instead of you hiring someone else to manage the Kitty Kat, why don't I train Addison to do it?"

"You want that instead Addy?" Gage asks her.

"I do. I've been watching Bailey with the computer part. I saw how she auditioned the girls, and I know what she expects out of everyone working here. I can do this Gage."

"Okay. You'll train with Bailey on the management side and be taken out of the dancin' rotation as of today. We open in a few hours, so you're gonna have to set up a new one. You better follow what Bay does to the letter because I'm not goin' through this shit again."

"I promise; I won't let you guys down!"

Now that I have that all taken care of, I guess it's time to let Addison in on the computer and see how she does inputting the information. That's the only way she's going to learn it. Plus, she needs to make up the new rotation, check on the bar, make sure the girls have everything they need, and once we open, check on customers. It's a lot of work, but I think she can handle it.

"Addison, here's a list of everything you need to do today. I've written everything that I would do and that's what you have to do every day. Now, the only other thing you need to do is make sure that you don't let them run your ass over and do what they want. You have to let the girls know you're in charge here."

"I can do that. The only one that's not here yet is Maddison. She was here for practice and then ran out. I'm hoping that she'll be back." Addison says, looking unsure of what to do.

"Okay. Put her on rotation towards the end. I think she's the best one we've got so far. Then if she doesn't show up, we'll figure out what to do. You might have to go on in her place." I tell her, trying to get her to calm down a little bit. "Now, go out there and do your thing. I'm gonna try to get some more of this in the computer before I make an appearance close to opening. If you need me, come get me."

Addison scurries out the door. I return to the desk and take a seat so I can work on getting more accounts set up. There's definitely going to be more than enough for me to work on it and then have her complete it. I'm interrupted by a commotion going on in the bar section of the club though.

"What the hell is going on out here?" I yell, walking out to whatever is going on.

"Maddison showed up." Addison says. "But she's not alone."

I look over to see Maddison holding a pretty young looking baby. Looking up at her face I see blood dripping down her face. What the fuck?

"Maddison in my office now please." I tell her, looking at the rest of the girls. "You guys make sure you listen to Addison and do your job. Come get me if you need me."

Leading Maddison to the office, I close us in and sit her down before I go in the bathroom. Getting the first aid kit and some wet wash clothes, I make my way back to her to see Trojan sitting with her. Good, he can help me get her cleaned up and then I'll boot his ass so I can figure out what's going on.

"Trojan, take the baby so I can clean her up and see if she needs stitches." He looks at me like I'm crazy. "Listen, either help me out here or go get someone that will."

"I've never held a damn baby before Bay and you know it." He says.

"It's not that hard. Make sure you support her head and neck and sit back. She's not going to wiggle out of your arms and disappear."

Trojan does as I ask and holds the baby for me while I get Maddison cleaned up. It doesn't look like she's going to need stitches, but I'll keep an eye on her to make sure that the butterfly strips hold it together.

There's no way in hell she's dancing tonight though. Already I can see a huge bruise forming on her cheek under where the cut on her head is. Someone tried to beat the fuck out of her.

"Alright Trojan, you can leave now. I'll call you again if I need you." I say, cleaning up the mess I made until he closes the door behind him. "Want to tell me what happened to you? And don't try to bullshit me. My sister Skylar has been through it all."

"Well, I rushed home after practice so that my boyfriend wouldn't know I was stripping. Our neighbor was watching the baby and I didn't make it inside in time. He questioned me and didn't like the answers I gave him. So, he backhanded me and I fell through the table. I'll be okay. I just didn't have anywhere to take Zoey while I came back to work." Maddison says while looking down.

"How often does he hit you?"

"This is the first and last time. Usually he just tells me what to do, won't let me out of the house without him, and calls me names. I'm done with him though. I just don't have anywhere to go until I can make some money."

"You just sit tight in here with Zoey. Don't move. I'll be back in a few minutes."

Making my way out to the bar, I see Gage standing there talking with Crash and Trojan. I quickly go over what she told me and ask if she can stay in my room at the clubhouse. She'll be leaving with me as long as she's willing to uproot her life. Gage tells me he can handle that. I don't think it's going to take Addison long to catch on to things here since I can already hear her getting the girls in order in the back. So, I go to her before going back to Maddie.

"Addison, a minute."

"Am I doing something wrong?" She asks nervously. "I've gotten the bar-tenders filling everything up, the girls are getting their costumes ready, everything is spotless. All I have left to do is give the DJ the playlist they gave me."

"No, you're doing fine hun. I need to let you know that as of now Maddison is done. She won't be dancing here."

"O-okay. Do you want me to go on tonight?"

"Nope, you figure it out. You can do it. I need to call Grim and then I'm heading out."

I find a quiet corner to make my call. I'm not sure what he's going to say, or if Maddie is even going to want to come home with me, but she's not staying here. If she doesn't want to move away from family or whatever maybe I can talk Crash and Trojan into keeping an eye on her.

"Hey crazy girl! I wasn't expectin' to talk to you until later." Logan greets me.

"I think I'm bringing someone home with me babe. As long as she agrees to come home with me, we're gonna need room for her and a baby."

"What are you talkin' about?" He asks, moving to a quieter location.

"One of the new dancers came in today with her little girl. She had a cut on her head and her man backhanded her. Maddie said she's done but she's got nowhere to go. So, if she'll go for it, I'm gonna bring her home with me."

"Always tryin' to save the world. Yeah, I can put her up. I've got an apartment not far from us."

"What are you talking about? I didn't know you had an apartment." I ask him confused.

"No one does. That's what makes it perfect for this stripper. I barely crash there, and that's all it was, was a crash pad. There's only a couch and a bed in the damn place babe. I think I used the damn thing like two or three times since I got it when we first moved to town. I'll get it cleaned out and have Summer and Storm clean it up for her to move in. How are you gettin' her things here?"

"I honestly don't know how much she's going to be bringing with her. I'll let you know if I need anything else. I'm gonna head out to the clubhouse with her so we can get the baby out of the Kitty Kat."

"I love you crazy girl. Oh, by the way, Ma, Pops, and Tank are on their way there. They actually should be there in about a half hour or so."

"Why are they coming here?" I ask, getting pissed.

"Pops hates the fact that none of us were there to protect you. Tank just went along for the ride. I had nothin' to do with it babe."

"I'm fine. I told you I haven't seen anyone out of the ordinary. Gage has Crash and Trojan on me at all times. What do you guys think is gonna happen if I'm out of your sight for the slightest bit of time?" I ask, becoming even more frustrated.

"Nothin' babe. We're just worried since we don't know what Bull's next play is. He could be down there already." He says.

"I haven't seen him or anyone wearing a Soulless Bastards cut baby. I'd tell someone if I had."

"I know babe. I'll talk to you in a little while. Go handle your business and listen for Ma. She's gonna be in the strip club. They aren't goin' to the clubhouse first."

"Great, just what I need!" I groan. "Okay, I love you and I'll talk to you later to let you know what's going on."

"Love you too."

Quickly making my way in to Maddison, I see her lying on the couch with the baby sleeping. I can only imagine what's happening to make this girl turn to stripping when she has a baby at home. My only hope now is that I can talk her into coming home with us. She needs a fresh start I'm guessing and that's what I want to give her. As gently as I can I grab the blanket I put on the back of the couch over her and little Zoey. I'll let them rest for a while and go wait for Ma and Pops.

The show has already started on stage, Ma and Pops along with Tank have shown up, and now I'm just waiting for Maddie and Zoey to wake up so we can talk some more. I've let Ma, Pops, and Tank know what's going on and Ma is fully on board with me in getting her to come with us. And people wonder where I get my meddling from!

We're sitting at the bar when the front door opens and in walks a group of guys. They look around while letting their eyes adjust to the darkness. After looking at us for a minute, they make their way to a table on the opposite side of the room. I can vaguely make out the back of their cut and it's a Soulless Bastards cut. What the fuck? Why are they here?

Tank and Pops look at one another and then motion for Crash, Trojan, and Gage to go to the hallway. I know they're gonna talk about them being here after knowing that Vicky just told them Bull wants Skylar and me. Ma gives me a worried look and we make our way to the office. I'm hoping to hide out from them for now and make sure that Maddie doesn't come out here with the baby. They don't need to know about them.

"I'm so sorry I fell asleep." Maddison says as Ma closes the door. "I must have been more tired than I thought."

"It's okay baby girl. I'm Bailey's mom, Ma. I just got to town today. Who's this adorable little thing you have here?" Ma says, sitting down next to her.

"This is my daughter Zoey. It's nice to meet you ma'am."

"Hush that ma'am stuff now dear. You call me Ma just like everyone else does."

"Maddie, we need to talk. I don't want you working here. You're too sweet and innocent for this place. So, I have an idea I want to run by you. I'm gonna be going home here in a day or two. How about you and Zoey come home with us? My old man already has a place he can set you up in and then we can worry about finding you a job."

"I don't know what to say Bailey. I mean, I don't have anyone here to help me and I don't have anywhere to go. So, I guess I can go with you. If I don't like it, I can always save some money up and move on."

"Where's your family honey?" Ma asks her.

"My mom died when I was seventeen and I never knew who my daddy was. All I know is he was a biker that ran at the first opportunity. At least that's what my mama used to tell me. She said I look more like him than I do her, and used to yell and scream at me that I should have been aborted instead of her having me." Maddison tells us, looking down at her lap.

"Well, you have a family now dear." Ma tells her, making her look up at her. "Oh my, you do look like someone I know. You say your daddy was a biker?"

"That's what she told me. Said she met him at some rally and thought she had it made with him. But as soon as he got back home, she never heard from him again. I don't know if she tried to reach out about being pregnant with me or not. I'm just used to not having a dad. It's always been me against the world."

"Not anymore. How much do you have to move honey?" I ask her.

"Nothing. Brad wouldn't let me take anything out of the apartment when I left. Even if it was for Zoey. He's convinced she's not his since he never wanted kids to begin with. Always told me I got pregnant on purpose. I didn't mean to get pregnant, I swear it." She tells us, with her eyes filling with tears.

"It'll work out baby girl." Ma says. "You got us now and we're not gonna let you do this alone. Let me get my husband in here and we'll make a run for diapers and things for you both."

"I can't pay for it. I'm supposed to dance and that's what I was going to use."

"I'm not asking you for nothing in return honey. We'll get you two set up for tonight and the ride home. Grim, Bailey's old man, will make sure that everything is set up when you get there."

Ma no sooner finishes talking when Pops and Tank walk in the room. Pops comes to a dead stop as soon as he lays eyes on Maddison, then he shares a look with Ma. I'm confused as hell as to what's going on between the two of them right now. Tank has my attention though. He didn't look up from his phone until he almost ran Pops over. As soon as he saw Maddie, no one was going to take his attention away from her. I've never seen Tank look at anyone like he's looking at Maddison and Zoey.

"Pops, we gotta make a run to get Maddie and Zoey here some clothes, diapers, and other things to get them through the move back with us. Bailey's gonna call Grim to have him go get everything she'll need there."

"You okay sweetheart?" Pops asks her.

"I'm fine sir. Thank you." Maddison says, sneaking a peek at Tank and quickly looking away. Interesting.

"We'll be back to take you girls to the clubhouse as soon as we can. Let's go get their stuff Pops." Ma says, pulling him away and taking the wad of cash Tank just handed her. "Is Zoey on formula dear or are you breastfeeding?"

"Um… I'm breastfeeding."

They don't say another word as they walk out the door. Tank pulls up a seat in front of Maddison and I leave the room to check on everything in the back. There's no way in hell I'm going out to the bar when I don't know if the Soulless Bastards are still out there. Crash follows me to the dressing room and stands guard outside the door. Addison looks to have everything under control though, I'm really just giving Tank and Maddison a minute. Well, and to make sure that Addison stays back here for right now. We don't need her going out there if they know that she's the sister of Irish.

Tank

When I heard that Ma and Pops were making the trip to Dander Falls, I figured I should probably go with them in case someone decided to follow them. So, we got ready and made an uneventful trip down there. I followed Pops on my bike while he and Ma drove his truck. I'm not sure why they didn't take the bike unless something more was going on that I don't know about.

Walking into the office behind Pops, I'm reading a text that Grim just sent about being vigilant around Bailey since the Bastards just popped their heads up down here. So, I send a text back saying that they're at the Kitty Kat. When I look up I see the most beautiful woman I've seen in the longest time. With light blue eyes and blondish red hair down to her waist, she is tiny like a pixie with curves in all the right places, and an overwhelming urge to protect her comes over me. The girl is holding a sleeping pink bundle close to her chest and looks like she just woke up. The only thing I focus on is the bruise on her cheek and the butterfly strips holding her head together farther up. Who the fuck would lay their hands on this innocent looking woman?

As Ma and Pops were leaving, I made sure to hand one of them a wad of money to buy the things with. Pops gave me a knowing look before ushering Ma out the door. Shortly after they left, Bailey left to go check on things in the dressing room. Now, it's just Maddison and me.

"Um… Can I have a minute please?" She asks, pulling me from my thoughts.

"What sweetheart?" I ask.

"My daughter needs to eat. Can I have a minute please?" She asks, with a blush creeping up her face.

"I'll turn my back until you get covered, but I can't leave you alone in here. Is that okay?"

"Yeah. I'll let you know as soon as I'm covered up."

I keep my word and turn my back to give her some privacy. There's no way I'm scaring her away when all I want to do is get to know her. I've never just looked at someone and felt this undeniable pull towards them before. Not even with my son's mother. She was just kind of there and we were together one minute and not together because of her addiction the next.

"You can turn around now." She says timidly.

"Relax sweetheart. I'm not goin' to hurt you." I say, sitting down on the couch with a little bit of space between us. "You wanna tell me what happened to you?"

"It's nothing. I'm done with it now and Bailey's helping me out obviously."

"Doesn't look like nothin' to me sweetheart. Who patched you up?"

"Bailey did. I'll be fine." She tells me.

This one's gonna be tough to crack. She keeps stealing glances at me, but she's gonna push me away at the same time. I'm gonna have to fight harder than I've ever had to for Maddison to open up to me. I guess it's a good thing that I'm good with waiting and fighting for what I want. It's just been a long time since I've had anything to fight for. Not since my son.

Maddison

After rehearsal ran over, I ran to the apartment I shared with my boyfriend Brad. He's been acting out and weird since he lost his job and Zoey was born. I don't know what's going on with him, but I tend to stay out of his way. Unfortunately, he got home before I could pick Zoey up from the neighbor and get in the door to start dinner. That went well!

Then, I take Zoey to the strip club with me because I had no other choice and fell asleep on Bailey's couch in the office. When I woke up, I was alone and Zoey was still sleeping. Bailey and her mom came in and I fell in love with Ma. She's just one of those women that takes it upon herself to make everyone comfortable and loved. And, I think she may know who my dad is by the looks she keeps giving me. Wouldn't that be nice? To at least know who my dad is and see what I get from him. If he's even still alive.

What really has my attention though is the man that walked in a few minutes later. He is the most gorgeous man I have ever seen with shoulder length blond hair and the clearest, brightest blue eyes I have ever seen. He's got his lip and eyebrow pierced, and on his tanned skin it looks amazing. The man is built like a tank, I guess that's why they call him Tank, and I can see tattoos adorning every inch of skin I can see. Tank looks like someone that knows how to protect those he cares about, but he holds himself back. Even if he opens up once in a while, you can tell that he doesn't give anyone all of him.

After deciding that I would go home with Bailey, Ma and Pops left and Tank handed them money. I guess, for whatever reason, he's paying for my stuff. While Bailey was out in the club, Tank stayed with me and Zoey woke up. I didn't know how to handle the breastfeeding issue in front of him, so I just used the blanket to cover myself up. Tank was a gentleman and didn't even try to sneak a peek.

"Um… I wanted to say thank you for giving them money to buy stuff for us. I'll pay you back as soon as I get settled and find a job." I say, not quite looking at him.

"I don't need your money sweetheart. You just worry about you and that precious baby girl. What's her name?" He asks, leaning in a little closer to me.

"It's Zoey."

"Such a pretty name. She's gonna be a heartbreaker if she grows up to look half as beautiful as you."

I can feel the blush spreading through my body at his words. I've never known how to take compliments since I've never received many of them. "Thank you."

Tank leans back against the couch and puts his arm behind me. I can feel the warmth coming off of him and I just want to lean in and soak it up. I'm sure he's got a woman back wherever they're taking me, but it's nice to sit here and not have him expect anything from me. Hell, I feel safe for the first time in my life just sitting here next to him. Maybe moving with Bailey won't be so bad.

Chapter Eighteen

Grim

BAILEY'S BEEN BACK now for a few weeks and I'm so happy. She's been so happy since being back too. Most of her time is helping Maddison settle in and watching her daughter while Maddie's working. Almost as soon as they pulled up and Maddison moved in, she got a job at the diner in town. She's never been a waitress before, but she caught on real quick and everyone loves having her there from what I've heard.

I've been spending as much time as possible with Bailey, but it hasn't been a lot, between trying to figure out what Bull's doing, opening the garage back up, and all the drama with Vicky. She's still trying to show her ass around the club and tell people what to do and it's not happening. If she doesn't stop it soon, Bailey's gonna go off on her. I've already had to pull her ass away several times.

Today's another doctor appointment and I don't think I'm going to be able to make this one. It sucks, but there's so much to do and I'm only one person. Bailey is going to flip her shit when I tell her, but I hope she'll understand. I'm pulled from my thoughts by screeching and yelling coming from the common room. What the fuck is going on now?

I run out of the office to see Irish and Caydence helping Vicky out of the clubhouse. I'm guessing she went into labor and we're that much closer to getting rid of her ass. Bailey is sitting at the bar eating some fruit and reading a book. She's been doing that when she's not with Skylar or Maddison.

"Crazy girl, they takin' her to the hospital?" I ask, walking over to her.

"I don't know. Probably." She tells me looking up.

"Okay. Well, I'm gonna head on over to the garage. Come see me when you get back from the doctor?" I ask her.

"What do you mean Logan? You're not coming with me?"

"I can't this time baby. I've got so much to do over there. And, Cage and Joker need help with the bikes. If there was any way I could go with you I would and you know it." I say, leaning in and wrapping my arms around her.

"I know. I just thought you'd be going with me. It's not a big deal, go do what you gotta do and I'll see you when I'm done."

"Blade's with you. Don't leave without him and make sure he knows what time you have to leave."

"Okay babe. I love you."

"Love you too. I'll see you in a while. We're goin' out when I'm done at the garage though. Don't ask, because I'm not tellin' you where we're goin'."

"I can't. I'm watching Zoey tonight. Maddison has to work and I already told her I'd be there early since she has a few things to do on her way to work."

"Bailey, come on. We haven't really spent any time together since you got back and that was weeks ago."

"I don't like it any more than you do. I keep busy so I'm not sitting here waiting for you to get a minute. We'll have to do whatever you had planned another time. I'm sorry."

Tank comes up behind me and grabs a water from over the bar. He looks between the two of us like he wants to say something but doesn't know if he should. Finally, he opens his mouth and stuns us both.

"I can go watch Zoey tonight. You guys go do your thing and I'll head over to Maddison's after I check in at the hospital with Irish."

"Why?" Is all Bailey asks.

"You guys need your time too. It's not a big deal for me to watch Zoey." Tank says, walking out of the clubhouse.

He's been spending a lot of time over at the apartment since Maddison moved in. We all thought that Kenzie and him had a thing for a while, but he was just hanging out with her. I don't think that's the case with Maddison though. I've watched him watch her whenever she's been at the clubhouse. If a brother gets too close to her or Zoey, Tank's there with a warning in his eyes. I don't think it's going to be too long before those two are together.

"Well, if you're sure. I'll call Maddison and let her know of the change in plans." Bailey says, half yelling and picking up her phone.

"No. Don't worry about callin' her. I'll make sure I'm there early so she can go over whatever she needs to. I'm not plannin' on stayin' at the hospital that long. Just want them to know if they need anythin' I'm there." He answers before the door slams shut.

Bailey just looks at me with a knowing smirk on her face. "Crazy girl, leave it. They'll work it out on their own if they want to be together. You've got enough to worry about."

I kiss her goodbye and Bailey tries to make it more. I groan into her mouth as she starts rubbing me through my jeans. Damn her! She knows that I'm not going to deny her ass. So, I stand her up and lead her into the office. I'm not having someone walk in on us. Especially not Ma or Pops.

Instead of taking her to the couch, I lead her to stand in front of the desk. Gliding my hands up her back, I pull her shirt up as I go. Since she hasn't gotten dressed yet for the day, I don't have to worry about a bra, just removing my tee from her. Bailey raises her arms to help me get it off of her and I immediately bring a hand to her tit, squeezing and massaging it before moving to her nipple. They've already gotten bigger and I love it, knowing that she's going to be feeding our baby from her body.

Bailey throws her head back and lets out a little moan. Yeah, I found out she has sensitive breasts and can almost cum from me playing with them. Now, it's even worse. Looking down at her, I see that she's only wearing a pair of panties. I can't even begin to stop the growl at the fact that she was in the common room barely dressed.

"Crazy girl, you can't be wearin' shit like this around the guys."

"Babe, I knew there wasn't going to be any reason to dress in anything more when it was just gonna come back off. Besides, your tee is more than long enough to cover everything."

Instead of letting me continue to play, Bailey decides that she wants to play. So, she wrenches my tee over my head after setting my cut on the desk. In the next instant she's got my jeans down around my ankles and is starting to kneel down before me. While I love getting a blowjob from her, that's not happening today. She's going to have to take it fast, I'm not waiting. Later she can have sweet and more play time.

"Lean over the desk crazy girl. Fast and hard now. Play more later." I grit out between clenched teeth.

Without saying a word, she does as I tell her to. During sex is the only time Bailey does what I say without saying a word if she doesn't agree with me. I don't give her time to think about anything before sliding my hand between her legs to make sure she's nice and wet for me. I'm not disappointed, she's so wet it's starting to drip down her creamy thighs. Pushing her hair out of my way, I kiss and suck her neck at the same time I push into her. Bailey pushes back into me taking me as far as I can in her while bringing her arm up around my neck to keep me close. Meeting me thrust for thrust, Bailey speeds up when her other hand disappears to her clit. Not only is she playing with herself, she makes sure to grab my shaft every time I pull out of her. Fuck, I'm really not gonna last long if she keeps that up.

"I'm close Logan, so close." She pants out. I love hearing her breathy little moans better than any easy pussy screaming my ears off.

Instead of answering her, I start thrusting faster and harder bringing an arm around her stomach to hold her closer and make sure that we're not pressing her stomach into the edge of the desk. Bailey starts pushing back faster and faster against me telling me to pick my pace up. I can feel everything in me start to tighten as I get closer to my release and I know Bailey's about ready to fly by her breathing and the little moans escaping her opened mouth.

"Now crazy girl." I growl out, just as I feel myself swell inside her and know there's no stopping my release.

Bailey cums with me and we fall with her chest against the desk. I know she's not comfortable so I pick her up and walk to the couch for a minute so we can catch our breath. She lays her head on my chest and wraps an arm around my side. I've never been into cuddling, especially after fucking someone, but that all changed with Bailey. I want her in my arms as long as possible. I just know that I have shit to do today, so it's gonna be cut short this time.

"I can't resist you crazy girl and you know it. You don't play fair." I say as my breathing starts to even out. "Now, I've gotta get to Spinners and you need to get ready to go to the doctor."

"I know. I'm just ready for a nap now." She says while her eyelids flutter shut.

"Nope." I say smacking her ass. "Up to the room and shower to wake up. You don't want to be late. Are you takin' Ma with you?"

"No. I'll go alone. You said Blade's with me, so I'll be fine." She says, sitting up and going to get the tee from the floor by the desk. I can't do much else other than watch her ass sway back and forth as she walks across the room.

"Call or text when you get there. I want a text at least when you guys leave too. I'm headin' out. I'll see you when I'm done at Spinners." I say getting up and giving her a kiss while reaching for my shirt and cut.

Heading out, I make sure the office is locked up tight before I make my way out to Spinners. I really need to see how much work needs to be done there so I can get my hands dirty and try to figure out what to do next. I'm just pissed as fuck that there's so much to be done and I can't make it to the doctor with Bailey.

Bailey

I'm heading out to the doctor's office with Blade trailing me on his bike. On the way past the house, I pull in the driveway. I want to see the work that Rage has accomplished on the house. The way he's been busting through things, it shouldn't be long before he gets it finished and we can start moving in. I'm getting tired of living at the clubhouse. Don't get me wrong, I love the guys and spending time with them. But, if I want to be alone, the only space I have is our room. I can't just go sit outside with a book or something because you never know when someone's going to walk out.

Pulling through the field from Sky's yard, I see that the outside of the house is completely done. Rage jogs over as soon as he sees my truck. So I park and roll the window down. I really don't have time to get out and take a look around.

"Hey Bailey. I didn't know you were gonna be stoppin' by today." He says leaning his arms on my open window.

"Neither did I, it wasn't planned at all. Um... I'm heading to the doctor and just wanted to take a look at what's been done so far."

"We're workin' on puttin' the walls up for the office now. I'm gonna say about another month or less and we'll be done with it and you can move in. The only reason it's gonna be that long is because I need inspections done and everythin' like that. Have to wait on them to get out here."

"That's great! How's Kasey doing?" I ask, leaning back in my seat.

"She's doin' good. Been askin' about you though."

"I'll make my way over to see her in a little while then. She with Skylar?"

"Yeah. She and Reagan were playin' dress up or somethin' like that when I left." Rage says chuckling. It's so good to see him happy.

"Well, I'll make sure I go visit her then. I'll see ya later Rage."

"Bye Bailey." He answers, heading back to the house.

I pull out and head to the doctor's office. One more month to go and then we'll be in our own spot. When we get to the hospital, Blade makes his way into the office with me and sits down while I check in. I'm glad he didn't wait outside and came in with me. He's not going in the exam room with me, but I'll be more comfortable knowing he's waiting in the waiting room for me. Damn, I wish Logan were here with me.

"Bailey." A nurse calls almost as soon as I sit back down.

Standing up I make my way in back to get this exam done with. When the nurse weighs me, she makes a sound that I don't think is a good one. I know I've still been having morning sickness like crazy throughout the whole day, but I do eat. My clothes are getting tighter too and there's a ton of things I just can't wear anymore.

"Everything okay?" I ask her.

"You've lost some weight since last month. Are you still getting sick?" She asks me.

"Yeah. But I've been making sure to eat more in order to help what I lose when I do get sick."

"We'll see what Doctor Bell has to say honey. She'll tell you if she wants you to change your diet or something like that."

I follow her into a room so she can do her thing before the doctor comes in. I'm ready to get out of here after making sure that everything is okay with the baby so I can go have lunch with Logan and then spend time with Kasey. I miss the hell out of that little girl!

After Doctor Bell does her exam, she looks at my chart and sees that I've lost weight instead of gaining it. "Bailey, you're still sick?"

"Yeah."

"Is it better, worse, or the same." She asks.

"It depends on the day. Some days it's really good and other days it's worse."

"Okay. We'll keep an eye on your weight and at the next appointment we'll see if you're starting to gain. If not, we may have to think about admitting you to make sure that you're getting the proper nutrients and can start keeping more food down."

"Really?" I ask. "Don't some women lose weight in the beginning of their pregnancy?"

"They do. But, you're just over three months now so you should be gaining and not still losing."

"Okay. Well, I'll try to eat more at home and see if I can find something that helps with the morning sickness. I'll try keeping crackers and ginger ale or something with me to see if that settles my stomach."

"If that doesn't work for you, try a few different things. Dry toast, water, some juice, yogurt."

"Okay. Thank you. I'll see you again in a month." I say getting off the exam table and starting to gather my purse to leave.

"Bailey, don't forget, if you need me, call."

"I will. Thank you."

I grab Blade after making my next appointment and we head over to Spinners. Logan isn't going to like the fact that I've lost weight and I might have to go in the hospital if I don't start gaining weight. But, I'm not going to keep it from him either. He needs to know. Once we pull up, I sit in my car for a minute trying to just stop my head from reeling at knowing I have to figure out something to get past this morning sickness. Joker doesn't let me sit there alone for long though. He makes a beeline for my truck and opens the door scanning me from head to toe.

"What's wrong Bay?" He asks with concern etching his handsome face.

"I'm okay. I just have to talk to Logan. You can come in too so you know what's going on."

Getting out of the truck, we go into the office with Cage following us. Logan sits up straight in his chair seeing the three of us make our way through the door. Like Joker, he scans me from head to toe trying to figure out what's wrong. He's not going to see anything, so I just sit down in a chair across from him. Joker sits next to me and Cage stands behind us.

"Nothing's really wrong baby." I begin. "I've lost some weight and they're going to monitor it by seeing what I weigh in a month. If I haven't gained any, I might have to go in the hospital for a little bit. Nothing to worry about." I say, trying to downplay how scared I am.

"That's it? You've got to be kiddin' me that it's not a big deal crazy girl. Why are you losin' weight?"

"Probably because of the morning sickness."

"What do we do now?" Joker asks.

"I'm going to see if I can figure out what to eat when I start feeling sick to help calm my stomach down. Otherwise there's nothing that I can do and we'll have to wait and see what happens in a month."

"Let's go get some stuff then." Logan says, standing up.

"I'm fine. I don't feel sick and I'm heading over to Skylar's to see Kasey. Rage said she's been asking for me while I was gone. So, I'm going to spend the day with her. There's stuff I can try at Skylar's and there's things at the clubhouse I can try too. Calm down, all of you." I say looking at the three men in the room. "Women go through this every damn day and I'm no different."

"Crazy girl, if you need to go get shit, then we'll go."

"No! You have things to do and I'm going to have a play date with Kasey. Later on I'm probably going to check on Maddison and Zoey to make sure she's doing good and that Tank didn't piss her off by watching the baby. I don't know what time I'll be back but I'll let you know where I am."

"I don't like this shit." Joker says standing up. "You've been through enough and I'm tired of seein' you look like shit!"

"Thanks big brother. I love you too." I say dryly.

"You know I love you Bay. I just don't want to see you admitted to the hospital. I'll call ahead and make sure Sky knows to get things ready in case you need to eat somethin' for your stomach."

I can see how this next month is going to go already. These men are going to drive me up a fucking wall and I'm going to end up losing it on one of them. Pops doesn't even know yet, so I can only imagine what the hell he's going to have to say about it. Hopefully he's not the one that I happen to go off on.

My day has been exhausting! Little girls sure know how to wear a person down and make them ready for a nap. I want to go see Maddison though, so I'm pushing myself to make it to her apartment across town before I head back to the clubhouse to rest. Logan would flip a gasket if he knew I was tired and not taking a nap so I'll keep it to myself. He's got enough going on and doesn't need to worry about me.

Pulling up to the apartment building, I park and Blade follows me up to her apartment. I know that she just got off work a little bit ago so I don't know why Tank's bike is still here. Must be she's taking a shower or something. Oh well, he'll keep me company until she's done.

Knocking on the door, I hear Zoey crying and whoever is holding her is walking to the door since her cries are getting louder. Tank pulls it open and I can see Zoey squirming in his arms. He's not fazed by it though, he just steps aside and closes the door behind Blade.

"What's wrong little mama?" I ask.

"She's hungry and Maddison is just finishin' up in the shower. I already let her know so she's hurryin'." Tank says taking a seat on the couch Logan left here.

"I can hold her if you want me to." I tell him watching him with Zoey.

"I'm good." Is Tank's only response.

Tank looks so comfortable holding a little baby. He knows exactly what to do to get her to even remotely calm down. Zoey's already starting to slow her crying down as Tank rocks her back and forth and hums to her softly. I don't know the song he's humming, but I'm sure it's not a normal lullaby.

"Hi Bailey. Everything okay?" Maddison asks as she rushes into the room taking Zoey from Tank before sitting down in the chair and covering her chest and daughter up.

"Everything's fine honey. I was just stopping by to check on you and see how you've been settling in."

"I'm tired as hell honestly." Maddison says, peeking below the blanket to check on Zoey.

"Do you want me to keep the baby while you take a nap?" I ask her.

"No. Tank's going to stay for a while. Unless you got a call or something." Maddison answers while looking at Tank.

"I'm good sweetheart. While Bailey's here I'm goin' to go get our dinner. I'll be back in ten." He says walking out the door.

"So, wanna let me in on what's going on with the two of you?" I ask her while shifting to get more comfortable on the couch.

Maddison ducks her head, but not before I see the blush creeping up her neck. "Nothing's going on. He's been a real big help since we got to town. He came here and kicked everyone out so he could finish putting the furniture together. Then he went and bought me groceries. Today, he's been a big help with Zoey. Honestly, I wasn't sure about him watching her while I was working, but they both survived."

"Uh huh. You like getting to know him though don't you?"

"What's not to like? I mean he's gorgeous!" Maddison quickly looks around and sees Blade standing in the kitchen trying not to laugh.

"Don't worry, Blade won't open his big mouth about what he's heard." I say, looking at him with a glare.

"Nope. I don't hear anythin'." He says sitting at the table and leaning back in the chair.

"Well, I'm not going to complain to have Tank around as eye candy." Maddison continues. "I'm just not going to be in a relationship with him. Or anyone else."

"Where's that coming from?" I ask her confused.

"I'm just not going to put myself out there. Tank will be a good friend and that's about all I'm looking for now."

"We'll see Maddison. I'll tell you right now that if he's like my brother, Cage, and Grim, Tank is not going to give up until you're his. Tank's a real sweetheart and has been a shoulder to lean on for Skylar and me in the past. You'll be treated really well by him Maddison. Believe me, Tank is one of the good guys." I tell her my honest opinion of Tank.

308

"Then I'm going to talk to him. I'm not ready and I don't know if I'll ever be ready for a relationship with anyone. I've not got a good past and my track record with men is obviously not a good one. Considering the one relationship I was in was abusive. Just because he only hit me once, doesn't mean that he wasn't an abusive prick."

"We'll help you with whatever you need honey. But, I'm going to take Blade here with me as soon as Tank gets back. I need to go see if my man has a few minutes to breathe and relax with me tonight."

"I appreciate you stopping by Bailey. I'm so glad that I decided to come home with you. I needed a new, fresh start." Maddison says with tears in her eyes while switching Zoey to the other side.

We continue to just bullshit about random things as she finishes feeding the baby and wait for Tank to return. As soon as he does, Blade and I head back to the clubhouse so I can see my man and take advantage of him. He's going to give it to me tonight and I don't want to hear any bullshit about me needing to worry about gaining weight or anything else. If he doesn't want to give it up, I'll make sure that I drive him insane and leave him no other choice but to get involved, or watch me handle it myself.

Chapter Nineteen

Grim

IT'S BEEN ALMOST two months and things are coming to a head with the Soulless Bastards. We've put feelers out and we're pretty sure we know where they're bunking down now. Slim and his club along with Gage's club are going to come in and help us take them out. They should be here in a day or two. Plus, we have a toy drive coming up in the next month or so in order to help out the children's wing of the hospital for Christmas. Bailey's been talking to different businesses around town to help out, other clubs are coming in, and we're going to have a carnival at the end of it. It's a good thing that the weather stays pretty warm and we can do this on the bikes.

"Babe!" Bailey calls out. "I'm heading over to look at the house. Rage said he's just putting the finishing touches on it."

"I'm comin' crazy girl. I told you I was goin' with you." I say pushing up out of my chair.

"You're busy. I can go."

"No! When you see the house, I'm goin' with you. We're goin' to see it together." I tell her, wrapping my arms around her. "I can take time out to do this with you. Plus, I want to know when we can have the furniture delivered."

"Then let's go!" She says almost bouncing on her toes.

"You shakin' my baby up in there with all of your excitement?" I ask her.

"He or she is not getting shaken up in there." She says looking at me. "Speaking of which, don't forget we have the ultrasound coming up in a few days."

"I won't forget crazy girl. I'm tryin' my hardest to arrange everythin' around that day. I can't wait to see what we're havin'!"

"Me either. Are you sure you want to find out?"

"Absolutely!" I tell her leading her out of the clubhouse. "Let's head out so we can get back. I've got calls to make."

I hate having to rush her going over to look at the house, but I need to make calls, get gear ready to ride out, and a ton of other things that need to be done before the rest of the guys get here and we head out. Thankfully Blaze and the nomads are coming in so that I can leave them at the clubhouse while we ride out and rid the world of Soulless Bastards. Blaze knows that they're staying here and has no problem with it. His guys are going to do security and make sure that Bailey and Sky are guarded at all times. Blade is going with us and Rage is staying behind with Kasey. He really wants to ride with us, and he will next time, but I want him with his daughter this time since she's still getting used to everything that goes on around here and a bunch of guys she really hasn't seen are going to be around.

Walking across the field, Bailey and I make our way to the house that Rage has been busting his ass on finishing for us. I know that Bailey has been waiting and waiting for it to be finished, but she hasn't been bugging Rage about it at all. She's kept her distance and stayed away at all costs other than checking the progress a few times here and there.

"Rage, where you at Brother?" I call out when we get close and I see the front door is standing open.

"Grim, I'm in here. Come on in guys. I'm just finishin' up on the kitchen since the appliances are gonna be here in a few hours. So, I'm just hangin' the cabinet doors." He tells us as we walk in to the kitchen.

We walk in and Bailey's mouth drops open at the progress and the way the house looks. She picked out a tiled pattern for the kitchen with dark granite countertops, and oak cabinets. There's a ton of cabinets in here, plus a pantry. Bailey wanted an extra big refrigerator for when we have parties and things like that. Along with an industrial size stove and oven. I think she just wants

Skylar to come over and help her cook. Whatever she wants is what she's going to get though, nothing's too much for my girl.

"Rage, I love it so much! You've done an amazing job in here!" Bailey says in awe of everything that she's seeing.

Looking through to the living room, dining room, and to the office in the corner, all I can see is hardwood floors and the color scheme that Bailey picked out. Downstairs is all beige with wood accents all around. She even wanted exposed beams in the ceiling in the living room and dining room. The only room that is different is my office, which she had the guys paint a dark gray with the Wild Kings on one wall. She's not touching anything else in that room, her words not mine.

Bailey leaves us and walks through the rest of the house. She is eager to get moved in and I'm with her on that. I want us to have our own space to live in where we can do our thing without worrying about the brothers wanting our attention every two minutes. After a minute without a sound from her, I go in search of Bailey leaving Rage to finish his thing in the kitchen.

"Bay, where are you crazy girl?" I call through the house.

"I'm in the master bedroom." She answers me so I follow the sound of her voice.

Walking in, I see the huge empty space. Bailey's walking around looking like she's planning where to put everything. I can see her mind working overtime trying to make sure she gets everything placed exactly where she wants it. I wander around the room and take a look at everything they did in our space. There's a huge walk-in closet that will fit Bailey's clothes, and only her clothes.

"Crazy girl, where are my clothes supposed to go?" I ask her, kidding around.

She comes running in to see me. "Right here baby. See, this little three-foot section is all yours. So, make sure you choose wisely which clothes you're gonna hang up."

My girl is being completely honest with me right now. I'm getting a dresser and that's really all I get for my clothes. I guess it's a good thing that I don't have a lot of clothes that I need to worry about putting away.

"It's alright crazy girl. I'm sure eventually you'll need that section too." I tell her.

"Probably. But right now, it's gonna be all yours."

I can't help it, I need to kiss my girl. She's being so cute right now that it's impossible not to want to kiss her. So, I do.

"You haven't seen the best part Logan." She says, dragging me into the bathroom.

As soon as we get in there, my eyes are immediately drawn to the shower and the tub. The shower looks big enough to fit at least six people in and the tub is just as big. There's his and hers sinks along one wall with a ton of drawers under the sinks. Tucked away in one corner are shelves for towels and things I'm guessing.

"I so ripped off Skylar's bathroom with this." Bailey tells me. "But when I saw it I fell in love with her bathroom and she knows I wanted the same thing for us."

"I love it babe! We're gonna be breakin' this shit in sooner rather than later." I tell her pulling her to me.

"I want to show you the nursery." Bailey says leading me away from my thoughts of all the ways we're going to be breaking the tub and shower in.

"Lead the way ma'am." I say, as I guard my stomach waiting for her to elbow me. She can't stand being called ma'am.

"I'm going to pretend I didn't hear that because I'm so happy right now." Is her only response though.

We walk in to the room next to us and it's a huge room. Almost as big as our room is. The walls are painted white with no color of any kind on them. There's a closet off to the back corner of the room and two huge windows along the back wall.

"I love how big the space is." I start "But, why are the walls just white? You don't have white really anywhere in the house."

"Rage is going to paint the walls and lay carpet once we know what we're having and what color we want to have in here."

"Okay. You're not doin' the paintin' though. Right?" I have to ask because I know how impatient Bailey can be when she wants something done.

"Nope. He's going to do it as soon as we tell him what we want. Kasey is going to help him. She's really excited to get to help him paint our baby's room."

"You've grown attached to her haven't you?" I ask, pulling her back in my arms.

"I have. She's so cute and tiny. I love her big heart and she's always following me around when we're together. She just wants some attention from someone other than Rage and I have no problem giving that to her."

I look at her with amazement in my eyes. She's come so far since she's been going to counseling and I couldn't be more proud of everything she's accomplished. Bailey has a heart of gold and wants to help everyone and worry about herself last. For a while she was in no shape to help anyone, but she still wanted to. Now, she's almost back to her old self, but better than before. Bailey's always going to have days where the loss of Ryan is in the forefront of her mind and she can't deal with things. But, we'll all be there to help her on those days and get her through them.

"I love it and can't wait to see what we're havin'." I tell her kissing her forehead. "Now, I've got to get back to the clubhouse and get some work done. You hangin' here or are you goin' back?"

"I think I'll go back with you. I'm getting tired and want to lay down for a bit."

"You feelin' okay?" I ask concerned about her.

"Yeah, I'm just going to get tired more easily as I get farther along. It's all a part of it daddy. You heard Doctor Bell say that she was happy with the weight I've been putting on. My morning sickness is almost non-existent now. I'm okay. We're okay."

"You'll tell me if you feel off?"

"I will, I promise. Now let's get you back so you can get some work done."

After saying bye to Rage, we make our way back across the field and I walk Bailey up to our room. She's already got most of it packed up and ready to move over to the house when we can start moving things in. Within a week, that should be happening. Rage just has one last inspection to get through and then we're ready to go. Hopefully the inspector doesn't come out until after the ultrasound appointment and we get back from dealing with the Soulless Bastards.

"Alright, you relax. I'm goin' to call Slim and Gage. Blaze should be here with his guys later today. You need me, you come get me and I'm yours."

"Okay baby. I'll be fine. When I get up, Skylar and I are making dinner for everyone. Then we're going over to the house so she can see it. Hopefully Rage has most everything done. It's just the last minute, tiny details he's working on now anyway. I might talk to him about getting the furniture moved in throughout this week."

"I won't be here crazy girl." I remind her.

"I know. Blaze and the guys can help us. I won't even lift a finger unless I'm pointing out where I want something to go."

"You would take that shit away from me?" I ask her.

"Absolutely! I know you hate that shit. So, if I can have it done when you get back, all you'll have to worry about is your office."

"I love you! Now, I'll see you in a while."

After making sure she's settled in bed, I make my way to the office to handle my calls, go over last minute plans for Bull and his crew, and wait for Blaze to pull in. I'm hoping that we can get there, handle business, and get back within a day or two. I don't want Bailey to have to do everything with Blaze and the guys at the house. I hate doing that kind of stuff, but I will for her. As long as she gets everything where she wants it and is happy, I'll be happy.

Bailey

Taking a nap is just what I needed after being up most of the night before with Logan and then walking over to the house today. I love everything that Rage has done to the house and I didn't even walk through the whole thing. The basement is going to be another surprise for Logan and I'm happy that he didn't walk down there. I know we said we were going to make it a game room, but really it's a game room for the guys and him.

As soon as I know he's leaving to go take care of business, I'm having a pool table, all the accessories for it, a poker table, a bar and all of his favorite alcohol, and some tables to scatter throughout the room delivered. He's talked about wanting something like that before and I just thought it would be a nice surprise for him. There's going to be some posters from the room at the clubhouse down there. Along with some pictures of the members of the club throughout the years. I've been debating on putting a t.v. down there, and I think it will make a good addition to the room. That way the guys can watch games or whatever they want to and not disturb the women of the club. He knows nothing about it and the guys have kept quiet about it. Which is surprising because most of the time they gossip more than any female I know.

After taking care of business, I make my way in to the common room to see if Skylar made it here yet. The first person I see is Blaze. He stops talking to my brother and makes his way over to me scooping me up into a huge hug and spinning me around. When he puts me down, he kisses my forehead and leads me to where he was sitting with Joker.

"It's good to see you again Blaze. Hey brother, your woman here yet?" I ask sitting down.

"She's on her way. Cage is helping get the kids loaded in the SUV to get them all here. You feelin' okay? Grim said you were sleepin' when I got here a little while ago."

"I'm good. You know how Skylar got tired more often the farther along she got."

"I know, but you're like five months."

"I know that. I didn't get a lot of sleep last night is all. And you don't want to know why so don't ask."

"That's an image I didn't need in my head Bay."

"Look at you though Bailey. The last time I saw you, you were skinny as a rail. Now, you've put weight on and that little baby bump looks cute as fuck on you." Blaze says staring at my stomach.

"You hittin' on my girl Blaze?" Logan asks walking over to us.

"Hell no! I'm just sayin' how the baby bump and pregnancy glow she's rockin' works on her. We all know who she belongs to." Blaze responds as Logan pulls me up and sits down in my chair before pulling me onto his lap.

"You won't be sayin' that when she puts your ass to work while I'm gone. She's got plans for you there big guy."

"What's that?"

"Rage is just about done with the house. So, I'm going to use the muscles of the guys that are left here to help me move everything in."

Blaze groans out loud making the rest of us laugh. "I think Grim said he wanted me to go with him and you to stay behind Joker."

"Nah. He knows I won't get anythin' done because I'll be with my old lady the entire time."

"You guys still workin' on makin' that football team?"

"No, we're not!" Skylar says, walking in the door followed by the kids and Cage.

"Whatever you say baby girl."

Skylar walks over to me pulling me up and leading me into the kitchen. She doesn't say anything to my brother, Blaze, Grim, or the other guys on our way. What the hell is her problem? She's usually not like this.

"What's up mama? You just ignored everyone out there except for your outburst walking through the door." I ask her, walking over to start pulling everything out of the refrigerator.

"The guys want more babies and I'm not ready yet. So, there's been some tension at the house."

"You just had the boys and they want more?"

"Yep. I'm thinking we're done having kids though. I want to get my tubes tied and they don't want that."

"Too fucking bad. Six kids is more than enough!"

"That's my thinking too. They want a huge ass family though. I'm over the pregnancy and shit. Breastfeeding is bad this time since Kyle hates feeding and more times than not we have to bottle feed him. I don't want the pressure."

"Then we'll go and you can get your tubes tied no matter what they say. But I know you won't do that. You'll make them come around to your way of thinking, and you'll have the kids you have now."

"We'll see. They're sleeping on the couch tonight, I know that for a fact!" Skylar says, pulling the pots and pans out we need to make dinner for everyone that's going to be here.

For the next two hours we keep conversation light and cook our butts off. Tonight's dinner is meatloaf, mashed potatoes, green beans, and Skylar's biscuits. For dessert, she's making cheesecake, a pumpkin pie for my brother, and some cookies. Meatloaf is her go to meal when there's a lot of extra people in the clubhouse. She knows it won't take forever to cook, it makes a lot, and the guys all love it.

Summer and Storm have come in to help us while Cage brings the boys in to Skylar to feed. Brandon eats like a champ while I feed Kyle. He's really fussy while I'm bottle feeding him. So, I see where Skylar's coming from. As soon as she's done feeding Brandon, we switch babies and she takes Kyle up to Joker's room to finish feeding him and get him changed. I don't know what's going on, but she's about in tears when she leaves the room.

I hope that Joker helps her out in there since she had to get the keys from him and I saw him following her. Brandon is cooing in my arms until Cage comes in to get him from me followed by Jameson. He needs to know where his brothers and sisters are at all times.

"Hey handsome!" I say lifting him up. "How are you?"

"Good auntie Bay. Ky is sick and mommy's upset."

I can't say anything to that. Jameson watches everyone and everything around him. He's like a little Cage in that regard. I'm surprised he's not trying to get in the room with Joker and Skylar right now.

Setting him down, I grab some juice boxes for him and the girls so I can talk to Cage for a minute. "Cage, we need to talk."

"What's up?" He asks, following me into the back corner away from Storm and Summer.

"Skylar's tired. You guys need to calm down on the baby thing. Please! I know you all want a big family, but six kids is a lot of work when you're alone with them for the most part. You guys are getting ready to leave and it's just going to be four of us taking care of them."

"Bay, why are you talkin' about this with me?" He asks getting pissed off by my intrusion.

"Because I love you all and I'm telling you that she's tired and doesn't want to have any more kids. It's not because she doesn't love the hell out of the two of

319

you. It's because she's physically and mentally exhausted. Especially with whatever is going on with Kyle right now. She was just about in tears when she took him from me."

Cage doesn't say anything to me in response. Instead he makes his way to the rooms to check on his woman. So, I leave the other two in the kitchen and go see my nieces and nephew. They're in the common room hanging off of their favorite brothers. Tank just walked in with Maddison and Zoey in tow. So, Reagan goes running over to him.

He scoops her up and gives her a huge kiss on her cheek. "How's my favorite girl doin'?"

"Good. You Tank?"

"I'm good baby girl. You want to meet someone?" He asks her.

"Yeah."

"Maddison and Zoey, this is Reagan. Reagan this is Maddison and Zoey."

"Hi." Reagan says, burying her face in Tank's chest. Her shyness still comes out most of the time.

"Hey cutie." Maddison says, stepping just a little bit closer so Reagan can see Zoey in the car seat.

"She pretty." Reagan says in a whisper to Tank.

"I think so."

Reagan starts squirming to get down and after Tanks sets her on the ground, he makes sure she's steady on her feet before letting her take off. Making her way over to Grim, she climbs up on the chair next to him and grabs her crayons from in front of him. Tank has always been her favorite, her gentle giant, so I'm sure him showing up with Maddison is hurting her. She just doesn't know what she's feeling or how to explain it.

"Hey pretty girl" I say, quietly to her sitting down on her other side. "He's always gonna think of you as his baby girl, you know that."

"I know." Reagan says back quietly.

"Don't you want your Tank happy?" I ask her.

320

"Uh-huh. She pretty."

"She is pretty. And she's nice. You can talk to her while the guys go away this week. Does that sound like a plan?"

"Yeah."

I look over Reagan's head at Logan and he's smiling at us. We all know that Reagan loves Tank and any female that comes around is going to be hated by her. Just like we all know that Tank likes Maddison and is going to do whatever is necessary to win her over. I just hope he doesn't get his heart broken in the process. Maddison is trying to stay strong and stand on her own two feet right now. I just don't want to see her push him away because she's afraid to open herself up. She's a tough one to get to open up and I don't know why. I'll work on that while the guys are away this week. She already said she was going to come help us out at the house. Yeah, I'm planning on having everything moved in before Logan gets back, he just doesn't know it and we're going to keep it that way.

Since all of the kids are occupied, I go back in the kitchen to make sure that everything is ready. The meatloaf should be about done and the potatoes should be ready to turn off now too. The desserts have been made and are either cooling down or in the refrigerator. Summer is pulling the meatloaf out of the oven and Storm is already mashing the potatoes when I walk in. So, I make myself busy checking on the biscuits and green beans. Everything is done and ready to dish up. The three of us get the kids' plates ready and then set everything else out so the men can get their own plates. I sneak a plate for myself and Logan before I go in the common room with Reagan and Haley's plates. Summer and Storm bring the rest of the kid's plates out and set them on the big table that Joker, Cage, and Skylar usually sit at with them.

Logan comes up to me and wraps his arms around me while I put our plates with the kids. He kisses me, despite the kids saying 'ewwwwww', before sitting down. I'm not going to bother the guys and Skylar. They'll eat when they're done talking their situation out. Taking my seat between Haley and Alana, I watch the other two kids start eating. Tank sets his plate down by Reagan and Maddison sits on the other side of him.

"Where's Sky and the guys?" He asks.

"In Joker's room. Kyle was fussy so they took the boys in there until they can get him fed and settled down."

"Everything okay with him?" Maddison asks. She met Skylar and the guys when we got in to town.

"I don't know. She said he's been having a hard time breastfeeding and I was bottle feeding him earlier and he was fussy as hell."

"She might have to put him on formula. I know she doesn't want to, but that could be the problem he's having."

"You can talk to her about it when you see her. She'll appreciate any ideas you can give her I'm sure. From what she's said, none of the other kids have had a problem like this."

"Some babies just can't tolerate breast milk and need to be put on soy formula or something like that. Even regular formula may make a difference. Zoey hasn't had a problem with that, but one of the girls that I used to live by had a baby that had a problem with breast milk. As soon as she changed him to formula, the fussiness went away and he was a happy camper."

"Well, like I said, you can talk to her about it this week or something."

The three of us sit back and watch the kids eat. When they're done, I'll take them to our room and give them baths so that it's one less thing that Skylar has to worry about doing. Logan can help and get some practice with it before our little one is here too. He's never given a kid a bath and I think it's gonna be hilarious.

"Bath time is fun right?" I ask Logan.

"Yeah, tons." He says drily, glaring at me from the bathroom.

He's got Alana and Haley in the tub and I don't know who has more water on them, him or the girls. I took care of Reagan a little while ago and Jameson is getting in after Alana and Haley are done. Since Logan's covered in water, he can take care of Jameson too. I turn my back for a second to finish getting the girls' pajamas out and hear a loud shriek followed by a huge splash of water. Spinning around, I see Logan covered in water and the girls giggling at him. They're only two so I have to laugh since they're really pulling all the punches with him. They never give me this much trouble.

"You want some help baby?" I ask innocently.

"Nope." He grits out grabbing the washcloth and baby wash. "Give me five minutes and then you'll be rethinking laughing at me."

"Nope. You have to help Jameson after the girls. He'll probably want a shower though."

"How the hell am I supposed to help him in the shower?"

"The same way you are now. You just hold the curtain to the side and don't let any water out. Although I don't think it really matters at this point in time if you let water out or not." I say laughing.

"You'll get yours crazy girl. Just remember when you wanna have fun later." He says, trying to get even with me for laughing at him.

"Baby, I have ways to make sure that you'll give in to me. Remember the last time you wanted to deny me?"

"You don't play fair!"

"I know that. Get the girls done and I'll get Jameson showered and ready for Skylar and the guys. You can quit pouting now."

"No, I'll take care of it. You go do whatever you need to and I'll get the three of them washed up."

"I'm waiting on you so I can get the girls dressed baby."

Logan moves his ass to get the girls washed and rinsed off so that I can get them in their pajamas and take them back out to the common room. Jameson comes running in the room out of breath and laughing. I catch him and start taking his shirt off.

"What's going on little man? Why are you running in here like that?" I ask him.

"Glock chasing me."

"Why?"

"We're playing. I'm faster than him auntie Bay."

I can't help laughing at him. He's so excited that he beat Glock. Jameson is all about competition when he's not watching out for his siblings. It's one of the things he has in common with everyone in this place. Everyone always trying to prove they have the bigger dick.

Glock makes it to our door trying to catch his breath. "You got lucky little man. Next time, there won't be as many legs for you to weave through that I have to push out of my way."

"Sure." Jameson says, lifting his arms so I can get his shirt off him.

"Next time, we're outside. Maybe I'll set up an obstacle course." Glock says, acting like he's mad at losing to Jameson.

"And I'll still win!" Jameson says excited at the prospect of running an obstacle course.

"We'll bet."

"Anything?" Jameson's little eyes light right up at that.

"We'll see." Glock returns before leaving the room.

I go in the bathroom and take the girls from Logan and usher Jameson in to him. Jameson closes the door and I can hear him telling Logan about beating Glock and the obstacle course. He's talking a mile a minute. Logan is laughing and talking back to him but I can't hear what he's saying. Probably telling Jameson what he should make the bet for. Glock's going to be sorry if Logan, my brother, or Cage have any input in Jameson's part of the bet.

While I'm dressing the girls, Skylar comes in the room. She's been crying and I know that she needs a break. Especially when the guys leave. So, looks like I'm going to be taking the kids from her for a night or two so that she can sleep and just relax.

"I'm sorry for disappearing." She says helping me finish.

"You take care of you and don't worry. Jameson's in there with Grim right now and then all the kids, except for Kyle and Brandon, will be done. It's not a big deal."

"I'm going to take them home when Jameson's done. The guys are going to follow me back to the house."

"They still sleepin' on the couch?" I ask her.

"No. Whatever you said to Cage worked and he talked Joker around to my way of thinking. So, we're going to be looking into possibly getting my tubes tied."

"Good. I'm happy for you that this is out of the way and you stood your ground with them. Oh, while you were in Joker's room, Tank showed up with Maddison and Zoey in tow."

"Okay." Skylar says, drawing the word out because she's confused.

"Tank broke Reagan's heart because Maddison is pretty."

"My girl's first crush broke her heart already!"

"She was upset and wouldn't let him hold her. But, I don't think anything is ever going to take away her crush on that man."

"I know. I feel sorry for any boy that likes her. They're going to have to measure up to not only her daddies but to Tank too. It's going to be hard for anyone to get near her with the three of them being used as a measuring stick."

"Yep. At least you won't have to worry about her dating then!" I say, starting to laugh.

"True."

At that moment Logan opens the bathroom door and I swear he's covered in more water than he was with bathing the girls. Skylar and I look at him and then bust up laughing so hard we have to hold our sides. He doesn't see what's so funny though.

"Did you get in the shower with Jameson?" Skylar asks.

"No."

"How did you get covered in water then?"

"It started with Alana needin' to splash every time I moved a muscle. Then I couldn't get the shower to stay where I put it when I was washin' Jameson."

"He usually washes himself and I just help him get spots he missed and rinse him off." Skylar tells Logan.

"What?" Logan asks, trying not to shout.

Jameson comes out covered in a towel and laughing his little butt off. He's in heaven right now. Not only did he beat Glock, but he got one over on uncle Grim too. Jameson's going to be telling anyone that will listen to him about this day for a long time to come. I love it!

"Okay little man get dressed so that we can head back to the house. It's about bed time and mommy's ready to go to sleep. Tomorrow you can have more fun and play around."

"Okay mama." Jameson says getting his pajamas and going back in the bathroom to get dressed.

"I don't know how to do it." Logan says to Skylar. "I'm soaked and feel like I'm the one that took a shower and I didn't."

"It's easy and comes with practice. You'll get used to it when your little one gets here. Just don't be afraid you're going to hurt them or anything and you'll be fine."

Logan walks out the door shaking his head. He doesn't even bother changing his clothes. I'm sure he's just going to grab a beer and have a sit down with the guys before they leave and then he'll come in to shower and get ready for bed. It's early but he tries to lay down with me when I'm ready to hit the hay every night. I'm still tired, so we'll see if he makes it back before I'm sleeping. I don't even want to take a shower I'm so tired. Yawning, Skylar hurries Jameson up and gives me a hug before leaving the room. As they're leaving the room, I can hear Jameson telling his mom about beating Glock in a race and the obstacle course.

I go out to get my hugs goodbye from the kids and let Logan know that I'm going to bed. He can stay out here and do his thing, but I'm ready to get away from the craziness. More and more guys are just going to be showing up and I'll need my rest to do everything to get ready for them showing up and everything I want to do while Logan's away. He tells me that he'll be in as soon as he's done with his beer and kisses me on the neck before I walk out of the room.

Chapter Twenty

Grim

I STAYED OUT in the common room until Slim and his crew showed up and then I had a beer with them. Once my beer was gone, I joined Bailey in our room. She was passed out so I get ready to hop in the shower real quick to warm up and get clean. Giving the kids a bath tonight was definitely an experience I won't soon forget. How such little things can get so much water all over the place is a mystery I don't think will ever be solved.

Walking in the bathroom, I can see that Bailey cleaned up the mess made earlier and I feel bad that I didn't take a minute to clean it up before I went out for a few drinks. Stripping my clothes, I make sure they land in the hamper before starting the shower. I look in the mirror and see the weariness lining my face. The only thing I want is to get the Soulless Bastards taken care of so we can relax and I can enjoy the rest of Bailey's pregnancy. I hope like hell we can leave in two days and nothing is going to make us move before then.

After a quick shower, I climb in bed and pull Bailey to me. She burrows farther into my chest and wraps her arm around me. I love when she gets as close to me as she can so that she wraps her entire body around mine. It's amazing that even in sleep she turns to me and burrows in.

I'm just settling in to go to sleep and I'm startled by a loud pounding on the door to our room. Quickly I leave the bed, not even caring that I'm not wearing a single thing. If whoever's pounding on my door wakes Bailey up, I'm going to be beating some ass. Naked or not!

"This better be fuckin' good!" I growl out, opening the door enough to see Slim standing there.

"You know I wouldn't bang your door down if it wasn't. We got word that we need to move now. The

Soulless Bastards are gettin' ready to move and we don't know where they're goin'."

"Fuck!" I growl. "Wake everyone up, emergency church. I'll get dressed and let Bay know we're headin' out. Cage and Joker are home so I'll call them on my way down."

Slim turns and starts pounding on doors up and down the hallway. I shut the door, really hating the fact that I have to wake my girl up when she's been so tired. But, there's no way in hell I'm leaving without telling her goodbye. That's something I won't ever do to her no matter what we got going on, I'll always tell her goodbye.

"Crazy girl." I murmur next to her ear. "Wake up crazy girl. You can go back to sleep in a few minutes."

"Huh?" She asks, slowly opening her eyes.

"Just got word we gotta head out now. They're gonna be movin' and we don't want to lose them."

"Okay. You go do your thing and I'll pack your bag." She tells me, sitting up and pulling my tee farther down on her.

I kiss her forehead and throw some clothes on before calling the guys to come in now. I know they'll be a few minutes so they can tell Sky goodbye and pack their bags. We'll wait for them to get here before we do anything. It will give me enough time to get a cup of coffee in me before we make plans to head out.

Walking into the kitchen, I see Storm standing by the coffee pots making sure they are filling up. Once they're ready, she's filling up the carafes so we can take the coffee in the meeting room with us. I grab the mug she hands me and add my creamer and sugar. I no sooner walk into the common room, where the rest of the guys are trying to wake up, and Cage and Joker burst through the doors. They got here a lot faster than I thought they would. Their bags must've already been packed and ready to go.

"Meetin' room. *Now!*" I call out over the dim roar of conversations going on.

Everyone files in and my crew take their seats. Slim's crew lines up along one wall and Gage's crew lines up along the opposite wall. They weren't here when I went to bed, so they must have gotten here in the last little bit. I've only been in my room a few hours at the most. Once I take my seat, I bang the gavel and call the meeting to order.

"Slim, you woke me up, so you can explain what the hell's goin' on." I say giving him the floor.

"You know we sent Wood and Boy Scout up ahead to scout locations for us. About a half hour ago, they were in a bar and in walked a few Soulless Bastards. Since neither one was wearin' their cut, the Soulless Bastards walked in talkin' about makin' their moves and headin' out at first light. It's gonna take us at least a few hours to get there so we need to head out."

"All in favor?" I ask.

The response is a round of 'yays'. So, I tell them all to gather their hardware and be ready to roll in five minutes. That will give me enough time to say goodbye to Bailey again and drink one more cup of coffee. I stay in my seat until everyone else has filed out of the meeting room. There's no sense in fighting everyone else to get out of the same room.

I finally walk out and see Bailey sitting at a table holding Kasey. So, I make my way over to her and see that my bag is sitting on the floor under the table. She must have packed my guns and didn't want Kasey to get at it. When I get outside, I'll put them in my saddle bags until we get closer to wherever the Soulless Bastards are. Wood and Boy Scout are going to meet us when we're about a half hour out from where they're staying.

"Crazy girl, where's Rage?" I ask, so I can have a minute alone with her.

"He's in the kitchen getting Kasey a drink before we go up and lay down in our bed."

"Okay. Kasey, why don't you go see daddy so I can talk to Bailey a minute."

"Okay." Kasey says running into the kitchen to find Rage.

"Come on crazy girl. Let's go outside." I say pulling her up and grabbing my bag at the same time.

"I'm gonna miss you." She says. "But, I know you need to go kick some ass and come back to me."

We walk out to my bike and I put my go bag in one of the saddle bags and my guns in the other one. As soon as I'm done, I turn and face her pulling her into me. I wrap my arms around her and hold her close. This is one of the reasons why I didn't want an old lady. I don't want to have to worry about making it back to someone, or having them worry about me the entire time I'm gone. Bailey's worth it though.

"Crazy girl, I'm comin' home to you. I'm gonna try my hardest to get this taken care of and be back for the ultrasound."

"You worry about taking care of business and I'll see you when I see you. I love you!"

"I love you too. Take care of our baby. Rage and Blaze are here if you need anythin'."

"I'll call Ma if I need anything baby. You go take care of business."

I grab Bailey around the back of her neck and pull her mouth to mine. She immediately opens up to me and gives me what I want. So, I take her mouth and the moan she gives me. No one needs to hear her moans and whimpers, they're all mine.

"I'll call you when I can crazy girl. I love you."

"I love you. I'll keep my phone on me."

Bailey walks back to stand near the door with Skylar and watch us leave. She immediately picks Alana up and cradles her to her chest. I know that Bailey's doing this so I won't see the tears in her eyes. She doesn't want me worrying about what's going through her head.

"Alright, let's roll!" I call out.

We all mount our bikes and start them up. Thankfully, there's only Alana outside because I'm sure that none of the other kids would tolerate the noise from fifty plus bikes starting almost at once. It's loud as hell going down the road. Starting them within the compound is even louder.

Bailey

It's almost the middle of the night and the guys have been gone for a little while now. Kasey is lying in my bed with me passed out. Rage and some of the other guys are still awake walking the grounds making sure that nothing happens since there's not really that many guys left here. So, they've split up and are going to be taking turns standing guard. Rage is going to be going to sleep soon though because he has Kasey and because he has the inspector coming in tomorrow.

Hopefully tomorrow afternoon we'll be able to start moving things in the house. I've already let the furniture company know that the inspector is coming in and we'll be ready for the furniture tomorrow afternoon. If something goes wrong, they're willing to hold off. They're just waiting on my call as soon as Rage lets me know what the inspector says.

I'm trying to go to sleep and it's not happening. I know that Logan is going to have a ton of guys at his back, but that doesn't mean that I don't worry about things going wrong. All it takes is one guy to not pay attention for a split second and someone's gonna catch a bullet. The Soulless Bastards don't seem like the type of crew to worry about what's going on with the other crew other than taking them down.

"Bay, I'm not sleepy." Kasey says waking up from her short nap.

"What's the matter honey?" I ask her.

"I'm thirsty and my belly is rumbling."

"Do you feel like you're going to be sick again honey?"

"I don't know."

"Why don't you go in the bathroom and sit in front of the toilet? I'll get your daddy in here and we'll get you taken care of baby girl."

Kasey gets up and goes into the bathroom. I follow her and lay a towel down on the floor so she has something under her little knees. Then I open the door to see if I can see anyone in the hallway. Thankfully Summer is coming down the hallway.

"Summer, can you do me a favor?"

"Are you okay?" She asks, speeding up walking to me.

"I'm fine. It's Kasey. Can you get Rage for me please? She's not feeling real well right now."

"I think he just sat down in the common room. I'll send him right back."

Closing my door again, I go in to see that Kasey is in fact sick again. This poor little sweetheart looks so upset because she's getting sick. She's crying now which isn't helping the situation any, but most little kids do cry when they get sick.

Just as I'm about to kneel down next to her, there's a knock on my door. Rage pokes his head around it after opening it up a crack. He can see right in the bathroom, so he sees that Kasey is throwing up again while I hold her hair back.

"I'm sorry Bay. I didn't know she was sick when she asked to come in here with you."

"It's okay Rage. She fell asleep for a little bit and woke up saying she was thirsty and that her belly was rumbling. We got her set up in here and it didn't take long before she was sick."

"I can take her to my room if you want."

"Nope. You need sleep and to do what Blaze needs you to do. I just need some blankets to make her a bed on the floor and something in case she gets sick and can't make it to the bathroom. I've got her."

"You need sleep too. Grim would kill me if he knew you were takin' care of her while she's sick."

"You let me worry about him. Just get me things to make her comfortable. Or, you stay in here with her and I'll get what I need."

"I'll stay with her."

Making my way into the hall, I run into Dozer. Literally. He steadies me and then continues on his way down the hall to a room he's staying in. Dozer reminds me a lot of Tank with the way he acts and how little he speaks to most people. Going to Joker's room, I gently knock on the door. The last thing I want to do is wake up the kids.

After a minute, Skylar opens the door and pokes her head out. "What's wrong Bailey?"

"I need any extra blankets you might have. Kasey is staying with me and she's sick. So, I'm making her a bed on the floor."

"Yeah. Give me a minute and I'll be right back."

I'm waiting in the hall and Blaze comes down the hall. He stops when he gets to me and I tell him what's going on with Kasey. Blaze stays with me and carries the blankets Skylar hands me back into my room. Setting them on the bed, he waits so that he can talk to Rage before they both go get some sleep. Must be the other guys that came in with him are on watch right now.

"Thanks Blaze. I could've handled it though."

"I know you could have. I wanted to help."

"I'll be out in a minute man." Rage says from the bathroom.

"Take your time. Your daughter's more important than anythin' we gotta talk about." Blaze tells him.

"I'm gonna go get a pan, some water and crackers for later, and some movies I saw in your room Rage."

"Okay. I'll get her blankets set out on the floor while you're gone."

While I'm in the kitchen, I hear a small commotion coming from one of the bedrooms. It sounds close to the kitchen, and my room, so I'm thinking it may be in Rage's room. Walking there, I see the door is slightly open so I peek in. Summer is laying in his bed waiting for him, and one of the club girls is standing there chewing her a new ass.

"Excuse me!" I say, moving in the room and closing the door. "Summer, Rage know you're in here?"

"Yeah." She says covering up.

"Then what the hell are you doing in here?" I ask the club girl.

"I was going to go to bed. This bitch won't get up so I can lay down."

"This isn't your room. You don't have a room in this clubhouse. In fact, I don't think I've ever seen you here before."

"This is the first time that I've been here. What the fuck is it to you?"

"Bitch, I'm the President's old lady. Everything that goes on here is my business. Now, I suggest that you leave this room and the clubhouse. No one needs your skank ass here."

"You can't tell me to leave."

"As a matter of fact I can. I'm in charge of the women in this clubhouse. Now, I'm telling you to get the fuck out!"

This dumb bitch actually tries to come at me like she's going to put her fucking hands on me. I go to defend myself until she gets yanked backwards by Summer, who leaped off the bed in all her naked glory. This is quickly turning into a cat fight that I don't need to deal with.

"Bitch, she's pregnant with the President's baby. You really wanna put your fuckin' hands on her?"

About this time Blaze and Dozer come busting through the door and take in the scene. "Bailey, what's goin' on in here?"

"Rage knows that Summer's in here waiting for him. This other bitch decided that she was going to kick Summer out of his room her first time here. Then she lunged at me when I told her to get the fuck out because it doesn't matter what I say here."

"Really? Dozer, why don't you take hold of the bitch so Summer can cover herself up." Blaze says. "Now, not only is she the President's old lady, but her brother and father are members of this club. In fact, her mom's right in the kitchen. That makes her untouchable. You want to put your hands on her?"

"I-I didn't k-know." The club girl stammers out. "I'm sorry!"

"Too late for that now. Dozer escort her off the property. I'll wait until you get the movies and walk you back Bay." Blaze says, moving out of the way of the bitch Dozer is now escorting from our sight.

"I'm sorry Bailey." Summer says.

"It's not your fault honey. It's that bitch that doesn't know what the hell she was doing. Don't worry about it. Rage should be here in a few minutes."

"Okay."

I quickly grab a few of the movies that I know Kasey loves before going to get the rest of the stuff from the kitchen. Ma follows me into my room. She wants to know what's going on, and I'm not gonna keep anything from her. As soon as the guys leave the room we'll talk.

Rage has Kasey laid out on a pile of blankets and is sitting next to her. So, I hand him the pan to put by her and take the rest of the stuff to sit on Logan's stand next to the bed. Blaze quickly recounts what he walked in on in Rage's room before the two leave the room so I can relax with Ma and Kasey.

"Baby girl, you get in bed and relax. I'm gonna stay in here to help you out with Kasey. You need your sleep for my grandbaby."

"Yes mother." I say, leaning down to kiss her cheek.

It feels like I no sooner lay down and cover up and I'm out cold.

Chapter Twenty-One

Grim

WE MET UP with Wood and Boy Scout about an hour ago. As soon as we stopped everyone pulled out at least one weapon. Yeah, we know we're gonna surprise the Soulless Bastards, but we're not gonna get caught unaware either. Wood had Killer pull every blue print he could find while working his magic to the warehouse they're staying in so we can form a plan of attack.

"Slim, you got the information we needed, what do you think?" I ask him.

"I think we separate into three teams. One for the front door, one at the back door, and the third stays back a bit to get anyone that tries to run. The third group can be the biggest so that they can spread out around the warehouse."

"Gage, you good with that?" I ask, turning to look at him.

"Yeah. I think one of us should lead each team. Pick the guys we trust the most, and then the rest spread out on team three."

"Okay. Slim, what door you want?"

"I'll take the back."

"Alright. Gage, you pick whose team you want to be on and we'll get the guys in groups before we head out so we can split up where we need to."

"I'll go with you Grim."

The three of us turn and face the guys we brought with us. I already know without a doubt I want Cage, Joker, Pops, Tank, Irish, and Glock with me. Gage picks Crash, Trojan, Steel, and Fox to come with us. Slim picks Wood, Killer, Des, and Whino to go with him. I guess we're taking more guys since we're going through the front doors. If they're planning on leaving at first day light, they will probably be up and getting ready to go when we come busting through.

After explaining where everyone is going, we all mount back up to get to the warehouse. Since Wood and Boy Scout know where we're going, Wood leads the pack. Then the guys that are going to be spread out around the warehouse follow before the guys going in with me. Wood is going to let them know where they need to pull off and hide their bikes before moving into position. Thankfully, Slim and Gage didn't choose Grizzly, Strip, Playboy, Stryker, and Ghost. They've been through this before so they can lead the rest of the guys and make sure they're on point and know what they're doing. Besides, you rarely find Ghost without seeing Shadow up his ass. Those are two sneaky fuckers.

Before we left, Blaze set us up with a few charges we would need to open the doors. Not exactly subtle, but they'll blow the doors off the hinges. If we're lucky, it'll take out a few of the Soulless Bastards too. Steel is going to go up and set the charges at the front door and Killer is going to do the same at the back door. Slim will do the countdown so that we can blow them at the same time.

Once Steel walks back over to our group, I hear Slim begin his countdown in my ear piece. Just so I know that the guys behind me know what's going on, I hold up my fingers and do the countdown at Slim's pace. He no sooner hits one and Steel is pushing the button to set off the explosives he rigged on the door.

As the explosion occurs and we can move, we're on our feet running towards what used to be the door. Inside, the warehouse is nothing but utter chaos. The Soulless Bastards are trying to run, but we're taking them out faster than they can get away. The only one I want alive is Bull. He's going to answer the questions we have regarding Skylar and Bailey and what their end game is in all of this.

Seeing Cage in the corner fighting off two men, I make my way over to help him out. I'm not going to shoot and hit him by accident. Skylar will shoot my ass if that happens, and I like being on her good side. Pulling

338

one guy off, I step out of the way of the knife he's waving in the air towards me. Just as I go to take care of him, he drops to the floor. Looking up, I see Joker aiming his gun at him. Giving him a nod I make my way through the chaos in search of Bull.

No matter where I look, I can't find him anywhere and I'm running out of places to search. We've opened all the doors and let the women that were here go. There's no basement to the place and everything is pretty much open. Where the fuck is the bastard?

"Pres! Pres!" I hear Blade yelling "I got him!"

"What?" I ask, heading toward the back door where I hear Blade coming in.

"He tried gettin' out and I got him." Blade says, dragging an unconscious Bull behind him.

"Blade, you need to let go of him and sit down. Now!" I yell at him. Not only does he have blood pouring out of his shoulder, but there's blood pouring down his leg too.

"What? Why?" He asks me thoroughly confused.

"Man, you're bleedin' like crazy from your shoulder and leg. What the fuck happened to you? Cage, Tank, and Joker, over here now!"

"I don't know what happened." Blade says, sliding down the wall to a sitting position.

"What the fuck happened?" Cage asks when he sees Blade on the floor and Bull not too far from him.

"Blade caught the coward tryin' to sneak away out the back. I don't know who the fuck shot him, but he's got one in the shoulder and one in the leg. We're gonna have to take him to the hospital. We've got no choice with two holes, and doc couldn't come."

"Have Shadow take him. He can say they were in a bar fight or some shit. Ask Wood what bars they went to last night and name one of them." Gage says, walking up to us.

Joker goes running over to Wood to ask him some bar names. Meanwhile, Gage goes out and gets the cage we brought with us to carry the explosives in, and in case something happened like this. Tank's busy tearing strips of his tee off to try to stop Blade's bleeding. So, I make my way over to Slim to get him to string Bull up while we tend to Blade and see how many other guys are injured or worse.

Walking through the wreckage, I count a few guys that have nicks and scrapes from guns or knives. The only dead bodies I see so far belong to the Soulless Bastards. Outside is a different story. Most of the guys that were surrounding the warehouse are whole and just relaxing after being braced and waiting for something to happen. Until I see a circle of Slim's guys standing off to the side.

Making my way over to them, I see a guy on the ground. Strip is lying there with his eyes closed, and if you didn't look closely at him, you would think he was knocked out. Unfortunately, I know this isn't the case. His chest is completely still and the patch of red on his chest is huge. The guys surrounding him are filled with sadness and anger. Strip was one of the good guys. He went up through the club with Slim and they were close. This is going to gut him.

"I'll tell Slim." I tell the remaining guys. "What happened?"

"Before Blade could get that fucker knocked out with his gun, Bull went after Strip as soon as he walked out the door. There was no warnin' or anythin'. Didn't even think twice about shootin' his ass." Grizzly tells me, rubbing his hair out of his face.

"Okay. I'll go tell Slim. Find somethin' in the van to cover him up before they take Blade to the hospital. Bull shoot his ass up too?"

"Yeah." Is all I get from Grizzly before I turn to break the news.

As I walk back inside, my guys fall behind me in case I need them to help restrain Slim. This time though, I'm going to let him have his fun. He's going to get the shots he needs in while I question Bull. Bull is really going to regret taking out not only one of Slim's men, but his best friend.

"Slim, I need a minute." I tell him seeing that Tank and Wood are tying Bull up.

"What's up Grim?" He asks, making his way through the carnage to me.

"I need to tell you somethin'. You'll get your payback, but you gotta wait until we get everythin' sorted out and start to question Bull."

"What happened? It's not Playboy is it? Tell me my son is okay."

"Playboy is outside. He's fine. It's Strip."

"Where is he?" Slim asks, standing tall.

"He's outside with your men. I'm sorry Slim. This is on me for askin' you to help us out."

"It's not on you. We all knew what we were gettin' into when we talked, and agreed that we would help. I'm goin' to see him and Playboy. I'll be back. Tell me that's the fucker that killed him?"

I nod my head and Slim heads out. He's trying not to let his emotions show, which is when he's at his most dangerous. Instead of lashing out, he's going to hold it in and let it rage through him until he can get his hands on Bull. When he unleashes his rage it's going to take all of us to restrain him and stop him from killing him before we have our answers.

Shadow is staying at the hospital with Blade. He had to go in for surgery to remove the bullet that's still in his leg. Plus, they wanted to make sure that the main artery wasn't damaged. We'll make our way there when we get our answers from Bull.

He's just starting to wake up. We didn't wake him up before now so we could move the bodies to one side and set up the tools we're going to need during our interrogation. I'm standing next to Slim and he nudges me, letting me know that Bull is starting to come around. Thank God we can get this show started now.

The first thing Bull does is look around until he sees all of his men dumped like garbage in the corner. His rage-filled eyes find Slim, Gage, and me before he takes in the rest of our guys standing around him. Finally, you can see the resignation on his face, he knows that his time has grown limited and that can make or break the situation now. Bull's either going to eventually give us the information we want, or he's going to keep his mouth shut since he has nothing to lose now.

"Welcome back fucker!" I say, moving closer to him.

"Fuck you!"

"I think he doesn't understand the situation he finds himself in right this second Grim." Slim says, walking over to him.

Without any hesitation, Slim rams his fist right in Bull's face. "You're gonna pay for takin' Strip's life you dirty fucker!"

"I'm not payin' for shit. He deserved what I did, and if I had my way, he would've been tortured before I killed him."

"Wrong answer douchebag." I say, getting in his face. "What the fuck do you want with Skylar and Bailey?"

"Who?" He asks, playing dumb.

"You know who I'm talkin' about asshole. What do you want with them?"

"I'm not tellin' you fuckers anythin'." Bull responds before spitting in my face.

"Slim, do your worst, but keep him alive. You've got ten minutes before we head out to get dinner and check on Blade." I tell him walking away to clean up a bit. We need to regroup and I need to call Bailey to check on her.

I can hear Bull's grunts and groans as I make my way down the little hallway where I saw a bathroom in earlier. Closing the door to shut out the noise, I text Bailey and tell her that I'll call her later. She responds saying okay and that she loves me. Shoving my phone back in my pocket, I go to the sink and wash away all the blood and gore from my hands and upper body. We're all going to have to change clothes before we go find food and then go to the hospital.

It's been a week and Bull still hasn't talked. He's beat to hell and I don't know how he's still hanging on to life right now. Blade is recovering in the hospital with Shadow and Boy Scout staying with him. We visit every day, but he knows we need to get this shit handled so we can head home when he gets out of the hospital in a few days.

Slim is in with Bull right now trying to get him to talk. I'm ready to go in and end the fucker, but we need to know what's in play right now. So, I make my way in the main room of the warehouse to see Cage, Joker, Pops, Tank, and the rest of our guys standing around watching Slim cut Bull up now. He's been saving this in case Bull wouldn't talk.

"Slim, hold up. I'm ready to have my go at him today. He's still got his tongue right?"

"Yeah. I figured we'd leave it to the last thing to take out. He needs it to talk to us right?"

I laugh before I can stop myself. The things that come out of Slim's mouth sometimes kill me. "Yeah, we need him to talk."

I grab the bowie knife from Slim's hands and shove it in Bull's thigh making sure to miss anything vital so he doesn't die before we're ready. "You ready to answer our questions now?"

"F-fuck y-y-you!" He stammers out.

"Nope, you're not my type, and I got a woman I need to get home to. Now, what the fuck were you gonna go after Bailey and Skylar for?"

"You're not gonna win." Bull says. "The guys that want them aren't fuckin' around. They want those two and they want them bad."

"What guys?" I ask, leaning in closer.

"They're gonna be sold to the highest bidder motherfucker." Bull manages to grit out between his teeth.

"Who is?" Pops explodes from his spot leaning against the wall.

"You'll never guess, and I'm not tellin'. You got a better chance of suckin' my dick then you do gettin' me to tell you anymore."

"Who the fuck are you talkin' about?" I ask again, leaning all my weight on the knife sticking out of his leg.

Instead of answering, he just groans until he has no choice but to scream out through the pain. I really don't think we're going to get any more out of him. I'm honestly surprised we got that some men want to buy Skylar and Bailey. I'm not sure who it is, but we're going to find out who these fuckers are and stop them.

"Slim, you get all that shit out of your system?" I turn and ask him "I think he's done givin' anythin' up to us."

"Yeah."

"Good. Pops, Cage, and Joker you get to finish him off, but the rest of the guys need to get their shots in too. I'm goin' to call Blaze and tell him to lock the girls down."

Everyone around me nods their head and I head outside to make my calls. Once I'm done talking to

344

Blaze, I need to call Bailey and talk to her. I'm so fucking pissed I missed the ultrasound appointment, but we had to get this shit done too. Fuck! She's going to hate me.

"Crazy girl, I'm so sorry." I say as soon as she answers the phone. "We're almost done here and I'll be headin' home as soon as Blade gets released."

"I know you're sorry baby. It's okay, Maddison went with me." Bailey says, and I can tell she's been crying.

"She shouldn't have had to go with you though. I should have stayed my ass home and met up with the guys after the appointment."

"Did you get the job done? Find the information you were looking for?" She asks me.

"We did get the job done. We found out some of the information, but there's still things we need to figure out."

"Then you were where you were needed." She says, her voice growing stronger.

"You needed me too and I let you down." I say, dropping my head.

"Baby, I grew up in the club and I knew what I was gettin' into when I *chose* to become your old lady. It was an appointment you missed, not the birth. I'm fine, just come home when you get things wrapped up."

"I love you so much! I need you and Skylar to listen to Blaze and the guys until we get home. Bring Maddison in too. I want you to call the diner and explain that she's got an emergency goin' on and she won't be able to come in for a few days. We're goin' to find her a job with the club so she won't have to worry about losin' money too."

"Okay baby. I'll get everything handled until you come home."

"How's my baby?"

"Growing like he or she should be. They said we might have a Christmas baby since I'm about a week farther along than what they originally thought. Only about three and a half months left daddy." Bailey tells me and I can see the smile in her voice.

"A Christmas baby huh? Any more instances like the last one with the club girl?"

"Nope. Other than Summer and Storm, Sky, Maddison, and I have been the only women in the clubhouse."

"Okay. I'm gonna go see what's goin' on and then go see Blade. I love you crazy girl."

"I love you too baby. I'll see you when I see you."

Hanging up I take a minute to just calm down. I hate missing this shit with the baby appointments, and I know it disappoints Bailey. But, she's right, she grew up in the club and isn't really surprised when I have to cancel shit last minute or miss things. When our baby gets here, I'm going to do everything in my power to be around more for him or her.

It doesn't take long before Pops joins me. He leans against the wall next to me and stares at me for a minute. I'm sure he can detect the anguish I'm feeling right now.

"She knows you love her and would be there if you could, son." He says.

"I know. But, I missed the fuckin' ultrasound appointment Pops. We were goin' to find out what we were havin'."

"She understands. Is everythin' okay with the baby?"

"As far as she said the only thing she was told was that she's about a week farther along, and we could be lookin' at a Christmas baby."

"That's wonderful!" Pops says. "Schedule another appointment for an ultrasound when you get home and make sure you don't miss that one. Or did my baby girl find out already?"

"She didn't say one way or another if she did or didn't."

Pops doesn't say anything else. We just stand there lost in our own heads for a few minutes. I'm sure that he's thinking about everything he missed out on when Ma was pregnant with Joker and Bailey.

"I'm goin' to talk to Slim about havin' a memorial for Strip at our clubhouse when we all get back. Then they can do their thing when they get home."

"Sounds good son. I'll leave you to it. Bull's dead now. The guys are gettin' everythin' set to blow this shit up so we can leave and get to Blade."

"Okay. I'll help them finish it up. Then we'll head out. I wanna stop at a motel to clean up and I'm sure other guys will want to do the same. We'll get ten rooms and take turns since we're just cleanin' up."

I make my way in and we finish setting up the explosives to blow this warehouse up. Thank God Blaze set us up with a ton of shit to use to make sure nothing comes back on any of us. That's the last thing that we're going to need while we're trying to figure out who the hell is after Skylar and Bailey.

We all stop at a motel, the kind you pay for by the hour, so we can take quick showers before heading over to the hospital. Shadow sent a text to Gage earlier and told him Blade was goin' crazy. He wants to get the hell out of there and now. He's tired of being laid up. It's bad enough he's not gonna be able to ride his bike back home and is gonna be stuck with Glock in the van. Glock's one of the only ones I trust to drive the van with that kind of stuff in the back.

As soon as my crew's done with our showers, Slim tells us to head out and the rest will meet us there. They'll bring food and drinks to keep us until we can get home. Looks like one way or another most of us, if not all of us, are leaving today. So, we all mount up and head to see Blade. We'll see what the doctors say when we get there and if we can break his ass out. Doc is on standby to call and talk to his doctor so we can leave.

Walking into the hospital everyone moves out of our way. Must be these people don't see a lot of bikers around here. Even the people around Clifton Falls stop and talk to us every now and then now. They don't run away from us or plaster themselves to the wall while we pass by.

We don't talk to anyone as we pass by, we head straight for Blade's room and push through the door. He's sitting up in bed talking to Shadow and Boy Scout. They all stop laughing as soon as they see me. I stand there for a minute with my arms crossed over my chest before I smile at them.

"What's your doc sayin' Blade?" I ask, taking the seat Shadow was sitting in.

"I can go as soon as he comes in to do his final check of me. Doc didn't wait to hear from you, he called and talked to him already. That's the only reason I'm gettin' released today."

"You get to ride with me Princess." Glock says smirking at Blade, trying to make him uncomfortable.

"Oh yeah? I got ear buds I can put in when you won't stop talkin'." Blade says.

"Nope. I already took them out of your bag. That's the thing about givin' one of us your shit to hang on to." Glock says getting smug.

"Motherfucker!" Blade says. "Fine, just get me my clothes so I can get out of here as soon as the doctor comes in."

Glock hands him the bag he packed so he'll have his clothes. We're in here for about ten minutes before the doctor comes in and does his exam with a hot little nurse. Blade does what the doctor asks, as I watch through the window in the door, but he can't take his eyes off the nurse. That little fucker is gonna try and get a piece of strange before he leaves here. Sure enough, as soon as the doctor heads out, the nurse stays behind to 'help' him get dressed. So, I lead the guys away to go wait outside. Glock needs to bring the van around anyway. Once I tell the guys what we're waiting on, they all laugh their asses off because it's the same thing we have all done or would do for the single guys.

Chapter Twenty-Two

Bailey

AFTER GETTING A few hours of sleep thanks to my mom, I wake up to Rage calling me. He tells me that the inspector approved the house so we can start moving in as soon as we're ready. As soon as I get off the phone with him, I quickly make all the calls I need to make and take a shower. I'm wide awake now. Blaze is heading over to the house to start helping Rage get the basement set up for Logan while the rest of the guys hang out around the clubhouse. Even with most of them going over to help me move things in, some are still going to stay here and keep a watch. They don't want anyone sneaking in while we're busy.

Maddison, Ma, and Skylar are waiting for me in the kitchen so that I can grab something to eat before we head over to the house. The furniture store headed this way last night so it's only going to take them a few minutes to get to the house. I'm so happy we decided to go with the store in Slim's territory since I'm sure the one in town wouldn't be as accommodating as the one I went with is.

"You ready to get this done baby girl?" Ma asks, setting a plate of food in front of me.

"I'm so excited. I can't wait to see what the house looks like with all the furniture moved in!"

"Are you gonna stay there without Grim?" Maddison asks me.

"No. I'll be over there during the day, but then come back over here at night. Or when I get tired. I can't have him worrying about me being separated from the rest of you guys just to stay in the house."

"Okay. Well, I'll help when I'm not working." Maddison tells me.

"Thanks." I say around a mouthful of food. I know it's rude, but I want to get to the house. "But, you're not working right now. Grim wanted you pulled in with us, so I called the diner saying you had a family emergency and wouldn't be in for a few days. I'm sorry."

"It's okay. If Grim thinks I need to be pulled in, then it is what it is. Honestly, other than helping you, I'll be glad for a break. I've been pulling a few doubles and stuff lately. Carly doesn't want to work I guess."

I'm shoveling food in my mouth as fast as I can so that we can get our asses in gear and start getting everything in the house. To say I'm impatient would be an understatement. The girls can sense this so they let me eat and help Skylar load the kids up in her SUV. She's going to drive it across the field so we don't have to walk with the babies. Then we're setting up a play pen in the kitchen so we don't have to worry about them while we move in and out of the doors.

Right now the plan is to get all of the furniture set up where I want it. Then tomorrow we're going to go to the storage unit I put all of our new stuff in and bring that over to the house. The rest of my stuff is going to stay in storage until someone needs it. I'm already thinking of giving some of it to Maddison for the apartment she's staying in. My decorations and a few other things is all I'm bringing out of the storage unit.

I quickly finish eating and we head out. Ma is riding over with Skylar while I walk over with Maddison and Zoey. Thankfully Maddison is using Skylar's stroller so she doesn't have to carry the baby over. Just as we're walking up, with the guys behind and in front of us, I see the truck from the furniture store pulling up. Rage comes out and tells them where to back up so it will be easier to get everything inside.

"Bay, you just direct us where you want everythin'." Blaze says coming out of the house. "We're goin' to help the delivery guys get everythin' where you want it so Grim doesn't kill us all for you doin' somethin' you're not supposed to."

"Okay. Sky and Maddison are going to help with the light stuff. Let's get going!"

Everyone around me laughs because I'm so excited to get the house ready to start living in when Logan gets home from the run. I laugh with them because I know how excited I am and I know all of these guys are here to help me make our dream a reality. One I didn't think I'd ever have.

"By the way, how's the basement coming?" I ask Rage.

"It's almost done actually. Just a few more things left to be done. I'll take you down when we're done here."

All the guys busted their asses today to get all the furniture moved into the house. Rage took me downstairs as promised and showed me the basement and I fell in love instantly. I know this is going to be one of Logan's favorite rooms in the house. At least until we get the attic set up with everything we want. I'm still kind of on the fence about all of that though. We'll wait and see what Logan thinks when he gets home. The only other room I check out is the gym. Instead of having it in the basement, like we were originally thinking, Rage added another room downstairs for it. Other than Logan's office and the bathroom, it's the only other room with walls down here.

Now, it's time for me to head back over to the clubhouse. Skylar and Ma already made their way over there to start dinner for everyone. I'm exhausted and don't really want to eat but I know I have to. Logan sent me a text earlier and said he would call later, but I'm not worried about it if I don't hear from him. I know they got things to do. So, the guys follow me back over and I take a quick shower to rid myself of the sweat. As soon as I'm out, Kasey attaches herself to me. I really love this little girl.

"You tired Bay?" She asks me.

"Yeah, I'm tired. Tonight I'm going to eat and probably go right to bed if you're sleeping in my room again. How's your belly feeling?"

"I feel good. Daddy made Storm feed me toast with nothin' on it today. Sky's makin' something I can eat for dinner that doesn't upset my belly again."

"Sounds good. But, we'll keep everything in my room just in case. We'll talk to daddy at dinner about you sleeping in my room again, okay?"

"Yay!" Kasey jumps up and down and starts dancing around in her excitement.

We take a seat at a table with Jameson and Reagan. Blaze and Dozer join us and I can feel myself starting to doze off while sitting there. Skylar nudges me as she sets my plate down in front of me.

"Babe, eat and head to bed. Kasey is sleeping in my room tonight. I've already talked to Rage. You've had a big day today and a big day tomorrow with your appointment."

"I'm fine if she wants to come in my room Sky. You've got your kids to find spots to sleep in."

"It's more than fine. Kasey and Reagan are making a fort between the bed and couch. Alana and Haley are gonna be in their toddler beds, the boys in the playpen, and Jameson is going to sleep on the couch. We're fine Bailey. Go get your rest."

After eating, I make my way into our room and lay down on top of the blankets. I'm already in one of the shirts Logan wore before he left, so I set my phone on his stand and fall fast asleep.

352

I was hoping that Logan would call and tell me that they were on their way home and would be here to go to the ultrasound with me. But, that's not happening. So, I put a smile on my face and go about my routine before I have to leave. I'm not fooling anyone though. Ma can see right through me and she's trying to make me forget that Logan won't be here. It's not working.

"Bay, do you want me to go with you?" Maddison asks me. "Ma said she would watch Zoey while she's keeping an eye on Kasey for Rage."

"Sure. At least I won't be alone right?"

"He would be here if he could honey. I know I haven't been around long, but anyone that sees you two together knows that he would move heaven and Earth to give you what you want and need."

"I know. It's just these damn hormones making me crazy that he's going to miss it."

Maddison puts an arm around me and tries to comfort me. It's not working either, so we head out the back door and sit on the little patio area that was just added with a table and chairs. The quiet is kind of comforting, even if I do tend to go in my own head and think about everything. I really wish the guys were here damn it!

"What time do we have to leave honey?" Maddison asks me.

"In a few minutes. I better go get my purse and change into a pair of shorts. I'm already sweating to death."

Maddison gets up with me and we head our own way to get what we need. I stop in the doorway to the room as a sob rips through me. Logan is going to miss this and he swore he would be here. I know he tried and I know they're doing what they have to do, but it does bother me with all the hormones raging through me.

Rage comes up behind me and wraps his arms around me. He pulls my head to his chest as Kasey wraps herself around my legs. I'm glad that he stopped and held me for a second before I pull away. It was kind of what I needed, even if it came from him.

"Thanks." I say looking up at him.

"You're welcome Bay. Just don't tell Grim so I get killed."

I can't help the laugh that leaves me. He's trying to make me forget and it's working this time. I'll be fine, I just need to get through the appointment so that we can get the rest of the stuff for the house.

"I promise I won't say anything. You're following us right?"

"Right. Dozer and Blaze are going too. They wanted to know if you wanted the rest of the guys to head over to the storage unit with the rest of the new stuff you bought while we're with you. That way we can just head back to the house and you can do your thing."

"That sounds good. I'll get the keys and write down directions real quick. Or are they taking Sky with them?"

"I think they can take Sky if Ma and a few of the guys want to watch the kids."

"She knows where it is, so that might be easier. Twist and Snapper can go with her and the rest can stay here. Everything is in bags or boxes so it shouldn't be too hard for the three of them to load it all up."

"I'll talk to Blaze while you get your things." Rage says backing away and going in search of him. Kasey stays with me.

Grabbing my purse, keys, and changing into a pair of shorts, I make my way into the common room. Kasey is still holding onto my hand and doesn't seem like she's going to be letting go anytime soon. Rage and Ma sees this, so Ma walks over to us and kneels down before Kasey.

"Kasey, I'm going to need your help today for a while. Are you gonna help me?" Ma asks her.

"What are we gonna do?"

"Well, I need you and Reagan to help watch the younger kids. Plus, we're gonna make cookies." Ma says with a twinkle in her eye.

"What kind?" Kasey asks in a whisper like it's the world's biggest secret.

"I think chocolate chip. So, are you with me?"

"Yes!" She answers letting go of me so I can head out the door with my escorts.

Pulling out, Maddison watches me and I know she wants to say something. So, I wait until she's ready to talk. It doesn't take her long.

"Can I ask you a question Bailey?"

"Sure."

"Why do your parents look at me weird every time they see me? At first I thought it was just me. But, it's every time I see them that I notice it now."

"Oh, I don't know. I've noticed it too though. They started as soon as they found out that your daddy was a biker. We can ask Ma later on."

"No, that's okay. Maybe they knew him and don't want to tell me he's dead or something. I was just curious."

"Well, if you want me to talk to them, just let me know and I will."

"Thanks."

We remain quiet the rest of the drive. Pulling into the office, I park as close as I can and we walk in. Rage is the only one that stays outside. He's got his phone out so he can call if he sees anything suspicious. I don't know what the big deal is unless the guys didn't find the Soulless Bastards like they wanted. Logan hasn't said anything to me about what's going on, so I don't know.

I give the receptionist my name and she tells me to have a seat until they call me back. We sit close to the door leading in the back and I watch all of the other women in the room. Some are alone, or with a friend, like me and others are with the father of their baby. We're all in various stages of pregnancy from the you can't tell they're pregnant to the ready to pop pregnant women. My eyes start to mist as I look at the women here with their men. But, I can't change the way things work in life within the club. So, I blink away the tears and pull up my big girl panties. We'll get through this and I know I can still make this special for Logan. We *will* find out the sex of our baby together.

"Maddison, don't let me forget to talk to the ultrasound tech please."

"Everything okay?" She asks me.

"Yeah. I just thought of a way to still make this special for Grim and me."

"Okay. Do you want me to know or not?"

"As long as you can keep this to yourself, you can know."

I fill her in on my idea and she squeals in excitement at the way I want to be able to learn the sex of our baby. I'm guessing she likes the idea and thinks that Logan will too. I hope I'm doing the right thing here and that we can still have our moment.

Soon, I'm called in and when the guys try to follow me, I motion for them to remain sitting. I'm sure between my dad, brother, and Logan they were told to keep me in their line of vision, but this moment isn't for them. Maddison is one thing, but nomad bikers is a whole other story.

After getting everything set up, I talk to the ultrasound tech about my idea and she loves it. She's going to make sure that I get pictures without showing the gender of the baby, and then she's going to put my idea into motion and do as I want to make sure that we can have our moment.

"Everything looks good Bailey. The only thing I'm going to dispute is that I think you're about a week farther along than we originally thought. So, next week you'll be five and a half months along. Looks like you could have a Christmas baby."

"Really? That's exciting!" I say looking at Maddison.

She's just sitting back and watching everything the tech is doing. "Okay Bailey, I need you to turn your head now. Then we'll be done and you can set up your next appointment with Doctor Bell if you haven't already."

"Okay. Thank you."

"I'm going to put some tape on this so you know if anyone got in it."

"Great. Thank you again for your willingness to help me out with this. You've truly made my day and pulled me out of my funk."

"Anytime honey. I'll see you again if you need another ultrasound."

I wipe the goop off of my stomach and sit up putting my clothes back where they belong. We go out and I make sure that I don't have to make another appointment since I already did before we head out to my truck. I feel so much lighter than I have since the guys left. Now, it's time to go and make sure everything else that's been gotten from the storage unit is where I want it and then dinner time.

We've all been unpacking bags and boxes of everything that I bought the day I found out I was pregnant with this little peanut. The guys are down putting the finishing touches on Logan's man cave or whatever and all of the women are setting my kitchen, bathrooms, and bedroom up. The only furniture we have left to get is the stuff for the nursery and Logan and I are doing that together when he gets back and has a day free.

"Bailey, I think we're finally done upstairs. I love your bathroom!" Storm says coming back downstairs.

"Thank you. I stole the idea from Skylar when I fell in love with her bathroom. I plan on making the most of the shower and tub! Just like I'm sure Skylar and the guys have done more than once."

Skylar blushes at being called out for doing exactly what I know she's done in the shower and tub. She forgets I grew up with her two men and I know how they think. While I don't want to think of my brother and what he does with Skylar, I'm sure they've taken advantage of the bathroom multiple times. Now, Logan and I can do that in our home instead of having some tiny ass tub/shower to try to move around in.

"Mmmhmm. We know exactly what's going through your mind right now Skylar. Don't be getting all hot and bothered in a houseful of women though honey." Summer says coming in on the conversation.

"Oh my goodness!" Skylar says covering her face and burying her head while the rest of us laugh and joke about the size of the bathroom in our homes.

"Bailey." Blaze calls out. "Can you come down here for a minute? We want to see what you think?"

"Yeah."

We all walk downstairs to see Logan's surprise. Very few people know what I planned for down here. Now, I just hope they'll all keep their damn mouths shut and don't tell him before he can see it for himself.

"Wow!" I say coming to a stop at the bottom of the stairs. "This is absolutely amazing! Thank you all so much for helping me put this together for him."

The rest of the women are all seeing this for the first time and I'm glad so I can see their honest reactions. They all wander around and look at everything from the pool table, poker table, the bar complete with stools, and the few tables scattered around the room. Rage painted the Wild Kings on one wall and the rest are left bare so that I can hang the pictures I blew up around the room.

"If you tell us where you want the pictures to go Bailey, we'll get them hung up for you so this room is completely done before Grim gets home." Rage says wiping down the bar.

"I'll go around and set them on the floor below where I want them. That sound okay?"

"Yep."

I walk around and take a good look at all the pictures before selecting where I want them to hang. There's two that are going on the wall where Wild Kings is painted. One of them is a picture taken a few years ago of every member in the club. The other one is a picture of Logan, Joker, Cage, Gage, Irish, Glock, Trojan, and Crash. They all patched in around the same time in one chapter. When the club started expanding and adding chapters, Gage, Trojan, and Crash went to Dander Falls. The rest of the pictures are just random shots from parties, runs, opening days of businesses the club has started, and just some candid shots.

Once I'm done making sure I have them all where I want them, the women all head back upstairs to finish working up there while the guys hang the pictures so we can all head back to the clubhouse. Kasey hands me a picture that she's been working on since they arrived at the house earlier and I hang it on the fridge with some magnets that I bought. Next to her picture I put up the latest picture from the ultrasound. It looks like the baby is waving with one hand while sucking the thumb of the other hand. I think it's cute as hell.

"Bailey, the guys are going to hook up the t.v.'s, surround sound, and everything else Grim has for it tomorrow afternoon." Storm tells me.

"That sounds good." I say, trying to hide my yawn.

"We're just about done in here. You wanted to get the rest of what you're bringing tomorrow or later this week from your storage unit so we can finish up then. Let's get you back to the clubhouse baby girl. Dinner and bed for you." Ma says pulling me out the door with everyone following us.

I lock up after the guys did a walk through to make sure all the windows and doors were locked. Ma leads me over to Skylar's SUV and I plop in the passenger side while the kids get loaded up. As soon as we pull into the clubhouse, I park my butt on one of the couches and within minutes I'm passed out.

Chapter Twenty-Three

Grim

WE'RE FINALLY ALMOST home. Bailey doesn't even know we're on our way back yet. The last day or two it's been hard to catch her. Ma and Blaze assure me that she's doing well, she's just been exhausted and heads to bed almost as soon as she's done with dinner. During the day she's been working non-stop in the house to get it done before I get home. I could care less if the house is in shambles when I walk through the door as long as the baby and Bailey are doing okay.

I talked to Slim while we were waiting for Blade to get his piece of strange about having a memorial for Strip at our clubhouse and he thought it was a good idea. Then they'll do their own thing at their clubhouse and we'll all get together for the funeral.

About a half hour from the clubhouse, I pull over and we top off our tanks before making the last leg of the journey. I'm hoping Blaze and Ma didn't open their mouth about us being almost home. So, I text Blaze.

Me: No one opened their mouth right?

Moving my bike so Cage can fill his tank up, I wait for him to text me back. It only takes him a minute.

Blaze: Nope. We've all been really busy. She has no clue.

I'm glad that no one spilled the beans to her. But, now I'm curious as hell about what's been going on to keep them all so busy. It can't be just the house. Maybe Bailey has had them helping her out with organizing the toy run and carnival. I don't know what all she has left to do since most of it was done before I left on this run.

"You okay Pres?" Cage asks, parking his bike next to mine.

"Yeah. Just tryin' to figure out what's been keepin' them all so busy while we've been gone."

"What do you mean? How do you know that?"

"I asked Blaze if anyone spilled the beans to crazy girl about us bein' almost home. He said no because they've all been too busy."

"Who knows what our women have had those guys doin' while we've been gone." Pops says walking up to us. "I'm sure the house took up a large portion of it though. Bailey wanted to make it perfect for you before you got home."

"She knows that I didn't expect that Pops. I would've helped when I got back and she knows that."

"I know. But Skylar and her probably wanted to keep their minds occupied so they weren't thinkin' about you guys. It's fine. Let's just go so we can get home and you can see for yourself instead of worryin' about it." Pops says heading to his bike while I go in and pay for everyone's gas.

The roar of our bikes brings everyone running outside when we pull up at the clubhouse. I'm looking all over for Bailey as soon as I back my bike in and I don't see her anywhere. Rage or someone can grab my shit, I need to know where my girl is. Usually she'd be right out here welcoming me home and she's not.

"Where's my girl Blaze?" I ask rushing past him.

"She's in your room man. She was exhausted and couldn't keep her eyes open so Maddison took her in to lay down."

"Everythin' okay with her?"

"Yeah, she's just tired man."

I don't say anything else to anyone as I make my way to our room. Opening the door slowly so I don't wake her up, I see that almost everything is out of the room. I guess they really have been busy as hell getting the house ready to move in. Now, I can't wait to see what our home looks like. But that can wait until Bailey is up and she's not exhausted. If that takes us staying in bed for a few days, I'm down with that.

Maddison looks up from the couch and gives me a small smile. Picking up her things, she moves past me and leaves the room as I close and lock the door and move to the bed and my girl. I push some hair out of Bailey's face and she stirs. Since I don't want to wake her up, I back-up, grab some clean clothes, and go in to take a shower. Once I'm done there, I slide in to bed with Bailey and wrap her up in my arms. Again, she turns over and burrows into me. Best part of my day right here.

Bailey

I slowly wake up and I feel like the room is over a hundred degrees. It wasn't this damn hot when Maddison ushered me in here and I promptly fell asleep. What the hell is going on? Opening my eyes, I see Logan curled around me and I can't stop the scream from escaping my mouth.

"Baby, you're home! I missed you so much!" I get out between plastering kisses all over his face and neck. Anywhere that I can reach on him.

"Crazy girl, I'm home. I missed you too and I love you so much!" He says in his sleepy, growly voice.

"How long have you been back? Why didn't you wake me up?" I ask him sitting up in bed.

"I've been back a few hours now." He says looking at his phone. "I didn't wake you because Blaze said you could hardly keep your eyes open. You and the baby need your sleep, so I got cleaned up and joined you."

"I can't wait for you to see our home baby!" I say excitedly.

"Hang on a second crazy girl." Logan says laughing. "I have a question first."

"What's that?"

"Did you find out the sex of the baby while you were at the ultrasound?"

"No. You weren't there and I wasn't going to do that without you."

Logan just looks at me. He has no clue about the surprise I have waiting for us at our home. That's only part of the reason I can't wait to get over there. The other part is that I want to show him his room. I want to see the look on his face when he sees what I did for him.

"Well, we're havin' a memorial for Strip tonight crazy girl. I sent some guys out shoppin' for food and things so you girls don't have to cook. It's just goin' to be somethin' low key and then we'll go to their club for the funeral and memorial."

"Okay. Do we have time to go to the house first?" I ask again.

"Yeah crazy girl, we can go take a look before."

"Good. Go get everyone ready to head over and I'll meet you outside." I tell him going into the bathroom.

"You want everyone to go?" He asks me amazed.

"Absolutely! I'm not going to leave people out just because it's our house. If they're here they're going over."

I wait until Logan leaves the room and then I go into the bathroom to freshen up a little bit and change out of the clothes I fell asleep in, figuring Logan wouldn't approve of me going out in his tee and a pair of panties. So, I find a cute little summer dress and throw my hair up in a messy bun.

Everyone is waiting outside for me except for Joker. He's halfway across the field. What the hell is he doing? Logan grabs my hand and we all make our way over to our new home. Both of us have keys and I didn't bring mine, so he has to open the door up. Those of us that have been working here during the week or so they've been gone stand back so the rest of the group can see what we've accomplished.

"Crazy girl, this looks amazin'!" Logan says coming out of his office. "Come look upstairs with me."

We walk up to our room and there's a huge box sitting on the bed that wasn't there before. I look around to see if anything else is different in the room. Not seeing anything else, I go to move in the bathroom but Logan grabs my hand.

"Joker did it crazy girl. Open it." He says pulling me to the bed.

I don't have to open it to know what it is. It's my rag. Really, I don't care if I have one or not. But I know what it means to the guys and it's for my protection too. So, I tear into the wrapping and pull it out, sliding it over my arms. I turn around so Logan can see everything before he pulls me to him and crushes my mouth with his. Hmm, this could turn out very good for me!

"Crazy girl, I want you so bad. But, we have a houseful of people and I want to take my time seein' my name on your back. Tonight, your ass is mine!"

"Absolutely!" I say, breathless from his kiss. "Come on. I have a few surprises myself Pres."

I lead him to the basement stairs and everyone follows us down. Rage is already down there making sure that everything is wiped down, picked up, and just the way I wanted it for him. Logan gets to the bottom step and stops dead. Joker and Cage almost run us over since no one was expecting this.

"Are you for real crazy girl? I thought this was gonna be a gym or somethin'."

"I still have my gym. This is all for you. I thought you could use a space to relax and just hang out away from the club once in a while. Go take a look around."

Logan leaves my side and wanders to look at every picture in the room. Most of the guys follow him going from picture to picture sharing their own story about that day or just laughing at what's going on in front of the camera lens. I'm so happy that they all seem to like it. My dad wanders back over to me and pulls me into a side hug.

"You feelin' okay baby girl?" He asks.

"I'm just tired more often. But, I'm doing good daddy. You doing okay?"

"I am. You did real good with this for him. Especially all the memories up on those walls."

"I tried to make it special for him. This is all for him down here."

"Crazy girl, you said you had more than one surprise for me. What's next?"

"Well, I told you that I didn't find out the sex of the baby because you weren't there with me."

"I'm sorry about that." He says lowering his voice.

"Don't be baby. Follow me upstairs. Everyone follow us and find a spot you can see the t.v. Rage, did you do as I ask and set the video up for me?"

"It's ready to go Bailey." He answers hanging back.

"You too Rage. Let's go!"

We all pile into the living room and I sit Logan down on the couch. Sitting next to him I grab the remote. Everyone else finds somewhere to stand around us other than Pops and Ma. They sit down next to us with Joker, Cage, and Skylar right behind us. I wish Maddison was here with us, but she chose to stay at the clubhouse with the kids. Pressing play on the remote, our baby fills the screen. Logan just looks at me for a second.

Ma throws her hand over her mouth at the image of our baby moving on the screen. It takes a few minutes, and a few different angles, but then letters start appearing on the screen. Logan sucks in a breath along with me, and we wait to see what we're having. The words start appearing; 'I'm a baby boy."

"You're givin' me a son?" He asks me in shock.

"I guess so baby."

"You really didn't know?"

"Nope. Ask Rage."

"Why would I ask him?"

"Rage, when you set everything up for this moment, was the tape on the case still intact?"

"Yeah Bailey. No one got into it. I used my knife to cut through one piece of tape."

Logan stands up with me in his arms and spins me around the room. He buries his face in my neck and I can feel his breath catch. He's really trying hard not to show his emotions right now. Soon, we're surrounded by our family, blood and extended, getting congratulations from everyone here.

"I wanted us to know and it be a special moment for everyone we love and consider family. I didn't want to do a traditional gender reveal since we didn't know either. I hope you like my surprises." I tell Logan as everyone starts making their way over to the clubhouse.

"I love your surprises crazy girl. You definitely made this a special moment for everyone involved. Where's Maddison though?"

"She's with the kids. I think she didn't want to be around such a large group of people right yet. She's still nervous around people and has a hard time."

"Well, let's go tell her the news together."

Maddison

When everyone went over to see the new house with Grim and Bailey, I decided to stay and watch the kids for everyone. I'm not good with a lot of people that I don't know. Hell, I'm not good with a lot of people period. So, I avoid large groups at all costs unless I'm working at the diner. There I can't help when large groups of people come in to eat, I suck it up and do my job.

I can hear the excitement from everyone as they start pouring in the clubhouse. Grim and Bailey make their way over to me at the table I'm sitting at and sit down with me. The smiles on their faces are contagious and I can't help but smile in return.

"So, we wanted to let you know what we're havin'" before everyone else opens their big ass mouths." Grim says.

"I can't wait to find out!"

"It's a boy!" Bailey says beaming at Grim and leaning in closer to him.

"That's great!" I say switching the way I'm holding Zoey until Tank comes over and takes her from me.

"I hope he looks just like his daddy." Bailey says.

We all sit there in our own thoughts until an older man comes over to our table. He pulls the remaining chair out and plops down like he has the weight of the world resting on his shoulders. Even though I'm looking at Tank holding my little girl, I can feel the older man's eyes on me. Not in a creepy stalker way, but in a way that shows he's trying to figure something out.

"I don't think we've met yet sweetheart. I'm Slim, the President of the Phantom Bastards."

"I'm Maddison." I say ducking my head.

"You okay?" He asks me.

"Yeah, I just don't do well in crowds of people. Bailey I think I'll go to my room." I say starting to stand up.

"Wait, can I ask you a question?" Slim asks.

"I guess so." I say, still not looking at him.

Slim gently tilts my head up with a finger and stares in my eyes. I look into eyes that I see in the mirror every day. What the fuck? Who is this man?

"Are you sure we haven't met before?" He asks me. "You look so familiar. Maybe I know your parents."

"I don't know who my dad is." I say stepping back a little bit. "I'm not sure you'd know my mama or not."

"What's her name?"

"Roxy Miller."

I can see the eyes bug out in Slim's face. He moves his hand closer and I flinch until he withdraws his hand. Still looking at me, he asks "From Dander Falls?"

"How did you know that?" I ask, becoming confused and looking to Bailey and Grim for help.

"How old are you?" He asks.

"I'm twenty."

"Did Roxy ever tell you who your daddy was?" He asks sitting back down.

"No. All she said was she met him at a bike rally." I say looking into identical eyes to me.

"We may need to talk more little girl." He says.

"O-okay. I'll be around for a little bit. I'm going home tonight Grim, if that's okay."

"Not right yet honey. There's some things we need to figure out before we can allow that."

"Oh." I say with my heart dropping into my stomach. "Well, I'm going to take Zoey and go lay down for a while." I say leaving the three at the table and going to find Tank.

I'm so confused at Slim asking me all those questions. I want to know what's going on, but I'm afraid to find out the answers. Maybe a nap will help me out and it will get me away from everyone at the same time. That's probably what's going on. There's so many people here that they're spilling out the front and back doors. I'm overwhelmed and need some alone time. Finding Tank by the bar, I tap him on the shoulder and step a little closer.

"What's up sweetheart?" He asks.

"Nothing. I'm going to take Zoey to my room and lay down for a while." I answer reaching for my daughter.

"You sure you're okay? I can come with you if you want." He says.

"No. I'm fine. I just need to be alone for a while. Too many people and all that."

Tank watches me disappear into the hallway leading to the rooms. I can feel his eyes on me whenever we're in the same room. It's comforting in a way because I know he's watching out for me. He makes me feel things I'm not ready to deal with though. With Tank, I feel safe, like a woman, and like there's no one else in the surrounding area. Meanwhile, he's probably just looking for a quick fuck and I'm not going to be a notch for any biker. I learned that lesson from my mom. It's probably one of the only things she taught me growing up.

Closing my door, I let out the breath I was holding and lay Zoey down in the playpen Skylar is letting me borrow while we're here. I'm so happy that Bailey let me come with her. The people that I've met so far are kind and willing to help people out no matter if they can be repaid or not. I'm thinking about all of this as I get in bed and pull the covers up tight around me.

Slim

"You okay Slim?" Grim asks me.

"I don't know." I answer as I see Pops and Ma making their way over to us.

They've seen the girl. Pops will tell me if I'm crazy for thinking that she looks a little too much like me. I did meet a woman named Roxy at a bike rally many years ago. It was one of the best weeks of my life. We met at a bar when a guy was harassing her and then spent the entire week together. When it was time to leave, I tried to get her to come with me. Roxy laughed and told me that she was just looking for some fun, she didn't want to wind up an old lady that was forgotten and left alone at home all the time. So, we went our separate ways and I still think about her all the time. She had my number so I don't know why she didn't call me and tell me if she was pregnant. It makes no sense.

"You look like you just saw a ghost Slim." Pops says sitting down and pulling Ma on his lap.

"I think I did. You've seen the girl, tell me I'm crazy and not seein' what I think I am." I say looking at them, desperately wanting to know if I have a daughter.

"I think the same thing you are right now Slim." Pops answers. "The only reason I didn't say anythin' sooner is because I wanted to be sure."

"You seen Roxy?" I ask them both.

"No. Bailey went down to help Gage at the Kitty Kat. She hired Maddison. Everything was fine until the night they were gonna open again. After rehearsal, Maddison disappeared until just before opening. When she walked in, she had her daughter and the side of her face was red and turning into a bruise with a gash in her forehead. So, Bailey brought her home with us and she's been here ever since. She works at the diner in town." Ma tells me. "She told us she didn't know who her daddy was, just that her mom told her he was a biker. Never gave her mom's name though. The only thing we've heard about her mom is that she died when Maddison was seventeen of a drug overdose. And we just learned that."

"Why wouldn't Roxy tell me? I gave her my number before we left."

"I don't know Slim." Pops says. "Maybe she thought it wouldn't matter to you."

"Then she didn't listen to a damn thing I said that week. Fuck! I'm gonna go find Maddison and talk to her."

"Slim, I know you want to know if she's your daughter. But, she really does have a problem with crowds and she's probably not ready to face anything yet. Just give her some time and I'll go talk to her in a little bit. Please, for her." Bailey pleads with me.

"Why doesn't she like crowds?" I ask, wanting to know everything about her.

"I don't know. I don't think she had a great upbringing and that might play a part in it. Maybe you should give Playboy a heads up in case he runs in to her." Bailey says.

"Yeah. I'll go find him and talk to him. I don't know how he's gonna take this shit. God, they're the same fuckin' age."

"Who's the same age?" Playboy asks coming up to the table we're all sitting at.

"Son, we need to talk. Let's go outside."

"You okay?" He asks me.

"I am, I think. Just got the shock of my fuckin' life."

We walk out the back door and find a quiet place by the fence. I lean against it and try to find the words I need to say to Playboy. He's my son in every way and I know this is gonna be a shock. It's a fucking shock to me. I met his mom just after we got back from the rally. It was love at first sight and I'm happy as fuck that I married Brittney. Playboy was born later that year.

"The year I met your mom, I went to a rally close to Dander Falls. While there I met a woman named Roxy and we spent the week together. That's the last time I heard from her. When I was just inside, fuck I don't know how to say this to you."

"What's wrong dad? You can tell me anythin' you know that."

"I know that son. I think you have a sister. Her name is Maddison. She said Roxy is her mom and all she knows about her dad is that he's a biker."

"O-okay. What led you to ask about her mom?" Playboy asks.

"She has our blue eyes and the same dimple you have when you grace us with your smile son. I can feel it in my bones this girl is mine."

"Where is she? I wanna see this for myself." Playboy says.

"She's laying down. Apparently she has issues bein' around a large number of people. I don't know what that's about. So, when you see her tread lightly. I don't want her scared away before I get answers."

"I got it dad. If she's yours, what are you gonna do?"

"That's up to her. She's buildin' a life here and I'm not gonna interrupt that for her."

"I'll follow your lead then." Playboy says as we walk back inside.

Damn! I need to wrap my head around this and think of the best way to handle everything. I don't want to scare Maddison away, my only goal is to get to know her. When I told Playboy I could feel it that she was my daughter, I wasn't lying. I feel that shit deep in my bones. I'll keep an eye out today and tonight and see what I can do about getting to know her. Maybe she'll talk to me and we can work this out.

Chapter Twenty-Four

Bailey

THE MEMORIAL WE had for Strip was good. Everyone got together and celebrated his life and we spent a relaxing night together. Maddison stayed glued to my side when she came out of her room and Tank didn't go far from her. Slim and Playboy kept watching her from afar and I know this situation is tearing Slim up. He's convinced that he's her daddy and wants to talk to her but doesn't want to push her. Maybe I need to have a conversation with her.

Before we all went our separate ways for the night, I pulled her aside so we could talk. Tank was taking care of Zoey, so we sat close, but out of hearing range. Maddison looks so uncomfortable that I want to ease her mind, but I'm not sure how.

"Honey, I think we need to talk." I start out.

"Are you making me leave here?" She asks, and I see the terror and pain all over her face.

"What? No. What would you ask that?"

"Because I'm causing problems being here. That man is more upset because of me." She says looking in Slim's direction.

"Honey, he's not upset with you. The reason he was asking you all those questions earlier is because he thinks he might be your daddy. He met your mama at that bike rally."

"What? Then why didn't he want me until now?" She asks, trying to blink away her tears.

"From what I gather, he didn't know about you honey."

"My mom said she told my dad and he told her to get rid of it. Why would she lie to me?"

"I don't know. But, he's very adamant that he knew nothing of you until he saw you earlier." I say, pulling her into my arms.

Tank, Slim, and Playboy all act like they're going to head our way, but I shake my head telling them to give me a minute. I need to calm her down and see what she wants to do. Then we'll go from there and I'll help her through this the best that I can.

"What do you wanna do honey?" I ask her.

"Should I talk to him?" She asks, looking up at me, confusion written all over her face.

"I think you should. Slim is a good guy. But, it's your decision. He's the only one that can answer questions you have though."

"O-okay. I'll talk to him. But, only him. I don't know who that other guy is staring at me."

I look up to see Playboy standing next to Slim. He hasn't taken his eyes off of Maddison. "That's Slim's son honey. I'm guessing Slim told him his thoughts and Playboy is trying to see what Slim sees when he looks at you."

"Oh. Well, I'll talk to Slim now and maybe the other guy later."

I stand up and lead Maddison over to where the two are standing around the fire. Nodding my head, they both start heading our way. So, I put my hand up until they stop. Walking over, I tell them what she said and I can see understanding flash across both of their faces. Playboy is actually handling this a lot better than what I thought. Slim walks over to Maddison and leads her over by the fence. She's far enough away they can talk without being disturbed, but close enough that Tank, Zoey, and I are in her sights.

Suddenly I feel Logan wrap his arms around me and place his hands on my belly. He kisses the side of my neck and I move my head to the side giving him more room. I love when he wraps me in his arms and kisses nowhere other than my neck. We stand watching Slim and Maddison for a few minutes before he leads me to a seat by the fire and pulls me on his lap.

"Everythin' okay over there?" He asks me.

"Yeah. I think so. I explained to her why he asked her the questions and why he was watching her. She said she wanted to talk to him. Playboy will add in to the equation later on. She's too nervous and confused right now."

"Poor girl. But, I know you'll be there for her. How's my man takin' this situation?" Logan asks nodding towards Tank who's holding a sleeping Zoey.

"I don't think she's talked to him about anything yet. I don't know what to do with that either. It's not my place to talk to Tank about it."

"Nope. I'll keep an eye on it. If I think he needs to, I'll have him call Slim and they can hash that shit out between them."

"Tomorrow we need to go shopping for food. That's the only thing I didn't get for the house yet. I wasn't sure when you were coming home and didn't want everything to spoil."

"Okay crazy girl. We'll go as soon as we wake up." He says nuzzling into me and grinding himself on my ass.

"You tryin' to tell me something Pres?" I ask.

"I need you crazy girl. It's been too long and I don't care if I bury myself balls deep right here."

"Follow me." I say standing up and leading him to the fence at the back of the property.

There's hardly anyone out this far. Ma and Pops definitely aren't back here. Without waiting for Logan to do anything, I drop to my knees and undo his pants while he rips his shirt over his head. Damn, I could look at his body all day long. So, I plant my lips on his abs and feel the ripples that go through his body at my touch while I shove his jeans down enough to get his cock out. Following his six-pack lower, I stop only to lick each side of the V he has leading me to his throbbing cock.

"Crazy girl, you don't have to. Get up off your knees." He tries to tell me.

"I want to baby. I'm fine. You just relax and let me take care of you."

Without waiting for his response, I take him in my mouth as far as I can get him. Using my hand, I make sure I don't leave a single part of him untouched while stroking the part of his shaft I can't get in my mouth. Instead of using my other hand to play with his balls like I usually do, I slip it under my dress and find my clit.

"You touchin' yourself crazy girl?" He grits out as I swirl my tongue around him.

Nodding my head, I don't miss a beat. I start sucking him as I pull my head back and I see him throw his head back and feel his fingers dig into my hair grabbing on harder. He knows that I love when he starts to lose control enough to pull my hair. Just as I start to move faster, both on his cock and while shoving my fingers in my dripping pussy, he pulls me off of him.

"I'm not blowin' in your mouth crazy girl. Knowin' that you're touchin' yourself has me ready to blow. Turn around, ass out, hold on to the fence."

I immediately do what he says and I feel him yank my dress up over my hips and my thong rips away from my body. "Hard and fast crazy girl. That's what you want, isn't it?"

"Yes!" I moan out, feeling his tongue on my bare back and I can't even hide the shiver that runs through my body.

With one thrust, Logan is in me as far as he can go. Both of us moan out at the feeling of each other. He didn't lie when he said hard and fast. Logan is setting a punishing rhythm and his fingers are holding me back, bruising the skin at my hips. I've been thinking of this all day, so I've been on edge. Now, I'm ready to blow and my orgasm is there, I just can't seem to reach it.

"More baby." I moan out.

Logan starts thrusting in me harder and faster. He releases one hip and brings his hand to one of mine at the fence. Pulling my hand away he brings it down so I'm rubbing my clit with him. He's going to control everything tonight and I love when he does that.

"Touch yourself crazy girl." He grits out, taking his hand away from me.

So, I lower my finger to stroke him as he's pounding away before moving my fingers back up to my clit. I can hear him growl, so I start a rhythm of rubbing and pulling my clit then moving my hand down to stroke him and back up. Before too long, his movements become erratic and I can feel myself get that much closer to finding mine.

"I'm close." He grits out. "Find yours crazy girl."

Before I can do anything to find mine, he removes a hand again and pulls my dress down enough to pull out my nipples so he can play with them. At the same time, he starts kissing and biting my neck. And, that's what pushes me over the edge. Moaning out my release, I can feel him thrust a few more times before he swells in me and goes rigid.

"Bailey!" He moans out.

Once he's done, he slides us to the ground so we can catch our breath before making sure our clothes are put right. The entire time, he holds me and doesn't let me touch the ground. I'm resting on him and he's making sure that we're covered enough in case anyone walks by.

"Nice show Pres." I hear called out after a minute or two.

We both lift our head to see a group of about twenty people standing around us. Apparently we were so into ourselves and what we were doing that we didn't realize anyone else was that close. Oh well, I could be embarrassed, but what's the point. They already saw us.

"Get out of here now." Logan yells out. "My old lady needs to get dressed."

They all disappear into the shadows while we start laughing about putting on a show. Not our intention, but it happens. Logan helps me stand before he stands in front of me so that we can fix ourselves. The last thing I want to do is let my parents know what we were doing out here.

"Let's go say good night and head to bed crazy girl." Logan says, wrapping an arm around me.

"Sounds good." I say, trying to stifle a yawn unsuccessfully.

As soon as we get back with everyone, we make our rounds and tell everyone good night before heading up to our room. Logan leads me into the shower and cleans me before leading me to bed and curling around me. Within a matter of minutes, we're both out cold.

Grim

Waking up, I see that Bailey is nowhere to be found in our room. Where the hell could she be already this morning? So, I take a quick shower, after being woken up by her a few times last night I need one, and make my way into the kitchen. Skylar, Maddison, and Bailey are all standing around the island talking about whatever happened with Maddison and Slim last night. Not wanting to interrupt them, I grab a cup of coffee and snag my girl around her neck and give her a kiss, making sure that I leave her breathless.

"I'll be in my office when you're ready to go shoppin' crazy girl." I tell her leaving them alone.

Once in my office, I pull up my email and find that Fox has emailed me some documents and pictures about different contacts the Soulless Bastards were meeting with before we killed them all. I don't recognize a single person in any of them other than Bull and his guys. So, I email Fox back and let him know to see if he can find out who they are and that I'll let Irish know on my end so he can do his own research. He'll like staying home since Caydence and the baby are going to be here. Those two have really taken to being parents.

They named the little girl Cassidy Rose. She's perfect and now we don't have to worry about anyone coming back saying that she's theirs. Vicky definitely won't be coming back and even if she does, all the paperwork for little Cassidy has Caydence and Irish's name on it. Hell, we even checked Vicky in under Caydence's name.

There's a knock on my door and I'm expecting it to be Bailey. It's not. Instead it's Pops, Ma, Joker, and Cage. I wonder what the hell they're up to. Fortunately, I don't have to wait long to find out since Ma lays a box down on my desk and looks around for her daughter.

"She's not in here Ma. Last I knew she was still in the kitchen with the other girls. What's this?"

"You can't open it until she gets in here." Ma says going to the door and calling for Bailey.

The rest of us laugh our asses off since Ma has probably just woken everyone else in the clubhouse. Including all of our visitors. She doesn't care though and she'll smack anyone that tries to chew her a new ass. Unless it's Irish and Caydence since they have the baby here. She's got a soft spot for babies and Cassidy is no exception to that.

"What do you want Ma?" Bailey asks coming in the office. "I just got out of the shower."

"You need to open this with Grim baby girl." She says standing with her hands on her hips. "Since you planned a gender reveal without telling anyone, we got you this."

Bailey walks over to me in a little sun dress under her rag and she looks amazing. It just barely hides her little belly and I know it's only a matter of time before she gets bigger and I can't wait to see her getting bigger and bigger with my son in her belly. I'm sure she won't feel the same, but I can't wait.

She pulls the ribbon off of the box and we tear off the paper together. Inside is the little onesie and hat that Ma gives anyone in the club that's having a baby. I should have expected this but, I honestly wasn't even thinking about it until now. Looking at my girl, I see tears in her eyes and she runs over to her parents giving them both hugs and kissing Ma on her cheek. Today's going to be a good day.

"Alright, Bay and I have to get out of here for a while. Joker, Cage, and Rage are with us. Ma, you got Kasey?" I say standing up.

"Yes I do. We've got things to do and you guys need to leave. Give me a key to the house so Pops can run this over and put it in the nursery." Ma says, holding out her hand to me.

"We're gonna be there in a little while. As soon as we're done at the grocery store, I'll pick it up and take it over." Bailey says going to leave the office.

"Nonsense child of mine. Let Pops run it over now and we'll meet you over there when you get back to help put everything away."

"Crazy girl, you know there's no use fightin' Ma. She's gonna get her way no matter what."

Bailey grumbles but hands her set of keys over to Pops and we head out of the office. I tell Bailey that I need a minute and go to Irish and Caydence's room knocking softly. Irish opens the door and he looks haggard. Coming into the hallway, he gently shuts the door and takes a breath.

"Everythin' okay brother?" I ask him.

"Yeah. Just a rough night with Cass. She didn't want to sleep and was fussy as fuck. Caydence just got her to sleep and is layin' down with her now."

"You need a break, you let us know. Anyway, Fox sent an email I forwarded to you. It's got some pictures I need you to look at and find out who the people are in them. Don't worry about it right this second though. You rest up and I'll get with you later about it."

"Gotcha Pres. Need me, just text or knock."

"We won't disturb you. Need us to pick up some different formula or anythin' while we're at the store?"

"Yeah, why don't ya. That way we can try somethin' else tonight before we end up in the hospital because she's havin' a hard time."

I nod and give him a man hug before turning and making my way to Bailey. Everyone is outside waiting for me at her truck. Guess it's a good thing I have a key to it since Pops took her key ring. Cage, Joker, and Rage are gonna be on their bikes so they head to them while I head to the truck.

"Baby, get on your bike. I can drive over and you can have four bikes instead of three on lookout."

"It's all good crazy girl. I just was on my bike for the run." I say trying to get in.

"Give me your key for the truck and take your bike. We'll be fine." She says, resting her hand on her little bump.

"You sure?"

"Absolutely. Hand it over." She says hopping up in the truck.

We get back to our house after two hours of shopping for groceries. I sent a text to Pops letting him know we were on our way back so they could meet us at the house like Ma requested before we left. Pulling in, we start to unload everything only to have all the bags taken from Bailey and myself. Hell, they won't even let us in the damn house!

"What's goin' on crazy girl?" I ask.

"Your guess is as good as mine baby. Let's make the most of it though and take a walk towards the pond. It feels like I haven't been there in ages."

I grab her hand and tell Joker where we're going before leading her away from our house and through the path in the woods. Coming out at the pond, Bailey takes a seat on one of the benches so I sit next to her and we just sit in silence. My girl looks like she's thinking hard about something and I wonder what's going through that pretty head of hers, but I'll wait until she decides to open up to me.

"Baby, did you ever think we'd be here?"

"At the pond?" I ask her confused.

"No." She says laughing, a sound I could listen to forever and never get tired of. "Us, together and getting ready to have a baby in a few months. Did you ever think we'd be together and experiencing this together?"

"Honestly, I dreamed about it every fuckin' night crazy girl. Even when I was tryin' to protect you and push you away, I saw us together. In my dreams there were little boys that look like me and little girls that look just like their gorgeous mama. I just didn't think I could ever act on it."

"Was it all about what Pops and Joker would say? Is that why you never went after me?"

"No. I always imagined you with a citizen and the house with a white picket fence. But, I know that you would never be able to settle for a life like that. The club is too ingrained in you for you to be content with a citizen." I say looking at her. "When you started seein' Gage, my heart broke into a million little pieces and I knew I would never have it put back together until I had you. You're the glue that holds me together and you always have been."

Tears are running down her face and I pull her into my lap. Bailey is not a girl that cries. Well, she wasn't until she got pregnant. Now, I've learned that every little thing sets her off in a crying ball of Bailey. I say that because she curls up in my lap as small as she can get around her little belly and tries to stop crying.

"I love you more than I ever imagined I would love another person crazy girl. I need you to breathe and center myself. Without you, I would've gone in like a mad man when we did that last run and not have cared about the outcome."

"I love you baby. You are my entire world and I thank anyone that will listen every day that we found our way to one another." Bailey says, calming her tears down and taking a big breath.

We're sitting here in complete silence holding one another when Joker comes down the path and takes us back to the house. He said they got most everything put away except for the dry goods because they didn't know where Bailey wants them. I stand up taking her hand back in mine and we head over to the house.

As soon as we get up to the door, everyone stands up and yells "Surprise!"

Bailey and I look at each other and try to figure out what the hell is going on. Ma comes forward and hugs us both before turning us in the direction of the stairs. She pulls us up them and we're followed by everyone here.

"What's going on Ma?" Bailey asks.

"You'll see." She says leading us to the nursery and opening the door up.

Walking in, Bailey gasps and I have no words. Sitting in the once empty room is a crib, rocking chair, and changing table. Everything is hand-made and has little motorcycles carved in the ends of the crib, on the back at the top of the rocking chair, and on the solid end of the changing table. Once again, Bailey has tears streaming down her face as she runs her hands over the crib before moving on to the chair.

"This is from Pops. He knows a guy that custom makes furniture and had him do this set up as soon as he found out he was gonna be a granddaddy again." Ma says putting her arm around both of us.

"Daddy!" Bailey says going to him and hugging him with everything she has in her. "Thank you so much for getting us this. It's so beautiful!"

"You're welcome baby girl!" He says hugging her tighter.

I make my way over to him and thank him while giving him a hug. This furniture is more than I ever thought possible. We were just planning on getting a set that matched from one of the stores. The set Pops got us will last forever and is better than anything we could find at some store.

"You outdid yourself here Pops." I tell him. "This is amazing!"

"Anythin' for my little girl." He says.

Ma leads us all back downstairs and shushes everyone so she can say whatever she needs to. "Now, we've had a rough patch here and before Slim, Gage, and their respective clubs all leave we decided to throw a baby shower and house warming party all in one. Guys, you can party down in Grim's room or you can stay up here with us."

Most of the guys head down to the basement to play pool and cards while the women do their thing. I hang back for a minute watching everyone around us. These people are our family and they are doing something so special for us. I couldn't be happier of the people that we have surrounded ourselves with.

Bailey

Today has just been full of surprises. Waking up, I met with Skylar and Maddison in the kitchen so she could tell us about her conversation with Slim and later meeting Playboy. They are going to stay in touch and get to know one another. Slim instantly fell in love with Zoey and Playboy is excited to be an uncle. I just hope that Maddison doesn't leave. She's become a friend and I would miss the hell out of her. But, she's gotta do what's best for her and little Zoey.

We've played games and the guys are outside starting to cook the meat to go with the mountain of other food we have to eat today. Now, I'm surrounded by presents for the baby and the house. There are so many that it feels like it's going to take me forever and a day to open everything. Maddison is sitting next to me writing everything down so I can send thank you notes later on.

"Guys, this is all really too much! We don't need all of this." I say to everyone.

"Hush baby girl." Ma says. "Open your gifts and thank everyone for them."

It takes forever, but I finally get through all of the presents we received. My goodness we have more than enough of everything we could need for the little guy now. I honestly don't know what Logan and I have left to buy.

To go with the amazing set in the nursery, we got a ton of sheets and blankets for the bed, a mobile with little motorcycles, and a bumper set with motorcycles on it. One of the old ladies from Slim's club made a blanket with the Wild Kings colors on it. Other than that we got some toys for him, onesies, clothes, binkies, bath stuff, bottles, bottle cleaners and warmers, diaper bags, diapers and wipes, a high chair, car seat, stroller, bouncy seat, floor mats with toys on them, and I can't even remember everything else. Ma of course got the cutest little outfit for him. It's a little pair of jeans, boots, and a tiny leather jacket with the Wild Kings colors on the back. He'll have a cut from Ma by the time he's one too. I know Ma.

Logan, Joker, Cage, Gage, and Pops carry everything upstairs to the nursery so that I can put it away a little at a time. As soon as they're done Logan makes sure that I've had plenty to eat and drink before they head back downstairs. I think they're getting ready to play poker or something like that so I suggest that the girls and kids go over to the pond and swim for a little while before it gets too dark.

Skylar runs down to let the guys know where we're going while I go up and put one of my bikinis on. It's not gonna be much longer before I won't be able to wear them. Throwing on one of Logan's tees I make my way back down to see that most everyone has decided to go to the pond with us.

"You ready crazy girl?" Logan asks grabbing my hand.

"Yeah. Let's go so we can get in the water. You getting in with me?"

"I will get in with you this time. I don't want you swimmin' without me around in case somethin' happens."

"Yes sir!" I say smiling up at him.

"You want a spankin' later crazy girl?" He asks.

"Maybe I do."

As soon as we get to the pond, I take his tee off and he can't take his eyes off of me. Tons of people are already in the pond as I start to walk in. This makes Logan quickly strip of his shirt and take everything out of his shorts before jogging over to me.

"I told you not without me crazy girl."

"You were right there baby."

"Not without me with you." Is all he says.

We're all in the water playing around and racing with the kids for a while before someone starts a bon-fire. Soon the pond clears out as stuff to make s'mores come out and we all gather around the fire to warm up a little. Logan makes sure that I've dried off and sits me as close to the fire as we can stand without feeling overheated.

"You tired crazy girl?" He asks me.

"Starting to get there. We had a busy day today."

"Yeah we did." He says standing up. "I'm takin' crazy girl home. I'll catch up with you all before you leave tomorrow."

Everyone's 'bye' rings out and Kasey runs over to hug me. It's not until Rage comes over to get her before she lets go of me. I look up and see Maddison sitting between Tank and Slim. Hmm. That's got to be a little awkward. I'll talk to her tomorrow when things calm down about it.

Chapter Twenty-Five

Bailey

IT'S BEEN A few months and things have been crazy with the holidays coming up and everything going on with the club. Logan has been spending a ton of time at the clubhouse. When he's gone, I have a full patch and usually Rage with me. Maddison has been spending a ton of time here with Zoey too. Caydence and Irish are settling in just fine as awesome parents and Cassidy has started sleeping better since they found a formula that will agree with her. Skylar and the kids come over to visit, but she spends most of her time at home with Blade and a full patch too. Kenzie is doing her own thing. We haven't really seen too much of her since she started working closer to Slim's club. He's got protection on her there. I miss my girl, but she needs to be happy too.

I'm seven and a half months pregnant now and I've got the nursery exactly how I want it. Everything for the baby has been washed, sterilized, and put away. Pops ended up bringing over a toy box that goes with the rest of the furniture in the room. The only difference is it has 'Wild Kings Future Prospect' burned into the top.

Today is another doctor appointment and Logan's trying to get some work done before he picks me up for it. If he doesn't go, Maddison already said she would go with me. At least I won't be going alone, again. Something is going on that's driving the guys crazy and none of the women know about it. All we know is that we're not to be alone ever and we're to stay hyper vigilant when we're away from the clubhouse. The guys that aren't on babysitting duty for us do continuous drive by's of those that live away from the clubhouse. It's bad enough that Irish talked Caydence into moving into the clubhouse for now. Ma and Pops have been splitting their nights between our house and Skylar's.

"Can I ask you a question?" Maddison asks me.

"Sure. You know you can ask me anything."

"What am I supposed to do about Tank?"

"What do you mean?"

"He's a great guy. Always at the house helping me and Zoey out, he watches her while I work, does things around the apartment, and I feel so safe with him. I just don't know that I'm ready for what he wants. Plus, Slim has been talking about me going to stay there for a while so we can get to know one another and he can get to know his granddaughter."

"And what do you think Tank wants from you?"

"I think he wants us to be together. He hasn't tried anything with me, but I see the looks he gives me and he wouldn't do everything he does if he didn't want more."

"If he's there for you and you feel safe with him, why don't you want more?"

"I don't know. I'm so confused when it comes to him. Maybe I do need to go visit my dad so I can wrap my head around this thing with him."

"Have you tried talking to him?"

"No. I don't know what to say. What if I do and I'm wrong? Then I won't be able to look at him again."

"You have to figure out what you want and then you need to talk to him about it."

"I think I'm going to call dad and have him come get me. Or Playboy. He wants me to visit them too."

"You do what you gotta do for you. I can't say I'm happy you're leaving, but I get it. Just let me know when you leave, yeah? And talk to Tank and let him know why you're leaving. Don't just leave him hanging. Please!"

We sit there in silence for a while before I have to get ready to leave. I've already taken my shower and stuff so all I have to do is change and get my purse. I'm trying not to get ready yet because if I do and Logan doesn't show up, I'll be disappointed. But, I keep watching the clock and it's getting to the point that I'm going to be late if I don't get around in the next few minutes.

Maddison watches me and knows that I'm getting upset that it looks like Logan isn't going to make this appointment. So, she gives me the nudge I need by starting to get Zoey ready to leave. Thankfully we put a car seat in my truck for her a few weeks ago so we can just go without worrying if one of the guys switched it from the club's vehicle, which ever one brings her over and takes her home. Now, we can just go when we want to and if she wants to go home, we go there and hang out.

Grim

I woke up before Bailey did this morning, like most mornings these days, and made my way over to the clubhouse. We still have no clue who the people are in the pictures and I'm getting pissed off. The women are getting tired of having to have babysitters, as they call them, and it's to the point not a lot of work is getting done in our businesses. We're using all of our resources to figure out who wants our women to sell them.

"Pres, you got a minute?" Tank asks, poking his head in the door.

"Yeah, I need a break from lookin' at this screen for a while. Talk in here or in the common room?"

"In here." He says sitting down. "I've been lookin' at the pictures Fox emailed you. I found somethin' none of us have noticed it yet."

"What's that?" I ask perking up.

"They all center around Dander Falls. All of the background buildin's are in Dander Falls. Street signs too."

"You sure about that?"

"Yeah. I've been lookin' and lookin' at them tryin' to figure this shit out. I've seen them when we've gone there." Tank says pulling out a stack of pictures much larger than what Fox sent me.

He takes half the pictures and lays them on one side and the other half right next to them. Somehow he's gotten pictures of the buildings around Dander Falls that line up with the pictures I was sent. Even the things around the street signs are the same as I look through what he has.

"Fuck! Good catch Tank. At least we have a general direction to look in now."

"Blade helped point it out to me. I knew that I had seen the background images, but he pointed out the gas station in the one picture."

"He's gettin' patched. Rage too. They've done enough time, more than enough. And they have proven themselves enough. We're votin' this shit now. Call everyone in for emergency church. Get the guys on the phone that are with the women and see how they want to vote. I want everyone else here in ten minutes or less."

Tank leaves the office and goes to get everyone here. Now I have to call Gage so he can step up even more on security and keep an eye on the women around them. He's not happy when I get off the phone with him. Fox should have caught the buildings and he didn't. We're definitely going to be spending some time in Dander Falls in the next few days and weeks to come. Gage agrees and says he's going to start getting things ready for us to show up.

Walking into the meeting room, I see everyone that should be here sitting around the table already. So, I quickly take my seat and call church to order.

"First things' first. Tank and Blade put together somethin' from the pictures you've all seen. All those meetin's took place in Dander Falls. I just got off the phone with Gage so he knows. He's steppin' up security on their women and gettin' things ready for us to get there. We'll be leavin' in a day or two so we can finally try to put this to rest once and for all."

Everyone around the table is pissed off with the news that they've been that close. Obviously there's a sex trafficking ring there and none of us have known about it until now. Until Bull gave us one tidbit of information before he met his maker.

"Second piece of business we need to talk about is makin' sure that we have people in place here to run our businesses until we can get back on track with them. Before we leave, I want Tank and Irish to go to them all and make sure the managers know they can still call us but that we'll be out of town for a little bit. We have to be back for the toy drive for the hospital though."

Tank and Irish nod to me that they'll get on that as soon as we're done here. We really don't have a ton of businesses here right now, but they still need to know that we haven't abandoned them. I would never do that to any of our businesses. There's too much more I want to do in this town to piss people off like that and make them not believe in us anymore.

"Last piece of business for now. There's goin' to be a discussion so hold whatever you have to say in until I open the floor." I pause to make sure that they all know I'm serious. "We've been talkin' about it for a while now and its time. I want to patch in Blade and Rage. They've both done their time and proven their worth to the club. Now, who has somethin' to say about that?"

I look around and most of the guys are smiling and nodding that the two men are finally going to be patched in. All except for Pops and Glock. Pops steps up first.

"I'm all for patchin' Blade in. He has proven himself multiple times to all of us. But, Rage has been gone dealin' with his shit and now, he's not steppin' up as much as Blade with his little girl here. He's done more construction and shit than bein' here."

"Construction is his job Pops. You know he has to earn money to support his daughter and him. When we were gone, he did his rounds and the women kept an eye on Kasey. You know he lost his mother and had to take care of that crazy bitch."

"I do know that. I'm not sayin' that he isn't helpful to the club or that I don't want him patched. I'm just sayin' that he's been gone and now has his daughter."

"Then I guess none of us deserve a patch that have kids. Irish hasn't been pullin' his weight in that case then since they got Cassidy. No disrespect intended brother."

"None taken Pres. I know I've been busy tryin' to help Caydence. But, I'm comin' back around now." Irish says.

"Glock what have you got to say?" I ask him.

"I was thinkin' the same as Pops." He mutters.

"Anyone else?" I ask. "No? We vote all in favor of patchin' Blade in say 'yay'."

Everyone goes around the table with a 'yay'. I'm last and add my 'yay' to them. Tank gives me the votes of the members that can't be here, all 'yay'. Banging the gavel on the table I announce that he'll be patched in before we leave for Dander Falls. I look directly at Pops and Glock.

"All in favor of patchin' Rage in, say 'yay'."

Once again, everyone around the table says 'yay' and the members that aren't here are 'yay'. We all know that Rage is more than pulling his weight around here. He might not hang out as much, but I probably won't either once the baby gets here. Rage deserves it though and everyone in this room knows it. I don't get why Pops is against him getting his patch. When it comes to Glock, he adds in his 'yay'. So does Pops. Adding my vote in, I announce that Rage will be patched in at the same time as Blade. Then I adjourn the meeting and everyone goes to get everything ready so we can leave.

"Pres, I have nothin' against him patchin' in. I honestly don't." Pops says, remaining in his chair.

"Then what's goin' on?" I ask him leaning forward.

"I don't want him off of watchin' Bailey. He pays attention to her and helps her when she needs it. Other than checkin' in on her and Kasey, he stays outside and guards your house and woman, my daughter."

I can't help the chuckle I let loose. "Is that the only reason you brought that other shit up?"

"Yeah." He says looking down. I knew he was worried about crazy girl, but I didn't expect that.

"I'll still keep him on her watch Pops. I didn't have any plans on takin' him off her. I know that she trusts him and loves the extra time with Kasey."

Pops lets out a breath and visibly relaxes in his chair. "How is my baby girl doin'?"

"Good." I say looking at the clock. "Fuck! I was supposed to pick her up almost an hour ago for a doctor's appointment."

"Get lost." Pops says "Go see where she is and meet her. We got this handled."

Pulling out my phone I call Rage to see where they are with my girl. He tells me that they got back to the house about ten minutes ago and Bailey went up to take a nap. Fuck! That means she isn't visiting with Maddison any more even if she's still at our house. She's upset, pissed, and this isn't going to go good when I tell her that we have to go to Dander Falls for a while. Bailey is not going to want to leave with a month and a half left until her due date. I can't leave her here alone though.

I run across the field and make my way into the house. Rage is walking the outside of the house and Crank is walking in the opposite direction. Walking in I see Maddison sitting on the couch feeding Zoey under a blanket. Saying hi I make my way up to our room and see Bailey curled up in the middle of the bed fast asleep. Shit!

Toeing my boots off, I climb in bed and wrap around my girl. This time she doesn't turn to me or burrow her way into my embrace. She's hurt beyond belief right now that I missed another appointment. Hopefully she understands when I tell her what happened this morning and that I was late because of that.

Laying here watching Bailey sleep, I ignore calls and messages coming through to my phone. I know things are going on and I shouldn't be ignoring anything right now, but Pops is at the club and one of the guys would come find me if it's something needing me right away. If it's Gage or Slim, they both have Joker's number if they can't reach me. I need to make sure that Bailey's okay. And find out what happened at the appointment today.

Bailey slept the day away and I did nothing but watch her sleep. She didn't move one single time and the only time she usually does that is when she's curled around me. But, her back is flush against the front of me and I have one hand resting on our boy. He's moving around and kicking up a storm. I start remembering the first time we felt him move.

We were sitting on the couch watching a movie. Well, Bailey was watching a movie and I was watching her. Every day she gets just a little bit bigger with my boy growing in her belly. The changes in her have been amazing to watch and experience right along with her; her belly growing, her tits getting bigger (definitely my favorite part), and the glow that she has whenever she lays her hand against our boy. She gets a look in her eyes and the smile I love so much shows up on her face.

All of a sudden Bailey starts giggling like a schoolgirl. At first I think something funny is happening on the movie, so I move my attention to the t.v. I don't see anything going on that I would consider funny, so I lift my head and look down at her. Instead of telling me anything, she grabs my hand and sets it on her belly. I don't feel anything for a minute and I'm about to move my hand away when I feel it move. Looking down at her,

395

smile coming out full force, I can't help the smile spreading across my own face.

"Is that our boy?" I ask her, full of amazement and awe.

"Yeah, it is." She says holding my hand in place with hers.

Every few minutes we can feel him move again. For the rest of the day we just lay there and wait for the next time our boy moves around. The movements aren't as strong as they're going to get, but it's amazing as hell and I can't wait until we feel them more and more. Getting stronger and stronger every day as he grows bigger and stronger.

I'm jarred out of my memory when I feel Bailey start to stir next to me. She slowly opens her eyes and looks at me. All of a sudden she tries to move away so I wrap my arm around her just a little bit tighter, making sure that I don't hurt her or the baby.

"I'm sorry baby. We got a lead on shit and I had to call emergency church."

"I know. Crank told me." She says pulling away and sitting up.

"What did the doctor say?"

"Everything's on track for a probable Christmas baby. I've been feeling some Braxton hick's contractions and that's not going to stop any time soon. So, I can expect to feel uncomfortable until he decides to grace us with his presence."

"I wish I could've been there with you crazy girl." I try again.

"I know. Club business and all that comes first. I get it Logan. Is Maddison still here?" She asks, heading into the bathroom.

"I'm not sure. I've been up here with you."

"Oh."

"Got more to talk about crazy girl." I tell her sitting on the edge of the bed.

"What's going on?"

"We have to all go to Dander Falls for a little bit."

"Why?" She asks coming out of the bathroom.

"Tank looked at some information again and the person we're lookin' for is in Dander Falls. Gage already knows we're gonna be headin' that way."

"Oh. How long will you be gone this time?" She asks stepping between my legs.

"Not the guys and me, crazy girl. Everyone in the club is goin'. Includin' the old ladies, Storm and Summer, and Maddison and Zoey."

"When are we leaving?"

"Tomorrow. I've decided that I want to leave sooner so we can get there and back before you have the baby. Tonight we patch Blade and Rage in. But, we're not gonna celebrate until we get back for obvious reasons."

"Go let everyone know and I'll get us packed and ready to go." She says moving to the closet.

"That's it? You're not gonna fight me on this?" I ask her shocked as hell.

"Nope. I'm not exactly comfortable leaving my doctor this close to my due date, but we have a month and a half right? I'll just switch my appointments to the doctor she suggested before until we come back home."

"You sure?"

"Don't really have a choice do I? You might want to talk to Maddison though. She was talking about going to visit Slim."

"I'll go down now and talk to her. I love you crazy girl!" I say heading for the door.

"Love you too."

Making my way downstairs, I see Maddison still sitting on the couch watching a chick flick. So, I sit down next to her and hold my hands out for Zoey. She hands her to me and I cradle her close to my body as I turn more to face her.

"Something wrong Grim?" She asks me nervously.

"No. I have to talk to you though."

"Okay."

"Crazy girl just told me that you want to go see Slim. When were you thinkin' of doin' that?"

"Oh. Well, he just mentioned that he wanted to get to know me and Zoey more. Playboy too. I was thinking of going next week or something. I need to talk to Tank first."

"What's Tank got to do with it?" I ask confused.

"Nothing. I just need to talk to him about something."

"Okay. Well, we're all headin' to Dander Falls for a while. You were gonna have to come too. But, if you want to go to Slim instead I get that. It might make it easier for your protection."

"I can do that as long as Slim agrees and I can talk to Tank first."

"I'll get him over here and you can talk in the basement. Call your dad and let him know what's goin' on."

Maddison digs her phone out of her diaper bag and dials Slim. While they're on the phone, I text Tank telling him to come over here. He replies that he'll be here in a few minutes. That should give Maddison time to get off the phone so Tank and she can talk. What the fuck is going on between them? I know he hasn't been around the clubhouse as much because he's been with her, but I didn't know they were together.

"Slim says it's all good and he'll be waiting for me to get there."

"Sounds good sweetheart. Tank will be here in a minute or so." I tell her right before the door opens. "Or, he's here now. You two go downstairs and I'll keep Zoey with me."

Maddison

I'm nervous as hell to talk to Tank. But, Bailey was right, I do need to talk to him and let him know why I'm leaving for a while. I follow him down to Grim's room and he pulls out a seat at the poker table for me. After I sit down he sits next to me, angling his chair so he can look at me.

"Everythin' okay sweetheart?" He asks, grabbing my hand in his large one.

"I don't know Tank. What are you expecting from me?" I blurt out.

"What do you mean?"

"You help me all the time, spend most of your free time with me, and you watch Zoey and won't let me pay you. What are you expecting in return?"

"Sweetheart, I don't want anythin'. I like spendin' time with you and I love watchin' Zoey while you're at work. You need a break every now and then too. Even if it's just to take a little bit longer in the shower, or get housework that I didn't get a chance to do done. What brought this on?"

"I'm so confused by you. When I'm with you, I feel safe and comfortable in a way I've never felt before. Zoey adores you even though she's only a few months old. You do things around the apartment that my ex never did and you don't live with me. I'm just not sure I'm ready to give you what you're going to eventually want." I say looking down at our entwined fingers.

"Maddie, I'm in no rush. I like gettin' to know you. If we develop into somethin' more than friends, I'm definitely all for that. If a friendship is all I ever have with you, then I'm fine with that too. Just know that I'll always be there for you and Zoey no matter what happens between us."

I blow out a breath knowing that this is going to be the hardest part of the conversation. "I need to tell you something. When you all leave to go to Dander Falls, I'm going to my dad's. Playboy and him want to get to know Zoey and me."

Tank doesn't say anything. In fact, he doesn't move a muscle. Looking up into his face, I see a whole range of emotions flitting across his features. It happens so fast that I can't even figure out what he's feeling.

Finally, he speaks. "Are you comin' back?"

"I am. I'm not leaving here for good. It would just be nice to get to know my family. I didn't have them growing up and I'm not going to deny Zoey having her family in her life."

"When are you comin' back?" He asks.

"I don't know Tank. I have to think about work and talk to them if I even still have a job. And I need to figure out what's going to be best for Zoey. She's my number one priority."

"I know she is sweetheart. But, I don't think you have to worry about callin' the diner before you leave. Grim's givin' you a job here when we get back. Bailey's 'bout ready to pop, so he's gonna have you take over the office at Spinners."

"Oh. I didn't know that."

"He just figured it out. Since we more than likely cost you your job, he wanted to make sure you had somethin'."

"I'll have to thank him. I hated workin' there anyway. I'll have to find a sitter before I come back then."

"Skylar." Is all Tank says.

Tank

This girl is breaking my fucking heart and she has no clue. Yeah, I'm gonna take this shit at her pace because Maddison is mine. She's been mine since I first laid eyes on her at the Kitty Kat. I haven't even touched a club girl since I met her. Haven't had any desire to touch nasty when I can wait for a piece of heaven.

Telling me that she's going to Slim's club feels like she's telling me good bye for good. That's just not gonna work for me. But, it might work out if I can talk to him when I drop her off. Cause she damn sure isn't heading there by herself. I'll just take a few guys with me when we pull off and head to his clubhouse.

"We're gonna patch a few guys in before we leave, but I doubt we'll have a party like usual. I'm gonna take you home so you can pack for Zoey and you and then we'll come back here. Sound good?" I ask her.

"Yeah. Um… How am I gettin' to my dad?" She asks me.

"I'll take you there on our way to Dander Falls."

"O-o-okay." She stammers, like I'm giving her a gift.

Maddie has given me the gift. Every day that she allows me to spend with her and Zoey is the best gift that I've ever received in my life. These two females have quickly become the most important things in the world to me and I'm not going to live without them. Do I care if she visits her dad and brother? Absolutely not! Is it gonna be hard as fuck to leave them there, where I can't see them? Every fucking day is gonna be hard to get through.

"Let's go get the princess and get things rollin'." I tell her.

She stands up and leads me back upstairs. Grim and Bailey are sitting on the couch with Zoey between them. I notice their bags are packed and I look at Grim to see what's going on.

"I wanna leave earlier than we first thought. We're leavin' later today." He says.

"Okay. We just came to get Zoey to go pack them up and get ready to go to Slim's." I say. "I'm takin' her there and droppin' her off."

Grim can see that I'm not gonna budge on this so he nods and tells me that he's going to send Rage and Joker with me. They'll stop not far from our turnoff so that we're not alone and sitting ducks for long. Since

Bailey's truck is going, we're gonna hook a trailer up and my bike can go in that with his. He's not letting her out of his sight to drive the few hours to Gage's club.

Maddie goes to pick Zoey up and we head out to my truck. I already switched the car seat over so she puts Zoey in and we take off. Not being able to help myself, I grab her hand and lay it on my thigh. She doesn't pull away, so I'm thinking that she doesn't mind.

Bailey

I was so upset that Logan missed the appointment, but once he explained I understood. Even if I did come off sounding like a bitch to him. They've all been trying to get something taken care of since they came back from dealing with Bull and his club. If something comes up regarding that, I know Logan's going to stop whatever he's doing and take care of that.

Since none of the women know what's going on, I'm assuming it's really bad. Especially with the way the guys are acting and guarding us all. The only ones that aren't under supervision all day, every day are the club girls and strippers. So, it must just mainly concern the old ladies of the club.

After packing our bags, I call Logan up to carry them down. He's carrying Zoey when he enters our room, so I take her from him so he can grab the bags and take them down to the door.

"You get everythin' you need in here crazy girl? Fuck, how many things did you stuff in here?"

"Well, we don't know how long we're gonna be gone and I'm not going to suffer and be more uncomfortable then I already am."

"I'm sorry crazy girl. If I could take it from you, I would."

"I know. Right now I just mainly can't stay cool and it's getting harder and harder to sleep. Between being hot all night long and the baby deciding that my bladder is his own personal trampoline, I have to pee every five minutes these days."

"I know. I feel you get up all night long. And, before you say it, I'm not bitchin'. I'm just sayin' I know that you're gettin' miserable. But, we're almost to the finish line. Little bit longer and we'll be meetin' our boy."

"That's the only reason I'm getting through this part baby. If I felt like this the entire time, I'd be crazy right now. Instead of just hormonal."

Logan laughs at me and pulls me down next to him on the couch, making sure that Zoey doesn't get hurt. I slide away from him and lay her between us. He starts tickling her and I start looking around for Maddison. Where the hell did she go?

"Who you lookin' for crazy girl?"

"Maddison. Where is she?"

"Down with Tank. She said she needed to talk to him."

"She's going to Slim's instead isn't she?" I ask him.

"Yeah. What's that got to do with Tank?"

"I don't know what's going on between them, but something is. I told her to talk to him before she went for her visit so he knew she wasn't running and that it was only to get to know her family."

"She into him?"

"I think so. But, something has her scared shitless to pursue it."

We just sit there and continue playing with Zoey until they come back up. After Maddison takes her daughter, Logan and I head over to the clubhouse with Crank and Rage following behind us. They're carrying our bags to load in the truck while we go inside. Logan nods his head to Joker, who nods back. Must be making sure everything is ready to patch the guys in later. It sucks that we can't throw them a party like normal, but I'm sure they'll understand. We'll just make sure it's even better when we get back and throw them a huge blowout.

Everyone is back at the clubhouse after gathering what they'll need to leave. I'm sitting at a table with Maddison, Skylar, and Caydence. Summer and Storm are behind the bar so the guys can at least have one beer when Blade and Rage get their patches. It's not much, but it's enough for now.

"Settle down, settle down!" Logan shouts over all the noise, waiting until everyone is silent. "Blade and Rage bring your asses forward. *Now!*" He calls out.

The two men scramble through the crowd of men, who aren't making it easy on them, and come to a stop in front of Logan. I can't see Rage's face, but I can see Blade is looking at everyone and everything from the corner of his eyes. He's suspicious of what's going on, trying to figure out if he did something wrong. I'm sure Rage's mind is racing to come up with ideas of what's going on right now.

"You two have been with us for a while now. You've lasted longer as a prospect than most of these fuckers could handle. So, you should know what you can and can't do. Right?"

"Yes Pres!" They both reply simultaneously.

"Then what the fuck are you thinkin'?"

"About what Pres?" Blade asks.

"About finally bein' patched the fuck in?" Logan says, a huge smile spreading across his face.

I visibly see both men relax and let out the breath they were holding. Joker steps up behind Logan with the patches they'll need to put on their cut. Both men are smiling and accepting all the man hugs and backslapping. I'm so happy for both of them. Pretty soon Logan and

Joker are leading them over to us so we can congratulate them.

"I'm so happy for you both." I say standing up hugging first Rage and then Blade. "As soon as we can, you know we're gonna throw you a huge ass party."

"We understand why it can't be now." Blade says hugging me.

"Are you sure you got Kasey in the truck with you guys?" Rage asks Logan and me.

"She wouldn't have it any other way Rage and you know that. Ma is riding with us too so I'm going to sit in the back with her. You got the DVD player and some movies packed right?"

"Yeah. She picked her favorite ones already. I need to run to the room and grab the bags and make sure she packed enough. She wanted to do it alone."

"You stay and have your beer with the guys. I'll grab Kasey and we'll go double check the bags."

"Thanks Bailey. I don't know what I would do without you, Skylar, and Ma." He says, dipping his head while Logan throws an arm around him.

"Don't think anything of it honey. You're one of us which makes her one of us. Now, let me get the princess and make sure we got everything we're going to need."

After sitting around for an hour or so, we all start to load up in the vehicles and the men on their bikes. There's a trailer on my truck and one on Skylar's SUV. Cage is driving her and their kids and Irish is driving Caydence, Cassidy, Summer, and Storm. So, four bikes needed to be loaded in the trailers so the guys have them at Gage's. Plus, I'm sure that they have other equipment, parts, and tools that they're going to need on this trip.

Ma tries to get in the backseat with Kasey, but I push her to the front. She doesn't want to budge, but I pull the grandbaby card and she moves. Pops starts laughing his ass off at me because I just got my way and Ma is moping in the front seat.

"Ma I love you and I'll see you when we pull over at a diner." Pops says to her kissing her long and hard.

"Ewww!" I pipe up from the back seat with Kasey.

"You hush baby girl!" Ma says. "Sitting back there acting like I don't know you manipulated me. You're not as smart as you think you are."

"Of course I am. Who do you think I learned that shit from?" I fire back.

"Well, she has you there woman." Pops says leaning in for another kiss. "Love you."

"Love you too. Even though you do nothing but encourage her!"

"So do you darlin'." He responds before shutting the door and walking over to his bike.

Rage gives Kasey hugs and kisses and tells her he loves her before shutting her in and going to his bike. Logan jumps in and we head out. Pops and Joker are riding in front of us, at least until Joker, Rage, and Tank pull off to go to Slim's. I settle in for the long ride and am asleep before I know it, leaning on Kasey's little pillow with my head next to hers.

Chapter Twenty-Six

Grim

I WOKE BAILEY and Kasey up when we got to the diner to wait for Tank, Joker, and Rage. I'm not comfortable enough to keep going without them with us when we don't know who we're looking for. We know the place, but we don't know who. Gage and his club have been putting out some feelers since I called and gave him the news. So, I'm hoping that they have some news when we get there.

After we all ate and the guys met back up with us, we're heading back out for the rest of the journey. We're still about an hour and a half out. With all of our stomachs full, the three riding with me immediately passed out. Looks like I've only got music as my company for the next hour and a half or so. If we haul ass, a little bit at least, we can cut that time down so the women can get a bed instead of sitting up or laying in awkward positions in the vehicles.

Fortunately, the hour and a half was cut down to just over an hour before I find myself pulling into Gage's. They're all waiting outside for us to help us unload and show us all to the rooms we're staying in. Gage walks directly over to the truck and opens the back door thinking Ma is sitting back there. When he sees Bailey, he grimaces at the position she's in. I've been doing the same thing since she fell asleep.

"Hey man." I say, getting out and stretching.

"Glad you're here. We're set up in the meetin' room already to go when you are."

"Good. Let's get the women, kids, and bags in and get down to business. The sooner we can get home, the better. Crazy girl doesn't want to have the baby here."

"How much longer?" He asks.

"Month and a half."

"Damn! That flew by."

"Yeah. Well, we've had a lot goin' on. She's so uncomfortable now it's not funny. I hope you got extra fans and shit for her."

"I'll have Shadow pull them out and take them to your room."

"I can hear you two talking you know." Bailey says sitting up.

"Damn sweetheart!" Gage says when he sees how big her belly is.

"I know I'm a fat ass, you don't have to comment." She snaps.

"Not what I was thinkin' honey. It's just the last time I saw you all you had was a little baby bump. Can't say the same thing now."

"Get out of our way." Crash says, stepping up and helping Bailey out of the truck before hugging her.

Trojan is next and he spins her around. Much to my amusement, Bailey starts acting like she's going to throw up on him and he immediately sets her down. After he makes sure she's steady on her feet, Trojan backs up and watches her.

"Gotcha smart ass!" She says, slapping him on the chest.

"What?" He asks confused.

"You were shakin' our boy up doin' that shit." I say.

"She could've said that." He says acting pissed but he's trying to hide his laughter.

We wake all the women and kids up to get them inside and into each of our rooms. Most of us are going downstairs to the newly renovated basement. Gage and the guys split it up so that now there's about fifteen more rooms down here with a small section with a t.v, game systems, and a crap ton of movies and things for the kids. The only ones from my club staying upstairs are the single guys, the rest of us are down here.

After making sure Bailey is settled in the room to continue resting, with Kasey, I head back upstairs with the rest of the guys so we can have church. Gage and I sit together at the head of the table while everyone else spreads out around the room. Thankfully his meeting room is bigger than the one we have so most of us have a chair to sit in. He looks over at Rage and Blade noticing the new patches they're rocking and opens the meeting up by congratulating them. Now, it's time for business though. So, Fox takes over talking and we all turn our attention to the screen on the side wall.

"I've been pourin' over the photos since you called Grim. I can't believe I didn't notice that before. I'm a dumbass! Anyway, I've been starin' and starin' at them for hours. Most of them all have one other common factor in them." Fox says, using a laser pointer to circle the guy the Soulless Bastards are meeting with. "This guy right here is in most of the photos I got. Because we can't really see his face, we still don't know who he is."

"Any distinguishin' marks on him?" I ask.

"I can make out part of a tattoo on his right arm, but that's it. When I try to blow it up, it gets distorted and blurry. To me it looks like it's tribal, but I'm not sure."

We all sit there and stare at the guy's arm for what feels like forever. Fox is right though; you can't really make out the tattoo. And the guy dresses like any other guy walking on the street. Jeans, usually a dark shirt, a plain baseball hat, and either sneakers or boots. Not a lot else to try to figure out a way to identify him.

"What now?" Cage asks.

"I guess we start combin' the streets when it starts to get dark out. That seems to be when Bull met this guy. We put feelers out like we've got some girls to 'get rid' of." Gage says and looks at me.

"I like it. Who's stayin' back to watch the women and kids?" I ask.

"Why don't most of tonight's crew be my guys. That way you guys can get some rest after drivin' half the day."

"Sounds good. Everyone keep your phones on if you're stayin' here in case they get in trouble. Wake me up with a text when you get back and we'll meet again." I say starting to stand up.

My guys follow me out of the meeting room and either head downstairs to our family or find a piece of strange for the night. When I walk in our room, Bailey and Kasey are passed out cold. Rage follows me in and lifts his daughter out of the bed to take her to his room. I strip and climb into bed next to my girl. Once again, she turns and burrows into me. Before too long, my brain shuts down and I'm asleep wrapped up in my girl.

Bailey

We've been here for almost a week now and I don't think the guys are any closer to finding what they're looking for than when we got here. Logan comes in the room, or wherever I am, when he returns and I can see the frustration and rage rolling off of him. The rest of the guys aren't much better than him either.

The second day we were here, Gage led me outside to show me the memorial that they put together here for Ryan. It's almost the same exact thing as what was set up at our clubhouse. While Logan's gone I spend most of my time out here. I feel bad because Kasey knows this is my special spot, like back home, and she waits for me to go back inside to spend time with her. Other than that she spends her time with either Skylar or Storm.

There's been a few run-ins with some of the club girls from Gage's club and Summer and Storm. Yes, they are club girls, but they're also a tremendous help to Skylar and me. So, when we go on lockdown, they're on lockdown. When we go somewhere like this, they come with us. Logan does run the club a little different from other Presidents because no one else would bring club girls with them like this. So, as of now, Trixie and Peaches are banned from coming here. None of the guys want to deal with the drama so that was the best thing to do.

Tomorrow I have to go see the doctor here to make sure that things are still going good. Doctor Bell told me that we'll probably start my weekly appointments now because of my nervousness about something happening to the baby. So, I'll probably see the doctor here at least twice. Hopefully it's not more than that because I don't want to have my baby here and we have the charity run coming up in a little over three weeks.

Thanksgiving is coming up too. We're all prepared to make dinner here for everyone, but I'd rather be home. It is what it is though and we'll all deal with what we have to work with. I'm sitting in the room Logan and I have watching some cartoon with Kasey when Skylar comes in.

"You got extra blankets in here?" She asks me all flustered.

"I think so. What's wrong?"

"The kids want to make a fort. I'm running out of ways to keep them occupied and Cage and Joker are both out working. Pops and Ma can't even keep their attention this evening."

"You can send some in here with us if you want."

"I'll ask, but I don't know if any are going to want to leave our room. Maybe I can talk Reagan into it though."

"You look in the closet for the blankets, and I'll get Reagan, Alana, and Haley to come in here with us. When we get back, we'll the start the movie over again Kasey."

"Okay." She says, not looking away from her movie.

By the time Skylar finds what she's looking for I have the girls with me in my room. They settle in to watch a movie with Kasey and Storm brings them in popcorn and some juice to have with it. I sit at the desk in the room and read. Kasey and I have watched the same movie a dozen times already and I'm done watching it. I just want to go home honestly.

Grim

We've been driving around and around Dander Falls, putting feelers out trying to make contact with this guy. Not a single one of us have had any luck so far and we're all giving up hope of ever finding him. The women are starting to get miserable from being kept inside with the kids and the kids are starting to go crazy. Bailey is even more tired every day and she doesn't do half the things here that she does back home.

"Pres, when is it enough?" Glock asks. "We can't find the fucker. All we're doin' is wastin' time and burnin' fuel."

"I'm not restin' until we find the motherfucker gunnin' for Skylar and Bailey!" I say, pounding my fist on the table.

"I get you want this guy, but maybe we should back off for a while and then start again. Go back home and let him come back out. Gage and his guys can continue doin' shit here and we'll be on standby, ready to leave at a moment's notice." He continues.

"I'll think about it. Can't do anythin' until after crazy girl's appointment tomorrow."

Maybe Glock's right and we should go home for now. Thanksgiving is in a few days and then we have the toy drive. I'm going to talk to Gage and the guys from my club and we'll head out tomorrow afternoon. I've got to trust that Gage and the guys here will continue their questions and trying to find him. I know they will though because Bailey and Skylar are loved everywhere they go. They want this asshole found as bad as we do.

Chapter Twenty-Seven

Grim

WE'RE BACK HOME and Thanksgiving is here. Skylar, Bailey, Summer, and Storm are cooking up a storm while the guys do their own things. Some are watching a football game, some playing pool or poker, and others are in their rooms with club girls who will come and go through the back door. The kids are playing and running everywhere.

I really don't want Bailey cooking, but she's going to do what she wants to do, so I guess I'll keep my mouth shut. The doctor told us that she's already starting to dialate and she still has over a month to go. That worries me, but Doctor Bell knows and assured us that it could take the next month for her to get far enough that we'll have to go to the hospital. So, I guess it's a good thing that we came home. She'll kill me if she doesn't have the baby here.

"Pres, Gage sent me a text earlier." Tank says, taking a seat next to me at the bar.

"Why didn't he text me?"

"Didn't want to wake your girl up if she was still sleepin'. They got nothin' new on this fucker. No one's talkin' either."

"So, same shit as when we were there. Who the fuck is this guy that he can hide in plain sight and no one will point his ass out to anyone?"

"Your guess is as good as mine. How's your girl doin'?"

"She's miserable as fuck. Sleep is gettin' harder and harder for her to find. I'm gettin' ready to take her up for a nap. How you doin' without your girls here?"

"Not my girls." Is all he says.

"Not yet. You goin' after Maddison?"

"I am. Already talked to Slim and told him when she's ready I'm claimin' her."

"What did he say?"

"Not much. Just told me if I hurt her he's puttin' me to ground. But, he's goin' to watch her and make sure no one there touches her. I'm not gonna stop her though if she meets someone there and wants him."

"Why?"

"I'd rather see her and Zoey happy than make sure she's mine. From the little I've gotten her to open up, she hasn't had a lot of happy in her life, and most of what she's had is centered around her baby girl. I'm not standin' in her way from findin' her happy."

"You're better than me. You need anythin' I'm here. You wanna go to Slim's let me know and I'll figure shit out to cover you while you're gone."

"Nope. I'm lettin' her have this time."

The two of us just sit there and drink our beer while we get lost in our own thoughts. Mine center around Bailey and everything that I've done to hurt her. I've been such an ass and I'm lucky as fuck that she even gave me a chance. Tank is a good guy and the woman he wants isn't here for him. I know Maddison isn't his, yet, and has some things to work through, I just hope he gets his happy sooner rather than later. Tank deserves it.

Pretty soon, the women come out of the kitchen and announce that everything is ready and we need to help them get it all out here. I move to Bailey and help her sit down by the head of the table. She looks dead on her feet, but she hasn't rested at all yet today. Instead, she's been in the kitchen 'pulling her weight around here'. Her words, not mine.

"You sit here and I'll be right back." I tell her.

She doesn't even have the energy to do much more than smile at me. It's not even a full smile. My girl is eating and I'm taking her ass home. Someone else can bring dessert over later or something. This is ridiculous! Looking up, I see Ma watching us and I nod down at her daughter so she makes her way over to sit next to her.

"Not many of us are here today. Some are with family and others are doin' their own thing." I say once the food is all set out. "Usually we go around the table and say what we're thankful for. I'd like to start that today."

Everyone stops filling their plates with all the food, and there's a crap ton of it. The weight has to be about as much as the table can hold. "This year I'm thankful that I have an amazin' old lady rulin' this club by my side and we're makin' our family grow. In just over a month we're welcomin' a baby boy to the family. I never thought we'd get this far, but my crazy girl is the best thing that has ever happened to me. I love you baby."

"I love you too baby. Okay. This year, I'm thankful that we were introduced to new members of our family in Maddison and Zoey. And I'm thankful that I have every single one of you by my side. Lastly, I'm thankful that I have an amazing man that's going to make a great father to our baby and will do everything in his power to protect all of us and still show me his love every day. Even when I'm mad or upset."

Everyone around us chuckles because they know I piss her off more than anything else these days. Each person around the table takes their turn telling everyone what they're thankful for. Some are goofy, some are sad, and some are nothing more than a few words to each member of this extended family as a whole. As soon as the last person goes, we all dig in and eat as much of this amazing food as possible.

I see Bailey slowing down so I pick her plate up and finish it for her. She hates wasting food! So, she just sits there trying not to fall asleep while the rest of us talk and laugh. Nodding to Ma she nudges her while I move my plate away and go to pick her up.

"Where we going baby?" She asks.

"Home. You can't keep your eyes open. We're goin' to bed now crazy girl. Sky will make sure to save some dessert for you. Right?"

415

"Absolutely. I actually already put a cheesecake in your fridge. There's different toppings on the counter for you."

"I love you." Bailey mumbles as I head for the door.

Walking over to the house, we're being followed by Rage, Joker, and Pops. I don't know if they're just making sure nothing happens to us in the dark, or if they wanna talk when I get crazy girl to bed.

Pops leans over my arm and kisses his daughter on the forehead and Joker does the same. They hate seeing her this tired as much as I do. Walking upstairs, I put her in bed and pull her shoes off before sliding the shorts she's wearing off too. Bailey's already in one of my tees since most of hers don't fit her at the moment.

Walking back downstairs, I see the three men sitting on my couch waiting for me. "What's wrong?"

"Nothin'. We were just thinkin' that maybe we should up the number of guys on Bailey for right now. If you can't be here, I want to make sure that one or two can be inside and still have some outside." Joker says.

"Okay. I couldn't agree more. But, I'm gonna try to stick close to home as much as possible."

"We get that son. But, there's gonna be days you gotta go out. In two days, you're gonna be at the park in town to make sure the rides and games get here and set up on time. That day it's gonna be Rage, me, Joker, and Cage inside. Tank and Glock will be outside." Pops says.

"Think she's gonna go for that old man?" I ask him.

"She won't have a choice. If she's like her mama was, in the next few days and weeks she's going to be movin' and cleanin' up a storm. You'll be spendin' more time at the clubhouse than you will here."

"No I won't." I tell Pops.

"Yeah you will. She'll boot your ass so fast your head will spin. Nothin' personal, she'll just say you're in her way. I went through the same shit with Ma both times." He says, chuckling to himself.

"We'll see. But, I do have to be at the park day after tomorrow to make sure they get all set up and shit. You guys make sure my girl is comfortable and doesn't overdo shit. Rage, you know what you'll be doin' already."

"Yep. I got the paints and everythin' ready to start whenever you say to."

"If you want, you can start when you're ready."

"I'll go get started then. Ma is watchin' Kasey and the other kids while the girls clean up."

Rage takes off upstairs and we can hear him moving around in the nursery. I'm glad I shut the bedroom door so he doesn't wake Bailey up. Joker, Pops, and I sit there and shoot the shit for a while about nothing important. Today was a good day. No drama, no worries about being attacked, and my girl is up in bed sleeping. As soon as Rage is done for the day, I'll go up and join my girl in bed.

Chapter Twenty-Eight

Bailey

THE TOY DRIVE was an absolute success. We got a ton of toys to deliver to the hospital and the kids there loved all of the attention and toys they got to open up before Christmas. I had talked to the hospital and most of the parents before the drive and they were accepting of my idea of having an early Christmas party so we could watch them open their presents up. Most of the families there had tears in their eyes as the kids got to go crazy for a little while and play with new toys and games. Their kids got to act like kids instead of being sick. The smiles on their little faces were what made the day. Eventually we'll go back and arrange a ride for the kids that are able to on the motorcycles. And the parents were so thrilled to be able to forget for a little while that the children they love more than anything are suffering for different reasons.

When we left the hospital a few hours later, we all rode out to the carnival. Since I can't go on a bike right now and Skylar had all the kids, we were in her SUV with a group of guys surrounding us during the ride and on the way to the carnival. The way Logan's been acting, I'm surprised I even got to go. He's so overprotective and in daddy mode that he doesn't take his eyes off me if he has the option. But, he's been spending more time at home which is nice.

Any day now I could go into labor. I'm so ready for this shit to be over with! Not only am I uncomfortable, but now I have all this energy burning through me. Our house is so clean you could literally eat off the floor and not have to worry about dirt or anything else. Logan stays in the house until I boot his ass out so I can get things accomplished. The only two rooms I don't touch are his office and the room down in the basement.

Today, Pops found me in the kitchen on my hands and knees scrubbing the kitchen floor with a toothbrush. As soon as he saw me he threw his head back and roared with laughter until he had tears falling down his face. I didn't see anything funny about it and I let him know that.

"Daddy, this is not funny. What is wrong with you?"

"I wasn't expectin' to see you on the floor on your hands and knees usin' a toothbrush to clean. Your mama did the same thing though." He says, wiping the tears away.

"Well, I have to get this place clean. When I'm done here I'm going up to the nursery to clean that from top to bottom."

"No. We're goin' for a walk when you're done here." He says, pulling out his phone and texting someone.

"I don't have time for that today daddy. The nursery needs to get cleaned up and I have a desk being delivered in a little while."

"What do you have a desk bein' delivered for? Where the hell are you puttin' it?"

"I'm putting it next to the doors leading out back so I can have a nice view while I work."

"What work are you plannin' on doin'?"

"I won't be at Spinners, but I can use the computer to stay on top of things there."

"Baby girl, when Maddison comes back, she's takin' the office over." He tells me.

"Oh." I say, feeling like they're replacing me for a little bit. "Well, then I can do the books or something while your grandson sleeps."

"Calm down. Let's get you off the floor honey." He says coming over to help me up. "Grim's on his way over here now."

"What for?" I ask

"He wants to show you somethin' is all I know. And he might have received a picture of you usin' his toothbrush to clean the floor."

"Oopps. I didn't have an old one so I just picked one up."

"Uh huh. And we see that you definitely didn't pick your toothbrush up." Pops says laughing hysterically again.

Before any more can be said, Logan bursts through the door. You can tell he ran the whole way here as he bends down and rests his hands on his thighs to catch his breath. Finally, he can stand up and he looks at me holding his toothbrush in my hand.

"I piss you off or somethin' crazy girl?" He asks, coming over to me for a kiss.

"No. I just didn't have an old one and grabbed one."

"I see. And that just happened to be mine?" He asks starting to laugh. "Pops said you wanted to clean the nursery today and that you have a desk bein' delivered?"

"Yeah. I was planning on working from home. But, I guess you have Maddison to cover that when she gets back."

"I do. But, we're movin' you to manage Mystic. Plus, I'll talk to Wild Kings Ink and the Royal Lush about you doin' the books if you want me to."

"That sounds good." I tell him, wrapping my arms around him.

"Now, got somethin' to show you crazy girl. It's a surprise and I haven't even seen the work yet." He says leading us up to the nursery where the door is closed yet again.

Logan knocks on the door and I'm looking at him like he's stupid. It's our house, our son's room, and he's knocking on the door. I don't understand until we hear a muffled 'hang on a second' come through the door. The only thing I can do is look at him and my dad trying to figure out what the hell is going on.

Rage opens the door up just enough for him to get out. "It's done. I just finished it."

"Can we show her now?" Logan asks.

"Yep. Close your eyes Bailey." He says.

I do as he says and feel arms on either side of me, making sure I don't trip or anything. They lead me through the door and place me in the middle of the room I'm guessing. After a few seconds, Logan tells me that I can open my eyes. When I do, I can't help the gasp that leaves me and the tears that start streaming down my face. Rage has been in here painting a mural on the walls of the nursery. On the wall between the two windows is a replica of Spinners with motorcycles parked outside. Over the crib is another motorcycle, but what really makes my heart stop is the bright yellow star painted above the motorcycle. The words painted between the two make my heart race. It says: 'Baby Wilson watching over and guiding you.' This is the best thing that I have ever seen. There's also two new pictures hanging on the wall by the door. So, I move to them. One is the ultrasound picture of Ryan and the other is the ultrasound picture of our new son. Sitting right next to one another with the words: 'Brothers 'til the end' above and below the pictures. My guys really did an amazing job on this.

"I love it! Thank you both so much. You don't know how much this means to me." I say hugging first Rage and then Logan.

"Are you sure Bailey?" Rage asks, looking the most unsure I have ever seen him.

"I'm positive. These are happy tears, trust me. You got it perfect. I love the star and the pictures. The motorcycles too."

"I'm happy you like it crazy girl." Logan says. "Now, let's figure out where this desk of yours is goin'."

Grim

Rage did so much more to our son's room than I anticipated. He didn't tell me what he was going to do when I approached him about adding a little something to the walls of the nursery. Bailey and I both fell in love with it as soon as we saw it. He has so much talent. Before he left, he cleaned up his mess and opened the windows to get the smell of paint out of the room. I'll close them before we go to bed tonight.

Bailey leads me downstairs and shows me where she wants her desk to go. It's along the back wall across from my office. She can look outside while she works or catch the breeze from the open doors. I can watch her sexy ass while I'm in my office. It's a win-win for everyone. Pops and I move the few things that we have on the wall already so the desk and filing cabinet can go there. We no sooner get done and there's a knock on the door. Rage opens it after looking to see who it is.

"We have the desk, chair, and filing cabinet." One of the delivery men say.

"We're ready." Bailey tells him. "It's going over here on this back wall."

We stand back and let them do their thing. Thankfully the desk is already put together so we don't have to set that up. All we'll have to do is put Bailey's computer up and set it up how she wants is. Tank and Glock can do that shit later. The rest of the day is going to be all about my girl and me.

Once the guys are done putting everything where Bailey wants it, I kick Pops and Rage out. Bailey and I sit on the couch and watch a movie before I convince her to go for a walk with me. I lead her to the pond and we sit on one of the benches for a while, not talking or moving. Just me holding my girl and watching our surroundings. I feel for the ring in my pocket that I've been carrying around for a few weeks now. Never thought I'd be doing this, and I'm not sure I can find the words I want to say, but here goes nothing.

"Crazy girl, you know I love you yeah?" I ask her, sliding off the bench and landing on a knee.

"I do Logan. I love you too."

"For the longest time I didn't think I deserved to have your goodness, kind heart, and the light that shines from you in my life as more than a friend. When you shattered my heart and walked away from me I knew I'd never breathe again until you were home and by my side. I couldn't push you away any longer. Now, we're gettin' ready to have a little boy, the greatest gift you could ever give me, and I can't wait any longer. I want you by my side in everythin' I do. Will you do me the honor of becomin' my wife?" I ask, pulling the ring I had made out of my pocket.

"Oh my God! Yes, yes, yes Logan I will marry you!" Bailey says, holding her hand out for me to slide the ring on.

Instead of just having a normal ring, I had the jeweler make the center into a crown with a diamond in it. There's diamonds around the crown and along the band are the birthstones of the three of us with placeholders for any other kids we have.

"When do you wanna get married?" She asks me.

"When you're ready. As long as I know my ring's on your finger, I'm content to wait."

"As soon as we can after I have the baby, we're getting married." She says, jumping up and wrapping her arms around my neck and pulling my face down to hers. "I love you so much Logan."

"I love you too crazy girl. You ready to go to bed now?"

"I am." She says, as I pick her up and carry her back to the house and straight up to bed.

Chapter Twenty-Nine

Bailey

I'VE BEEN GOING to see the doctor once a week for the last few weeks and she says I'm ready to go into labor any day now. So, I've been staying close to home, cleaning, setting my desk and computer up, getting all the bags packed for when it's time. When Logan's working in the office, I've also been cooking extra meals and freezing them so I won't have to worry about cooking after we get home. Skylar's been helping with that.

Even more people are surrounding me when Logan does have to leave. Mainly it's Ma, Pops, Rage, Cage, Tank, and Glock. Slim Jim, the prospect, is here too but he stays outside. Ma has been helping me out when she can but I usually push her away and do it myself.

Maddison is coming home today. I know Tank knows, but he's not talking about it. They've been talking on the phone since she's been gone, but it's not the same. He's not the same. Logan told me they had a talk and that he's willing to step aside if Maddison finds her happy in someone else. I don't think that's something he has to worry about though. She's told me that she misses him so much she can't stand it.

So, I'm trying to get my housework done so that I can spend the afternoon with Maddison and Zoey today. Ma and Skylar are helping because they know I'm excited as hell to see Maddison again. It's been too long. We were planning on going Christmas shopping but I'm not feeling good enough for that. We've already been once and I don't want to go again. Besides, I've been having little twinges in my back on and off all day so far. No, I haven't said a word to anyone about it.

"Bay, I think she's here." Ma calls out going over to the front door.

I waddle as fast as I can over to the door so that I can wrap her up in my arms first. Tank is already at the truck Slim drove her back in helping her get Zoey out. Figures he would have to beat me to her!

"Maddison, let Tank and Slim get Zoey and everything else you need out of the truck!" I yell. "Come give me some hugs, I missed you!"

Maddison turns and breaks into a huge smile at how fat I've gotten since she's been gone. "How's my number one bitch?" She asks.

"Still fat and miserable."

"You're not fat! You're pregnant." She says running up the front steps. "I missed you all so much!"

"We missed you and Zoey too."

I drag her in the house and upstairs to show her Rage's work in the nursery. Like me, she breaks into tears at the star and the pictures. It's safe to say all the women love those parts of peanut's room. Logan and I have decided on a name, but we're not telling anyone what it is yet. And they've all tried to get it out of us. As we go to leave the room, I have to stop and hang on to the wall for a minute as another pain shoots through my back.

"You okay?" Maddison asks me.

"I'm fine. Just lost my breath for a second."

"You in labor Bailey?" She asks, rubbing my back.

"No. I think it's just more of those Braxton hick's contractions. They've come and gone all day. I'm fine. Let's go sit out back and talk. You can fill us in on your visit with Slim."

"Okay. I think he said he's planning on staying a day or two."

"Grim will like that. I think he wanted to talk to him about whatever's been going on anyway."

Making our way downstairs we head out back and sit around the table Logan put out here for cookouts. No matter what I do today, I just can't get comfortable. So, every time one of the women go to get something from inside, I go instead. Just so I can stand up and walk around without letting anyone know that I'm in pain. My back is killing me. I don't think it's time yet, so there's no point in letting anyone know. But, that doesn't stop Maddison from watching me like a hawk until Tank takes her and Zoey home before dinner.

Ma and Pops are staying with us for now. Just in case something happens. Last week Logan went on a run and was gone for a few days. He's not going on any more now, but he had to take care of something. Right now, Ma's in cooking a simple dinner for us and then we're going to veg out in front of the t.v. and watch chick flicks until Logan gets home. I don't know if I'll make it through even one movie, but I'm gonna try.

Grim

Going to the clubhouse this morning, I need to do more work on this sex trafficking ring before the baby gets here. So, Irish and Joker are helping me go through photos and trying to pick out anything that will tell us what kind of car this guy drives, if he has more tattoos, anything that can help identify him.

"I'm not seein' anythin' Grim." Irish says after going over a stack of photos again.

"It's just the one tattoo. You don't ever get a shot of the direction he's walkin' in from or where he heads when he leaves." I say in frustration.

"We need to catch a break sometime Pres." Joker says setting his stack of papers on the desk. "Someone is gonna come forward and tell us what we're missin'."

"Not soon enough." I mutter. "We've been at this for hours. Maddison is probably gettin' ready to head home with Tank and Slim's gonna be stoppin' in. Let's pick this back up tomorrow. Send picture to everyone's phone so they have it in case someone strange starts showin' up or askin' questions."

"On it." Irish says.

There's a knock on my office door and I call out for them to come in. Slim steps through the door and takes a seat on the couch. "Have a good visit with your daughter?"

"Yeah. Her and little Zoey are too much sometimes. Zoey's startin' to assert her independence and doesn't want to be held as much. But, she's so tiny for bein' seven months old. I want to wrap her ass in bubble wrap and never let her down."

We all laugh and lose a little of the tension we've been feeling throughout the day. It's good that I won't be bringing all that home to crazy girl. She's got enough going on and doesn't need this shit tainting her.

"Maddison happy to be home though?" Irish asks.

"Yeah. She knows she can come back whenever she wants. But, she wanted to get back to Bailey since she knows she's ready to pop any day now." Slim answers Irish before turning to me. "Your girl don't look so hot today Grim. I caught her more than once while I was there stopping to catch her breath. She hasn't said a word to anyone though. My girl was watchin' her like a hawk too."

"What? Why didn't she fuckin' tell me if somethin' is goin' on?" I yell, standing up so fast my chair crashes to the floor.

"She might not know she's in labor. I've seen it, but I don't know why Ma hasn't asked her."

"Fuck! I should be there and not here."

"You're doin' your job son." Slim says. "Bailey's not worried about it, so you shouldn't be either. They were gettin' ready to eat when I was leavin'."

"I'm goin' home. You guys deal with this and let Slim know what's goin' on too." I say heading for the door.

Running through the field, I don't stop to talk to anyone until I get inside and see my girl curled up asleep on the couch. Ma is rubbing her back and Pops and Cage are sitting close by. I don't know what's going on, but something is.

"She's in early labor and hasn't said anything yet." Ma tells me. "Even though she's resting, she's been having contractions and they're becoming more regular."

"Then let's get to the hospital." I say going to pick her up.

"Logan, you need to follow her lead in this. She'll tell you when she's ready to go. The best thing to do right now is take her to bed and make sure everything is ready to go." Ma says.

"It's been ready for two weeks now. Can you make sure the truck is gassed up and ready to go in case we need to leave?" I ask Cage.

"Already done. I took it out earlier and filled it up. Go to bed Pres and we'll see you when we get the call."

Picking Bailey up, I take her up to bed and don't bother removing either one of our clothes. I can hear Ma and Pops talking to Cage downstairs, but I can't go join them. Bailey needs me even if she doesn't know it yet and I'm not leaving her side.

"Ahhhhhh!" Bailey's scream wakes me up.

"What's wrong?" I ask sitting up.

"It's time Logan."

"Time?" I ask still half asleep.

"Baby time Logan!" She says frantically. "My water broke."

"What do you need crazy girl?"

"I need new shorts and a different top. You better change too. I think some of it got on you."

Looking down I see that the side of my clothes are soaked through. "Okay."

Running to the door, I yell for Ma and Pops as Bailey makes her way to the bathroom. They come crashing in and I tell them it's time to go, her water broke. Turning they go to get dressed as I hand Bailey her clothes and get changed myself. As soon as I'm changed, I grab the bags that have been sitting just inside the closet and run downstairs and out to the truck. Jumping in, I start it and send out a mass text before starting to back up. Pops waving frantically from the porch is the only thing stopping me from leaving.

"You forgettin' somethin' son?" He yells out and I look to my side.

"Fuck! I'm sorry." I say parking the truck again and going in to get Bailey.

"Don't worry, I was the same way. She's on her way down now."

Running back through the door, I see Bailey and Ma on the last step as Bailey bends over and yells through the pain she's feeling. Ma is rubbing her back and murmuring to her. I feel so useless and out of control right now. It's not a good feeling at all.

"Did you try leaving without me baby?" Bailey asks me with a gentle smile on her face.

"I did. I'm so sorry crazy girl. I don't know what to do or what you need from me."

"I only need you next to me. We'll get through this and then our son will be here. Help me out to the truck." She says as another pain shoots through her.

There's no way I'm waiting for her to walk outside, so I pick her up and move my ass to get her loaded up. Pops is already in the driver's seat as I put my girl in the back and climb in next to her. I hold her hand and rub her back. When a contraction hits we time it and I remind her to do her breathing. This is going way too fast as far as I'm concerned, but Pops has us to the hospital in just a few minutes and there's already nurses waiting outside for us.

"I called ahead while you were gettin' my girl outside." Pops explains.

The next few hours are a blur of activity between nurses checking her and making sure she's as

429

comfortable as possible and Bailey yelling at me and throwing everything she can get her hands on at me. But, finally just after five in the morning our little guy is here and lets us all know with his cries. Bailey has tears streaming down her face and I can only assume that she's thinking of Ryan right now. For a few minutes we get to hold our son before a nurse takes him to get cleaned up and do whatever else needs to be done.

"I'm so proud of you crazy girl! You did such a good job." I tell her, kissing her like I haven't kissed her in forever.

"He's so tiny, baby." She says. "Are they sure he weighs eight pounds?"

I laugh and tell her that I saw the scale myself and he weighs eight pounds and four ounces. He's long though. Bailey tells me to go let everyone that's here know that our guy is here and to take them to see him while the doctors finish up with her.

Going out to the waiting room I see everyone is still here. Even the kids are here still. They're all sleeping on couches and chairs in the waiting room the club was moved to. Ma sees me first and comes rushing over to me.

"He's here weighing in at eight pounds four ounces. If you want to see him, we'll go to the nursery." I tell everyone while Ma wraps me in a hug.

"How's our girl?" Pops asks.

"She's doin' good. They're cleanin' her up now and then I think she's gonna pass out. So you all might have to wait to see her."

"We'll see the boy and come back in a few hours to visit. She needs her rest."

The nurse is just finishing up with my boy when we line the nursery windows. So, she brings him over to show us. All the women ooh and ahh over how cute he is and how tiny. Ma and Pops have tears running down their faces, like they do with every new grandbaby. After a few minutes everyone heads out to get some sleep and I go back in to crazy girl. She's already passed out. So, I pull a chair up by her and lay my head on the bed by her side.

Bailey

Once I was cleaned up, I promptly fell asleep and didn't wake up until this morning. I feel pretty good, but I'm ready to see my baby boy. Logan is still sleeping with his head lying next to me and holding my hand closest to him. When he feels me stirring next to him, he wakes up and kisses my hand.

"How you feelin' crazy girl?"

"I want our boy." I tell him.

"I'll go get him. Be right back." He tells me, kissing me before leaving the room.

Minutes later a nurse follows Logan back in the room with a bassinet. She checks on me before she leaves us with the baby, telling us to call if we need anything. Logan hands him to me and I sit up higher so that I can look over our baby. Pulling his hat off his head, Bailey asks me to hand her the hat Ma gave us. We see a head full of dark hair, it looks so soft so I run my fingers through it. Just as I'm pulling his hat on him there's a knock on the door before Ma pokes her head in.

"You want us to come back?" She asks.

"No. You can come in." I tell them.

Everyone pours in the room not leaving a whole lot of room for anyone else to squeeze in here. Ma and the rest of the women surround me on so they can get a better look at the baby. Knowing better than anyone else, I hand our little guy over to Ma who goes right over to Pops and they beam down at our little blue bundle.

"So, you gonna let us all know his name yet?" Pops asks, his voice full of emotion.

"What do you think crazy girl?"

"I think so. We can't have them calling him baby or something all the time." I say looking at him.

"His name is Zander Roman Elliott." Logan says looking up at Tank.

431

"That's perfect!" Ma exclaims. "An absolutely perfect name for this larger than life little guy."

Tank stands there and just looks at us. He doesn't know what to say to us for using part of his name in our son's name. Maddison wraps her arm around him and lays her head against his side with Zoey in her arms. Ma walks over to him and hands little Zander to him. Tank holds him and looks down into his little face.

"Such a strong name for a strong little guy." He says. "I'm gonna teach you a lot of things growin' up."

I can't help the tears that start rolling down my face. Tank is going to be such an amazing role model to all of the kids involved in the club. He does have a lot to teach them. Every member of the club has a lot to teach each child that we are bringing into our world. Logan looks at me while I watch as each member of our family holds our son and tells him a little piece of their own wisdom. Pops is the last to hold him and he sits down in the chair by my bed and talks to him about bikes, women, and love. Zander will hear this speech more times than he can count. But, he'll love his granddaddy as much as his daddy.

Epilogue

Bailey

WE'VE BEEN HOME with Zander for about two months now. I've taken so many pictures that I'm sure everyone is tired of seeing a camera in my hands. But, the kids aren't going to be little for long and I want to capture as many memories as I can of Zander and the rest of the kids. Jameson now has a new little one to watch over. Whenever he's around, he tells Zander what they're going to do when he gets bigger and how they need to protect the girls. Jameson has things all laid out and is just waiting for the rest of the boys to get big enough to help him. He's such a smart guy for not being quite six now.

Logan has taken to being a father like he was born for the role. If he's home, Zander is with daddy. Unless it's time to eat. Then they're both with mommy. He told me one night that he loves watching me feed our son because he loves seeing the bond form between us. Plus, you know, he gets to see my tits. There are a ton of pictures that he hasn't seen yet of him sleeping with Zander on his chest in bed or on the couch, him sleeping in the rocking chair after changing him, and a ton of him holding Zander with love and raw emotion pouring from his face.

Our story may have started out rough, and things aren't always going to be easy in life, but I wouldn't trade anything in the world for watching my soon to be husband and son grow and learn every day.

Grim

I didn't think life could get any better than it was before, but I was wrong. So fucking wrong. Watching my woman and our son together is something that I won't be able to get enough of. The only thing that would make it better is when we add a few more kids to the mix.

Eventually, I want a daughter that looks just like her mama and has the same big heart.

Bailey doesn't think I know about all of the pictures she has of Zander and me, but she's wrong. She's the one that doesn't know about the pictures I have of her and our son together. My favorite has to be when I got home late one day. Bailey had been home with Zander all day while I was working at Spinners and trying to figure out who this guy is still. By the time I could get away, it was way past dinner. But, I didn't hear one word from Bailey. At first I thought it was kind of odd that she didn't text asking where I was. Then I got worried that I didn't hear from her. Finally, I rushed home. When I burst through the door followed by Joker, Tank, and Pops, I found them upstairs in our bed. My girl was laying down with Zander on her chest. Both of them were fast asleep. She had one hand on his back and the other one supporting his head. Zander had one little fist in his mouth and the other one over his mama's heart. Not being able to stop myself, I took a picture of them. Pops made sure that I sent it to him too. I'm sure it will be up on the wall in their house.

My days are now spent getting back into the swing of things while Bailey is starting to get ready to go to work. Since she's helping Glock out managing Mystic now, she's going to take Zander with her until I can get free. Our main priority is finding out who this guy is though and then taking care of him before he can hurt anyone else. All three clubs are working endlessly at trying to figure this thing out and it's taking its toll on all of us.

Maddison

I had a nice visit with my dad and brother, but I was more than ready to come home. For the most part, I missed Tank so bad my chest hurt wondering what he was doing. We talked all the time on the phone and he always told me he missed me and that he would wait forever for me to give him a chance. No matter how much I want that, I don't know if I'm ready to risk that again. I have to think of Zoey. And if all Tank's looking for is a good time, then he needs to move on because that's not me.

Being back home has been nice. I've gotten closer to the women and I'm starting to talk to a few of the members of the club. Grim, Joker, Cage, and Pops are the main guys I see and it's still hard to talk to them even at Spinners. This shyness is killing me and I don't know what to do to help fix it.

It's been a long day. I worked, picked Zoey up from Skylar's, and then went to see Bailey and Zander until Tank could take me home. Zander is getting so big already. He's such a cute baby that hardly fusses unless he's hungry or tired. Bailey is an amazing mom. I know she worried about how she would handle being alone with him, but she's so good with him and gets so much done during the day since she set up her own little workspace. We laugh and talk and she plays with Zoey while I hold Zander. Often times we joke about them being so close that they might have to become a couple when they get older. Don't know how Grim's going to feel about us planning his boy's wedding already though.

"Hey, we're all getting together tomorrow night here to plan the wedding." Bailey says.

"Okay. You need me to take Zander for a while?" I ask.

"No! You're coming here and helping us out. It's going to be fun. We even get to use Grim's room downstairs."

"Oh, okay. Need me to bring anything?"

"Just you and Zoey."

We're sitting at the desk when Bailey's phone goes off. There's a picture message so she opens it up and shows me. I gasp and stand up so fast I scare both Zoey and Zander. Bailey rushes to me after checking on her son.

"What's the matter honey?" She asks. "You look like you've seen a ghost."

435

"Why did you get sent a picture of Brad?"

"Who?" Bailey asks confused.

"The picture you just got, why did you get it?" I ask, feeling like I'm going to pass out.

"Who's Brad, Maddison?"

"He's my ex. What's going on?" I ask, starting to feel like the room is spinning.

"I'm calling Tank and Grim." Bailey says sounding a million miles away.

Before I can do anything else, I feel my legs buckling and I'm going to the floor. All I see is black and I know I'm passing out.

Tank

Bailey calls us flipping out about a picture we sent her and Maddison passing out and knowing who it is. Every person in the meeting is now running like a bat out of hell to get to Grim's house. No one is beating me over there though. Maddison is mine and I need to find out what happened to make her pass the fuck out. Bailey wouldn't exaggerate something like that just to get us to the house.

Running through the door, I see Maddison laying on the floor not moving at all. Fuck! Stopping I pick her head up and put her head in my lap brushing her hair out of her face and talking softly to her. Bailey has water ready for her when she wakes back up and the rest of the guys are surrounding us trying to get what happened out of Bailey. Zoey is in her arms and Zander is starting to cry so Grim picks him up and cradles him against his chest.

After about a half hour, Maddison starts to wake up. We've heard Bailey's version of the story but we want to know what made her flip out the way she did. Picking her up, I move to the couch and sit her in my lap.

"Maddie, can you tell me what happened sweetness?" I ask her gently.

"B-b-bailey got that picture on her phone in a message. Is he here for me? Is he gonna try to take Zoey from me?" She asks. "Tank, don't let him take my baby girl from me!"

"Who sweetness?"

"Brad!"

"That's your ex?" I ask her. "He's the one that smacked you around and made you hit your head in Dander Falls?"

"Yeah. And now he's here to take my baby isn't he?" She asks again.

I look at Grim and he's standing completely still not knowing what to say or do right now.

"Honey, no one is takin' your baby girl from you. I can promise you that right now!" Pops says, kneeling down in front of her. "You're sure that's your ex?"

"I am. I bought him that hat and he's had that tattoo on his arm since before we were together."

"What's the tattoo of?" I ask her.

"It's a mixture of skulls, tribal, and Zoey's name is added in around his wrist. Why do you have that picture of him?"

"He's in to some bad stuff that we're not gonna get into right now. We're gonna get you home to relax and we'll talk about it later." I tell her.

Grim pulls me aside real quick and tells me not to pressure her to tell me more. In a day or two we'll call church and bring her in to tell us everything she knows about Brad. Finally, we have some information that will help us put this fucking puzzle together. Hopefully it's before anyone gets hurt.

The End

Note to the Readers

Dear Readers,

First of all, thank you so much once again for using your hard earned money to buy my book. I hope that you like it as much as I did writing it. This book took me on a whole bunch of twists and turns that I didn't see coming at all. But, I wouldn't change it for the world. I love the story and the portrayal of what some women go through after losing a child.

Personally, I have suffered a miscarriage and I had a son that was still born. I was torn apart when I had my miscarriage. But, I lost myself when I had my son still born a little over a year later. Even though I had one son that was a toddler, I didn't see a way past my depression for a long time. Thankfully, my family and his father were there to help me with him. He's ultimately the one that got through to me with his love and wanting to bring mommy back. A lot of the things that Bailey does in the story, I also did. When I didn't have my son, I drank myself to oblivion. Other than a few certain people, I pushed everyone in my life away. And I didn't get help from a grief counselor at all. If you, or anyone you know, are suffering through the loss of a child, I urge you to get help from someone. Please! I don't want to see anyone go through what I did during this hard time in my life. Still to this day, almost 14 years later, I have days that I can't stop thinking about him and going through all of the 'what ifs' and wondering so much about him. What would he look like? What would he be interested in? Would he have as big of a heart as my other children? So many thoughts and feelings that never go away.

I would also like to take a moment to remind everyone that I am donating a portion of all the royalties I get from now until November to an MC. This donation is going towards their toy drive for children for Christmas.

Any and all support, sharing, and getting the word out is greatly appreciated!!! Thank you in advance.

Thank you so much! I can't wait to hear from you all.

Erin

Bailey's Saving Grace Playlist

The House Rules – Christian Kane
Beam Me Up – Pink
Broken – Seether (Feat. Amy Lee)
Photograph – Ed Sheeran
Let Me Go – Christian Kane
Let's Take A Drive – Christian Kane
Unbreakable – Jamie Scott
Like A Wrecking Ball – Eric Church
Break On Me – Keith Urban
Let It Hurt – Rascal Flatts
Dear Agony – Breaking Benjamin
Fall Into Me – Brantley Gilbert
Just As I Am – Brantley Gilbert
Home – Phillip Phillips
Never Let Her Go – Florida Georgia Line
Drink A Beer – Luke Bryan
Breakdown – Seether
Skin – Rihanna
S & M – Rihanna
Wild Wild Love - Pitbull

*Not all songs are named in the book. Some I listened to while writing particular scenes or parts of the story.

Acknowledgements

First and foremost, I need to say what wonderful kids I have. They not only support me, but they give me the time I needed to finish writing the book and do what I need to do to fulfill my dreams. Their love and unconditional support mean the world to me and I can't thank them enough. My kids are my world and life and I love them more every day.

Next, I have to thank Tracy-Lisa. You have become a friend and a tremendous support. Not only in my journey of writing, but on a personal level as well. You have talked me down when I have been ready to give up on everything and make me feel stronger. Thank you for being there for me!

There are also some amazing authors that I need to thank. Liberty Parker, Vera Quinn, L Ann Marie, and Shelly Morgan. These amazing ladies have given me advice, answered questions that I had, given me help with not wanting anything in return, and have gotten my name out numerous times. Thank you ladies from the bottom of my heart! There are a ton more that I haven't named, and I'm sorry for that. I thank you too! It would honestly take me forever to name all of the authors that have helped me.

During a release party I did a post to help me come up with songs for strip clubs. The winner of that contest was Sacha. Thank you for helping me come up with songs to everyone that participated though. I also have to thank Michelle, Daphne, and Kelly for helping me come up with some amazing names. Two names from Michelle, one from Kelly, and two from Daphne made it in this story. I plan on using more of the names in future books.

My beta readers have been amazing. Darlene you always go above and beyond with your comments, help with editing, questions, and everything else you leave me. Mel, Michelle, Sherry, Daphne, Vicky, April, Sherry H., and Jeanette thank you all from the bottom of my heart for wanting to read the story and help me make it better for the readers that take a chance on my books. Right now, I have only had three of you beta read for me before. After this book, hopefully I can get your help again on the next book! I really cannot say thank you enough for your hard work.

Finally, I have to say thank you to the readers. Thank you for taking a chance on me while I learn and grow in this amazing journey, for commenting on posts, and showing me support every day. Without all of you, none of this would be possible! I can't wait to see where this journey takes me and I hope to connect with all of you in some way.

About The Author

Growing up, I was constantly reading anything I could get my hands on. Even if that meant I was reading my grandma's books that weren't so age appropriate. I started out reading Judy Blume, then graduated to romance, mainly historical romance, and last year I found an amazing group of Indie authors that wrote MC books. Instantly I fell in love with these books.

For a long time, I've wanted to write. I just never had the courage to go through with actually doing it. During a book release party, I mentioned that I wanted to write and I received encouragement from an amazing author. So, I took a leap and wrote my first book. Even though this amazing journey is just starting for me, I wouldn't have even started if it weren't for a wonderful group of authors and others that I've met along the way.

I am a wife and mother of five children. Only one girl in the bunch! My family and friends mean the world to me and I'd be lost without them. Including new friends that I've met along the way. I've lived in New York my whole life, either in Upstate or the Southern Tier. I love it during the summer, spring, and fall. But, not so much during the winter. I hate driving in snow with a passion!

When I'm not hanging out with my family/friends, reading, or writing, you can find me listening to music. I love almost all music! Or, I'm watching a NASCAR race.

I look forward to meeting new friends, even if I'm extremely shy!

Here are some links to connect with me:

Facebook:
https://www.facebook.com/ErinOsborneAuthor/
Twitter:
https://twitter.com/author_osborne
My website:
http://erinosborne1013.wix.com/authorerinosborne
Spotify:
https://open.spotify.com/user/emgriff07

Made in the USA
Middletown, DE
23 June 2019